TWO CAN PLAY

By Kate Kessler

TWO CAN PLAY

AN AUDREY HARTE NOVEL

KATE KESSLER

REDHOOK

www.redhookbooks.com

Redhook Books/Orbit
Hachette Book Group
1290 Avenue of the Americas
New York, NY 10104
www.HachetteBookGroup.com

First Edition: November 2016

Redhook is an imprint of Orbit, a division of Hachette Book Group.
The Redhook name and logo are trademarks of Hachette Book Group, Inc.

The publisher is not responsible for websites (or their content) that are not owned by the publisher.

The Hachette Speakers Bureau provides a wide range of authors for speaking events. To find out more, go to www.hachettespeakersbureau.com or call (866) 376-6591.

Library of Congress Cataloging-in-Publication Data

Names: Kessler, Kate, author.
Title: Two can play : an Audrey Harte novel / Kate Kessler.
Description: First edition. | New York, NY : Redhook, 2016. | Series: An
    Audrey Harte novel ; 2
Identifiers: LCCN 2016026142| ISBN 9780316302531 (trade paperback) | ISBN
    9781478940234 (audio book) | ISBN 9780316302517 (ebook)
Subjects: LCSH: Police psychologists—Fiction. | Women
    Psychologists—Fiction. | Murder—Investigation—Fiction. | BISAC: FICTION /
    Suspense. | GSAFD: Mystery fiction. | Suspense fiction.
Classification: LCC PS3611.E8456 T89 2016 | DDC 813/.6—dc23 LC record
    available at https://lccn.loc.gov/2016026142

ISBNs: 978-0-316-30253-1 (paperback), 978-0-316-30251-7 (ebook)

Printed in the United States of America

LSC-C

10 9 8 7 6 5 4 3 2 1

For Mum—I miss you.
And for Steve—I love you.

CHAPTER ONE

Ian Monroe didn't look like a serial killer.

Audrey Harte stared at the mugshot in Monroe's file. He didn't have a vacant expression like Gacy or Bundy's crazy eyes. He didn't have that seventies gay porn star look like Dahmer, or the full-on nut job vibe of Ramirez. He looked preppy and stylish—smart, like he was posing for his high school senior class photo.

In fact, Monroe had been out of high school for only two months when he was arrested for the murders of five girls in Portland, Maine. The yearbook, in which he wore a smile much like the one in his mugshot, had been dedicated to the memories of four of his victims. He'd gone to their funerals, the little prick.

Someone (a reporter) had given him the title of Maine's youngest—and handsomest—serial killer—like it added prestige to the violence done by the then seventeen-year-old. Monroe, a fairly textbook psychopath, didn't need his ego stroked by being singled out. Like most psychopaths, he already believed himself superior to most of the world. As a subject of study, he was fascinating. As a human being, he was one of the worst.

He was finally going to trial, and the prosecution had asked Audrey to be an expert witness. They said it was because she was from Maine and understood the people there—that she would be invaluable in helping select jurors, but when a tabloid magazine ran a photo of her next to one of Monroe with the caption *Killer Doc to take on "Boy Scout" Monroe at trial*, she wondered if the DA wasn't trying to stir up some publicity of his own.

If someone had told her when she was in college that having committed murder when she was thirteen would actually make her professionally desirable, Audrey wouldn't have believed it. But with the murder of her former best friend, and partner in crime, Maggie Jones, that summer, Audrey's past had bit her on the ass so hard, she still had a bruise. She didn't like to think about Maggie, or the particulars of her murder, but she couldn't deny it was partly responsible for her now having her own office at the Beharrie Center. Her boss, Angeline Beharrie, had put her in charge of the East Coast location—a position in which she felt like a fraud at thirty-two. And she was well aware that there were those at the center who didn't think she deserved the promotion.

Which meant she was going to have to prove that she *did* deserve it. She might be slightly notorious, but she loved her job, and worked hard at it. She was going to do everything she could to make sure the prosecution's case against Monroe was airtight.

A knock on her office door—which was open—made her lift her head. It was Lauralyn, who ran the front desk and handled appointments, calendars, and client concerns for the clinical psychologists in the office. Basically, no one there would know what to do without her. She was forty-something with curly blond hair and a youthful round face. She smiled as she stuck her head in.

"It's two o'clock."

Audrey glanced at the clock on the wall. She'd asked Lauralyn to remind her that she wanted to leave early. Traffic around Boston was horrible at the best of times, and she didn't want to turn a three-and-a-half-hour drive into five by being stupid enough to leave at rush hour.

"Thanks," she said, closing the folder. "I'm staying at that B and B in Rockland, right?" It wasn't far from Warren, where Ian Monroe was incarcerated, and an hour and a half from Portland, where the murders had taken place.

"Yep. I e-mailed you the details and the Google map, and here's your travel mug." She set the tall mug on the desk. "The coffee's fresh and I added that Italian Sweet Crème that you like."

Fetching coffee wasn't part of Lauralyn's job; she was just that nice. "You are an angel," Audrey told her with a grin.

The older woman winked. "I'll remind you that you said that at my review. Safe travels, and good luck in Portland." Then she left the office.

Audrey stood, gathering up Monroe's file, along with several others, and the binder in which she kept her notes. Her hand hesitated over the latest *People* magazine that had an article on Ian and the events leading to his arrest. The FBI and Portland police had gathered enough evidence against him for a warrant, and barged in while he was toying with his latest victim, whom they rescued before Monroe could kill her. The writer spoke in depth to Victoria Scott—*The One That Got Away*—and several other people close to the case. Since a good part of her involvement in the trial consisted of assessments and interviews, the article would be a good one to have as a reference. Plus, it mentioned her. Audrey tossed it in her leather computer bag before slipping her laptop inside as well.

She slipped into her dark red peacoat and wrapped her scarf around her neck before slinging her bags over her shoulder and grabbing her coffee. She turned down the heat, shut off the lights, and locked the door behind her.

The clinic was located in Cambridge, a bit of a walk from Harvard. Angeline chose the five-story building for its location, and for the fact that its redbrick facade was both academic and inviting. The first time Audrey had seen it, she thought it looked like money, and vaguely pretentious, but she wasn't the one paying the rent. She had to admit, though, it was a nice place to work.

And she had been working. A lot. Mostly to avoid going home. And because her work enabled her to continually psychoanalyze herself without anyone noticing. Of all the killers, violent offenders, and victims she'd interviewed, the workings of her own mind were what confounded her most. She could be very good at her job. She was capable of being a good person, but the place she felt the most comfortable was the place she'd run away from years ago—the place that knew just how terrible she could truly be.

She had a reserved spot in the parking garage attached to the building via a covered walkway, which helped her avoid the damp cold that had settled over the city for the last couple of days. As she approached, she hit the remote starter for her Prius so it would be nice and warm when she got in. Jake had laughed at her for getting the remote, but he hated to wear shoes, even in the winter, so obviously he was a freak of nature. A guy with that little body fat should not be warm all the time.

The drive to Rockland was uneventful except for the thermometer dipping a couple of degrees the farther north she drove. In another couple of weeks it would be Halloween. She remembered it would sometimes snow while trick-or-treating as a kid. They had loved it, little freaks that they were.

After more than a decade in California, she wasn't prepared for a New England winter. Hell, she wasn't even prepared for fall.

It was getting dark when she pulled into the B and B's drive. Hers was the only car in guest parking. This place probably did extremely well in the summer given its picturesque view of the water. The trees had turned color, and most of them still had an abundance of leaves. It might be colder than LA, but the air was clean, and it was a hell of a lot prettier. Not that LA didn't have its moments.

Pulling her coat closed, Audrey got her bags out of the backseat and locked the car.

The door was opened by a smiling woman who looked to be in her sixties. "You must be Audrey."

"I am." She returned the smile. "Mrs. Fletcher?"

"Indeed. Come on in. It's going to be a nippy night, I think."

Audrey stepped inside. The interior was very English countryside—plush and rich but inviting. And was that roast beef she smelled? And apple pie? Her stomach growled.

Mrs. Fletcher showed her the dining room and common areas before taking her up to her room. Decorated in shades of plum, cream, and dark green, it had the same relaxed opulence of the rest of the house. It had its own bathroom as well, complete with a large, claw-foot soaker tub. *Much* better than staying in a cheap hotel.

"It's lovely," she told Mrs. Fletcher. "Do you suppose I could trouble you for some ice and directions to the nearest good restaurant?"

"I can bring you an ice bucket. And you needn't worry about going out again after your long drive. If you like roast beef, I'll bring you up a tray of our dinner. I always make too much."

The inherent kindness of this part of the world always surprised her, even though she'd grown up with it. When she was a kid, though, it always seemed intrusive, and was counterbalanced with the nosiness and gossipmongering of small-town life. "That's very kind of you. If it's no trouble, I'll take you up on it."

Mrs. Fletcher smiled. "No trouble at all! It's so nice to have someone else in the house. Did I read that you're part of the prosecution against Ian Monroe?"

Audrey froze as she set her bags near the bed. And there was the flip side of small-town hospitality. "Yes." She met the woman's pale blue gaze. "I am."

All the mirth drained from Mrs. Fletcher's round face. "Terrible business. Do you actually have to see him? Is that why you're here?"

Was there any harm in being honest? Audrey couldn't tell, but she also couldn't think of how this nice woman could possibly make trouble for her since she would be leaving the next day. "Yes. I'll be interviewing him tomorrow."

Graying curls bobbed as she shook her head and clucked her tongue. "I'm going to bring you a slice of pie as well. Do you like ice cream?"

Do bears shit in the woods? The voice of her father rang in Audrey's head. "I do. Thank you."

The older woman's smile returned just before she closed the door, leaving Audrey alone. She took her toiletries from her overnight bag and set them in the bathroom. Then she took her suit for the next day out of her garment bag and hung it up. It was simple and well cut and had cost more than some people made in a week. It had been a worthy investment, though. With a crisp white shirt, she looked professional, put together, and slightly intimidating, but not like she was trying too hard. She called it her *Grosse Pointe Blank* suit, because when she wore it, she felt like John Cusack's character from the film. Hopefully she wouldn't have to assassinate anyone.

She had just kicked off her boots and taken off her coat when Mrs. Fletcher returned with a tray bearing dinner, a bucket of ice, and a bouquet of flowers. Audrey quickly took the heavy tray from her and set it on the small table near the window.

"I forgot that those were delivered for you earlier today," the older woman told her, her face a little flushed from carrying the tray up an entire flight of stairs.

Audrey checked the flowers. "Really?" No one but work and Jake knew where she was staying. "They're very pretty." Actually, white roses always made her think of funerals, but they still smelled nice.

Mrs. Fletcher looked disappointed that she hadn't opened the card. "Well, I'll leave you to it. Just leave the tray outside the door and I'll collect it later."

After thanking the woman once again, Audrey put the bottle of wine she'd brought with her in the bucket of ice, and sat down to eat. It was as delicious as it smelled—and way too much food. Cooks in Maine seemed to operate under the thought that every meal was for a lumberjack—or a teenage boy. Every time she came home she had to double up on gym time when she returned to Boston.

When she finished the last bite of pie and melting vanilla ice cream, she set the tray on a table outside her room and went back to the flowers. There was a small card inside a white envelope. She opened it.

Looking forward to playing with you.

What the hell? That wasn't cryptic or creepy at all.

The card wasn't signed, but the phone number for the florist was embossed in silver on the bottom. They could be from Jake. Though she couldn't imagine him writing something so cheesy, or picking white roses as a gift. He had more color to him than that, and he'd probably go for something more exotic.

Like a carnivorous plant. A pretty one. And he'd tell her it reminded him of her.

Audrey smiled at the thought of him, even though her stomach fluttered like a hive of neurotic bees. It wasn't a new sensation. Jake Tripp had fascinated her, scared her, and held a firm grip on her heart for almost twenty years. They'd been friends for even longer. His grandmother, Gracie, had appointed herself Audrey's fairy godmother even before she and Maggie had been arrested for killing Clint Jones. Audrey wouldn't be where she was if not for Gracie. God only knew how she might have turned out.

She ran a bath and called Jake while the tub filled.

"Are you in Rockland?" he asked when he picked up. The sound of his slightly scratchy voice loosened her muscles more than any bath ever could. He was like her grounding wire. Always had been, even when he was the one setting her nerves on edge.

"Yeah. Got here a little while ago. Hey, did you send me flowers?"

There was a pause. "No. Was I supposed to?"

"No. But the owner gave me a bouquet that had been delivered earlier with my name on them."

"What did the card say?"

Now she was the one who hesitated.

"Aud?"

"It said, 'Looking forward to playing with you.'"

"That combination of words would never find its way out of my mouth." He sounded offended that she'd even asked.

"I didn't think so, but I wanted to ask before I let paranoia set in."

"You think someone related to the Monroe case is trying to unsettle you?"

"I don't know. At least I know they didn't come from Monroe. I can't imagine they let you send flowers from prison."

"He could have paid someone to do it. It's a classic taunt."

Oh, shit. "Not helping with that paranoia."

"You want me to tell you it's nothing? That you're imagining things?"

"Yes."

"Can't do it. It's weird, and you should look into it. You should also tell the prosecution. Take a photo of the flowers and the card." He sounded concerned, but not freaked out, which was exactly the right reaction to make her feel the same.

"I will." She took a corkscrew from her bag and opened the bottle of wine. "You still want me to stay at your place this weekend?" Though she spent most of her time in Edgeport at his house, she did occasionally stay with her parents. She trusted him to tell her if he didn't want her around, but after years of being hung up on him, the reality of being with him seemed... tenuous. They were still trying to find their way—or she was.

"You get a better offer?"

She smiled at his teasing tone. "No."

"You just want to hear me say it, is that it?"

"Would it kill you?"

He laughed. "Yes, Aud, I want you to stay with me. It would

fair render me distraught if your boots found their way under someone else's bed."

Audrey's brow pulled as she poured wine into one of the glasses on the table. "I've heard that before."

"Gran used to say it to Gramps when he accused her of trying to get rid of him."

Gracie and Mathius Tripp had one of those loves that they made movies about. The sort that ran down to their bones and even death couldn't shake. In another life they would have gone out together in a hail of bullets during a gunfight with the police. Instead, they both went quietly in their beds, far too many years apart. "Good thing I wore boots, then."

They talked for a little while longer and then hung up. He hadn't said he loved her and neither had she. There was a small part of her that wanted to say it—wanted to hear it—but deep inside she already knew it. She and Jake had loved each other since they'd been kids, long before either of them knew what romantic love was.

After plugging her phone into the charger, Audrey took a photo of both flowers and note, sent each to Will Grant, the prosecuting attorney, and then headed for the bath with her glass of wine. She soaked for almost an hour before getting out, her skin gone pruney. After drying off, she slipped into a T-shirt and pajama pants, and slathered on her nightly skin care before climbing into bed with her tablet and another glass of wine. She read for a couple of hours before deciding to call it a night.

But before she went to sleep, she climbed out of bed, picked up the vase of roses, and put the creepy arrangement on the table in the hall. They were not going to be the last thing she saw before going to sleep, and they sure as hell weren't going to be the first thing she saw in the morning before heading to Maine State Prison to interview its most dangerous inmate.

Margot Temple had a shrine to Ian Monroe.

Actually, it was a scrapbook, several DVDs, and a wall in her basement covered with his photographs, but "shrine" sounded pure and holy while the truth made her sound more like a teenage girl than a full-grown woman. A fourteen-year-old's devotion to a member of a boy band could not begin to compare to the deep, almost spiritual connection she had with Ian. No one understood it—not her family, her friends. Her therapist tried to understand, but when she said they'd work together to rid Margot of her "obsession," Margot canceled all future appointments.

She didn't *want* to be rid of Ian.

He had done horrible things, she knew that. Judging or forgiving him wasn't her responsibility. She wanted only to help heal whatever wound had turned him into the sort of person who hurt women. He was broken, but he could be fixed—she was sure of it.

Her psychologist (the one she'd fired) said she had hybristophilia, and suggested that she had a history of being sexually drawn to dangerous, even criminal, men. Really? What woman hadn't lusted after a bad boy once or twice in her life? Maybe she was attracted to danger, but it didn't feel that simple. She didn't just want to sleep with Ian, she wanted to *heal* him. The age difference between them was enough that she could guide him, but not so vast that she was old enough to be his mother. Not that it mattered.

She could count the weeks until his trial on both hands. She would be there every day if she could manage it. She'd already booked her vacation for that week so she could be there for him if he needed her. He *would* need her too; she felt it in her bones. He would need to know he had a friend in the courtroom—one who could pass on the support of the more than a dozen supporters he had in the city.

Margot unlocked the door to her apartment and crossed the threshold. Her cat—a large fluffy Persian named Mr. Beans— came to greet her. She picked him up and hugged him to her chest, pressing little kisses all over his velvety head. She turned the deadbolt and carried sixteen pounds of purring cat into the living room.

She ordered Chinese for dinner and then went to her bedroom and changed into her pajamas. While waiting for her food, she began wondering about Ian's trial, and what to wear. She wanted to look good. Polished. Not crazy—because she knew that's what people said about her when they found out that she had started a support group for Ian Monroe. They called the Freedom for Ian Coalition a "fan club" and made fun of her. The only person who hadn't talked about her like she was a joke had been Chris James, who had interviewed her for the book he was writing about Ian. At the time it had been obvious that he didn't understand her attraction to Ian, but at least he tried.

Because of her involvement in the support group, Margot got a lot of mail—both e- and snail. Most of it was friendly. Some of it was weird, and some of it was downright hateful. She didn't have an assistant because she couldn't afford one—it wasn't like she charged people to be part of the support group—so she read and answered all of it herself. Sometimes, the letters left her sobbing and shamed, or cursing and furious. People called her crazy, stupid, delusional. They said the world would be a better place if she killed herself. What sort of freak was she to support a monster like Ian Monroe? A compassionate one, she had to remind herself. She didn't answer those awful letters, but she did save them just in case, and she took screen shots of every threatening or mean post on her social media sites as well. Many times the ones who were the most vocal about how crazy she was to support Ian were the very same ones threatening to rape or kill her. It was because of these scary communications that she kept her phone number unlisted and never mentioned where she lived—not even the neighborhood.

So when eating chow mein straight from the carton and checking her mail, she was surprised to find an envelope from Maine State Prison.

Margot's heart skipped excitedly in her chest, like two young girls playing double Dutch. Her fingers trembled as she slipped one beneath the flap and tore the paper. When she opened the letter inside, tears sprang to her eyes.

Dear Miss Temple, I've added you to my visitor list. I look forward to meeting you at last.

Sincerely, Ian Monroe

Margot giggled, then laughed. She was still laughing when tears trickled down her cheeks.

She was going to meet him. Finally. She was going to be in the same room with Ian. He wanted to meet her. Talk to her. She would be able to tell him just how much she cared for him. Tell him that she would do anything for him.

Anything.

CHAPTER TWO

Audrey woke up early the next morning, a small knot of either anticipation or anxiety—she couldn't discern which—in her stomach. She took a shower, did her hair and makeup, got dressed, and went downstairs for breakfast. Mrs. Fletcher was in the kitchen. She looked up when Audrey entered the room, and smiled, lines around her eyes and mouth creasing. "I hope you like French toast."

Audrey smiled. "It's my favorite. You really don't have to go to that much trouble."

"It's no trouble at all. I made it for my husband and myself as well. Would you like to join us for breakfast? Or would you prefer to eat in the dining room?"

Eating alone would give her a chance to mentally prepare for her upcoming interview with Ian Monroe, but Audrey didn't much feel like sitting at that big table all by herself, or making the older woman wait on her. "If you and your husband don't mind the company, I would like to join you. Thank you."

The older woman seemed pleased by her decision. "We don't mind the least bit. I hope *you* don't mind, but I told my husband why you were here. He's very eager to meet you. He watches all of those crime shows on the television—you know, those ones about the criminal profilers and forensic investigators."

While Angeline wasn't a big fan of such shows and their portrayal of forensic psychologists, Audrey sometimes watched one or two of them herself. She realized they had to take a lot of dramatic license, but she appreciated when they actually got it right.

"I hope he's not expecting me to be like Gil Grissom or Clarice Starling," she said with a smile. "He's going to be very disappointed if he is."

"Oh, I suspect he will be more than thrilled to hear about the real thing. That is, if you don't mind him asking you questions?" She actually looked a little anxious.

"Of course not. I have a little time before I need to leave for Warren, so I will try to give him as much of an accurate description of what I do as I can."

The anxiety disappeared from the older woman's face. "He'll enjoy that so much! You are a dear to indulge him."

Audrey helped Mrs. Fletcher carry the coffee and French toast into the family dining area. It was a small nook off the kitchen with a square table and four chairs and a window that overlooked the water. Very cozy.

Mr. Fletcher was a tall thin man with gray hair and spectacles. He wore a plaid shirt and gray trousers and a pair of highly buffed oxfords. He smiled when he saw Audrey, and rose to his feet.

"You must be Dr. Harte." He offered his hand. Audrey

accepted the handshake, pleased that he didn't limp-fish her like many older men did, as though they thought themselves so strong they might break her delicate female bones. "It's a pleasure to meet you."

"Call me Audrey. It's lovely to meet you. You have a beautiful home."

"If it's lovely, it's all because of the missus," he said with a twinkle in his eye. "Please, have a seat."

Audrey set the coffeepot on a trivet, and took the chair on Mr. Fletcher's right. Mrs. Fletcher sat across from her and offered her the platter of French toast. She took two thick slices, and doused them both with a heavy deluge of maple syrup.

"It's all local," Mrs. Fletcher told her with a touch of pride. "I made the bread myself, the eggs are from a farm just outside of town, as is the cream, and the syrup was made by my son-in-law."

Audrey cut into the golden brown egg-soaked bread and leaned forward as she shoved the bite in her mouth to keep from getting any syrup on her shirt. She couldn't help closing her eyes in pleasure at the taste.

"It's delicious," she said after she swallowed. "Thank you."

Mrs. Fletcher cut into her own breakfast. "I couldn't help but notice that you put the flowers on the hall table. Mind if I ask why?"

Audrey hesitated before replying, "I think they were meant to be more of a taunt than a gift." Even as the words left her mouth, she realized she shouldn't have said them.

"A taunt?" Mr. Fletcher asked. "From who?"

"Someone trying to unsettle me." Audrey cut another bite as she tried to sell that it was nothing. "Attorneys do it all the time." They didn't, but the Fletchers probably wouldn't know that.

Mr. Fletcher frowned. "Should we call the police?"

She shook her head. "I sent a photo of the card to the prosecuting attorney just in case, but I think it was meant as a prank—to throw me off. No threats were made. Please, I didn't mean to upset either of you."

"Upset?" Mrs. Fletcher echoed. "We're not upset, my dear, we're angry! To think that someone might actually sympathize with that monster...well, it's disgusting."

"It happens more often than you think," her husband replied. "There are people out there who have fan clubs for serial killers. Why, even Charles Manson found some poor soul to marry him."

Audrey couldn't argue that, but she could change the subject. Instead, she commented on how comfortable and lovely the house was, and asked how long they'd lived in Rockland. By the time she'd finished her breakfast, the older couple was all smiles, and Ian Monroe—and serial killer groupies—was forgotten. Though, she felt as though she'd given Mr. Fletcher a twenty-minute crash course on forensic psychology.

She went back to her room, brushed her teeth, packed up, and left for Warren. It was about a fifteen-minute drive to the prison. Even though her appointment time wasn't until nine thirty, she was there at nine, per the instructions given to her for visiting the facility.

Maine State Prison was a large, white building, slightly grayed from the elements. If you ignored the wire, fences, and armed guards, it would look more like an industrial building than a maximum-security facility. Audrey pulled into the parking lot and found a spot. Before getting out of the car, she checked to make certain her hair and makeup looked presentable. She didn't care if Ian Monroe was impressed with her—his taste was in blondes—but she wanted to make certain she looked put together and professional.

And maybe a little intimidating. What was the point of having "resting bitch face" if you were afraid to use it?

She had two messages on her phone. She read them while standing between the car and the open driver's door. One was from Margot Temple, president of Ian Monroe's fan club. Technically it was called the "Freedom for Ian Coalition," but it meant the same thing. Audrey had already told them she couldn't speak at one of their meetings while she was working for the prosecution. Now, the woman wanted to know if maybe she'd visit after the trial. She thought it might be interesting for the members to hear both of them discuss their meetings with Ian.

If Monroe was meeting with the president and founder of the FIC, his ego must be in need of stroking, because according to the information she'd been given, he hadn't had any visitors other than his mother since they'd locked him up to await trial.

Maybe meeting with the woman before the trial would be a good idea. If she could find out what Ian said to her, it might prove useful to the prosecution.

Audrey didn't immediately reply to Margot—she wanted to check with Will Grant, the assistant DA, first—and went to the next message. It was from Christopher James, the crime writer, asking if she'd grant him an interview. She didn't respond to that one either. It was better to let a little time pass so that both of them would think she was busy, which she was. But also, she didn't want to give the impression of holding either of them important enough to warrant an immediate response. There was nothing wrong with not wanting to appear eager where those who might be mentally unstable or parasitic were concerned. She needed to be focused on the job she'd been hired to do, and not encouraging the small cult of celebrity that had sprung up around her since her past became public knowledge.

People found out you killed someone, and all of a sudden you're interesting.

It was a surprisingly warm morning for mid-October. Her coat hung open as she slung her bag over her shoulder and headed for the prison entrance. Inside, it was decorated in what Audrey thought of as "corpse colors"—grays, creams, and fleshy pinks. It looked better than some institutions she'd visited. But it still set her teeth on edge and made her eye twitch. Every time she stepped foot in a prison, she had the irrational fear that when the time came, they wouldn't let her leave—that they'd force her to stay, because a cold-blooded killer like herself deserved to be locked away for life.

She didn't regret what she'd done, but no regrets wasn't the same as no guilt.

She went through security, and tried to look disinterested as the guard inspected her purse and another patted her down. Her coat and nonnecessary items were secured in a locker in the lobby.

"Is this your first time visiting the facility?" the older guard asked.

Audrey nodded. "I've conducted prisoner interviews at different prisons, though. And I've read the procedure document on your website."

"You know the drill then. There will be a guard in the room with you, and he'll escort you there and back." He nodded at a younger male guard a few feet away. Audrey tried not to smile; she knew that face. It had been a long time since she last saw it, but Kenny Tripp didn't look much different than he had when he was sixteen—except that he had considerably less hair than he had back then. And more belly. He was Jake's cousin, but they looked nothing alike. Jake was tall and lean, with brown hair and hazel eyes. Kenny was several inches shorter, his hair a dark blond and his eyes blue.

It made sense now why Jake hadn't been nervous about her visit to Warren; he had someone on the inside to be his eyes. She didn't know how he'd managed to make sure Kenny was her escort, or if he'd had a hand in it at all, and she wasn't about to ask questions that might be overheard by the guard's superiors. What she wanted was to get this over with. While she found psychopaths as interesting as the next person, sitting across a table from one was an entirely different situation than seeing them on video or reading about them. A person would be stupid not to have some apprehension about sitting down across from a predator, even if he was only nineteen years old.

"You'll be in a private interview room," Kenny told her as he unlocked a door and followed her into a corridor. "Monroe will be restrained, and I'll be keeping watch out of earshot. If at any time you feel unsafe or uncomfortable, just say the word and I'll take you out of there."

"Thanks," she said. "Have you ever spoken to him?"

"Monroe?" When she nodded, he shrugged. "Yeah. He's a polite kid. Never gives the guards trouble. Quiet. Then again, the worst ones usually are."

"He's been here since he was seventeen. Has he ever been the target of other inmates?"

Kenny shot her a narrow glance that reminded her of Jake. Maybe there was a little resemblance after all. "Of course, but most of them think he's crazy, so they stay away."

"Why would they think he's crazy? Most psychopaths seem completely normal."

"Bit an inmate during a scuffle. Took a chunk of the guy's face off and swallowed it. I don't think anyone's challenged him since then, but he's been kept fairly isolated."

Audrey's breakfast shuddered in her stomach. "I thought you said he didn't make trouble."

"I said he didn't give the *guards* trouble."

Yeah, he was a Tripp, all right, splitting hairs right down to the follicle.

"What's this interview for anyway? I heard you're an expert witness in his trial."

"I'm supposed to assess him for the prosecution—let them know if he's competent to stand trial, and if he's lying about anything. I need to interview witnesses too. The prosecution wanted me because my experience is with juveniles, and almost everyone involved was under the age of eighteen during the times of the murders."

"So you're supposed to back up the decision to try him as an adult?"

"I'm supposed to provide an honest assessment of his competency." She smiled slightly to soften shutting him down.

They entered a room near the end of the corridor. Sitting at the table, arms and legs in restraints, was a young man in prison blues. He was good-looking despite being quite pale, with dark brown hair and eyes. His photos didn't do him justice. No wonder the press had nicknamed him the Boy Scout. He looked like a sweetheart. The kind of kid you'd want your daughter—or your son—to date.

"Hello," he said, meeting her gaze with a slightly mocking smile. Not so much a sweetheart with that expression. It was an amazing contradiction—in her opinion—that psychopaths tried so hard to appear like everyone else but then had such narcissistic pride over what they were and what they'd done. In their hearts they didn't want to be seen as a regular person; they wanted to be seen as the "monsters" they were.

"Good morning," Audrey replied. "Mr. Monroe, I'm Dr. Audrey Harte. I'm here to talk to you on behalf of the state."

"I know who you are and why you're here. Am I supposed to feel some sort of kinship with you because you offed some child fucker?"

If he was hoping to unsettle her, he was going to have to do better than that. She pulled the chair out from the table and sat down. "No. I don't expect you to feel anything for me at all."

"Good, because I don't." He studied her blatantly. "You've got freaky eyes."

"So I've been told." She resisted the urge to add "asshole" to the end of the statement.

"I'd bet you'd look good as a blonde."

Of course he did. All of his victims had been blond. "Actually, I tried it once. It's not a good look for me."

"Are you sure you want to be so close to me?" he asked. "I'm a sexual sadist. I raped all those girls."

Interesting. He taunted her with the rapes but not the murders? "I know what you've been accused of doing."

"Did the guard tell you what I've done since they locked me up here? I'm insane, you know." There wasn't a shred of madness in his dark gaze. In fact, there was very little of anything in his gaze. "You shouldn't get too close. I'm a monster."

Audrey gave him a patently false smile. They both knew she was too old for his tastes. "You're not my first monster, Mr. Monroe."

He leaned forward now. Out of the corner of her eye, Audrey saw Kenny's posture shift. He wouldn't hesitate to step in if she needed him. "Your first monster," Monroe began, his voice low and rough, "was he the one you killed?"

Did he think he was her first psycho? That apprehension she'd felt earlier vanished. She wasn't nervous to talk to him. He didn't scare her at all. He ought to have, but Audrey had known for years that there was something wrong inside her—a disconnect, for lack of a better term. She could shut down her emotions—and her morality—fairly easily.

"Yes," she replied, looking him in the eye. "But I assure you, you are perfectly safe from me while the guard is present." She pressed Record on her digital voice recorder as she tried to ignore the surprise on his face. "Shall we get started?"

In the hour and a half she was allowed to have with Monroe that day, Audrey learned that Ian Monroe possessed above-average intelligence—just enough for him to affect superiority—had been brought up in an affluent and reasonably loving home, and he liked the sound of his own voice.

Being kept isolated from the other prisoners after the face-eating episode, Monroe didn't have anyone to talk to, and it seemed he planned to make up for that with her. He used five words where two would have sufficed, and often veered off into segues that seemed to serve no other purpose than to bait her into giving away personal information. It didn't work, and it wasn't going to, but he kept trying.

And he took great delight in recounting his crimes. She had to shut off the part of herself that could still be horrified at the things people could do to one another, and listened silently as he spoke, interjecting only when he began to veer off onto another topic. She made notes as he talked. He watched her write, and that seemed to spur him on to give even more details. He got off on recounting how he'd raped those girls, but there was no way to avoid that when everything he said could also be used against him.

He was an attention-starved psychopath. But that didn't make him special either, as so many psychopaths were. His age made him an anomaly, but there had been younger—and worse—killers throughout history. It was simply more unsettling to see such lack of remorse in a kid. Audrey really didn't need to get this much in-depth information from him, but the longer he spoke, the more she began to understand him. And understanding was why she'd gotten into the field. She didn't know any forensic psychologist who would pass up the opportunity to talk to someone like Monroe.

"Kaylee's pussy had this smell that really turned me on. She'd just finished her period and there was this earthy scent—like dirt and metal. Fucking her felt like fucking Mother Nature."

Whoever first thought to use the word "pussy" as a euphemism for the vagina ought to have been shot. It was one of the most ridiculous words in the history of the English language.

Audrey tilted her head, her hatred of his vocabulary safely tucked away. "What did it feel like when you killed her?"

Until that moment, Monroe had kept an obviously mocking smirk on his face. She watched as it slid from his lips, replaced by a sneer. "That's not the important part. How many times do I have to tell you that? That's not what it was about."

"What was it about? Your love for these girls?"

This time his smile seemed genuine. Most people would be horrified by it, but Audrey wanted nothing more than to be inside his head at that moment, and see what exactly he remembered to make him smile like that. That was part of the disconnect; she looked at him like a puzzle—the *why* of why he'd raped and killed more important than the how, or even the who. "They were special—each and every one of them. Beautiful and perfect."

And dead. But Audrey didn't say that. It was actually fascinating, how he avoided discussing how he'd killed the girls when he gave her every stomach-turning detail about how he sexually assaulted them during the four days he kept each of them alive.

"Why the nineteenth of the month?" she asked. "You'd abduct them on the nineteenth and then leave them to be found on the twenty-third. Is there significance to those dates?"

"Yes."

Audrey waited, but he didn't elaborate. Suddenly, he wasn't so keen on letting his mouth run on any longer. That meant there was a significance behind the dates—something the prosecution might want to use. But really, she couldn't imagine it would come to that. The jury would listen to Monroe for five minutes and declare him guilty. They had physical evidence linking him to the crimes. They had his DNA, and despite his insistence that the girls had wanted him, each one of their bodies showed signs of torture and violent penetration. Tori Scott would be the voice of those dead girls. When she told the jury what he'd done to her, no one would have a doubt that he ought to be kept locked up.

"Would you like to share why those dates are important?"

His expression was totally blank—not a shred of emotion in his face or eyes. "You're the profiler. Can't you tell me?"

"I'm a psychologist, Mr. Monroe, not a mind reader. But I

would guess that these dates mean something very personal
to you. That they played a part in an event in your past that's
important to you."

He blinked, but otherwise remained unmoved. "Bravo."

Okay, she'd have to look into that herself. In his file he
said the dates just worked out like that for his first victim, so
he kept them as a form of tribute to that first girl, but there
was more to it than that. Audrey could feel it. She wanted to
know it.

And Monroe knew she wanted to hear more, the little
bastard.

"I'm done talking for the day, Dr. Harte. You can leave now."

"I have a few more questions."

"They'll have to wait."

She was annoyed, but she couldn't force him to talk to her.
She'd known from the beginning one visit might not be enough
to do a valid assessment of him, so she would be coming back
regardless.

"I'll put you on my visitor list," he told her after signaling
for Kenny to approach. "You can come by whenever you want.
I have a feeling you and I will be spending quite a bit of time
together over the next couple of weeks."

"Why's that?" she couldn't help asking, curious at the impish
tone of his voice.

Monroe smiled. "I can't tell you that. It will spoil it, and I
want our time together to be special. Don't you?"

"To be honest, Mr. Monroe, I haven't given it much thought."

"You will." He glanced up as Kenny approached, then leaned

forward across the table. "I'm looking forward to playing this game with you, Dr. Harte."

Audrey froze—just for a second. The note with the roses. She wanted to ask if he'd sent them, but couldn't give him the pleasure. "I don't play games, Mr. Monroe."

He grinned. "I think you'll like this one." Then, to Kenny, "We're done. I want to go back to my cell."

Audrey gathered up her things and left the room with Kenny, Monroe smirking behind her as he waited for his own escort.

"You okay?" Kenny asked.

"I'm fine."

They walked down the corridor side by side. "What did he say to you at the end there?"

"Just that he looked forward to seeing me again." It wasn't really a lie. "I think he wants to drag this process out as long as he can."

"You're the first visitor he's had in more than six months. I'd want to spend as much time with a pretty woman as I could as well."

She smiled. "Thanks, but I think Monroe's more interested in manipulating me than flirtation. His family hasn't come to see him?"

Kenny shook his head. "His mother used to come by, but he had her taken off his list after the last visit. She tried to get him to pray for God's forgiveness."

"Let me guess, it didn't go over well?" If he didn't have visitors, how could he have gotten someone to send the flowers? He wasn't allowed with the other prisoners, so he couldn't have done it through one of them. A guard? That was a chilling theory. A phone call, maybe? He wouldn't be foolish enough to do it through e-mail. Was he even allowed computer access?

"Like a lead balloon," Kenny replied. "He told her not to come back. She hasn't."

So much for his "good" family. Then again, it would be hard for a mother to reconcile with the fact that her child was a killer. Audrey made a mental note to hug her mother a little tighter the next time she saw her. Though comparing herself to Ian Monroe was a dive into a vat of self-loathing even she wasn't prepared to make.

"I did hear that he added that fan club lady to his visitor list."

"Margot Temple?" At Kenny's nod, she continued, "I'm not surprised. He needs the attention."

"Yeah, I've met a few psychopaths since I've been here—not too many obviously—but they all seem to have that attitude of needing someone to hear them talk about how great they are. You'd think if they were really so smart, they wouldn't have gotten caught."

"Ironic, isn't it?"

He smiled. "Just like that Alanis Morissette song."

Audrey collected the rest of her belongings from the locker and, after saying good-bye to Kenny, left the prison. He would have been working at the prison when Matt Jones, Maggie's brother, had been killed. She'd have to ask him about that the next time she saw him—only because she had a morbid curiosity as to whether or not the bastard suffered. He hadn't had a great life, but Matt Jones had been almost as much of an asshole as his father. The last time Audrey saw him he'd beaten the snot out of her. She'd put a good one into him as well, and not just out of a desire to protect herself. Once he threw the first punch, she'd been filled with a familiar desire to beat him into the ground. She was like her father that way—never one to walk away from a fight. Her therapist in Stillwater had said she had anger issues. Almost twenty years later she still had them. No amount of therapy, classes, or self-realization had succeeded in getting rid of them, though she liked to think she had better control of them in her thirties than she had in her teens.

The drive to Edgeport was roughly three hours from Warren. A tiny little town on the southern coast of Maine, it was a gorgeous place to be in the summer, and boring as hell the rest of the year—or at least it had been when she was young. Now she had to admit there was an element of quaintness to the place if you ignored the odd car rusting out in someone's yard, or the houses that looked ready to fall down around the people living in them. There were a lot of poor people in Edgeport, some middle class, and very few wealthy.

At one time Jake had been among the poor, especially when he lived with his mother, but his grandparents were better off, though they hadn't acted like it. When his grandmother died, she left him everything, and she had more money than anyone knew. He'd added to it considerably over the years, but it was strange to think of him as rich.

A woman walking down the road waved as Audrey passed. Instinctively, she waved back, even though she had no idea who it was. If she didn't know the woman, chances were she knew someone who did.

Jesus, they needed to repave the damn road. It was patched with so much tar now that it was said you could feel your vehicle sink into it during the summer. When it got cold, however, it was a damn rough ride. It would be even worse in the early spring after the winter's frosts had a chance to buckle it some more.

Her parents lived in the part of town known affectionately as "Lower Edge." There was Central Edge and Upper Edge as well. Lower Edge was closer to the rocky shore, and had the best view of the ocean. Audrey pulled into the driveway of her childhood home—a white Cape Cod with slate trim and shutters—shortly after two. Her parents were decidedly middle class, though her father had grown up without many luxuries. He would remind his children of how lucky they were every time one of them complained about the unfairness of their lives. Audrey knew all about how water had frozen on the counter in the winter, and that the windows had frost on the inside. And she knew way more about the outhouse they'd had than she wanted to remember.

She parked beside the minivan that sat there. Her sister, Jessica, had taken their mother to a medical appointment that morning, and had texted her just a few minutes earlier to let her know they were home. Audrey wanted to know what the doctor had said.

Her father's truck wasn't there, but that wasn't unusual in the middle of the day. John Harte wasn't the sort of man who liked to sit still for long. Retirement had been hard on him, and he often did odd jobs for neighbors to keep busy. In the winter—which Audrey didn't want to think about—he'd be busy plowing driveways. Standing still made him pensive, and that head of his was too full of anxiety, regrets, and fear to suffer much introspection. Whatever kept him sober was good by her, and since her mother confessed to Audrey, Jess, and their younger brother, David, that she had cancer, their father had done a fairly decent job of avoiding the bottle.

The front door wasn't locked—they only locked it at night—so Audrey let herself in. The cat—a fat ginger for which her father had a variety of monikers, none of which she was certain was the animal's actual name—sat just inside the foyer, as if to say, "What took you so long?"

"Hey, fat man," she said, and bent down to scratch behind his ears. He purred in response, leaning into her hand so that she was the only thing keeping him upright.

Tiny but forceful footfalls caught her attention. Audrey turned her head to see a familiar, sturdy toddler watching her with a grin. She smiled back. "Look at you, walking by yourself." She held out her arms. "Come see me, Livvie."

The little girl staggered forward, pitching headlong into her embrace. Audrey swept her up fast, coaxing a laugh. It tugged at her heart, though she'd never admit it. Just a few months ago she'd worried she'd never have the chance to know her nieces. She and Jessica had been estranged for a long time, and resentment had grown thick between them. Sometimes it raised its head, but their mother's illness had shoved their petty arguments to the back burner, and forced them to be civil.

Jessica came around the corner, drawn by her child's laughter.

She was a little shorter than Audrey, but not much, and her features were softer. Recently, Audrey had been told she had a "resting bitch face," which made her wonder what she looked like when she wasn't resting. Jessica didn't have the mismatched eyes either, though her oldest daughter did. "Oh, it's you. I didn't hear you drive in."

"I'm stealthy," Audrey replied, kissing Olivia's chubby hand when it grabbed for her face. It was sticky, but Audrey didn't care. "Where's Mum?"

"Upstairs getting changed." Jessica inclined her head toward the kitchen. Audrey, recognizing the gesturing for what it was, followed after her. The kitchen would give them more privacy.

"How did it go?" she asked in a low voice once they were by the stove. Jessica put the kettle on. All of life's challenges could be tackled over a cuppa.

Her sister's shoulders sagged. "She's not responding to treatment like the doctor had hoped."

Audrey's stomach dropped. "So what's the next step?" She kissed Olivia on the forehead. The feel of that warm, soft skin made her feel better. "A more aggressive treatment?"

"Surgery."

"She hoped to avoid that." Her gaze locked with her sister's.

"I know." Jessica shook her head. "Dad's going to lose his shit."

It was a very un-Jessica thing to say, and under different circumstances, Audrey would have laughed. "So's David." Their brother was very much his mother's boy, and the sweetest of the three siblings—everyone in the family knew it was true.

"Oh, God," Jessica murmured. "Will you tell him? You're closer to him than I am."

She'd rather stick a fork in her eye than be the one to give David news that would upset him, but Jess was the one that lived the closest to their parents—David was in New York—and was the one that did the most, sometimes to the neglect of her husband and her own children. It might not be pleasant, but telling David was the least Audrey could do for her.

The kettle whistled, and Jessica turned the burner off. "I know you just got here, and that Jake's expecting you, but could you give me a hand with dinner? I need to pick up Isabelle from school."

"I'll take care of it. You go home and be with your family."

The suggestion was met with a suspicious stare. "Well, I was going to have Greg meet me and the girls here for dinner and then go home. Mum likes to hear about Isabelle's day."

Audrey shrugged. "Whatever. I'll make dinner."

"What about Jake?"

"I'll see if he wants to come here."

Her sister's gaze brightened. "Do you think he'd make brownies?"

Jake had brought brownies to the Fourth of July barbecue her family hosted. They were made from his grandmother's recipe and were a favorite of their mother's—and Jessica's, apparently.

"I'll ask." She'd left her purse in the entryway, so she grabbed the cordless off the counter and dialed Jake's number. He picked up on the third ring. He didn't hesitate to accept when she made the invite, and laughed when she asked about brownies.

His culinary skills were becoming a thing with them. He really knew his way around a kitchen, which would have made his grandmother proud.

Their mother came downstairs just as Jessica was leaving to get Isabelle. Olivia was in the play area that Audrey's father had put together for her. Basically it was a kiddie corral around a cork mat, but it was big enough that she could run around and play with all her toys and not get immediately bored.

Audrey was just about to start cutting up chicken when her mother walked into the kitchen. "How do you do, babaloo?" she asked as she came in.

"Hi, Mum." When she hugged her, Audrey tried very hard not to wonder if she'd lost more weight, or if she looked more tired than usual, but the answer to both was yes.

"Did Jess make tea before she left?"

"I think she was going to have some when she got back. Want me to make you a cup?"

"Would you?" She sat down at the table as though the journey from upstairs had exhausted her. Something pinched tight in Audrey's chest. *I don't want to lose my mommy.*

Once her mother had her cup of tea and a biscuit with butter and molasses on the table in front of her, Audrey went back to work on dinner. She cut up chicken, rolled the chunks in flour, and then dropped them into a large frying pan that had hot, melted butter on the bottom. The chicken sizzled. Chicken stew with dumplings was one of the things she cooked quite well, and it was at the top of their family's comfort food list.

"Chicken stew," her mother commented. "Smells good already."

"Thanks."

"So your sister told you about the surgery."

Audrey paused in the middle of cutting up carrots. "Of course she did."

"Couldn't even let me tell you myself. God, I can't even go to the bathroom without her telling someone about it."

"She does it because she loves you and she's worried about you."

"You don't need to put on your patronizing psychologist tone with me, Audrey Harte. I know *why* she's fussing over me. I just want her to stop."

"She's not going to stop." She shot her mother a pointed look. "And I wasn't using my patronizing psychologist tone with you. If I'd wanted to be like that, I'd also tell you that the reason you want her to stop is more than likely out of a sense of guilt rather than annoyance. Guilt for taking so much of Jess's time, for taking her away from her own family. And that you're so used to taking care of people that it pisses you off when someone actually dares to try taking care of you because it might render you obsolete and no one will need you... Stop me if any of this is off the mark."

"You really are a smart-ass, you know that?" But her words were softened with a smile.

"You taught me well." She stirred the chicken. "So when's the surgery?"

"I have to decide if I want to have it first."

Audrey stared at her. "Why the hell would you need to decide anything? If surgery is what your doctor thinks is the best treatment, you're going to have it done. It's only your uterus—not like you need it. The poor thing probably has cobwebs and a good layer of dust by now."

Anne frowned at the joke, but it lacked real anger. "There are other treatments I can pursue."

"Why are you so against surgery?"

For a second, she hesitated, and Audrey knew her mother was weighing whether to lie or tell the truth. Audrey might have gotten her father's temper, but she got her aversion to vulnerability from her mother. "Because I'm afraid they'll open me up, find me full of cancer, and close me up again. If they don't look, I can tell myself it's not there and go on hoping it will all be okay and that I'll live long enough to see you and David have families of your own."

That moment would not be the best time to tell her mother that she had no intention of ever breeding. It was also not the right time to let her bottom lip quiver. Her mother didn't need her to fall apart; she needed her to be strong. "I want those things for you too, Mum. We all do, which is why you're having the surgery. End of discussion. If I have to knock you out and fireman-carry you to the hospital through snow in my bare feet, I'll do it. Uphill both ways."

She thought maybe her mother would fight her, but she didn't. "Okay, babe. If it means that much..."

"It does. To all of us."

Her mother nodded. She looked defeated and afraid. Audrey went back to her vegetables and pretended she hadn't seen it, because that's what was expected of her. "Jake's coming for dinner. He's going to make brownies."

"I do like that boy."

Smiling, Audrey cast a glance at her mother. God, she looked frail. It was terrifying. Maybe she ought to talk to Will about replacing her as an expert witness, and ask Angeline for some time off so she could spend more time with her mother. Helping put Ian Monroe away for life seemed a little less important to her at that moment. Maine didn't have the death penalty, so provided Monroe didn't get shanked, he'd still be rotting in prison when her mother died.

She'd talk to Will about it on Monday when she arrived in Portland.

Meanwhile, she began cutting up an onion for the stew, so that if her mother saw her crying, she'd have something to blame it on.

CHAPTER THREE

There was one thing guaranteed to piss Jake Tripp off, and that was disloyalty. He could forgive almost anything else but a betrayal of his trust, and someone close to him had done just that.

He kept day-to-day accounting for his businesses, and once a month he sat down and took a look at the numbers. There were a couple of places where the numbers didn't add up, and the one thing those places had in common was his older brother, Lincoln, a walking definition of Peter Pan Syndrome

Jake and Lincoln had never been terribly close. When they were kids, his brother had been a bully he avoided as much as he could, and then Jake went to live with his grandparents when their mother decided she didn't want her younger son anymore. It was years before he and Linc reconnected. He gave Lincoln a job at Gracie's—the tavern he owned—and Lincoln took care of some of the under-the-table aspects of Jake's businesses. He'd known that Lincoln sometimes skimmed a little off the payments he collected on various debts and services, and that was all right on occasion—a little something for his trouble. But the numbers for Gracie's were off. It wasn't just money either; there was booze unaccounted for, and food. There were even a couple of chairs missing.

Lincoln looked him in the eye every day and then stole from him. Blatantly. Anyone else and he would have done something about it before now, but they were family. He couldn't put off confronting his bother much longer, though he was going to put it off until Monday. Audrey was home for the weekend, and he wasn't going to ruin the couple of days he got to spend with her.

Plus, he had brownies to make for dinner with Audrey's family. Lincoln often teased him about being like their grandmother—like it was an insult that he liked to cook and keep a tidy house. Gracie Tripp had also been a crack shot, bloodthirsty, and loved by most of the town.

His grandmother had taught him to look after his own—and that included the land and people of Edgeport. The Tripps were one of the founding families, and took that responsibility to heart. Jake gave the locals jobs, and bought local whenever he could, and he didn't mind that his neighbors didn't know what to make of him. In fact, he preferred it. That uncertainty made most people hesitant to fuck with him.

Jake knew who he was. He had no delusions and few insecurities, but there had been only three people thus far in his life who accepted him exactly as he was and loved him despite it, and those were his grandmother, his niece, and Audrey.

So he'd make brownies, and he'd spend time with her family, because she wanted him to. And this shit with Lincoln would have to wait, because his brother wasn't as important to him as Audrey was. It was that simple.

He was icing the still slightly warm brownies when the front door opened and Alisha stomped in. Seriously, the kid walked like a lumberjack. She threw her backpack on the floor and her coat on top of it. "Brownies!"

"They're for dessert," he told her. "I'll give you a couple to take home for you and your mom. I'm going to the Hartes'."

His niece's blue eyes lit up. "Audrey's home? Can I see her?"

It had been a pattern ever since Audrey had first come home earlier that summer. Alisha had fallen in love with her and wanted to spend as much time as possible with her. He'd never had to deny the kid anything, but when it came to Audrey, he was selfish. He still had a lot of lost time to make up. "You can come for breakfast in the morning. Don't pout."

"Why can't I see her tonight?"

"Because we're going to be having sex, Lish. Incredibly graphic, HBO sex. And that won't happen if you're under the same roof."

The kid laughed. She had a big, earthy chortle that reminded Jake of his grandmother. "HBO sex. Yeah, keep dreaming, buddy." She stuck her finger in the bowl of chocolate fudge icing he'd made and licked it. "You'd put your back out, old man."

He set the icing out of her reach. He was only thirty-three. "Smart-ass."

The phone rang, and even though Jake was closer, Alisha dove for it. "Hello?" Her face lit up. "Oh, hi, Audrey!"

Jake went back to his brownies with a shake of his head. He

knew how this was going to end. When his niece hung up, he didn't even have to ask. "Make sure you call your mother and make sure it's okay that you come with me. And go do your homework or no deal."

He watched her practically skip from the room with a tight feeling in his chest. Somewhere along the way he'd slipped into a fatherly role with her, which was as terrifying as it was centering. Her own father had never been in the picture, and while Jake wasn't sure he was a great role model, he was pretty sure he was better than nothing.

They arrived at the Hartes' just a little past five thirty. In Edgeport, it was considered rude to arrive too close to the time dinner was to be eaten, or too early. You showed up at least twenty minutes early for conversation, and to offer assistance in meal preparation. Jake brought a bottle of wine as well. Alisha had the brownies.

Audrey opened the door. Her gaze met his immediately, even as Alisha launched herself into her arms. She hugged the girl fiercely, but she smiled at him. He stepped over the threshold once Alisha was pushed toward the kitchen to hand-deliver dessert to Anne. He closed the door with a stupid grin on his face. It wasn't smart to let her know just how happy he was to see her—not at all in the interest of self-protection. But when she moved toward him, closing the scant distance between them, he knew she felt the same.

Jake took a step, meeting her halfway. His free hand came up to cup the back of her head as her fingers caught at the front of his jacket. The kiss was over too soon, but full of just enough promise that anticipation scraped at his nerves. It was going to be a long evening.

When he followed her into the kitchen, a loud squawk cut through the conversation.

"Who's that, Livvie?" Audrey's sister, Jessica, asked her youngest.

"Ack!" her daughter responded. Jake grinned as the little girl staggered toward him on her sturdy legs. She gave him a squint-eyed, snaggletoothed grin and held out her arms. He picked her up as the others laughed. He didn't know what he'd done to earn the kid's affection, but every time he saw her—and he saw her sometimes more than he saw Audrey—she came at him like a two-cent whore on a dollar. She put her chubby hands on either side of his face—her fingers were sticky. They were always sticky. What the hell did the kid get into?

Isabelle, her older sister, was a mini-version of Audrey, right down to the odd-colored eyes. She smiled up at him. "Livvie likes you, Jake." Then she grabbed Alisha by the hand and asked her to color with her.

Jess's husband, Greg, came over and shook his hand, and Anne gave him a hug for the brownies. She looked tired, but otherwise okay. Her husband, he noticed, wasn't home. Jake didn't remark on his absence. He had a fairly good idea of where John—Rusty to most of the town—would end up. There was a chair at Gracie's that practically had the shape of his ass worn into it.

With Olivia perched on his forearm, he helped with last-minute preparations and then put the little girl into her highchair for dinner. They'd all just sat down when the phone rang.

"Let it go to voice mail," Jess said.

Anne looked worried. "It could be John."

It was Audrey who actually got up. "I'll get it."

Jake watched her as he took the plate of chicken from Alisha.

"Hello? Yes, this is she." There was a long pause as the person on the other end of the line said something. Suddenly, Audrey straightened, her back rigid. "What?"

Jake wasn't the only one watching her now. A dull flush crept up Audrey's pale cheeks. He went still, his attention completely focused on her face. He thought she was gorgeous, but there was a hardness that she tried to conceal—that hardness was in the line of her jaw and the narrowness of her eyes as she listened. It was the same look her father got before he buried his fist in someone's face.

"There's no proof those flowers were from Monroe, and if they were, you'll be doing exactly what he wants by writing about it...No, I'm not going to answer any of your questions. Don't call this number again. If you want to talk to me, call my office." She hung up.

"Everything okay, babe?" her mother asked.

Audrey sucked in a breath and slowly exhaled. Her expression softened. "Someone sent me flowers at the B and B last night. I don't know who sent them, but the lovely owners of that establishment called the *Portland Chronicle Herald* and told them I'd been threatened by Ian Monroe. That was a reporter from the paper calling to get a comment."

"Why would the B and B people do that?" Jessica asked.

"Advertising," Jake told her. "Monroe's case is high profile.

By linking themselves to it, they're hoping to attract customers." It would probably work in their favor, despite reeking of desperation. Jessica looked at him as though she was disturbed that he'd answered so quickly. It wasn't like it was some kind of secret business acumen, nor one that he would practice.

Audrey came back to the table. "I should have tossed the card, or kept it." She rubbed her forehead. "They were so nice."

Under the table, Jake nudged her foot with his. When she lifted her gaze, he said, "This isn't on you, and it's not going to affect the case against Monroe."

She nodded, but he could see that she wasn't convinced. Audrey had always been able to admit that she'd been wrong, but had a hard time getting over thinking she'd done something that might be seen as stupid.

"Let's not talk anymore about that awful boy or anything related to him," Anne suggested—forcefully. "If the phone rings again, Jessie, you answer it."

Greg asked Audrey how she was getting along in Cambridge and easily changed the topic. Gradually, she relaxed. The wine probably helped. Jake watched her, looking for any hint that she hadn't told him everything about the flowers. She wouldn't want him to worry about her.

But he was already worried. It was a big case and he knew she wanted to give the prosecution all she had. Whoever sent those flowers, they'd done it to fuck with her head, and throw her off her game. To scare her. That pissed him off.

He'd stay out of it until she asked for his help—or until someone crossed a line. Then he wasn't going to stay out of it.

He'd taken his grandmother's lessons about taking care of his own to heart. Audrey was his, and he'd do anything to protect her, even if it meant getting blood on his hands.

It wouldn't be the first time.

Had she liked the flowers? Probably not. Audrey Harte didn't look like a white roses kind of woman. That was fine. The flowers weren't meant to be liked. They were meant to be thematic; white roses were symbolic of new beginnings, of respect and reverence, and of secrecy.

They also went great with funerals.

This was a new beginning—one worthy of marking. It remained to be seen if Dr. Harte was worthy of respect. She had promise. How long would it take her to figure out what the flowers meant? That would be a good place to start.

Had she already started to piece together that something wasn't right? She wouldn't have talked to the lawyers about it yet, though. She would investigate more before passing on any concerns. She'd want to be able to back them up. But she'd have to act on her instincts when the game got going. The police were dogs begging for scraps, but Audrey was different. She knew what it was like to see the life leave someone's eyes. Audrey Harte was a killer.

This was going to be so much *fun*.

Jake left before Audrey did so he could take Alisha home. Audrey stayed behind to help clean up.

"Where do you suppose Dad is?" Jessica asked as they loaded the dishwasher. Their mother was with Greg and the girls in the living room.

Audrey glanced up as she dropped silverware into the basket. "You have to ask?"

Jess grimaced. "Gracie's?"

"That would be my bet." Audrey closed the dishwasher. "I'm going to check on my way to Jake's."

"Greg can go. You have plans."

Her older sister's generosity surprised her. It had been so long since there was any kind of peace between them that sometimes it felt odd. "You and Greg are already doing more than your share. I can take care of it."

Jess shrugged. She had a brownie stain on the front of her T-shirt in the shape of a tiny handprint. Miss Olivia liked to play with her food. "You handle Dad better than David or me anyway."

Audrey frowned. "Yeah? When was the last time you literally kicked him out of a car?"

"I don't even go to pick him up. He wraps himself around a tree or loses his license, that's on him. I can't even make myself afraid of him hurting someone else anymore."

"I know." What went unsaid was that sometimes both of them wished that he *would* hurt someone else—and that he would have to live with that. Audrey wouldn't want anyone to suffer just so her father could face the consequences of his drinking, but a little consequence would be nice.

As a psychologist, Audrey knew about addiction and was

sympathetic to those who had their demons to battle. God knew she sometimes had her own, but as the child of an alcoholic, she just wanted her father to stop and acknowledge the damage his drinking had done. Was doing. It didn't matter how futile she knew it was. It didn't matter that she knew he was driven to do it. All that mattered was that the people around him hurt, and that compulsion was stronger than any love he felt for his family.

Jessica glanced toward the living room. "But she needs him, so maybe making sure he doesn't hurt himself or anyone else would be good."

"Yeah." Sighing, Audrey stepped away from the counter. "I'd better get going then."

She said good-bye to her mother—promising to see her the next day—and Greg, and hugged Isabelle. Olivia was passed out in her father's arms.

It was a cold night. Audrey pulled her coat tighter around her as she jogged to her car. It was going to be so nice to curl up with Jake later. The man gave off heat like a furnace. He'd always been like that. She remembered so many times when they were kids, pressing her back to his chest, or leaning in with his arm around her shoulders. He'd been keeping her warm since before they knew what sexual attraction was.

Gracie's wasn't far—nothing in Edgeport was. It used to be a house, years ago, but Jake's grandparents had turned it into a take-out and pool hall after that. Jake had been the one to take the ungainly "Frankenstein" of a building and turn it into a tavern. It had been a smart choice. The town was full of drinkers, and people came from neighboring towns as well. The bootleggers didn't much care for it, because going to Gracie's was still cheaper than buying from them—unless they made their own.

Neon lights blinked in the window and along the front of the building. A sturdy veranda provided a shelter for smokers so they didn't crowd near the door, and in the summer, had a couple of tables on it for those who wanted to sit outside.

When Audrey walked through that door a few months ago, she'd felt like everyone stopped and stared at her. That night, she didn't even think about it; she simply walked right in. She was old news now.

Jake's older brother, Lincoln, was behind the bar with Donalda, the young blond waitress who was his current sex partner. Lincoln dressed like he was a rock star—lots of black and vests, and jewelry. He also wore his dark hair long, though tonight it was tied back. He and Jake didn't look much alike, unless you got them at just the right angle and light. Jake looked more like the Tripp side of the family and Lincoln resembled their mother—the woman who had dropped Jake off at Gracie's house and said, "He's your problem now."

Lincoln smiled when he saw her and pointed toward the back of the room. Her father was in his usual spot. She hadn't needed to come get him the last few times she'd been home. Stupid to think that meant he'd given up drinking. It would be easier for him to give up breathing. At least he wasn't passed out, so she wouldn't have to get Lincoln's help in carrying him outside.

Unfortunately, her father was engaged in his second-favorite pastime as she approached. He was trying to pick a fight with a man at least twenty years younger than him. Audrey didn't recognize the guy, so he wasn't a local, which was unfortunate. Locals knew her father and how to handle him. This guy was younger, and he was pretty well built, so he probably figured he could take an old drunk. He'd probably think that right up until the point where he got a chair in the teeth.

Audrey walked up to them, insinuating herself between them. "Time to go home, Dad."

Her father smiled at her. Anticipation sparkled in his eyes—one brown and one blue, just like hers. He was spoiling for a little blood. "Hey, kid. You might want to move."

She turned to his opponent. "I'm sorry for whatever he's done or said to try to goad you into fighting him. I'm going to take him home."

"He's an asshole," the guy told her. "I'm going to kick his ass." He smelled like AXE body spray and beer. And either he spent every minute of his life outdoors or he went to tanning beds. His biceps were so overly developed, his arms didn't hang right at his sides.

Her father sure knew how to pick 'em.

Audrey met Mr. Roid-Rage's red-rimmed gaze. Her father was an asshole, yes, and he'd be the first one to admit it, but he was still her father. "What are you trying so hard to compensate for that you'd fight a drunk guy probably old enough to be your father? Because I feel compelled to tell you that your insecurity about your penis size isn't worth the hurt he'll deliver."

The man scowled. "What the fuck did you just say?" A woman tugged on his arm, trying to pull him away, but he pushed her with enough force that she bumped into a table and spilled the drinks on it.

No wonder her father picked this guy—he was a douche. If he didn't watch it, he was going to have the entire bar on his ass. People around these parts could ignore almost any sort of violence if they wanted, but they didn't approve of a man getting rough with a woman or child—at least not in public.

"Just walk away," Audrey told him. "And we'll leave. No one has to get hurt."

"How about you just step aside and *you* won't get hurt."

Her father took a step forward. "Touch her and the next time you see your teeth will be when you shit them out."

Axe pushed closer as well. She was going to get sandwiched in a moment. Audrey shoved at both of them, with little luck.

"Look," she said to the younger man in a final attempt to defuse the situation. She was just going to start talking and hope that at least some of what she said was on point. "Just walk away. I know that's hard for you, probably because you were picked on as a kid. Who was it that abused you? Your father? Did he beat you and your mom? You were probably a skinny kid too, huh? Did he tell you that you were weak like her? I bet school sucked for you too. You got yourself all buff and badass so no one would hurt you again? You probably fight just so you'll stop hearing his voice in your head. But you just hurt your girlfriend, and I bet she's looking at you the same way your mom used to look at your father. You don't really want to be like him, do you? Because that's where you're headed."

The man stared at her, his jaw slack and his gaze startled.

She'd gotten a few guesses right, apparently. Hopefully it was enough. Then, he turned his head and looked at the woman he'd shoved. "Baby, I'm sorry." He went to her, and Audrey turned to her father.

"You're fucking magic," John said, breathy with whiskey-scented awe.

"You're fucking leaving," she said, grabbing his arm and pulling. He staggered after her, shouting at Lincoln to put his final drink on his tab. Audrey didn't even want to think of how much of his money was spent on alcohol. And who would she be to judge when she had a closet full of shoes, some of which she'd hadn't even worn yet?

Her father laughed as she opened the car door for him. "You didn't even throw a punch and he backed down," he chortled as he slumped into the seat. "That's a rare talent, kid. Your grandfather could do that. 'Course most people thought he was nuts."

"You're too old to pick fights," she told him as she climbed in the other side and started the engine. "And don't try to butter me up by acting like I've done something fabulous. Mum needs you right now, and look at you. How can she go through treatment and take care of herself when she spends so much time worrying and fussing over your sorry ass?"

His laughter died. "Hey, you don't talk to me like that. I'm your father, and you'll respect me."

She scowled, checking for traffic as she pulled out onto the main road. "I'll talk to you however I want until you earn that respect. Fuck, Dad. Mum needs surgery. You have to be able to take care of her. She needs to be able to depend on you. We all do."

He was quiet. Had he lapsed into sullen silence like he normally did when he got his gin-blossomed nose out of joint?

"I know," he said finally. "I know she needs me. I'm scared, kid. I always figured if I lost her, it would be because she came to her senses and left me, not because... *I'm* supposed to go first." His voice broke.

If he started bawling, she didn't know what she'd do. "The surgery is so she won't die, Dad. If you want her to outlive you, you need to be there for her now. This isn't going to be easy, and she's not going to be able to do a lot after surgery. Can she depend on you? Can we?"

He sniffed. "Yes."

"You say that now. You'll say it tomorrow, but what happens the next time you get scared? Jesus, you need to find a better crutch than booze."

"I want to be the man she deserves, Auddie. I want to be the father you kids should have had."

Fuck, now she was going to be the one bawling. "You can still be that man, but saying it doesn't amount to anything. You have to do the work. Are you willing to do that? Because Jess and David and I will help you if you mean it."

"I do."

"Good."

"You know I love you, kid, right? Jess and David too."

Emotion knotted in her throat. "I know." But she couldn't make herself tell him she loved him too. Until the day he could say it sober, she wouldn't say it at all.

The rest of the drive passed in silence. She dropped him off and watched him go inside. Through one of the windows, she saw her mother come to meet him. He grabbed her up in his bearlike arms and hugged her. Audrey looked away from their intimacy and, for the second time that night, set off for the center of town.

Jake lived down a dirt road called Tripp's Cove. He owned most of the land from the main road to the shoreline, where the resort he owned was located. His sister Yancy, Alisha's mother, managed it for him. His house had belonged to his grandparents. It was a big Queen Anne, with eggshell siding and slate trim. He'd renovated the interior, but the old porch swing was still on the veranda, and Gracie's wringer-washer sat in a corner of the kitchen.

The door was open, so she let herself in. He met her in the kitchen, took one look at her, and opened his arms. She started crying before they closed around her.

Audrey woke up the next morning alone in Jake's bed. The scent of coffee and waffles made up for his desertion. God, he was so domestic. She remembered the two of them baking bread with Gracie as kids—before Maggie came between them. No, that wasn't fair. Maggie had been a lot of things, and most of them hadn't been good, but Jake wasn't one of her victims. He'd known exactly what he was doing when he screwed her that night at the camp, and he'd known Audrey would run away. They'd already aired that laundry.

She glanced at the clock. Nine o'clock. She slipped out from between the flannel sheets and hauled on leggings, an oversized sweater, and a pair of soft, fuzzy socks. Then she hurried downstairs, down the hall, and into the kitchen.

Jake was at the stove in pajama pants and a T-shirt. One of his bare feet tapped the hardwood floor in time to the song playing on the radio. "Perfect timing," he said without turning around. "Want to get the coffee cream and butter out of the fridge?"

"Smells fabulous," she commented as she undertook the task he'd assigned. "Is there maple syrup?"

He shot her a look that told her she should know better. "It's on the stove."

He'd heated the syrup. "It just might be possible that you're the most amazing man on the planet."

"Might?" A smile lifted one side of his mouth. "I must be losing my touch."

Audrey helped put everything on the table. They sat across from each other, legs entwined beneath. The first bite of pancake was a taste-gasm of epic proportions. "I take it back. You *are* the most amazing man on the planet."

"That's more like it." He took a drink of coffee. "Those roses. Is that all there's been, or is there something else I should worry about?"

She blinked. "I didn't think you were worried at all."

His gaze met hers, direct and open. "I'm not—if you tell me I shouldn't be."

"Well, since Monroe's in jail, he's really not much of a threat. I think they meant to unsettle me. For all I know, the B and B people could have orchestrated the whole thing as a publicity ploy. I lived in LA, I know how far some people will go to be on TV."

"Nothing like death to bring the tourists," he remarked, dumping more warm maple syrup on the stack of pancakes on his plate. "We were at capacity for a couple of months after Maggie's murder. We still get calls from people wanting to see the site."

"You should start a package—the Edgeport Murder Experience."

"Lincoln suggested the same thing, only not as catchy. He was serious."

"I'm sure he was."

"I like money, but not enough to exploit you, Bailey, or even Maggie for it."

She smiled as she carved out another bite with her fork. "Anyway, I'm not worried. After some of the stuff that happened this summer with Matt and Isaac, flowers from a psycho are a pleasant change."

Jake glanced up at her face, and she knew he was looking at the fading scar just above her left eyebrow. She couldn't remember if it was from when Matt hit her, or when Isaac ran her off the road, but one of them had caused it, and it was a reminder of that summer she didn't need.

"What did Grant have to say about it?"

"Will thinks it's just posturing. Regardless, it's not going to stop me from doing my job." She cut another bite.

"You don't have to prove yourself, you know."

She chewed and swallowed. "Actually, I think I do. At the very least, to myself."

He arched a brow and Audrey smiled at how much the expression reminded her of Gracie. "I'm embarrassed that I didn't see what was going on with Bailey until it was shoved in my face. I'm supposed to understand human behavior, especially where teenagers are concerned. I dropped the ball."

"No one had a clue, Aud. Not even the kid's father."

"Fathers rarely do." She set down her fork. "Look, I just have to work it out. Make it up to myself."

He tipped the coffeepot over her cup, refilling it. "Whatever turns your crank."

She squeezed his calf between hers under the table. "That would be you."

When his gaze locked with hers, she lost a bit of herself in those golden-green eyes of his. They stood up at the same time, limbs untangling just as easily as they'd wound together. She stepped away from the table just as he came around it. He pressed her back against the wall, warm hands slipping beneath her sweater. Audrey's heart jumped in response when his mouth covered hers. They'd been doing this for months now, but she still felt like a teenager every time he touched her.

A few minutes later, he was inside her, her legs wrapped around his narrow waist. His eyes were bright and heavy-lidded, the lean planes of his cheeks flushed. She needed to wash her hair, and her leggings hung from her left calf—they'd been in too much of a hurry to remove them completely—but Audrey was shameless in that moment. There were so many aspects of her life that made her uneasy, plagued her with second thoughts, but her relationship with Jake wasn't one of them.

"I love you," she told him, the confession falling easily from her lips. It was like tossing a weight off her shoulders.

Jake went still—and for one split second she wondered if maybe she should have had second thoughts after all.

"Say it again," he demanded, voice low and raw.

Audrey smiled. "I love you, Jake Tripp. Always have."

He kissed her hard, fingers of one hand biting into her thigh while the others tangled in her hair. They came together fast, with harsh breaths and muffled cries.

Jake broke the kiss long enough to look her in the eye. "Always will," he rasped, breath warm against her mouth. "I always will."

And then they fell silent. They didn't speak again for a long time. There wasn't any need.

There was nothing else to say.

CHAPTER FOUR

The blade of the axe bit into the log, cleaving the wood almost perfectly down the middle. Only a few stubborn strips of bark tried to hold on at the bottom, so tenuous Jake didn't even bother to cut them; he pulled the two halves apart and stacked them with the other splits before reaching for another log to cut. Another hour or two and he'd have a cord piled at the side of the house. Rusty—John Harte, Audrey's father—had offered him use of his splitter, but Jake preferred using the axe. He liked the way his shoulders hurt after a day of cutting. Liked the feeling of accomplishing something with his two hands.

It centered him. Cleared his mind. Put everything in perspective.

It was a chilly morning, but he was outside in jeans and a T-shirt, which was starting to feel damp. He wore a pair of steel-toed boots that had belonged to his grandfather. He hated wearing shoes, but he'd hate losing a toe even more.

Sweat ran down his forehead, and he wiped it away with a grimy forearm as his breath misted before his face. He set another log on the tree stump his family had used for cutting wood for the last sixty years, and hoisted the axe.

The sound of a motorcycle driving down the road reached his ears as the log splintered. Edgeport was the kind of quiet little town where you could hear cars before you saw them, and people laughing on the beach sounded like they were in your backyard, yet a moose—or a guy with a gun—could sneak up on you in the woods. Jake knew the sound of that bike, so he wasn't surprised when it turned into his drive, nor did he look up from his chore.

"Can't you hire some kid to do this for you?" his brother asked as he approached. Lincoln's face was flushed, reddened by the wind. Jake couldn't judge him for driving a motorcycle in October when he wasn't even wearing a coat.

Jake straightened. This time, he let the trickle of sweat run down his temple. "I like it."

Lincoln was dressed like he was auditioning for an eighties rock band—leather jacket, scarf, skinny jeans, and black biker boots. His brother surveyed the scene with an amused glance. "Yeah, I bet you do. Then again, no one else would probably be able to do the job to suit you."

Jake shrugged. He'd learned a long time ago not to rise to low-hanging bait. "Probably not." He stuck the axe blade into the stump and pulled off his work gloves. "It's before noon. What are you doing up and around?"

Linc smirked. "You beckoned, so I came running like a good little grunt."

So this was how it was going to be. Fine. "You never come running, and you're sure as fuck not a 'good little grunt.'"

"What am I, then?"

Sighing, Jake put his hands on his hips. "My brother, which is the only reason you're still able to use both hands."

Lincoln stiffened, his face twisting into a bitter, angry mask. "You think I'm stealing from you, is that it? You summoned me like I'm your fucking servant and then you accuse me of ripping you off?"

Disappointment pressed on Jake's shoulders. No pretense of not knowing what was going on—Lincoln went straight to theft with the self-defensiveness only an entitled asshole could.

"Save me the drama. I asked you to come up when you had the time, and I'm not *accusing* you of stealing from me, I know you did." If his brother owned up to it like a man, he would at least be able to respect him for it, but this indignant outrage was an insult to them both.

"You bastard. I've done *everything* you ever asked of me." Lincoln jabbed a finger toward the ground. "You make Yance and me work for you while you sit back enjoying all the money the old bitch left you. She only left me five grand."

Jake's jaw clenched. Their grandmother deserved more respect than that. "She knew you'd waste it, and you did. You had it gone before the week was up. I've given you everything you asked for, Linc. If you needed money, I would have given it to you. You didn't have to steal it."

His brother took a step forward, his cheeks flushed from more than just the chill in the air. There had been a time—years ago, now—when Jake would have taken a step back from that anger. He used to be afraid of his big brother, but now he found him more pathetic than intimidating. "It's rightfully mine. I wouldn't have to steal if she hadn't left everything to you."

"That's how you're going to justify it?"

"You know it's true."

The wind came up, icing the sweat on his skin. He was grateful for the cold taking the edge off his temper. "I know she gave you money every time you asked and that you never paid her back. I know you've been helping yourself since the day I gave you a job and a place to live. You don't steal from family."

"Fuck off, Jake." Lincoln's face contorted into an ugly grimace. "Don't talk like we're family. It's not like we've ever actually been brothers."

Of all the things Lincoln could have said, that was the one thing that actually struck a chord. Jake stared at him, unable to think of how to respond, and embarrassed by just how hurt he actually was. Family, he'd been taught, was the only thing that truly mattered. Family was supposed to love and support you. Family was supposed to have your full loyalty.

"You're fired," he said finally, the words rough in his throat. "You can keep the apartment, but I want your key to Gracie's."

"No," his brother replied, his expression turning smug. "You're not firing me. In fact, you're going to give me a raise."

Jake arched a brow. "Why would I do that?"

Lincoln tossed his hair. "Because if you don't, I'm going to call that sexy Neve Graham and tell her you had Matt Jones murdered."

He hadn't seen that coming. He almost respected his brother for striking back instead of slinking away. "Why would you do that?" He rolled his shoulders back against the tension creeping down his spine. The last time Lincoln tried to blackmail him they'd had a huge fight that resulted in both of them being bruised and broken for days, and that had been over a girl.

Lincoln grinned. "My friend Ratchett just got out of Warren a couple of weeks ago. He was there when Matt got taken out. He said everyone knew it was a hit. Kenny got all squirrelly when I asked him about it. I knew then that you'd had Matt taken out for what he did to Yance and your fuck-nut girlfriend."

Jake stared at him. He wanted to punch him in the fucking throat. It was all posture, this blackmail threat, but it still pissed him off. If he reacted, he'd be giving his brother power over him, and that was *not* going to happen. The fucker was trying to blackmail him for doing what Lincoln ought to have done as the eldest.

"What are you getting at, Linc?"

Lincoln's smile twisted and drained from his face. "I'm saying you're not going to fire me, Jay. Not if you want me to keep your dirty little secret. It's going to cost you."

Jake backed up a couple of steps and picked up another log, putting it on the stump. He pulled the axe free. "If you think you have information about a murder, you should go to the police."

The smile slipped. "You think I'm joking?"

Jake swung, cleaving the log cleanly in two. "I think you're a sorry sack of shit with no honor and no concept of loyalty. You do what you need to do, Linc. You're still fired." He tossed the halves of the log onto the pile, and slowly turned toward his brother. "And I've changed my mind about the apartment. I want you out of it. Come to think of it, you should probably leave Edgeport altogether."

Lincoln came at him with a snarl. Jake swung at him hard.

He remembered to drop the axe first.

Monday morning found Audrey in Portland, the largest city in Maine, with a population roughly one-tenth the size of Boston, and one-fifty-ninth the size of Los Angeles. As a child, she'd thought it had to be the biggest city in the world. It had seemed downright magical. Now she had to admit she liked the slower pace, and the fact that she didn't have to add an extra thirty to sixty minutes to a trip to allow for traffic.

She'd driven down the night before and checked into her hotel—a somewhat upscale affair with a view of the harbor. She'd booked a suite, since she was going to be there for the week, and the extra living area would keep her from feeling like she was trapped in a box. It gave her a work space where she could spread out all of her information, and when Jake joined her on Wednesday for a couple of days, it would almost feel like a romantic getaway. There was easily room for two in the tub, she thought with a smile.

They hadn't said they loved each other again after the first time. There hadn't been a need. Her first serious boyfriend in college, Kurt, had told her he didn't think she was capable of love. She told him she was capable, just not for *him*. Funny enough, they'd broken up shortly after that. It was true, though, not just a mean thing for her to say. She hadn't been able to love him, because he hadn't known the truth about her and there was always this huge omission hanging over her head whenever she was with him. She'd known he wouldn't be able to accept what she'd done in the past, so what was the point in falling in love?

She had breakfast in her suite as she prepared for the rest of the day. Most of it was going to be spent interviewing three girls who had attracted Ian Monroe's attention in the past. Fortunately for them, he hadn't graduated to killing at the time, but unfortunately for two of them, he had already figured out that rape was his thing.

They wouldn't be terribly long interviews—a rehash of statements they'd made, and assessments based on their current psychological state, and juror sympathy. The prosecution wanted to lock Monroe up and throw away the key. The odds of that happening were in their favor, but the defense was going to try to portray Monroe as innocent of the crimes he *allegedly* committed, and these three girls of being willing sex partners. If that didn't seem to work, they'd take a mentally unstable approach. The prosecution wasn't going to let either one of those defenses fly, so they needed to make certain they had an airtight case. Witnesses had to be credible, believable, and—if not likable—sympathetic.

It was part of Audrey's job to determine with which witnesses the jury would empathize, which ones needed coaching, and which ones, if any, shouldn't be called to the stand. And then, she would be asked to testify as to her professional opinion on various points.

She dressed in black knit pants, black boots, and a pale pink cashmere sweater. Over it, she threw on her warm, black wool wrap. She wore simple silver jewelry, and had her hair in a loose bun at the nape of her neck. She'd put a lot of thought into what to wear—black would make her look chic and professional, while the pink sweater added approachability and softness. Pink was often associated with compassion, and pale shades often had a calming effect—she'd read the research. She needed the extra softness to counteract the resting bitch face she often wasn't even aware of wearing.

She wanted these girls to see her as professional enough to be impressed, but girly enough that they felt safe and supported. Her jewelry was plain, but expensive, and her boots were highly polished leather, with a fashionable heel. Even her makeup had been applied with the careful balance of power and kindness in mind. That balance was important when dealing with women, especially younger ones, she'd found. If she'd been meeting men, she would have worn something that tipped the scales more toward power. It was sexual profiling, of course, and sometimes backfired, but for the most part, it served her well. She wasn't trying to manipulate anyone, just put them at ease so that they looked at her as someone in whom they could confide.

Audrey drove to a Starbucks not far from the USM campus. All three of the girls she was about to interview attended the University of Southern Maine, though they rarely socialized with one another. Amber Gale, her first appointment, was two years older than the other girls. She arrived promptly at ten o'clock, dressed in jeans, boots, and a sweater underneath a navy peacoat. She was average height, with long blond hair and blue eyes. Pretty. She recognized Audrey right away, and smiled as she approached.

"Thanks for coming," Audrey told her. "I hope I'm not interfering with your class schedule?"

"I have Monday mornings free," Amber replied in her high, clear voice. "Do you mind if I grab a coffee?"

"Of course not. It's on me." Actually, it was on the DA's office.

A few minutes later they sat across a small table from each other, Audrey with her notebook opened to a fresh, blank page. She didn't plan on taking notes unless Amber told her something the prosecution might have to follow up on, or something worth noting. It was more important that she listen carefully to everything the younger woman told her and made notes later. Of course, she would record the conversation in case anything was called into question. In addition to gathering information for the prosecution, she would be expected to back it up and answer questions in court, so it was important that she be able to go back and listen to the witnesses rather than just refer to notes.

She pressed the record button. "Interview with Amber Gale, October seventeenth. Okay, so you went to high school with Ian Monroe?"

Amber nodded. She was drinking a venti Pumpkin Spice

Latte with whipped cream on top. It smelled good. "I was a year ahead of him. His parents live a few houses down the street from mine, so we'd see each other a lot."

"Would you say you were friends?"

She shook her head, golden hair falling over her shoulders. "No. We never hung out."

Audrey tilted her head, watching as the girl began picking at her fingernails. "But he asked you out on a date, didn't he?"

"The Homecoming Dance." She took a drink, licking away the whipped cream that stuck to her lip. "He asked me to go with him."

"You said no?" She already knew the answer—it was all in the preliminary notes she'd been given—but part of her job was to discern malingering or lying in each witness.

"Yeah. I was going with my boyfriend."

"Would you have said yes if you'd been unattached?"

The girl made a face. "No. Definitely not."

"Because he was younger?" As a teen, Audrey wouldn't have dated a guy who was even a couple of months younger than her, let alone an entire year.

"Because he was weird." Amber took another drink of her latte.

"Weird, how?"

She leaned her elbows on the table. "Have you ever met someone who made your skin crawl? You don't know why, but just the look of them makes you want to turn and run in the other direction?"

Audrey nodded. "I know the feeling." She resisted the urge to advise the girl not to go into a career in psychology.

"Well, that's how I felt about Ian. He was always nice, but he was intense. He would watch me and not care if I noticed. It was like he wanted me to notice—wanted me to be uncomfortable."

"How did he take your rejection?"

"I thought he was fine at first, but sometime during the Homecoming Dance, my boyfriend's car was keyed. He thought Ian did it." She leaned back in her chair and started picking at her nails again.

"Do you know if Ian was responsible?"

"I remember seeing him in the parking lot, smiling at us. It was a smug smile."

"Did he ask you out again?"

"No, but one night when I was getting ready for bed, I looked out my window and he was on the street in front of my house, staring up at me. He didn't look away when he saw me. He just stood there. Staring." Amber frowned, her fingers wrapping around her paper cup. "I closed the curtains, and went to bed, but it was a long time before I went to sleep."

Audrey didn't doubt that for a minute. "Did you know Leigh Martin or Petra Seiders?"

"Not Leigh, but Petra and I were cheerleaders together. She's a little younger than me. People used to ask if we were sisters." Her gaze locked with Audrey's. "That's why he raped her, isn't it? Because she looked like me? Leigh too. All those girls he killed. They were all blond, and they all looked a bit like me."

Audrey leaned her forearms on the table, maintaining eye contact. "You had nothing to do with Ian Monroe and those other girls. He picked you for the same reason he picked them."

Because of another blue-eyed blonde earlier in his life. He'd never told anyone who that was. All they knew was that it hadn't been his mother, because she was dark like him.

Wide eyes stared into Audrey's. "But he didn't hurt me."

"And he didn't kill Leigh or Petra. Then he evolved."

"Evolution is supposed to be a good thing, isn't it?"

Audrey shrugged, but she added a smile so she didn't seem dismissive. "It's just change. Adaptation to stimuli or environment. He hadn't become what he wanted to be when he approached you."

"I met that girl who got away from him. Tori. I went to see her in the hospital. She told me we were the lucky ones." She laughed tonelessly. *"Lucky."*

Audrey pressed Pause on her voice recorder. "Amber, are you familiar with survivor's guilt?"

"You mean like when someone survives a bombing or something, and they feel bad for being alive when other people are dead?"

"Yes. Sometimes people who survive, or avoid terrible things, have a hard time making sense of why they were spared, and they begin to think that maybe there's something wrong with them for not suffering the same fate as the other victims. If I told you that I was outside in a thunderstorm with, say, five other people and that those five people had each been struck by lightning while I remained unhurt, would you blame me for what happened to those other people?"

"Of course not," the younger woman replied with a frown. "I'd say you were lucky. I knew exactly where you were going with that, by the way." Audrey hadn't been trying to be subtle, so she only inclined her head. "I know it's not rational, but it's how I feel sometimes. And now with the trial coming up, I'm feeling it all over again."

"What do you think would help alleviate that feeling?"

The furrow between her pale brows deepened. "Knowing that I helped put him away for a long time. If anything I do helps keep him behind bars, I think that will help."

Audrey smiled at her. It was impossible to truly get a sense of a person's mental state with one meeting, or a smattering of facts, but she had a feeling this girl was going to be okay, and that made her happy. "I think you're right."

The girl was thoughtful for a moment. "You know, Ian seemed drawn to girls who didn't want him. Petra had a boy-friend, and I don't think Leigh was interested in dating any-one." She frowned. "I don't know the other girls. They were a little younger than me."

"Rape is often about power and dominance." And sometimes it was the only way the perpetrator could actually become sexu-ally aroused. For Ian, forcibly taking what he wanted—from someone who didn't want to give it—was the ultimate turn-on.

"That woman with the fan club—Margaret . . . no, Margot Temple. She e-mailed me the other day. She wanted to know if I'd talk to her, and maybe her group. She said she thought I could provide information that would help them 'better under-stand how to help Ian.' Can you believe that?"

"Unfortunately, I can." Margot's belief in Ian blurred her ability to see the situation rationally. There was no other explanation for her approaching Ian's victims—and Amber was one of his victims, even if he'd never touched her. "Did you respond to her?"

"I told her I wasn't interested. How can she feel sympathy for him after what he's done?"

"'Hybristophilia' is the diagnostic term," Audrey replied. She'd brushed up on it when Will hired her, because she'd known there was a good chance she'd encounter it. "It's a form of sexual deviancy that refers to being attracted to and aroused by someone who has committed an atrocious crime such as rape."

Amber grimaced. "God. That's sick."

"It's not all about sex. I suspect Margot Temple has the kind that makes her want to 'save' the boy Ian was. She wants to fix him." Audrey understood the psychology behind the paraphilia, and thought of it as a sort of a twisted, alpha male thing. "Many times the women with this paraphilia have experienced something in their pasts that draws them to this sort of man. They sometimes call it Bonnie and Clyde syndrome."

Amber blinked. "Who's Bonnie and Clyde?"

Good Lord. Was this a sign she was getting old? "They're gangsters from a long time ago. They were a couple who went on a real crime bender."

"Oh, like *Natural Born Killers*."

Audrey smiled slightly. "Sort of, but without Robert Downey Jr." The smile slid from her face when she remembered a high school dance during which Maggie told Audrey that she thought of her as Mickey to her Mallory. Back then, she'd made a face and went off to drink with Jake in the parking lot. Had Maggie's romantic obsession with her started with Clint's death? She shook it off. It didn't matter. Maggie was dead, and any questions would remain unanswered.

"There's no chance of them setting him free, is there?" Amber asked, anxiety tightening her features.

"I can't answer that, but I really don't see how that would happen. There's just too much evidence." And there was Tori Scott, who had escaped him by being rescued by police. "Amber, do the numbers nineteen and twenty-three have any significance for you?"

"He'd take them on the nineteenth and dump them on the twenty-third."

"Yes, but do either of those numbers have any significance for you personally?"

The girl shook her head. "No, sorry."

So whatever the purpose behind those numbers, it hadn't started with Amber. If not with her, then who or where? The mysterious blonde he never named? They were too much a part of his signature not to be important to Monroe, and their significance could not only strengthen the case against him, but provide some deeper understanding of his psychopathy.

Audrey understood killing out of rage or love, or even revenge, but not compulsion. She and Maggie had plotted to kill Clint several times, but never did it. Then Audrey walked into Maggie's bedroom that night and found Clint on top of her best friend. The decision to bash his head in had been an easy one, made in the heat of the moment. It didn't matter that maybe Maggie had set it up; all Audrey had needed was to see what he did to her. Her motivation had been clear, but murder as a way to scratch an itch baffled her.

Amber said something and drew her back to the present. The rest of the conversation was a going over of more facts, and what Audrey liked to think of as a little free therapy. Despite her lack of clinical work, she still had training in it, and a feeling of compassion for those who needed it. There was nothing as satisfying as the feeling that you'd gotten through to someone. Helped them.

She couldn't stop herself from trying to help Amber reconcile with what had happened and her feelings regarding it. On the more mercenary side, the more secure Amber felt in testifying, the better. The girl was smart, poised, and pretty. A jury would love her, and they would want to convict the monster who threatened her.

The girl took Audrey's card before she left. "Will you be at the trial?" she asked.

Audrey nodded. "I will be. Do you have a therapist?"

Blond hair brushed her shoulders as Amber shook her head. "I did for a little while after Ian got arrested, but I stopped going after a few sessions. I didn't feel like he helped me."

"I can give you a few referrals if you like—reach out to some colleagues."

Amber smiled hopefully. "That would be great. Thanks."

"Meanwhile, if you need to talk, call me." Would the defense accuse her of witness tampering? Maybe, but it wouldn't stick. She was just doing her job. She hated the idea of Amber carrying around all that guilt and shame with no outlet for it, and no one to help her unburden herself. It used to be that she liked not having to "treat" someone, that she could hide behind her research, but something had changed inside her when Maggie died, that left her questioning every decision she'd made since leaving Edgeport.

After Amber left, Audrey got something to eat and a bottle of water, made a brief bathroom trip, and then checked her phone. There was a voice mail from her brother. He had just spoken to their mother and was upset because she sounded so tired.

Shit. David was the most sensitive of the three of them, wearing his heart on his sleeve on a regular basis. Thank God he had his boyfriend Seth to lean on, because he was going to be a mess when their mother actually had the procedure. She refused to think about how hard it was going to hit him when their mother actually died.

It was going to hit her hard too.

She called David and talked for a few minutes, reassuring him that the surgery was their mother's best shot at defeating the cancer. "It has to be done, Davy."

"I know. I'm just scared."

"She's going to be fine. I believe it." She had—it was too much to think of a world without her mother in it. And the thought of her father on his own was one she refused to entertain. Her brother wanted to know if he should come home now or wait. Audrey told him to wait. She and Jess would be there right after the surgery.

"Maybe you could take a little time off at Thanksgiving," she suggested. "She should be feeling a bit better by then, and you know she'd love to have you home."

"I have lots of vacation. I'll see what I can do. How's trial prep coming along?"

She filled him in on what she could share. When Petra Seiders walked in, she had to let him go. "Love you," she said, before tapping the screen to end the call.

It was obvious why people sometimes thought Amber and the younger girl were related—both young women were pretty, with blond hair and blue eyes, but the similarities were only physical. Petra was brash, borderline belligerent, and stoned. Her black eyeliner was a little too heavy and her lip gloss a little too pale. She had an elastic around her wrist that she played with as she talked, occasionally snapping it. She broke Audrey's heart, because it was obvious the poor girl needed someone to talk to, and help reconciling what had happened to her.

At a house party, then sixteen-year-old Petra had been flattered when the good-looking Ian Monroe paid attention to her. He drugged her just enough so she couldn't put up much of a fight, and then he raped her in one of the bathrooms, forcing her to watch in the mirror as he did so. She never went to the police because by the time she sobered up, Monroe had already told everyone they'd had sex. Consensual sex.

"The other night, I saw this guy at a party that looked like Ian, right?" Her smeared eyeliner was more visible as her heavy lids drooped. "I didn't care who he was. I didn't want to know his name. I just wanted to fuck him. That's messed up, right?"

"Actually, it sounds to me like it was a way for you to regain some of the power Monroe took from you." God, what Audrey would give for five minutes alone with Monroe and a claw hammer. "Did you sleep with the boy?"

"I did. It was good too. Better than any sex I've ever had. After he left, I ran to the bathroom and threw up all over the place." She smirked, but her gaze was flat. "Then, I rolled a joint and changed the sheets. Still think I regained my power?"

"I think choosing a sexual partner that reminded you of Monroe was your mind's way of telling you that you are no longer a victim."

"Or that I'm really fucked up."

Audrey gave her a gentle smile. "We're all a little fucked up." Personally, she thought Petra was going to be okay. She also couldn't help thinking of how much this girl reminded her of Maggie, whose demons had destroyed her in the end. There was always a little of Maggie in the girls she interviewed, or maybe she looked for the similarities. She gave Petra her card and told her to feel free to call her if she wanted to talk. "No charge and no strings." Sometimes, she just couldn't help herself. Her weakness was messed-up teenage girls, which was a surprise to no one.

"Mr. Lawson said the same thing, but then I found out he was writing a book."

Audrey kept her expression neutral. "Barry Lawson? The teacher?"

The girl nodded as she chewed on the side of her thumb. "He just wanted details about what Ian had done to me. He kept saying he *couldn't believe* that Ian would rape me. Like what

Ian had done to me was some kind of fucking honor I didn't deserve."

"If that's what he really thought, then he's an asshole."

Surprise lit that defensive gaze. "Yeah, he is." She shifted in her chair; took the card from Audrey's fingers. Audrey couldn't help but notice that the skin around each fingernail on every hand had been chewed to the point of raw raggedness. "Have you ever been raped?"

She shouldn't have answered, but building a level of trust with this girl was suddenly more important to her than secrets or information that could be deemed "private." "One night in college I had too much to drink at a party and ended up having sex with a guy I really didn't want to have sex with."

She'd been too drunk to even put up a fight, which meant she probably would have died of alcohol poisoning if she'd been a normal person. A high tolerance for booze was ingrained in her DNA. "He didn't get violent, but he didn't listen when I said no."

"So you have."

"Yeah." That had been a hard revelation for her. She'd always prided herself on being tough and strong—ready to kick the ass of any guy who ever tried anything.

Petra actually smiled—it was more like a smirk, but it was still good. "You seem to have turned out all right."

"That depends on your version of all right. There are a lot of people out there who understand what you've been through. If you'd like, I could check out a couple of groups that might be able to help."

Petra's gaze was wary, but she nodded. "I guess there'd be no harm in checking them out. I can always leave if they're lame."

"Sure," Audrey agreed, acknowledging the girl's need to put on a tough face. How many spiritually, emotionally, and physically violated girls had worn that same expression? Audrey could easily name twenty, herself included. Sometimes, a tough face was all the protection you had.

Petra left a few minutes later as she had class. She was going to become one of those girls Audrey carried around with her after this—a reminder of why her job was important.

Leigh Martin was her last interview of the day. She had a waifish, yet blank, quality to her expression that Audrey recognized as easily as Petra's defiance.

The young woman drank espresso, and used it to chase what looked like a couple of Xanax, which she tossed into her mouth as soon as she sat down. Audrey wasn't certain what she hoped to achieve with that combination. She was fidgety and anxious and avoided eye contact. She'd been a virgin when Monroe raped her, and she hadn't even dated a boy since. She didn't want anything to do with the opposite sex—or her own. She spent all of her time studying and watching Netflix. She didn't go out at night, and avoided parties.

"Sometimes I dream that he comes back to finish the job— kill me like he did the others. I wake up crying."

"I can see how such a dream would be upsetting." She ought to have a banner that read QUEEN OF UNDERSTATEMENT across her chest.

"No, you don't understand. I cry because I'm still alive."

Fuck. Audrey took a good look at the girl. Her hair was a little lank, and there looked like there was a small bald patch partially concealed beneath some artfully placed strands. Trichotillomania? Her sleeves were long, covering arms that were too thin and, Audrey suspected, littered with scars. She wouldn't be surprised if Leigh had tried to kill herself.

Audrey got the name and phone number of the girl's therapist, so she could call the doctor later. She gave Leigh her card as well, but she knew the girl would never call, unlike the other two. There was a part of her that feared Leigh was one pill away from suicide—either taking one too many and overdosing, or not having enough to numb the pain and taking another way out.

But, if she had to pick one of them to testify, it would be Leigh because the jury would have no choice but to see what Monroe had done to her. But honestly, she didn't think Leigh could do it. Petra could, but her tough girl attitude might turn off those who couldn't see through it, and the defense would use her sexual history against her. It was a sad situation when a young woman who had suffered something horrendous was treated like the criminal rather than the victim.

Audrey packed up her things and headed back to her hotel. When she walked in, she was intercepted by a young man who had been working at the front desk when she checked in the night before. "Excuse me, Miss Harte, but you have a package in the business center."

"Oh, thanks." She wasn't expecting anything, but Will might have sent something over. She went down one floor from the lobby and entered the business office. She gave the girl behind the counter her name, and in return, was given a small box, well taped with a printed mailing label. Audrey had to borrow a pair of scissors to get through the tape. Then, she peeled back the layer of packing material to peer inside. There, on a layer of tissue paper was a silver charm bracelet. It looked familiar. And there was something else with it—a note. As she read it, the bottom of her feet prickled as all the blood drained from her face. As she pulled out her phone and dialed Will's number, she glanced around to see if anyone was watching her. Nothing. Will picked up on the second ring.

"Audrey?"

"I need to see you," she said, heart pounding in her throat. *"Now."*

CHAPTER FIVE

Will Grant was gorgeous. Male model, superhero, romance novel gorgeous. Dark hair, blue eyes, chiseled features, and an easy grin. The first time Audrey met him, she'd almost made the mistake of assuming he was egotistical and probably gay. Then, she'd talked to him, and suddenly his face wasn't the most attractive thing about him. He was smart too—and a genuinely good guy. She thought of him as Clark Kent in an Armani suit. She wouldn't be the least bit surprised to discover that he put on tights and a cape and fought crime in his spare time.

The funny thing was, as beautiful as Will was, Audrey wasn't attracted to him in even the slightest way. So when she spotted him crossing the hotel bar toward her, the sight of him did nothing more than make her smile in relief that he was finally there. Meanwhile, every woman in the place turned her head to watch him pass.

She stood up when he reached her, and she stepped into the brief hug he offered. They had become friends of a sort during their brief time working together—partners in their quest to put Ian Monroe away for good. Plus, when they'd discussed her past—and of course they'd had to—he seemed legitimately interested in how she felt that experience related to her ability to understand troubled or criminally minded teens. He didn't want to know about the cause—he wanted to know the effect.

Will draped his overcoat on the back of a chair and unbuttoned his jacket before sitting down. "I hear you got a phone call from the *Chronicle Herald*." His voice, low and smooth, held a trace of concern.

Audrey winced. "Sorry about that. I should have taken the note."

He smiled sympathetically. "Please. It's not as if you left sensitive documents lying around for them to look at. It was a note, and there's no proof that Monroe sent those flowers. The reporter obviously slanted the story in that direction."

"Do you think it was someone else?"

"No, I think it was him. He just covered his tracks very well, because so far we've found nothing to trace the purchase back to him. I am, however, sorry that you're getting swept up into the circus this trial is becoming. Every media outlet, blogger, and person with a Twitter account wants to get involved. Anyway, it sounded urgent when you called. What's up?"

Just as Audrey opened her mouth to respond, the waitress approached them and asked if they'd like a drink. Audrey had sat in that bar a good fifteen minutes before Will arrived and no one asked her if she wanted anything. She couldn't help but shoot the woman a "really?" glance. Of course, the waitress wasn't looking at her, so it was lost.

"Scotch, neat." Will turned his dark blue gaze toward her. "Rum and diet?"

It was a little early...Oh, who the hell was she trying to kid?

She came from a long and proud line of alcoholics. There was no wrong time for a drink. She smiled at the waitress, hoping it wasn't too much of a smirk since she finally had the woman's attention. "Yes, please."

As the woman sashayed away, hips swaying like church bells, Audrey turned to Will. "That woman practically ovulated right in front of us when you spoke to her."

Will laughed, deepening the lines around his eyes. "You're terrible."

"It's true."

He shook his head. Slowly, his smile faded. "Tell me what happened."

Right. For a moment she'd managed not to think about the reason she'd arranged this meeting. Where to start? She didn't want to leave anything out just because she was a little rattled.

"Earlier today, I interviewed Amber Gale, Leigh Martin, and Petra Seiders. Petra informed me that Barry Lawson is writing a book."

Will rolled his eyes. "Lawson. When the police suspected him of being the killer, he went on and on about how he was going to sue, and how much he'd suffered at the hands of the cops. When he couldn't actually get a lawsuit off the ground, he decided to write a book about being so close to the investigation. I expect it will be more about how badly he believed he was treated than the actual crimes."

"So he's not very popular with local law enforcement."

"That's an understatement. I heard he received six traffic citations in five weeks."

So he hated cops, and the cops hated him. "He's not on the list of people I'm to interview."

"Because he's not testifying. The defense considered it, thinking he'd make all of us on the prosecution side look bad, but in the end, there was no good reason to put him on the stand. He might hate the police, and me by association, but after Monroe setting him up as a potential suspect, he's not exactly looking to make nice with the opposing side. We have no idea if he'd help make the case, or help destroy it."

"I can see why both sides would want to avoid putting him in the box." It sounded like the man was quite the piece of work. "I should probably thank you for ensuring he and I wouldn't meet."

"You're welcome."

"So what do you know about Margot Temple?"

He shrugged. "She's actually a sweet woman, despite her misguided infatuation with Monroe. She's tried to get practically everyone involved in the case to speak to her group. The Scotts had to get a restraining order because she kept trying to see Tori. She just couldn't understand why Tori wouldn't talk to her."

"I suppose her obsession with Monroe makes it difficult for her to gauge her own behavior on a rational level. She doesn't see him as a monster, but as someone who needs help—her help. And her love."

"She's not my first prison groupie, but she's the first one I ever felt sorry for."

"Don't underestimate her. She's reached out to Amber, and

to me. If she thinks Monroe might love her back, she'll do just about anything for him. Maybe even be his accomplice."

Will frowned. "What do you mean?"

"This is the main reason I called. When I got back to my hotel after interviewing the girls, I was told there was a package for me in the business office. This is what I got." She set the box on the table in front of him. "Do you recognize it?"

Will opened the box, but didn't touch the jewelry inside. Instead, he took a pen from his inside jacket pocket and used the tip to turn the bracelet over. "You couldn't lead with this?" he asked, looking up at her. "It looks like the one Cassidy Ryan was wearing the last time she was seen alive, but I'd have to check it against the report to be certain. It wasn't on her body."

"Read the note," Audrey prodded.

He used his pen to open that as well. *"Sentimental as I am, I'm returning this to make room in my collection for a new piece. Window-shopping is so much fun."* His gaze met hers. "A new piece? Window-shopping?"

Audrey's heart thumped hard. "Tell me they really mean jewelry and not that there's going to be another murder."

Will rubbed a hand across the back of his head, ruffling his thick hair. It only made him look more delicious. "I seriously can't believe you told me about the interviews and Margot before you mentioned this. Audrey, this is evidence. Was it couriered or hand delivered?"

"I didn't know what it was, and to me those girls are more important. It was couriered."

"Then someone would have had to fill out paperwork." He

took out his cell phone and tapped his finger over the screen before putting the phone to his ear. "Anita, it's Will. I'm with Dr. Audrey Harte, who received a package today that you'll want to see. Can you meet?" There was a pause and then he rambled off the name of the hotel and told her where to find them before disconnecting.

"Was that Anita Grayson?" She was the FBI agent who had arrested Monroe, and delivered Tori Scott back to her terrified parents.

Will nodded. "She'll know if this is Cassidy's bracelet. She'll take it as evidence and have it examined." He was silent as the waitress set their drinks in front of them, but he flashed the woman a smile that was as sincere as it was perfect. The smile vanished when she walked away. "Anita's going to want to talk to you."

Audrey sighed. "I know." She took a deep swallow from her drink. It was strong. Good. "First the flowers, and now this." There was no point holding on to the irrational hope that the bracelet hadn't belonged to one of those girls, not anymore.

"Someone's trying to scare you. Or impress you."

"But why? I'm not a lawyer or a judge, or even a juror. If they wanted to affect the trial, why not aim for someone who could make a difference? Or better yet, why not aim for someone who would be more satisfying to unsettle?"

Will shook his head, the lines between his eyebrows deepening. "I don't know."

Audrey leaned forward. "Have you considered that it might not be Monroe?" she asked, voice low.

"Who else would it be?"

"When Monroe was first arrested, wasn't there suspicion that he'd had a partner?"

His gaze locked with hers. He knew where she was going, and it was obvious he didn't like it. "There was never any conclusive evidence to back that theory."

There'd never been enough evidence to the contrary either. And Will had already said they'd had no luck tracing the flowers to Monroe. She didn't think they'd trace the delivery of this bracelet to him either. He either had someone doing his bidding, or... "When I interviewed Monroe, he was fixated on the rape of his victims, not the killing." God, she couldn't believe where her head was going, but it refused to do so without taking her mouth along with it. "What if that's because the rape was the only part in which he was involved?"

Will regarded her closely, as though weighing his words before he spoke. "I've wondered if he had a partner, but he's never given me any indication of it. Maybe he wants all the attention, or maybe he's protecting someone, I don't know. I do know that the killings stopped when he was arrested. There's been nothing even remotely similar since."

"Not here."

"Not in any neighboring states or directly across the border in New Brunswick. Monroe had a very particular MO. Even if some of that was the work of another person, it would attract notice if another body turned up."

"Maybe they just haven't been found. The public staging of the victims could have been Monroe's idea." Maybe she was grasping at straws. Serial killers didn't just stop—not without a reason. So, if Monroe hadn't killed those girls, who had, and where the hell were they?

"Maybe. In the end—as far as this case is concerned—it doesn't matter. I have one goal, and that's to make sure Ian Monroe spends the rest of his life in prison. I hope you still plan to help me do that, but I won't blame you if you want out."

"Please. I spent part of my teens in a correctional facility for girls. It will take more than flowers, some creepy notes, and a bracelet to scare me off."

He looked pleased. "Good. I can talk to Anita about getting you some protection."

"Do it." When he arched a brow at her quick agreement, Audrey continued, "Make sure Monroe knows about it. I want to see if he gloats the next time I visit him. He's a psychopath, and one of the few emotions they can feel is pride. A lot of them simply can't resist the need to brag about their superiority over the rest of us. If he's behind these gifts, he wants to scare me, and he's eventually going to let me know how much that pleases him."

"I knew I wouldn't regret hiring you."

"Don't get too far ahead of yourself. It could be nothing more than my overactive imagination." Her intuition hadn't exactly been on the mark lately.

Will lifted his glass. "I'll take my chances."

Audrey clinked her glass against his and took a drink. She wore what she knew would appear to be a genuine enough smile, but that little voice at the back of her mind was whispering again. What if Monroe did have a partner? What if they were the one who sent the flowers, and the bracelet? And what if they were just getting started?

Anita Grayson took the bracelet and its note and all the packaging when she met Audrey and Will at the hotel bar. She was in her forties, a no-nonsense redhead with a shrewd green gaze and—Audrey was certain of it—a gun beneath her jacket.

"It definitely belonged to Cassidy Ryan. I knew the son of a bitch kept it as a trophy when she was found without it."

"Either Monroe had someone mail it for him, or we've got another player," Will said.

Agent Grayson arched a brow. "Convenient timing. The business office staff provide any information?"

"No, but the courier information is on the label."

"I'll check it out." She turned to Audrey. "Why you? Why send Cassidy's bracelet to you and not to me, or Will? We've been attached to the case longer."

Audrey took a sip of her second rum and diet. She was feeling decidedly more relaxed about the whole situation. "Will and I asked the same question. Maybe because Monroe thinks he can unsettle me, or because I'm the one asking questions and stirring things up." She shrugged. "Or because he wants attention."

"Or because you know what it's like to kill someone."

"Jesus, Nita," Will started. "That's out of line."

She'd been waiting for someone to say it, so Audrey wasn't surprised. Grayson looked at her like she was a snake slithering up her leg. It would have been nice if Will had warned her that the woman didn't think much of her, but then it was obvious he hadn't expected her to vocalize it. Regardless, Audrey wasn't intimidated. And it wasn't like the two of them needed to work together; there was no doubt Agent Grayson was a reliable witness, completely comfortable with testifying in court.

"Maybe," she allowed without a hint of defensiveness. "Regardless of why, it certainly sounds as if the sender is looking to acquire a new trophy, and since I'm fifteen years too old and a brunette, I think it's safe to assume I'm not the target."

"Who is?" Grayson inquired.

Audrey smiled—and didn't bother to make it sincere. "That's your job, not mine."

"It could just be posturing," Will interjected. He was obviously one of those men who felt the need to defuse conflict. "A scare tactic to put us all on edge. Whatever the purpose, I think we can agree that Monroe is rubbing our faces in it."

Grayson put the box back into its packaging. "I'll get our people on it ASAP, see if we can get anything useful off the bracelet. I'll put a call into the courier company as well. I'll keep you informed if I learn anything. Good night, Will. Dr. Harte."

"And will you keep *me* informed?" Audrey asked Will a few minutes later, when they were alone again.

"I will." He fiddled with his empty glass. "Anita's not usually like that."

She shrugged, swirling the little plastic stick in her drink. "I have that effect on some people."

He smiled. "Do you intimidate them with your psychological superpowers?"

"Ha. You know how there's always that guy at the party who has to prove he's got the biggest dick?"

Will's eyebrows rose. "I think you and I go to different parties."

"Come on, you know what I mean. There's always that guy who has the best this, the best that. He has to outdo everyone else?"

"Yes, I'm familiar with the archetype."

"Okay, so something about me makes other women feel like they have tiny penises."

"I prefer women with tiny penises, actually. Microscopic, even."

Audrey laughed, and Will smiled.

"Regardless of the size of your penis, I don't like the idea of you being alone while your admirer is running loose."

Anyone else and she'd wonder if he was flirting, but she knew he wasn't. "My boyfriend will be here tomorrow night." *Boyfriend.* Surely she was too old for that term, but "partner" sounded so fucking pretentious when she said it.

"Jake, right? Good. I'll sleep better knowing that. Speaking of sleeping, I should get going."

"Hot date?" she asked with a smile.

"Ha. Yeah, with depositions and leftovers."

"Sounds like the evening I have planned. I'm putting together the assessments I did earlier today and will have them for you tomorrow—hopefully before I see Tori Scott."

Will shook his head. "That poor kid. She's a big part of our case against Monroe, but there's a part of me—and this is completely between us—that sometimes thinks she would have been better off if he'd killed her. I don't know if she'll ever be okay."

For some reason his words made her think of Bailey McGann, locked up in Stillwater, her life forever altered.

"Yeah," she said, taking another drink. "Some of them are like that."

Will's words rang in Audrey's head the next day as she walked up the steps of Owen and Nancy Scott's pretty Cape Cod. She'd called the Scotts almost a week ago to arrange the meeting. Mrs. Scott had been quite concerned about the stress the assessment might have on her daughter and asked to be present while Tori and Audrey talked. Audrey was okay with that—provided Tori was.

Mrs. Scott opened the door when Audrey rang the bell. She was in her late thirties, with dark blond hair and blue eyes. A pretty woman—the sort of pretty that might make people think of her as waifish, or delicate. But there was a spark in her gaze that Audrey recognized. She'd seen it before in the mothers of other teens she'd interviewed—the look of a woman who would do just about anything to protect her kid, and saw Audrey as a threat to that.

So Audrey smiled and offered her hand. "Mrs. Scott, I'm Audrey Harte. Thank you for seeing me."

The woman gave her a once-over, obviously evaluating the quality of Audrey's shoes and suit, as though the fit were indicative of her character. Maybe she could let Audrey into the house first? It was raining. Not to mention rude. "Come in." She stood back, granting access to the house.

It was a perfectly average upper-middle-class house. Well decorated without looking pretentious, and smelling of vanilla. It reminded Audrey of a house that had been staged for sale. Was it all for her benefit?

"Victoria is in the living room. Do you drink tea?"

"I do," Audrey replied, following her. "But please don't go to any trouble."

"It's already made. My daughter likes to have a cup when she gets home. She drinks it while doing her homework." She stopped and turned to Audrey. "Are these questions of yours going to upset her?"

"There's a chance they will, yes. I need to ask about what happened after she was abducted in order to assess whether or not she's able to testify."

Cool eyes narrowed. "It's very important to Tori that she take the stand."

Audrey nodded. Of course it was. The poor girl probably needed closure. "Then I'll do whatever I can to make sure she's able to do just that. I promise you, I'll try to cause as little distress as possible."

The older woman shrugged and led Audrey down a hall. "I suppose this will be practice for being on the stand." Her shoulders slumped a little—as though a weight had literally been placed upon them. "I hate to think of what that bastard's lawyer will do to her. What facing *him* will do to her."

"I know she's been through a terrible ordeal, and that you all want to put it behind you, but Tori is alive, and because of her, Monroe is going to spend the rest of his life in prison. He won't ever hurt anyone again."

Mrs. Scott stopped and turned to face her. Audrey almost ran into her this time. "Dr. Harte, the monster hurts my daughter every day. She still has nightmares. She is afraid to leave the house. The only places she'll go by herself are school and the library. She's on medication and has been visiting a psychiatrist once a week since . . . *it* happened. She's been diagnosed with PTSD. Monroe won't hurt her again? I'm afraid he'll never *stop* hurting her."

Duly chastised, Audrey murmured an apology. How could she have dropped the ball so completely? She ought to have realized the extent of harm Monroe had done to the girl. She had shut down her empathy so that she could be objective—impersonal—about the girls Monroe had killed, and even though Tori Scott hadn't been killed, she'd still suffered—more so than even Leigh or Petra. Monroe had perfected his process by the time he grabbed Tori, and the poor girl would carry the memory of it for the rest of her life.

She thought of Leigh Martin and how she woke up sobbing because Ian hadn't killed her. Did Tori ever wish he'd finished the job?

In all the media coverage of Ian Monroe's terrible career as a killer, Tori got the most attention of any of his victims, but very little of it had been voluntary. She'd given only two interviews since being rescued—one to Oprah Winfrey, the other to the *Portland Chronicle Herald*. A mismatched pair, but she refused to talk to anyone else, instead letting her parents speak for her.

Audrey had no expectations of the girl. If she thought it would cause Tori more harm to take the stand, she'd tell Will, but what he did with that was up to him and his team. She'd like to think he wouldn't push it, but she knew he would if he felt he had to. That was where the two of them disagreed. Audrey would always put the victim first, while Will's top priority was getting justice.

Mrs. Scott led her into a large room with comfortable couches and chairs, a plush carpet, and a television that had to measure close to eighty inches against one wall. A girl sat on one sofa, textbooks spread out on the cushions beside her. She scribbled in a notebook, taking notes from something on the screen of the laptop perched precariously on her knee. A cup of tea—steam gently rising—sat on the end table on her right. It looked like a comfortable little nest.

"Victoria, Dr. Harte is here to talk to you."

The girl's head rose. Audrey had seen photos of her, but they didn't do her justice. Tori Scott had the height, frame, and face of a supermodel. She wasn't pretty. Her chin was a little too narrow, her eyebrows too fierce over eyes that were almost too big for her face. There were too many "too's" about her to allow her to be anything close to conventional, but Audrey only had to look at her to see why Ian Monroe had targeted her. For a second, as she met a gaze that was decades older than the eyes that contained it, she felt a flicker of a rare emotion. For a moment, Audrey was intimidated, and then she reminded herself that any emotion or attitude the girl projected was in the name of self-protection.

From a professional perspective, she was a psychological gold mine. There was a part of Audrey that couldn't wait to take a look inside her head, and didn't feel the least bit sorry for it. Another part of her was so very sorry for all the young woman had suffered, and only wanted to help. What she had to remember, was that her current task involved neither of those things.

Dark blond hair fell in loose waves over slim shoulders as the girl set aside her work and rose to her feet. She was a little taller than Audrey, but probably a good thirty pounds lighter. She offered her hand. Audrey took it. Her fingers were cold but firm.

"Thank you for seeing me," Audrey said.

Tori tilted her head. "I didn't think I had a choice."

"Of course you do." Audrey pulled her hand free. "I'm not interested in imposing on you."

That striking face was void of expression, but there was a little curiosity in her gaze. "So if I told you to leave, you would?"

Audrey nodded. "I would."

"Would they still want me to testify?"

"I have no idea." She watched as Tori's long fingers clenched into fists. "Do you want to testify?"

The girl straightened her neck. "I do."

Audrey smiled. "Then I should probably stay, don't you think?"

Tori nodded, then turned to her mother. "It's okay, Mom. You can leave."

"I'll bring some tea for Dr. Harte," Mrs. Scott said. It was obvious she had no intention of staying completely out of the interview. Audrey didn't mind, so long as her presence didn't make Tori censor herself.

"Sit down." Tori gestured to the other end of the sofa, bending to gather up some of the books that had found their way there. Once a spot was clear, Audrey claimed it. She took her notebook and voice recorder from her bag.

"You're recording this?"

"I am. Do you mind?"

"Why?"

"I like to have a recording of the interview in case any facts— or my integrity—is called into question. It's for your protection as well, since you were a minor at the time, and still are. Also, it's so no one can put words in either of our mouths."

"Okay." The girl's brow tightened. "Can I have a copy?"

Audrey blinked. No one had ever asked that before. Was it some sort of protection mechanism? "I don't see why not. I can e-mail it to you if you want to give me your address."

Tori wrote it down on a piece of paper she ripped out of her notebook and handed it to her. "Thanks."

Audrey put the paper in her bag.

"I used to watch you—on that TV show you were on."

"*When Kids Kill.*" Audrey had been their resident psychologist and commented on each of the crimes they showcased. She hadn't enjoyed it exactly, but the extra money had helped support her growing shoe and boot collection, and her heightened profile had helped generate interest in the center and Angeline's work.

"Yeah. You're not doing that anymore?"

"No." The producer had decided that a convicted murderer wasn't good for ratings. Apparently he'd been wrong, because the show's ratings had dropped since Audrey's departure—or so she heard. Not that the producer, or Audrey's former best friend (the producer's sister), spoke to her anymore. It wasn't as though she could blame them for it. She wasn't even bitter about it. Much.

"Why are you here?"

"Because the prosecution thought my background in juvenile forensic psychology would be beneficial given the ages of those involved."

"No, I mean why are you *here*—in Maine? Why not find something else in LA, or move to New York? Why come back to nothing?"

It was an attitude Audrey had taken many times as a teenager. She simply hadn't been able to see the appeal of small-town life. It had felt like a cage. A prison—so much so that even Stillwater had been an escape.

"I'd spent years away from my family. It was time to come home." *Because my mother is sick and I'm terrified she's going to die.* And then there was Jake. It always came back to Jake.

"You're from Portland?"

"No. Edgeport, up the shore."

Tori's smooth forehead wrinkled. "I think my parents took me there one summer when I was younger."

"It hasn't changed much." She smiled. "Why don't we get started?"

Audrey turned on the recorder. She began the interview with general questions, letting the girl relax a bit while trying to earn a shred of her trust. Once the tension in Tori's shoulders eased a bit, she moved to the more difficult part.

"Can you tell me what happened when Monroe abducted you?"

The girl's pale blue gaze latched onto Audrey's. "Didn't your boss give you a copy of my statement?"

"Yes, I've read it. I'd like you to tell me, if that's okay."

"Right, because if I can't tell it to you, I won't be able to tell it to a jury. I understand." She took a deep breath. "I stayed after school to work on a project in the library. When I left to go home, I bumped into Ian outside. He offered me a ride."

"Did you know him well?"

Tori shook her head. "He was a senior. I was a sophomore. I knew who he was, and he said he'd seen me around. He told me he always noticed the prettiest girls. I knew he was just flirting, but it was nice. Anyway, I got in his car. He didn't take me home. I thought he wanted to hang out. He gave me a drink and I drank it. Next thing I knew, I woke up in a tiny room with a bucket for a toilet and an old bed with a stained mattress. He waited until I woke up to rape me. The second time he told me he wanted to keep me, but he wasn't allowed."

Allowed? Did he need permission? Audrey kept her face relaxed. This was new information—at least to her. Did Monroe have a partner? And was that person still out there, taunting her? As a tear trickled down Tori's cheek, Audrey reached for a tissue from the box on the table and gave it to her.

"The police arrived after the third time. Apparently someone had seen me get into Ian's car. They took me to the hospital and called my parents." Tori shrugged. "That's it."

Audrey nodded. Everyone handled trauma differently, and Tori had obviously gotten to a point where she could detach to a degree. There'd been no emotion in her voice. Only that tear had given her away. It was a terrible thing to think, but that tear would grab at even the most callous juror's heart.

"Did you tell the police that Monroe said he wanted to keep you but wasn't allowed?"

The girl gave her that look all teenagers possessed—the "God, you're so stupid" look. "Of course I did. I'm their only living witness. I told them everything. When Ian Monroe is sentenced to life without parole, I want him to know I did it."

Brave girl. Angry girl. Audrey understood anger. Anger could get you through things you didn't think you could ever survive.

Suddenly, that anger evaporated. "Will he be in the room when I testify?"

"I imagine so, yes. How does that make you feel?"

The girl shrugged. She was slowly shredding a piece of paper. "I don't know. Scared. Eager." She glanced up from under her hair. Is that weird?"

"No, I don't think so. You feel what you feel."

"I guess. I'll be glad when the trial's over. I keep telling myself that I'll be better then. Do you think that's true?"

"I think it can be true if you want it to be."

"You shrinks always talk in circles," Tori accused, tucking her hair behind her ear. "Just be honest with me."

"I am being honest." There were weeks at a time when she didn't think about the fact that she'd killed someone. It used to be she could go only a few days. She didn't regret ending Clint Jones, but she'd never forget it. "I honestly believe that you can overcome what's happened to you, but it's not easy. You have to want it badly enough to do the work—even if it's painful."

"Did you do the work?"

Audrey cocked her head. "What do you mean?"

"You sounded like you knew what it was like to overcome what's happened to you. So did you?"

Those pale eyes were unsettling. So much so, Audrey almost admitted that she hadn't had to overcome anything, that she was the one who created a terrible situation that others had been forced to overcome. But she wasn't telling this girl anything of the sort. "I did."

There was a tiny pile of confetti in Tori's lap, made while they'd been talking. "I have panic attacks. If I'm not wired, I'm depressed. If my mother looks at me the wrong way, I start crying."

"You're being treated for PTSD, yes?"

"Yeah. I'm taking Effexor. Xanax for when I have panic attacks."

"What about therapy?" The girl needed more than just drugs.

"My doctor and I just started doing this eye movement thing."

"EMDR." When the girl blinked at her, Audrey elaborated. "Eye Movement Desensitization and Reprocessing."

"Yeah. That. I think it's helping."

"Good. It's been effective in helping treat post-trauma disorders." Since she wasn't a clinician, Audrey hadn't much experience with the treatment, but she'd read several articles, and one of her colleagues at the clinic had some success with it. "I'm glad you're finding it helpful."

The door to the room opened suddenly. Tori jumped, her confetti pluming into the air before raining down all over the couch, table, and rug.

"Oh, sweetie, I'm so sorry!" her mother cried, rushing forward. Tori visibly drew back.

Audrey's gaze narrowed. Tori hadn't seemed overly anxious the entire time they'd been talking. She'd exhibited other behavioral traits of PTSD, but nothing this obvious—not until her mother came in. Mrs. Scott had painted a picture of her daughter as emotionally fragile, but that picture didn't hold up against reality. Then again, Audrey didn't live with the girl. Maybe she'd put on a brave face for her interview. Or maybe she'd taken just enough Xanax to make herself a little numb. Medication would certainly explain her lack of emotion while recounting the hours spent with Monroe.

She could have asked Tori more about those hours, but she had Will's notes on it, and she wasn't there as a therapist. She was there to determine whether or not Tori would be a reliable and sympathetic witness, and she'd had no reason to doubt that until just a few seconds ago.

It wasn't uncommon for mothers—and fathers—to act as triggers for their children. If Mrs. Scott had this sort of effect on her daughter, they might want to keep her out of the courtroom while Tori testified. Audrey made a mental note to talk to Will about it.

"I'm sorry, Dr. Harte, but Tori has a doctor's appointment we can't miss."

Why would the woman schedule an appointment on the same afternoon as the interview? Whatever. It wouldn't do any good to protest. In fact, it might make both mother and daughter less inclined to cooperate with her, or Will, in the future. Still, she'd been looking forward to a cup of tea. Now she'd have to stop at Starbucks. "Of course." She turned off the recorder and put it and her notebook in her bag. As she rose to her feet, Tori stood as well.

"Will you come back again someday, Dr. Harte? Maybe we could talk some more?"

Mrs. Scott looked as surprised by the question as Audrey felt. "Of course." She would like to maybe get the girl out of the house and see how she fared away from her comfort zone—and her mother. "I'll call in a couple of days to set something up."

Tori smiled, which made her mother smile. Both those smiles looked a lot like expectation to Audrey, who outpaced Mrs. Scott to the front door.

"How did it go?" the older woman asked, reaching in front of Audrey for the doorknob and halting her exit.

"It went very well. She's a strong girl. I think if she continues on her current treatment, she stands a very good chance at recovery." One thing about her profession that Audrey had learned early on was to never speak in absolutes. There were very few absolutes in life.

Mrs. Scott let out a breath, visibly sagging. "Oh, you have no idea how good that is to hear. And please, do call later this week. I'll make sure there's nothing else on the calendar when you come by again."

Not like there was any pressure in that overly bright smile. She wasn't being snarky, just wary. Someone else's desperation was just as uncomfortable as your own. "Let me check my own schedule. I'll call as soon as I can."

With that promise made, Mrs. Scott opened the door and Audrey jogged down the shallow steps. She'd just reached her car when she felt someone watching her. She looked up and saw Tori in one of the second-floor windows. The girl smiled and raised her hand in a wave. She reminded Audrey of Maggie— lost and wounded. No one had been able to fix Maggie, and in the end she became the thing she hated most, and Bailey paid the price.

Audrey waved back and then yanked open the car door. She jumped in, started the engine, buckled up, and put it in Drive as fast as she could, but her past caught up before she'd gotten very far.

It always did.

CHAPTER SIX

Natashya Lewis liked to walk to school in the morning. The fresh air woke her up, and the exercise helped her focus on her classes. She was a senior at St. Catherine's and had her heart set on going to an Ivy League school the following year. She wanted to work in the growing field of neurolaw—the application of neuroscience within the legal system. She'd always had an interest in the brain and criminal behavior, and when Ian Monroe was arrested for murdering all those girls, her interest in it grew. She even had a YouTube channel where she posted videos about her interest in the field and popular theories. She'd done a couple of vlogs on Monroe since his arrest, using him as an example of how the psychopathic mind differs from that of the nonpsychopathic. She had just over a quarter of a million subscribers, which she hoped Harvard would see as one more reason to accept her.

It was a gray morning, cold and damp with drizzle. She huddled deep in her wool coat and picked up her pace. Her nose, which had started to run, was going to be as red as a clown's by the time she got to school. She didn't care—it wasn't like she was trying to impress anyone with her looks.

She listened to a download of a lecture on criminality and brain injury on her iPod as she walked, so she didn't hear the car slowing down behind her. She didn't notice it at all until it pulled up beside her and stopped. The passenger window came down and a familiar face peered out of it at her.

Natashya removed her earbuds. "Oh, hi."

"Want a ride?"

Normally she would have said no. Cold as it was, she felt the walk did her good, but the car was warm and dry, and she knew the driver. She could listen to her lecture in the hall. "Yeah, thanks." She opened the door and climbed in. She had just buckled her seatbelt when she felt a sharp pain in her neck. She clapped her hand over it, but the needle had already been removed. "What the hell?"

"Sorry, but I need to make sure you don't get away."

Confused, Natashya turned her head. "Why?"

"Because you're going to be a gift for Ian."

Natashya grabbed for the door handle, but the door was locked. She tried to fight, but her limbs were already growing heavy. She screamed, but there was no one around to hear the pathetic sound of her weak voice muffled by her thick tongue. She slumped back against the seat, tears leaking from her eyes as the car pulled away from the curb.

"It's okay," her captor said as they drove. Natashya's vision blurred as her heavy lids fell closed. "I'm not like Ian. I'm not going to rape you. I'm just going to kill you."

* * *

"Anita managed to get the bracelet rushed through testing," Will said. "It's Cassidy's. DNA confirmed it."

Audrey had him on speaker as she drove. "I don't think any of us are surprised. Did they find anything else?"

"A partial print that matches Ian Monroe's."

"So he took the bracelet as an additional trophy to the hair?" That didn't seem right, as Monroe took his victim's hair as a personal, intimate connection to each girl. Jewelry seemed a little too impersonal.

"Or he gave it to someone as a gift."

"And then gets them to send it to me? That seems weird, right?"

"Someone might have held them for him—or knew where he hid them."

Yeah, and that someone knew what Ian had been up to. "Tori Scott said something to me today that suggests Monroe might have had help."

"She told you what he said about wanting to keep her? It was what alerted us to a potential partner. Obviously, we never found any concrete evidence to support it."

"Well, at least now you know there's someone out there with a strong connection to Monroe. I'd like to know how they found out where to deliver the flowers and the bracelet. Either they're following me, or they're making a lot of phone calls." They'd only have to call a hotel and ask to be put through to her room to find out if she was there or not, but that would mean calling every hotel in the area just to find her. That seemed like a lot of work to her, but maybe the person doing this found it rewarding. She should probably be more off-kilter than she was, but she'd never been easy to scare—at least not where her physical safety was concerned.

"The police are investigating the deliveries. The flowers were ordered in person and paid for in cash. They have a description of the guy who placed the order and are looking for him. The bracelet was dropped off by an individual also. Sounds like it might have been the same guy. It's not much—about five nine, thin, wearing baggy clothes and a ball cap. He could be the partner, but I think he was hired to do both jobs. If Monroe did have a partner, he didn't avoid arrest by being reckless or stupid."

"So now what?"

"Anita wants you to give a statement. I'm going to come with you."

"Why?"

"Because she's distrustful and she thinks it's odd that you're the one getting mysterious deliveries."

"Of course she does." What the hell was it about her and the law? Even Neve Graham, who had been a good childhood friend, looked at Audrey differently once she became a police officer. Every cop she ever met treated her like she was a criminal. Okay, so she *was* a criminal, but that had been a long time ago. And if anyone deserved to have his head bashed in, it was Clint Jones. The point was that she was on the side of the good guys. "When does she want me to come in?"

"Are you free now? Better to get it over and done with so it doesn't interfere with your assessments."

"Sure. I'll meet you there." She hung up.

Twenty minutes later, she parked in front of the building on Federal Street. She'd just gotten out of the car when Will arrived. He walked toward her, overcoat billowing behind him like a cape. He looked like a cologne ad.

"Thanks for being my wingman," she said.

Will smiled. "I just want to remind the FBI that you're here because you're working for the DA. Anita's not going to interrogate you in my office."

His support meant a lot, but as they crossed the street, Audrey realized there was no way she could walk away now. She'd been pulled good and hard into the situation, and she would have to find a way to balance it with her mother's illness. At least she didn't have to travel up from Boston every weekend.

They walked into the courthouse together. They'd barely made it inside the doors when Anita intercepted them. Her face was taut with tension, her movements jerky. Something had her extremely agitated, but it wasn't anger. This was fear—Audrey could read it in every inch of her body.

"What's going on?" Will asked.

The detective looked from Will to Audrey and back again. "We just got a phone call from Judy Lewis."

Will glanced at Audrey. "Judy's a defense attorney."

Anita continued, "Her daughter Natashya never made it to school this morning."

Will frowned. "Isn't she the one who wants to go to Harvard?"

"Yeah. She's never missed school unless she was sick. Judy

said she left the house at her usual time this morning, but never made it."

Unease unfurled in Audrey's stomach. She'd been that kind of kid. Once she set her mind to what she wanted to be, she went to every class she could, every day. She took summer classes, just so she could cram as much learning as possible into her head. She never missed class unless she was sick—really sick. So she took extra care of herself to avoid colds and got a flu shot every year.

"Judy Lewis." Audrey frowned in thought. "I know that name."

Will nodded. "Ian Monroe tried to hire Judy. She refused him. She made a fairly public statement about it."

Audrey's phone buzzed in her bag. She took it out and glanced at the screen. It was a text from Jake, but that wasn't what got her attention. Her stomach fell as she looked at the numbers at the top of the screen. "Oh, no," she murmured. It couldn't be. Please let it just be her brain making a huge, unrelated leap.

"What?" Will asked, his tone sharp.

But it was Agent Grayson's gaze that Audrey met, horrified. "Today's the nineteenth."

"Jesus," Will whispered, rubbing the back of his neck. "Natashya—she's a blue-eyed blonde, isn't she?"

Anita nodded, her face even more pale than usual

Audrey's guts tied into knots. It couldn't be a coincidence. Was it a copycat? Or had Monroe's rumored partner gone solo? If it was the latter, they had only a few days to find her; otherwise, on the twenty-third, Natashya Lewis would die.

* * *

Jake glanced in the rearview before getting out of the truck. The bruise high on his left cheek was dark—red and purple giving way to green and yellow. The swelling had gone down a fair bit, but it was still ugly. His knuckles were battered too, as well as his ribs. Audrey was going to want to know what happened, and lying to her wasn't something he enjoyed, so he'd have to tell her about Lincoln's stealing, and about the fight that ensued. She didn't need his personal shit on top of the stress this trial put upon her.

He opened the truck door and climbed out. He slung the strap of his leather duffel bag over his shoulder and walked across the hotel parking lot. The place looked pricey. Probably enough that a beat-up guy in Doc Martens and a leather jacket might be looked upon as suspect. No one hassled him, though. He walked through the lobby, got on the first elevator that opened, and rode it up to Audrey's floor.

Hotels weren't really his thing. They felt like prisons—comfortable prisons, but institutions all the same. He didn't like knowing there were people all around him. He had the same issue with Audrey's condo in Boston. It was gorgeous, but how could anyone live with all those people? He lived alone in an old farmhouse and his nearest neighbor was probably a quarter mile away. He liked solitude. Privacy.

But there was something to be said for room service.

He found the suite and knocked on the door. He could hear her on the other side, moving around. "Who is it?" she asked.

Jake frowned. "Who else are you expecting?"

The door was unlocked and opened. Audrey wore dress pants and a light sweater. It still surprised him to see her—an adult her—even though this thing between them had been going on for a few months. He didn't rhapsodize about her looks, or her unusual eyes. Her face was his favorite face in the world because it was hers, and not because of any particular feature.

"Hey," she said with a tired smile, and stepped up for a kiss. She didn't even comment on the bruises, and when his mouth touched hers, she wrapped her fingers around his shoulder, as if she needed support. Something was wrong.

It wasn't until Jake stepped into the suite that he realized they weren't alone. Sitting on one of the plush sofas in the living area was William Grant, assistant district attorney. Jake knew who he was because he'd looked into the guy when he found out Audrey was going to be working with him.

One thing Jake had never lacked was a certain amount of confidence in himself. He wasn't vain, but he was comfortable in his own skin, and knew that he was considered attractive by some women—and some men. Grant was the sort of man that made other men mentally calculate their every shortcoming. He looked like he'd just stepped off the cover of *GQ* in a dark suit, white shirt, and high-polished shoes. He rose to his feet when he saw Jake and stepped forward, offering his hand.

"Will Grant," he said. "A pleasure to meet you, Mr. Tripp."

One look at the man told Jake he wasn't going to be a problem. He didn't act like he had a right to be there, or like Jake was encroaching on his territory. His first impression was that of a genuinely decent man who didn't need to prove his prowess to anyone, which should have made him dangerous, but didn't.

"Call me Jake." He glanced at Audrey when he released Grant's hand. "Am I interrupting work?"

"We were just talking," she said. "Do you want a drink?"

"Sure." He watched her as she walked to the mini-bar. He didn't like the set of her shoulders. "What happened? Did you get more flowers?"

Her rasp of laughter had no humor in it as she emptied a tiny bottle of rum into a glass of ice. "I wish. No, I got a dead girl's jewelry. And now another girl is missing."

What the hell? When had she gotten the jewelry? Jake's attention returned to Grant. "You think it's connected?"

The older man nodded. "Unfortunately, yes. Today's the nineteenth. Monroe always took his victims on the nineteenth. The note that came with the bracelet indicated that there was going to be an abduction. I'm very glad you're here. I don't believe Audrey's in danger, but for some reason this person has decided to make her his emissary, and I don't like that."

"Neither do I," Audrey replied before Jake could. "I wish I knew how Monroe and his partner are communicating."

"Did you ask Kenny?" Jake asked.

"Yeah. He said Monroe hasn't had any visitors in months. Very limited contact with other inmates as well."

Jake shrugged. "Then it's either a guard, or someone he contacts outside of the prison. Kenny could probably find out if he's calling or writing to anyone."

"I'm sorry," Grant cut in. "But who's Kenny and what's he got to do with Ian Monroe?"

He turned to the lawyer. "Kenny's my cousin. He's a guard in Maine State."

Audrey handed him a glass. Rum and Coke if he wasn't mistaken. "Margot Temple's been writing to Monroe for months. Is it a coincidence that he *just* added her to his visitor list?"

Grant didn't look convinced. "Margot Temple's misguided where Monroe's concerned, but I can't believe she'd do anything underhanded for him."

"Ordering flowers and dropping off a package are pretty mundane," Audrey allowed. "She may have told herself she wasn't doing anything wrong, even though she knows I'm connected to the trial."

"But our witnesses say it was a young man."

"Margot is tall for a woman, and slender. She could have altered her appearance, or hired someone."

"I have to admit the idea of Margot being a patsy sits a lot easier with me than Monroe having a partner. But I can't believe she'd kidnap someone for him."

"I can," Audrey informed him, taking a sip from her own drink. "If she thinks he's in love with her, she'll do whatever Monroe asks, and find a way to justify it."

"Would she kill for him, though? Several times?"

"Karla Holmoka helped rape and murder her own sister."

Jake couldn't wrap his head around that, no matter how angry he'd ever been at Lincoln or Yancy, torturing and killing them was simply not an option.

Grant frowned. "I wish we knew why Monroe chose to intimidate you with his gifts."

Audrey tucked a piece of hair behind her ear. "I'm not sure it's meant as intimidation. I think it's peacocking. He picked me because he thinks I understand him better than the police or the FBI. He wants to impress me."

"Because you're a psychologist?" the redhead asked. She'd been quiet up until this point, and Jake had no doubt she'd been studying him, committing everything she saw to memory. "I'm FBI. We practically invented profiling. Why not try to woo me?"

Audrey looked her in the eye, unapologetic and unashamed. Jake loved that look. "Because as far as he knows, *you've* never murdered anyone."

Grant was a little pale beneath his tan. "I put you right in his crosshairs when I hired you."

"You couldn't have known any of this would happen, Will."

"But I knew about your past, and I wanted to capitalize on it. I knew you were the best for the job, that you would treat Tori and the other victims with respect, and I knew that I could use your own experience to present you as the perfect professional witness. I used you for my own grandstanding, and now another girl might die. *Will* die, unless we manage to find her. That's on me."

Jake had to hand it to the guy, he owned his shit without asking for sympathy.

Audrey's cell phone rang. She took it from the coffee table and looked at the screen. "It's that same number that called earlier. I better take it." She touched the screen and brought the phone to her ear. "Hello?" She tapped the screen again as her gaze went to Grant. She was silent for a moment, and then, "Hello, Ian."

Jake stiffened. Why the hell was Ian Monroe calling Audrey at this very moment? That was one hell of a coincidence, wasn't it?

"Did you know it was going to happen? All right...I might be able to do that..." She hung up. "He wants me to visit him tomorrow. He says he can help us find Natashya."

"Did he actually say her name?" Grant asked, frowning.

"No. He asked me if a girl went missing today. Then he said he wanted to talk to me about it."

"How did he get your number?" Jake asked.

Audrey turned to him. "My cell is my work number. It's on my business cards, and it's the one I gave the prison. In hindsight, I probably should have given them the office number."

She didn't look worried. She didn't even seem angry—which was usually her go-to reaction when something caught her off guard. Seeing her detached like that brought back memories of when they were kids. Whenever something happened that Audrey wanted to avoid, she just flicked a switch inside herself and shut off her emotions. He was guilty of it as well—children of alcoholics were experts at it, having learned the skill at a young age, right along with lying like a pro.

"You don't have to see him," Grant said. "He just wants to toy with us. Like you said, he wants attention."

"Or he might actually give us something," she countered.

"I doubt that," Jake interjected as he took off his jacket.

"Why?" Grant turned to him. He actually looked interested

in what Jake had to say. Audrey looked at him too—with that little smile that had hooked him before he had even the slightest thought of girls being dangerous.

"Monroe only talks about the rapes, right? He's never actually admitted to killing the girls."

"How do you know that?" Agent Grayson queried, her gaze like a hawk's.

Jake met her gaze without trouble. His mother used to say that he had problems with authority. Gran said that he didn't have a problem with authority at all, but that authority had a problem with *him*. "I read," he replied. "And there's this little thing called YouTube. Monroe's done a few interviews. He brags about raping the girls, but he won't talk about killing them. Watch him being asked about it and he'll either avert his gaze and refuse, or get upset. He could have outed his partner at any time to help his case, but he hasn't. That's submissive behavior." Why yes, he had been reading psychology books. How else was he going to understand what Audrey did?

"He's right," Audrey added. She didn't seem the least bit surprised by it either. "Psychopaths are generally narcissists who don't like to share the spotlight. Monroe isn't about to let his partner steal his, which is why he called me. But the fact that he didn't take full responsibility for the murders to begin with makes me think he's afraid of—or devoted to—the person who did commit them. Your earlier suspicions were correct—he does have a partner. A more careful, dominant one."

"Maybe someone older?" Agent Grayson suggested. "A family member or mentor."

Grant turned to her. "Time to brush off your profiling skills, Anita."

She shook her head. "Not my forte, but I'd be willing to assist our forensic psychologist if she's game."

Audrey's expression changed—just a twitch of her blue eye. The agent's suggestion surprised her. Jake wasn't surprised. Aud didn't often play well with others. Authority often had a problem with her as well.

"Is that good with you, Audrey?" Grant asked.

"Sure. I haven't done much profiling, but if we go back over all the murders and remove the rape element, we might find some indicators as to who we're looking for."

Grayson nodded. "I'll get you the files."

"Meanwhile, I'll go to Warren tomorrow afternoon and talk to Ian."

"I'm coming with you," Jake said.

Audrey didn't argue, especially when both Grant and Grayson agreed that it would be a good idea for her not to be alone, just in case the partner decided to up his game.

A few minutes later, with plans agreed on, the two of them decided to leave. Audrey walked them to the door, flipping all the locks into place once she'd closed it behind them. When she came back, she had a predatory gleam in her eye that made his heart beat a little faster.

"I need some distraction." She slipped her fingers through the belt loops on his jeans and pulled him close. "Have I ever told you how sexy I find smart guys with black eyes?"

He smiled. "No."

"How'd you get it?"

"I'll tell you later. I don't feel like talking right now."

She grinned, coming up on her toes. "I do like a man who knows when to keep his mouth shut." Then she kissed him.

They made it as far as the couch. She pushed him onto the thick cushions and straddled him. As clothing disappeared, Jake maintained his silence, but he didn't keep his mouth shut.

Audrey didn't seem to mind.

CHAPTER SEVEN

So who gave you that eye?" Audrey asked. It was morning, and she and Jake were just getting up.

"Lincoln," he replied. "We got into it."

"Lincoln?" That was a surprise. She tied the belt of her robe. "What happened?"

Jake ran a hand through his hair, taming some of the bed-head he sported. "I caught him skimming."

Audrey went still. She paused for a moment, waiting for him to tell her that he was joking. "He *stole* from you?"

In Edgeport, there was a certain amount of pilfering that was socially acceptable. Audrey's father used to drive around and steal cucumbers or tomatoes, or beans—whatever—from people's gardens. Sometimes people would take a little fish from someone's catch, or "borrow" a neighbor's lawn mower without always asking first. That kind of thing was okay, depending on your relationship with the thief. But to steal money, to actually rip someone off, especially family, was low. Really low. She'd heard stories when she was younger of people being seriously hurt—or worse—over thievery. And to Jake, someone who would give his family anything they wanted, to be stolen from was a real betrayal.

He pulled a T-shirt over his head, covering the bruises on his torso. How twisted was it that she found his "battle wounds" hot? "Yeah. I knew he was skimming once in a while, but last time I did the books for Gracie's, I saw some discrepancies. He's been taking money, booze, food—basically anything he can get his hands on. I finally had to call him on it."

"Why? It's not like you wouldn't give him anything he wanted."

Jake laughed. "That's what I asked. You know what he said? He said I *owed* him. That he had only taken what was rightfully his, and that if I was a decent person, he wouldn't have to take it."

"Gracie's will," she whispered. Jake's grandmother had left him everything when she died, a fact that didn't sit well with most of his family, who had wanted a piece of Tripp land and Tripp money. But Jake had been Gracie's favorite, and the most like her. She'd known he'd take the legacy and build upon it, not squander it like Lincoln would have. "How much?"

"Once it added up to five grand, I stopped looking." His expression was stoic, but she saw disappointment in his eyes. The hurt. He'd never said it, but she knew how much he wanted a relationship with his big brother, how much family meant to him.

"Oh, Jake." She went to him and wrapped her arms around his waist, put her head on his chest. "Why didn't you tell me?"

"You've got enough going on," he replied, stroking her hair. "I needed to confront him first."

"How many bruises does he have?"

"I don't know. He took off that night. I think I broke his nose."

"Took off?" She looked up at him. "He's gone?"

"Oh, yeah. I wasn't surprised. I kicked him out of the apartment, so I knew he'd have to go somewhere."

"Are you okay?"

He smiled. "Yes, Doctor. I'm pissed, but not surprised. I suppose I'll miss him, but he won't stay gone." The smile twisted. "He'll be back when he needs something."

Audrey couldn't imagine feeling that way about Jessica or David, but then she and Jess hadn't been close for years. It was only their mother getting sick that made them forge a truce and try to get along.

"So I don't imagine I can talk you out of trying to track down this psycho, can I?"

"I have to do something. Plus, I don't think I can refuse the FBI."

"I know. But you haven't had much confidence since Bailey."

She pulled back. He was right, but it still stung to be reminded of it. "I missed the clues, but I don't have to identify who they're looking for. I just have to give them some parameters for their search." Surely she could do that without messing up.

He gave her a dubious look, as though he didn't believe she'd keep her distance. But he was right about her losing her confidence. How could her instincts have been so off? She thought she was better at seeing through malingering than that. Or maybe she unconsciously turned a blind eye.

Maybe she didn't know what the fuck she was doing after all. But that wasn't reason to give up. People were counting on her. And this was her job—her passion. Sort of.

"How can I help?" he asked.

She pulled completely out of his arms. She needed a shower. "Order breakfast? I'm going to do some work before leaving for Warren. You sure you want to come with me?"

"You've gotten two gifts from this guy. I'm not letting you out of my sight."

"You can't stay away from your businesses that long."

"Yancy's got the resort—and I've got someone looking after Gracie's."

Not Lincoln. "Donalda? Isn't she back in college?"

"She is. I hired someone new."

"Who?"

Did he actually hesitate? "You really don't know?"

She stared at him as she stood at the dresser, a pair of underwear from the top drawer in her hand. Then her bewildered brain made the leap. "Not my father?"

Jake nodded. "Yeah. He told me he was looking for some extra work that would allow him to stay close to home."

She shut the drawer—harder than she'd meant to. "Jake, he's a fucking alcoholic! You can't trust him to run a bar. What the hell were you thinking?" God, it was like trusting a crow not to steal shiny things.

He tilted his head the way his grandmother used to when someone challenged her. "I was thinking that Rusty needed help and so did I. He promised me he wouldn't drink on the job."

"And you believed him?" Good God, when had he lost his damn mind? She grabbed her bra off the back of the desk chair, where she'd left it the night before.

"He said he needed to take better care of your mother, and that he needed to win back his children's trust. Make amends. I couldn't deny him that."

Audrey opened her mouth, but closed it again. She was pissed off, but not at him. She'd spent years of studying psychology and applying what she'd learned to herself. Some of it had taken and some of it hadn't, but she knew why she was so annoyed. She was afraid her father might actually keep his word this time, and that it would be because of Jake rather than his wife or kids, because his family hadn't been reason enough for him to get sober during his thirty-five years as a husband and father.

And she was annoyed with Jake for having more faith in her father than she did.

"You're right," she said. "Regardless, that's between the two of you and has nothing to do with me."

"Doesn't it?" Jake's tone was cryptic. "Your old man knew you'd find out. There's something about you that makes people want to prove their worthiness to you, your father included."

She arched a brow. Had Lincoln beat him around the head? "Are you saying I have high expectations of people?"

"The only person you have high expectations of is yourself. The ones you save for the rest of us are pretty fucking low. We want to prove ourselves better."

Indignation stiffened her spine. "That's not true."

He smiled—the bastard. He actually *smiled*. "Liar."

"No wonder you want to be with me," she drawled. "Who wouldn't when you describe me like that?" He was right, though. Low expectations were safer.

"It wasn't an insult, so don't go making it one."

She nodded. "I know. I'm just raw." She knew he didn't judge her. He never had. It was a strange feeling, to be so secure. She'd never been so sure of anything as she was of Jake. He was the only person—living—who knew that she hadn't just helped to kill Clint Jones, as she and Maggie had claimed, but that she'd been the one to actually bash his brains in. There had been a moment when she could have stopped, but she chose not to take it, and she had hit Clint with the intention of him never getting back up. Jake knew this about her, and it didn't matter.

He pulled her in for a hug. "None of this is on you, and you're not expected to fix it."

"I don't think we're going to find her before he wants us to." She didn't need to say that she feared Natashya would be dead when that time came.

"Don't go there until you have to. If anyone can figure this bastard out, it's you."

His belief in her was humbling. "Thanks."

Jake pressed his lips against her forehead. "What do you want for breakfast?"

While Jake ordered room service, Audrey grabbed a quick shower. When she was done, she opened her laptop and pressed the power button. She typed "Margot Temple" into the search bar and scanned through the results. She didn't have to look very far down the screen—Margot's website for Ian Monroe was the second result.

The site was well done. Margot didn't come across as full-on delusional so much as naive. She didn't try to claim that Monroe was innocent—in fact, she was very honest about his crimes—but she believed he could be rehabilitated. Audrey didn't have the heart to tell her that a person's rehabilitation hinged on their ability to feel remorse. Monroe didn't have that ability.

Had Monroe confided in Margot? He was manipulating her for certain, but was he sharing his secrets? Maybe she should talk to Margot after all. If Audrey planted the right suggestions in just the right manner, Margot might prove to be an unknowing ally.

As she plotted out how to begin, there was a knock on the door. Jake went out into the living room area to answer it. When he returned, he had a courier box in his hands. "From Grant," he said, handing it to her.

"Who brought it up?" she asked.

"Concierge."

Audrey pulled on the cardboard tab to open the box. Inside was a file folder, stuffed fat with photos and documents. The accompanying note read, *Anita asked me to send this on, Will.*

"What is it?"

"Agent Grayson's file on the murders. A copy of it anyway."

"You up for that? It's not going to be pretty."

She met his gaze. "I've seen dead people before, Jake. One of whom I made that way." He didn't even blink—just kept watching her. She sighed. "I *have* to be up for it. A girl is missing, and she's going to be dead by the twenty-third if we can't find her."

"You're taking this personally." What he didn't need to say was that she made mistakes when she let her personal judgment cloud the facts. She knew that. She also knew there was no way to be totally impartial.

"Yeah. He sent me *flowers*, Jake. And a dead girl's jewelry. It's my chain he's yanking."

"I know. And you're looking to yank back. You sure that's not what he wants?"

"Of course it's what he wants! But maybe if he's in a tug-of-war with me, no one else will have to die." There, she'd said it. He could call her an egomaniac or accuse her of having a hero complex—she knew it. It didn't change anything.

He held her gaze for a moment. "Okay." He picked up the phone and pushed the button for the front desk. "Good morning. Would you happen to have an extra presentation board in your convention rooms that we could borrow? That would be great. Thanks." He hung up.

"A presentation board?" she asked. "What do you need one of those for?"

"If *we're* going to profile this bastard, I need the right equipment." He leaned down and kissed her. "I'm going to get a shower."

Audrey watched him walk toward the bathroom with a smile on her face. Then she glanced down at the photo of Jillian White's lifeless body. She shoved it back in the folder. As hard-ass as she tried to seem, the photos of the girls upset her, even though she had firsthand experience with making someone a corpse. The difference lay in the fact that Clint Jones had deserved to die. These girls hadn't.

* * *

Margot wasn't jealous by nature, but checking in on Ian's "girls" had her feeling somewhat chartreuse.

She hadn't volunteered to spy on Amber or Petra, and she had argued against surveilling that poor little Tori Scott. There was no way she was going to add that poor girl's suffering. The only person she didn't mind watching was Barry Lawson, even though he was a total douche. Seriously, the man needed to take it down a notch. She watched him talking to a couple of male students, nudging one with his elbow when a particularly pretty blonde walked by. *Greasy.*

The irony wasn't lost on her. Lawson had insisted that he could never hurt a woman when police questioned him before eventually arresting Ian, and here he was, leering at a sixteen-year-old while boys her age laughed at whatever he'd said about her. Pervert. But then, the boys elbowed each other as Lawson left them, the two of them laughing as they watched him go. He was a joke to them. Good.

Maybe he wouldn't hurt a girl, but if she had a daughter, Margot wouldn't leave her alone with Lawson for even a second. Why would a man in his forties hang around outside with students during their lunch break? Then again, from the way his peers looked at him, it didn't seem any of them were inclined to be his friend. He had been accused of sleeping with a student, so his lack of popularity wasn't a surprise, even though the rumor had never been proven fact.

Margot turned away. She might have made a promise to

Ian, but she'd called in to work saying that she had a doctor's appointment that morning and that she would come in after lunch. She'd spent her morning at USM watching Amber Gale and Petra Seiders. Leigh Martin hadn't left her house that morning. And then Margot pretended to take a walk around the perimeter of the high school to check up on Lawson and Tori. Tori stood by the fence, reading. She looked up only once—when Lawson walked by. He'd smiled at her. Tori hadn't smiled back.

None of it had been interesting or dramatic, but it left her feeling wrong, and now her stomach was growling and she had to get to work or her boss would be pissed. She'd go through a drive-thru on the way to the office and scarf down something quick.

She stood on the sidewalk, digging her keys out of her purse. She didn't even hear the man approach until she lifted her head.

"Oh!" She jumped back, heart in her throat. She almost dropped the keys. Barry Lawson was right in front of her—maybe a foot of empty space between them. "You scared me."

He looked angry—face all tight. He was really sort of ugly with that expression. "What the hell are you doing here? Are you spying on me?"

Margot used to be afraid of men. But since she found Ian, she wasn't so afraid anymore. She certainly wasn't afraid of a greaseball. "No, I'm not spying on you. Why I'm here is none of your business." She slung her purse over her shoulder, fingers of the other hand wrapped tight around her keys. He'd get them in the eye if he tried anything.

Lawson took a step toward her, but Margot sidestepped him, keeping as much distance as possible between them. His eyes narrowed. "I know who you are. You're that fan club woman. You're spying for Ian, aren't you?"

"I told you, it's none of your business. I'm not even on school property. You've no reason to harass me."

He sneered, upper lip curling in a way that made him look like a braying donkey. "Christ, what kind of pathetic bitch are you?"

Margot's gaze narrowed. "You must really despise women to objectify young girls and spit vitriol at me. I feel sorry for you."

He moved like a snake, rearing back and thrusting forward so that he was suddenly right in her face, his fingers biting into her arms. "Listen to me, you *cow*." His breath was hot on her cheek, damp and coffee-sour. "I don't care how crazy you are. Come around here again and you'll fucking regret it. Do you understand me?"

Before Margot could stop herself, her hand shot out. She didn't need to be able to lift her arm to grab him by the balls. She squeezed just hard enough to get his attention.

And then she squeezed a little harder. She smiled—sweetly, it felt like. "Oh, threats! How fun. How about this, threaten me again and you'll find out just how crazy I actually am."

Lawson let go of her and she let go of him. She stepped out of his reach. It was a good thing looks couldn't kill because he looked like he wanted to kill her at that moment.

Did he want to kill her? Maybe Lawson had something going for him after all.

Margot smiled. "I'm going to leave now, and you don't have to worry about me coming around again." Even if Ian begged her, she wasn't going to risk running into Lawson again—or anyone else who might know who she was.

"Good."

She stepped to the curb, checking for traffic before stepping out into the street. She was at her car, the door open, before turning to look back at him. He stood exactly where she'd left him, just as she expected. "By the way, Barry," she called. "Ian says hi."

Watching the color drain from his face was worth it.

"Okay, we know that Monroe was the face of the pair," Audrey said, writing the number *1* on the large pad of paper held by an easel. It wasn't as big as she would like, but it would do for now. She scribbled, *Monroe—face*, in the first slot. "All of the victims were girls he knew, but wasn't friends with."

"So he chose them then?" Jake asked, chewing on a strip of crispy bacon. He wore only a pair of pajama pants and didn't seem the least bit chilled, despite his bare torso and damp hair. He wasn't moving stiffly either, which meant that the fight with Lincoln hadn't done any serious damage.

Audrey made a *3* on the paper. "I think that's a safe assumption for now. We also know, thanks to exams done on Jillian White and Kaylee Soto, that Monroe experienced some degree of sexual dysfunction."

"How did they figure that out?"

"Well, it's believed to happen to just over one-third of serial rapists, but in Monroe's case, he left semen behind in the other girls, but with Jillian and Kaylee, he left behind pre-ejaculate only, and that was on their thighs. Also, the examiner determined that they had been penetrated by Monroe's hand rather than his penis. They found traces of skin."

"So he used his fingers."

Audrey glanced at him. "His fist."

Jake scowled. "Bastard."

She went back to the board. She probably shouldn't have told him, but he wanted to help, and she needed to share it; otherwise it was just too awful. "According to Tori Scott's statement, Monroe didn't restrain her, but he did threaten to hurt her and her family if she resisted."

"Where did he take her? Someplace isolated, like a cabin?"

She glanced at him. She really shouldn't be surprised that he'd figured that out. "His family's cottage in Falmouth."

He nodded. "No one around to hear any screams." He lifted his coffee cup from the desk and took a drink. "Did he take the others there as well?"

"Yeah. Close enough that he could drive up without anyone thinking much of his absence, but far enough away that no one took notice."

"Someone took notice eventually, though, right? A woman who saw Monroe with the Scott girl?"

She lifted her head. "How do you know all of this?"

He reached for another piece of bacon. "Alisha was terrified by the whole thing, but she wanted to know all about it. I'd watch the news with her. Talk about it with her. There was a woman who saw them, right?"

He was so good to his niece, it killed her. "She saw Tori's picture on the news and called the tip line. She saved the kid's life."

"Okay, so the cops got Monroe, but where was this mystery partner?"

"Well, that was one of the reasons that police didn't think there was a partner—no evidence of another person in the cottage aside from Monroe's family and victims. But the most common theory was that either Monroe took them elsewhere to be killed, or that the partner let him have his fun and only came by when it was time to end it."

"Do you deal with stuff like this a lot?"

Audrey shrugged, biting into a piece of buttery toast. "It's a little easier to stomach when you're advocating for the victim, or trying to understand the criminal. I've only been doing this on my own for three years. Before that, I was Angeline's assistant. I spent most of my time organizing her research, transcribing notes, and occasionally sitting in on interviews before she started letting me get more involved. I guess that gradual exposure better prepared me for something like this, but I'm not sure you're ever prepared to look at photos of a dead teenager who had been repeatedly raped before she was finally killed."

"How do you keep yourself from killing the bastard when you're face-to-face with him?"

"Adult prison is a lot rougher than juvy, and Monroe's not worth the consequences."

"No," Jake agreed, taking another strip of bacon from the

plate. "He isn't, but there's a part of me that would like to give it a go."

"Ditto." Audrey picked up her notebook. "I've fantasized about being alone with some of these monsters—just them, me, and a baseball bat. I try not to think about it if I can help it. It would be all too easy, I think." She'd only confess that to him.

He held her gaze. "I don't think you'd find it easy, but I think you could do it." There was respect in his voice, and certainty. It was almost as if they were discussing changing a tire rather than murder. He was the only person, other than his grandmother, who had never acted as though what she had done was wrong. Not even Maggie had been able to do that.

She turned her attention back to the board. "So if the partner waited for Monroe to be done with the girls before having his own fun, that means he's patient."

"Or he ran out of patience. Maybe he liked what Monroe did to them. Maybe that was part of his process too."

"Maybe, but what you said about dominance keeps coming back to me. Maybe the partner gave Monroe so many days to have his fun before pushing in and taking over."

"That seems pretty sophisticated for a teenager. I mean, when I was seventeen, I didn't have much patience at all."

"Seriously? You were so laid back, you were practically dead. Until someone picked a fight. Maybe the partner's older." She flipped the page and wrote the question at the top.

"I'm not sure that was a compliment." Jake picked up the file. "Didn't the police suspect a teacher at the high school when the killings first started?"

"Yeah." She turned toward him. "Barry Lawson, the history teacher."

"Found him." He set the folder down on the desk, open to a photograph of the man.

Audrey took a look. Barry Lawson was a good-looking man in his early thirties. His blue eyes gleamed with a manic glint in the head shot that had appeared in the school yearbook that year. "He looks a little intense. There were rumors that he had an affair with Madison Hall, the third girl, but they never proved it."

"Okay, we need more space to put this out," Jake said. "Let's make a Staples run on the way back from Warren."

"I'll never turn down a Staples trip, you know that." She loved paper and pens and everything that went with them. "We should talk to Lawson."

"Did you become a cop in the two days since I last saw you?"

She shot him an annoyed glance. "No."

"Lawson's not testifying. You've got no reason to talk to him, and he's got no reason to talk to you. He won't talk to you willingly if he knows you're with Grant. You'll have to corner him, and you'll have no backup or support. Confronting him blindly is not the right tactic."

"I'm not stupid, Jake." It came out a little pricklier than she'd intended.

"I don't think you are. But I'm not letting you meet a man who could be a killer by yourself. Not after Jones."

He was talking about the fight she'd gotten into with Matt. She'd held her own, but if Jake hadn't eventually come to her aid, Matt would have beaten her senseless—maybe to death. The realization made her feel weak and vulnerable.

It was difficult to be mad when she knew he was worried about her. "Okay. I promise not to approach Lawson, especially not alone."

He kissed her, and then let her go, leaving her with a hint of salt on her lips. Audrey grabbed a piece of bacon and returned to the initial page she'd started on Monroe. "First of all, we need to eliminate as much of the rapes as we can from each of these murders, and look specifically at how the girls were killed and where they were left. Even if the rapes were an overlap, we'll treat the murders like Ian had nothing to do with them. That will give us a better idea of who we're dealing with."

"Is profiling really that effective?"

"Sometimes it is and sometimes it isn't. In the case of Jeffrey Dahmer, it was way off the mark, but in other cases it's been helpful. Most serial killers have a signature—something that never changes from kill to kill. Finding that will play a big part in figuring out the killer's psychopathy. Constructing a profile might prove helpful. At least it's a place to start." But he'd brought up a good point. Sometimes profiling sent investigators in the wrong direction entirely. She didn't want that on her shoulders. But neither could she just sit on her hands when she could be doing what she'd been trained to do—which was to analyze criminal psychology. Her specialty was juveniles, but she'd studied adult behavior as well.

"Okay, how can I help?"

"Seriously?"

Jake shrugged. "If I can't talk you out of it, might as well jump in. What do you want me to do?"

"Can you separate each murder into its own pile and set the photos of the girls on top?" She pushed items around on the desk to give him more room.

As Jake began his task, Audrey stepped back and watched him. His brow furrowed as he sorted through the documents Grayson had sent. Even if he didn't agree with what she was doing, he helped her. That was a true friend, regardless of romantic attachment. His grandmother used to say that a good friend would help you bury a body, but a great friend would do it for you, so you could claim ignorance. She had no doubt that Jake would hide a body for her. And she would hide one for him.

Hopefully, it would never come to that.

CHAPTER EIGHT

The prison hadn't changed since Audrey's last visit, but walking through the door felt like every step was toward her own doom.

So melodramatic, she thought, but even berating herself couldn't shake the feeling. This wasn't Edgeport, and she wasn't weeding out the secrets of people with whom she'd grown up. Those girls hadn't been killed because of something they'd done. They'd been raped and killed because two psychopaths had liked the look of them, and that was it. And one of those psychopaths was still out there—with Natashya Lewis.

Psychopaths weren't normal—everyone knew that. But while movies and television tended to portray them as socially awkward, shuffling monsters, or brilliant masterminds, the reality was that most of them were extremely good at hiding in plain sight. Ian Monroe had been caught because of evidence, not because of anything he'd said, or because he was odd. In fact, he'd managed to fool the police during the investigation, pointing the finger at his teacher, Barry Lawson, who'd already snagged the cops' attention.

Was Lawson Monroe's partner? Possibly. Lawson was a little

older; he could have perfected his psychopathy. Being a teacher required patience, but also hinted at a need for authority. He was smart too, and talked easily to people. But there was something off about the guy, something that hinted at Lawson being not quite connected with the world, and certainly not honest about it.

"You okay?" Jake asked when they entered the main area.

She nodded. "Just thinking."

"That's when you're the most dangerous," he said with a slight smile. Just looking at him made her feel more centered. Part of her warned that it was stupid to be so attached. Jake didn't make little demands, only big ones. He would do anything for her, but it was all or nothing, and that was terrifying. Fortunately, a much larger part of her didn't give a flying fuck. She'd been attached to Jake for more than twenty-five years. The only difference now was that they were together.

Audrey returned the smile. "Yeah, I know." He must have heard something in her tone, despite the attempt at sounding normal, because he took her hand in his and squeezed. His warm fingers stayed clasped around hers as they approached the desk. He might demand all she had to give, but she would gladly give it to him. He would never abandon her, nor would she turn her back on him, and for two kids with abandonment issues, that was a huge promise.

Jake obviously couldn't go in with her, but he'd texted Kenny earlier and arranged to meet his cousin during his break while Audrey was with Monroe. She didn't plan on staying any longer than she had to.

It was a different guard who escorted her to the visitation room. He was young, and asked her questions about her job as they walked. "You must be really smart," he said to her. "To figure out what's going on in their heads? That's a talent."

Audrey studied him. No lines around his wide eyes. Razor burn on his jaw. A baby, really. "I don't always feel so smart." Like when faced with a teenage girl who had bashed in her stepmother's head and lied to her face about it. Audrey hadn't had a frigging clue. Not so smart then.

"Yeah, well, I guess the bad guys can be pretty smart too, huh? We've got a couple of guys in here who read like crazy. They don't care what it is, they just want to cram it into their heads. Those are the ones that scare me, not the big ones or the violent ones. You know where you stand with them, but the smart ones?" He shook his head.

She couldn't think of anything remotely intelligent to say. All of her attention was focused on the young man waiting for her. "They can be challenging, yes."

The guard opened the door to the interview room. It wasn't the same one as before, and smelled slightly of sweat, stale cigarettes, and vomit. No—not vomit. Coffee. Acrid, bitter coffee.

Monroe sat at the table, shackled and smiling, just as she'd expected. So smug. There was a part of her that wanted to pick up the chair and smash it over his head just to see what his reaction would be.

"Dr. Harte. It's so good to see you again."

"I wish I could say the same, Ian, but circumstances have cast a pall over our meeting."

"First names. Our relationship has progressed." His gaze was far too assessing as he looked at her. "A pall? Is that how you normally talk, or is that part of your professional persona?"

Audrey sat down. "I thought you deserved my best vocabulary."

He tilted his head, still smiling. "Flattery. Did you come here hoping I'd tell you how to save the new girl?"

Well, yes. A part of her had hoped just that, even though she'd known it wasn't going to happen. "Isn't that why you called me? To have me sit across from you and stroke your ego until you toss me a crumb?"

"Oh, Audrey. I'd rather have you stroke my cock, but that's frowned upon in here."

If he wanted to shock her, he was going to have to try harder than that, especially when it was obvious he didn't mean it. "Not to mention it would be highly unprofessional of me. If you didn't summon me to crow, why did you summon me, Ian?"

He leaned closer, shoulders over the table. "I wanted to tell you not to bother looking for the girl. She'll be left somewhere for you soon enough—like Santa leaving a gift under the Christmas tree."

"I always peeked at my presents. No matter where my mother hid them, I found them."

He smiled. "You won't find this one."

She believed him, and it scared her. "Is your partner going to rape her before he kills her? Or was that just your thing?"

"Partner?"

"I'm sorry. Should I have said mentor?"

He laughed—rough and abrupt. A strange sound to come out of his wholesome face. "Hardly."

"Are you saying that you called the shots? Come on, Ian. I've seen your IQ tests. You're smart, but not that smart. I mean, your partner has avoided the police this long. He didn't even leave any clues or evidence behind like you did."

"Oh, there is plenty of evidence and clues—you just haven't found them."

So he wasn't even trying to deny it anymore. "He'll leave something behind on Natashya, though. Won't he?"

"Natashya who?"

Audrey hesitated. Should she tell him? He actually looked curious—wary. A rare show of emotion. "Lewis."

Monroe paled. He knew her. Now there was a crack in his facade, and Audrey couldn't help sticking her fingers in it.

"You thought your friend was giving you a gift, didn't you? But instead, he's taken someone you know. Who's going to make videos about you and study you if Natashya is gone? This isn't a gift, this is a slap in the face. A warning that you'd better keep your mouth shut."

"Tashya gave me a lot of airtime. Losing her makes me sad, Doctor. What kind of monster would I be if I was incapable of mourning a friend?"

"You don't have friends and you don't have feelings—not healthy ones. So what does this person have on you to inspire such devotion? What do you have to lose by giving him up?"

"That wouldn't be fair play." His smile—what little there

was of one—was tight. "There are rules to the game. You need to learn them. Fast."

"A girl's life isn't a game."

He arched a brow, a gesture that seemed more practiced than genuine. "Are you preaching morality to me, Doctor? You already know I don't have any. You're being something of a hypocrite. After all, it's not as though you don't have blood on your hands."

Audrey had to force one of her own eyebrows *not* to rise. "Is this part of the game? To make me think we're somehow the same because I took a life? We both have brown hair, but that doesn't mean you know me."

"There's no need to get defensive."

"I'm not, but if you'd rather talk about me than your partner, that's fine. This will be our last visit and I'll put all of my time and energy into looking for him. He's already stealing your thunder. No one is talking about you anymore—they're all terrified of him. I mean, it's not like you can hurt anyone in here, is it? You don't matter anymore."

"I have an entire fan club who would argue with you."

"Oh, yeah. Margot Temple and company. They've asked me to come speak to them after the trial. I haven't given my answer yet." The lie rolled easily off her tongue. "Maybe Margot mentioned that when she came to visit."

Monroe watched her for a moment, sitting back in his chair. He looked comfortable, though there was no way he could be. "Somebody took her bitch pills this morning. What's up with the attitude, Audrey? It's not making me feel all that eager to talk to you."

It was completely likely that he had no idea of what was going on. If he truly had no contact, then his partner was acting without his approval or knowledge. "Your friend sent me a gift before he took Natashya."

Monroe blinked lazily. No change of expression. "Was it a piece of jewelry?"

"Yes."

"Whose?"

"Cassidy Ryan as far as we can tell."

At the mention of the girl, Monroe smiled, but only for a second. "Her bracelet."

"Yes."

"You know, I wanted to feel bad when she died, but I just couldn't. Do you know what it's like to do something horrible and not feel any regret?"

"No," she lied. "I don't."

"It was the moment that I knew I wasn't right. I mean, I've always known that I was different, but that was the moment I knew what I was." He was like an actor rehearsing his lines.

"Yay you."

Monroe grinned. "You know, I like this side of you. A little fight gets the blood up."

Audrey tilted her head. "You talk like an old man sometimes. Where does that come from?"

"I spent a lot of time with my grandfather as a kid. He played a big part in my . . . evolution. I remember the day I found a stash of porn in his garage—rape porn. I shook so hard I could barely turn the pages. My heart—I thought it was going to come right out of my chest. I jacked off to those magazines for months. When the old man died, I made sure I got his collection out of the garage before my grandmother could find them."

Audrey had to stop herself from telling him that was a nice thing to have done. The bastard hadn't done it to spare his grandmother any pain. He'd done it so he'd continue to have his favorite masturbatory material.

When she remained silent, he shot her a coy glance. "No comment? C'mon, you know you want to ask me questions. Want to get into my head and figure out what made me a monster. Really? Not even a little bit? What if I offered to tell you about my friend?"

Her heart skipped a beat. God, he knew how to play her. It was so tempting to take the offer. "I'm not your Clarice Starling, Ian. And you are *not* Hannibal Lector."

A dark brow arched. "Dude, he was old and funny-looking."

She laughed. Couldn't help it, but it quickly died. That was the first time Monroe had sounded his age. "Look, you called and I came. What do you want from me?"

"I meant my offer—I'll tell you about my friend."

She wasn't surprised, but she tried to look it. "So your loyalty only extends so far?"

Monroe shrugged. "Loyalty's what got me locked up."

"No, raping and killing five girls is what got you locked up."

He sat back in his chair. "I didn't kill any of them."

"Then who did?"

"Wow, no foreplay?"

Somehow, she managed not to sneer at him. "I'm not playing—fore or aft."

Monroe's face lit up as he laughed. "Oh, witty! Look, it's simple. I'll tell you about my partner, and all you have to do is tell me about Tori Scott. How's she doing?"

Audrey was pretty much at the end of her patience, and since she wasn't *technically* there in a professional capacity, she could act on it. He had no intention of being helpful. She leaned forward. "Listen to me, you little fuck. Do *not* jerk my chain. I'm the one who could get in front of the cameras and tell the entire country that your deviant behavior stems from a low IQ and the secret desire to actually be a woman, so you violate that which you most want to become."

He laughed, restraints jangling as he clapped his hands. "Oh, this is going to be *fun!*" But there was a gleam in his eye that wasn't amusement. It was fear, and dislike.

She stood up. "We're done."

He hadn't expected that. For a second, his guard was down and she saw the monster behind his facade. *"Sit. Down."*

Her gaze locked with his. "No."

Monroe's expression turned slightly desperate. He was determined to hold on to her attention. "She's going to die, Doc—Natashya. You're not going to find her alive. In fact, I'll bet she's already dead. You know those four days? They were *mine.* My friend's not nearly as patient."

Shit. He might actually be their best chance at finding Natashya, but she wasn't going to give up Tori to save someone else. She couldn't—not when she had already been through so much. Giving details of her life to Ian would be a horrible thing to do—and dangerous, especially if the killer planned to go after Tori again. Audrey had no illusions about how little scruples she could have, or how far her moral outrage extended. But she was supposed to be an advocate for Monroe's victims—she wasn't about to become his bitch.

"I'm leaving. You can give me what I want, or not. If Natashya's already dead, it doesn't matter, does it?" She was just wasting her time. She nodded to the guard, who came to escort her from the room. "You have my number if you decide you're ready to play by my rules. Good-bye, Ian."

He shouted at her as she left the room—that she'd be back. "I know what you are, Dr. Harte!"

She glanced at him just as she was about to cross the threshold. "No, Ian. You really don't."

The door closed behind her, but his shouts followed her down the corridor. Audrey kept walking, praying that her instincts were right this time and that she hadn't just ruined her only chance of finding Natashya Lewis alive.

When Kenny took his break, Jake went outside with him, and stood in the damp wind as Kenny smoked a cigarette.

"Marty's mouth cancer wasn't enough to make you quit?" Jake asked.

Kenny shrugged, obviously unmoved by his stepfather's unfortunate—and grotesque—malady. "Bastard deserves it." He took a deep drag. "What are you doing here, Jake? I thought we were square after Jones."

Jake smiled, shoving his hands into the pockets of his jeans.

"We are. I haven't seen you in a while, I thought it would be nice."

His cousin eyed him warily. It was an expression a lot of people wore when talking to him. Not quite sure if he liked it, to be honest. "You don't have to worry—I don't always find out about things right away, but if I hear of Monroe talking to anyone, sending messages, or making calls, I'll let you and Audrey know."

"Thanks."

"I did hear a rumor that he's added some people to his visitor list. I guess that's Audrey. He also asked to see the minister. Not sure what that's about."

"I'll pass that on."

Another drag. At least he was considerate enough to blow the smoke away from Jake. "I like Audrey. She's too good for you, you know."

He knew. "You think?"

"I dunno. The two of you might be the same kind of bat-shit crazy. I saw what she did to Jones."

"Yeah, I took a few cracks at him too." He wasn't trying to negate the beating Audrey had given Matt, just relieve her of some responsibility.

"I bet you did."

Jake wasn't quite certain what he meant by that, but he didn't ask; it probably wasn't a compliment.

Kenny lifted his chin at him. "Who gave you that?"

Right. The black eye. "Linc."

Ash fell to the ground. "I thought you two were getting along."

Jake rolled his shoulders. "We were until he ripped me off."

His cousin looked surprised. "Seriously?"

"Yeah. Tried to blackmail me too." He wouldn't share that information with Kenny if he wasn't involved. "Said he had a friend here that heard Matt's death was a hit."

The other man didn't blink. "We had an inmate die during surgery at a local hospital. There are people here who think that was a hit too. Prison gossip's not always reliable."

"Sounds like home. Anyway, Linc accused me of being involved in Matt's demise."

"And all you did was beat him up?"

"I'm not the fucking Godfather," Jake informed him with a scowl. "Of course that's all I did."

"He light out?"

"That night. I came in to open up the bar and found him gone." The bastard hadn't even left a note. He had, however, emptied the cash drawer. Fortunately, they kept only a hundred dollars in it at any time. He'd never given his brother the combination to the safe—which was smart on his part. He didn't lie to himself by hoping that Lincoln wouldn't have robbed it. It would have been so cleaned out, it would have smelled of Lysol.

"Sorry to hear that."

"Yeah, thanks. Listen, if he contacts you, will you let me know?"

Kenny fixed him with a blank gaze. "Planning on hunting him down?"

Christ, was this what his cousin thought of him? "No. I just want to make sure he's okay. We both know how much trouble that mouth of his can cause."

Another deep haul on the cigarette, flame chewing up paper and tobacco with a warm glint. Kenny didn't look anxious so much as he looked...annoyed. "Never been a big fan of gossip."

"Yeah, me neither. Not like he has any facts to back it up." He rolled his shoulders, tension easing as they popped. "You'll let me know if you see or hear from him then?"

A wispy stream of smoke parted Kenny's thin lips. "Yeah, I can do that."

"Thanks."

"I didn't tell him anything, just so you know."

Jake nodded. "I know." And then, once the tension eased a bit, "How's your dad?"

"All right. His arthritis is paining him. His knee's all fucked up, but he can't afford to have it replaced."

"He doesn't have insurance?"

"He does, but it won't cover the full cost."

Jake didn't hesitate. "Tell him to go ahead and book the surgery. I'll pay for it."

Kenny froze, cigarette halfway to his mouth. "Why would you do that?"

"To help out. He's family." It never ceased to amaze him how many people didn't understand the concept of family loyalty.

Ash fell to the ground. "What do you want in return?"

"Jesus, Ken—nothing."

"You swear on Gracie's soul?"

Jake ought to have slapped him for the insult. Instead, he resisted the temptation. "I swear."

"Okay." His cousin looked as though he at least *wanted* to believe him. Kenny dropped his cigarette and ground it beneath the heel of his boot. "I'll keep an eye out for Linc for you, but don't come here again, okay? I don't need anyone making more connections between me, Edgeport, and Matthew Jones. I've already been asked how I know Audrey."

Jake nodded. "Sure."

His cousin stood there for a second, then turned and walked away. Jake didn't follow after him. He was still standing there, contemplating taking up smoking so he'd have something to do, when Audrey came out.

"Why are you out here?" she asked.

"Kenny doesn't want to be associated with me." That was the simplest answer—one that didn't require talking about Matt Jones's unfortunate demise. "How'd it go with Monroe?"

She shuddered. "Fucking psychopaths give me the creeps."

One corner of his mouth rose. "Why did you become a psychologist? You don't really like people or their issues."

"Untrue. I'm fascinated by issues, but psychopaths aren't issues—they're wired wrong. They're really good at faking it, and they get off on toying with people."

"I slept with a girl like that once."

"Maggie wasn't a psychopath."

"I wasn't talking about Maggie."

"Wow." She shoved her hands in her pockets. "I so don't

want to know anything about that. Unless, of course, you'd like to hear about some of my sex partners?"

No, he did not, but he was saved from having to say anything by the ringing of Audrey's cell phone.

"Hello? Hey, Will. What's up?"

Jake watched the color drain from her face. Instinctively, he took a step closer to her.

"Yeah, I'll be there as soon as I can." She hung up, and turned her gaze to his. One look and he knew what had happened. "They found her. Natashya Lewis. She's dead."

CHAPTER NINE

Audrey had never been to a morgue before. It wasn't an experience she'd be anxious to repeat. The lighting felt glaringly harsh, the smells both familiar and alien—chemical, musty, old meat laced with copper. She was shown to an autopsy room by a police officer—she wasn't allowed to walk around unattended. Jake had gone back to the hotel. To be honest, she was glad he wasn't there. He thought she was tough, but dead bodies were difficult. It was one thing to see photos, but in person they were . . . different. And he'd been the one to sit with Maggie's corpse waiting for the police to arrive. That was enough death for the year.

Her cell buzzed while she was in the corridor. It was a text from Angeline, her boss. She had heard about Natashya's abduction and wanted to know how Audrey was doing. Audrey shoved her phone back into her pocket. Her response was going to require a little more time than she had at the moment. Words had to be carefully chosen when talking to Angeline; the woman could read between even the most carefully constructed lines. They'd known each other for more than twenty-five years, their first meeting having taken place at Stillwater, the correctional facility where Audrey had gone after killing Clint. How could she possibly hide anything from the woman who often seemed to know her better than she knew herself? Will and Agent Grayson were already in the autopsy room when she came in. The three of them wore protective masks, gowns, and gloves. Funny, how most of life was spent trying to exchange bodily fluids with at least one other person, but death changed all that. What was once desirable was now repulsive.

"Audrey," Will said. "Thanks for coming."

"Why am I here?" she asked, trying not to sound pissed. She had no business witnessing the terrible things that had been done to this poor girl. She wasn't a crime scene investigator.

Above his mask, Will's brow furrowed. "We thought seeing the body might help you figure out what sort of person we're looking for."

You're looking for a fucking sadistic psychopath. Isn't that obvious?
"Will—"

"Audrey," he interrupted. "The killer left you a message."

Horror hurt—like a kick to the chest. Adrenaline maybe? "What? Like an actual note?" She glanced at the dead girl. "Please, not cut into her."

It was in a plastic baggie. Anita held it up. The paper was a little wrinkled, the text was printed in Arial—big block letters. DR. HARTE—YOUR TURN.

"Oh, God," Audrey rasped. What was it about her that seemed to attract killers? Seriously. "This really is a game to him. To both of them."

"Yes," Anita agreed. "And you're the opponent."

Audrey waited for the accusation, the distrust and barrage of questions, but none came. Whatever else she might think of her, the agent obviously did not think she was voluntarily involved in the case.

Well, that was definitely an improvement over last time. She'd been the number one suspect in Maggie's murder.

"I saw Monroe earlier. He told me she was already dead. He said his *friend* wasn't as patient as him."

"Damn it." Will's voice was muffled behind his mask.

"Have you met anyone new recently?" Anita asked.

"Just the people I've interviewed."

"We haven't made it a secret that Audrey is working for us," Will reminded her. It sounded like a confession. "It's probable that she hasn't met our guy at all."

Audrey's jaw clenched. "I really don't like being his playmate."

"We'll keep you safe," Anita assured her.

"That's not what I'm worried about. I'm pissed off. If this is a game, he won't hurt me—he wants to play. This prick might go after someone else just to toy with me."

"I know," Will said. "That's why I wanted you here. I realize this is outside the scope of what you normally do, but we need to catch this guy, and like it or not, he's made you part of his game. Plus, I need you here to keep me from losing my neutrality. I can't do my job if I lose myself in trying to avenge her."

And he wanted to avenge this girl—all the girls, Audrey realized. Detective Grayson wanted the same thing. They all did, didn't they? Why else do what each of them did if not out of a need to help people? She nodded, expelling a deep breath. They were a team—or at least on the same side. She needed to remember that, but the law made her nervous. "Okay, but I've never stood in on an autopsy before."

"You never get used to it," Anita informed her tonelessly.

"Fabulous," Audrey muttered.

Will put his hand on her shoulder. "We don't need to stay for all of it. This is just so you can see firsthand what we're dealing with."

"Was she posed when you found her? And where did you find her?"

Anita nodded. "Found in her homeroom, sitting at her desk with an open textbook in front of her. The book was upside down. She was fully dressed, but in a schoolgirl's uniform. Her hair was in pigtails and there was a large letter 'F' on her forehead, written in the lipstick she was wearing. Given the condition of the body, we think she'd only been dead a few hours. She was still warm."

The poor girl. Audrey pictured it in her mind. "She was a smart girl, yeah? Placing the book upside down might have been a mistake, but I don't think so, given the 'F' on her forehead. The previous victims were all staged in a mocking way. I'm assuming the killer wanted to portray Natashya as a dumb little girl. There's a need to feel superior, which is common in psychopaths, but of course I have no idea of the drive behind that need in this case."

"I think it's a sound assumption," Will agreed.

"I don't want you to take everything—anything—I say as an absolute. I might be wrong about all of it."

Detective Grayson met her gaze. "You wouldn't be here if we thought you didn't know what you're doing. It would be great if you got on board with that thought as well."

Audrey blinked. "Okay, then." That was not what she'd expected.

The medical examiner began her work of examining the body. Natashya didn't look as bad as Audrey had expected. She'd been beaten, and strangled like Monroe's victims, but she hadn't been cut up. The lipstick "F" on her forehead was smudged.

"Rigor is setting in," the doctor said, lifting Natashya's hand as if to prove the truth of her words. "She's definitely been dead for less than eight hours. He cleaned her up before dumping her. I haven't found anything on her yet except a small piece of plastic—from a garbage bag, I think."

Of course. Clean meant less physical evidence. And garbage bags were great for avoiding picking up evidence, and leaving it behind.

"We didn't find much in the classroom either," Anita added. "And there were so many prints, we're going to be going through them for days. The teacher said the room was unlocked when she arrived. The lock hadn't been tampered with either. Either maintenance forgot to lock the room up, or our killer had a key."

"Was it a teacher who found her?" Audrey asked.

She nodded. "Poor woman's a mess. Luckily there weren't any students around."

Small favors, Audrey thought.

"Staging the victims in a fairly public place, where there's a good chance of getting caught, is definitely part of this guy's signature," Will remarked.

Anita nodded. "We thought it was Monroe who liked to clean them up, dress them pretty. I guess not."

Audrey tore her gaze away from the corpse on the table. "When I talked to the girls Ian raped before the murders started, neither of them said anything about him trying to clean them up. In fact, he just left them."

"We probably would have caught him sooner if not for this partner." Will shook his head. "I'm beginning to think we've got a seasoned killer on our hands."

Anita glanced at him. "We checked the MO with our databases. Nothing similar came up."

"She was strangled with something strong and thick," the ME interjected. "A scarf, maybe."

Audrey stared at the girl, so pale and bruised. The ligature marks around her throat were vivid and ugly. Strangulation was a tough way to go—and a tough way to kill someone. It took longer than people thought. Extremely personal. The killer wanted to watch Natashya's face as she died.

When Clint died, he'd been facedown. That had been bad enough.

"Our killer is probably strong." Will glanced at Anita. "It takes a lot of strength to strangle someone, yes?"

Audrey added, "Or a lot of patience."

"That's right," Anita said. "Usually it requires both strength and patience."

It was on the tip of Audrey's tongue to add that it probably required a location where no one would hear if your victim put up a fight, but this was Maine, and you were never too far from a place where no one would hear you scream.

"What's that mark on her chest?" Anita asked, pointing a gloved finger. There, right between the girl's exposed breasts, was an oddly shaped bruise.

"It looks like a heart," Audrey said, tilting her head. "It is."

A rounded, purple heart, right there, just below her sternum.

Anita turned to the examiner. "Was she hit with something?"

"Looks like it. Didn't break the skin, though. I can't think of any kind of instrument that would leave that sort of mark."

"A novelty hammer?" Will suggested. "Or a statue?" He turned to Audrey, as though waiting for her to add something to the conversation. She shrugged. How the hell should she know what made the mark? He looked disappointed.

There were people, and Audrey had met a few of them since leaving university, who watched too many crime-solving shows and believed that psychologists and psychiatrists had some sort of magic powers that allowed them to see inside every person they encountered and extract the information they needed from vague facts. She wouldn't have thought Will would be one of them. She wasn't certain that he was—maybe he was simply desperate. Ian Monroe's trial was a big thing for him, and if there was a partner, he needed to get in front of things, because the public and the press were going to want to know how the FBI and the justice system missed it the first time. Maybe that was why he wasn't looking at Grayson as though she should magically figure out exactly who they were dealing with.

Audrey didn't have the heart to tell him that most of her time was spent applying basic Psych 101 principles until she had enough information to dig deeper. A person's psychology was a puzzle, and if you didn't have all the pieces, you had nothing.

But they knew that Ian had a partner, and this partner meant that Ian was a serial rapist, not a serial killer, although he would have been an accessory. Regardless, this new murder changed the charges against Monroe, changed things for Will, and made his job all the more difficult. Audrey wished she *did* have the answers he wanted.

"Nothing under her nails," the ME told them. No hairs on her clothing except for one long blond one that we've sent for analysis. It was a little lighter than her own, but I'd be remiss if I didn't check. And there was absolutely no sign of sexual assault."

That only solidified the theory that Ian had been the rapist and his "friend" the killer.

Audrey's cell buzzed, indicating a message. She sneaked a peek at it while Grayson, the ME, and Will discussed possible causes and implications of the bruise. The text was from Bailey. Audrey's heart clenched at the sight of the girl's name. She hadn't given Bailey the attention she'd wanted. She'd meant to, but shortly after that whole mess in the summer, she'd begun to see Bailey not as someone who needed her help, but as a walking, talking example of her own shortcomings as a psychologist. She'd missed the clues.

Maybe she was missing clues now as well. What had she been thinking taking on a job with such a high profile? If she fucked this up, she would never forgive herself.

She slipped her phone back into her pocket just as Will turned to face her. "Audrey, what are your impressions of our guy?"

She opened her mouth, ready to remind them that profiling wasn't an exact science, but Anita's words still rang in her head. She didn't have to be right, she just had to give them enough "maybes" to start with. "I'd guess that Natashya's killer knew her."

"You're thinking he picked her up?"

"It makes sense." Audrey glanced at Grayson before continuing, "She was smart, and smart kids rarely miss school unless they're sick. Natashya wouldn't have missed that day if not for the killer. It was a cold, wet morning. I bet the inside of a warm car looked good even to a girl who probably used her morning commute to get herself wide awake and alert. Plus, no girl with any sense is going to willingly get into a stranger's car."

"Okay, so that's something." Will looked pleased—relieved.

"Though she might have been forced," Anita reminded them.

Audrey nodded. "That's true. If she was grabbed walking to school, though, there had to be people around. Did she walk through a residential area?"

"She did," Anita replied. "No one on the street heard or saw anything. Two people saw Natashya walking, but no one noticed her get picked up, or if there had been a strange car on the street."

"This guy's smart, and he wants us to know it. He's also daring, but only because he's concealed himself so well. We wouldn't even know about him if he hadn't decided to play Secret Santa with me. And he's intimidating enough that even protected by prison, Monroe won't give him up. Though Monroe did offer to give me information if I reported back to him with news on Tori."

"Son of a bitch," Anita seethed. "Tell me you said no."

That was vaguely insulting. Audrey frowned at her. "Of course I said no."

"You could say yes and feed him false information." God, Will really had to be desperate to suggest it.

"There's no guarantee that what he gave us would be any more truthful," Audrey informed him. "People like Monroe lie easily, and they're more interested in manipulation than making deals. He'd probably lie just for the pleasure of frustrating us. Take a look at some of the older men in his life. He looks up to this person and has some loyalty to him—that's not something a psychopath usually gives. Look at the women in his life as well."

"A female serial?" Agent Grayson made a scoffing noise. "That's a unicorn."

Audrey shot her a sharp look. She didn't want to be there, didn't want to be in that position, and she most certainly did not want to be arguing over a dead girl's body. Grayson was a federal agent, she had to have seen female killers before. "Tell that to Aileen Wuornos or Jane Toppan. Toppan reported actually being aroused by the process of killing."

"Never heard of her," the detective replied.

"She confessed to thirty-one murders." Audrey had a bit of a "thing" for female killers. She didn't idolize them by any means, but she'd spent a lot of time researching female killers before narrowing her focus to female teenage killers. At the time she'd needed to find people who had done worse things than she had, and to make peace with the fact that no matter how much she knew she should feel remorse for killing Clint, she didn't feel the least bit sorry.

"I can't see Monroe being intimidated by a woman," Will remarked.

Audrey shrugged. "Maybe he wanted to impress her. Look, this isn't an exact science, and it's not like it's any harder to look at the strong women in Monroe's life than it is to look at the strong men."

"You're right." Coming from Grayson, Audrey was going to take it as a compliment.

"The killer likes to play with their victims." She would have to remember to use gender-neutral pronouns from now on. "Look at all those little marks and bruises on her arms—they make me think of a bully poking at a smaller kid with a stick."

"The previous victims didn't have any of those," Anita commented.

Audrey nodded. "Without Ian, he—or she—is able to stretch their wings a little."

Will nodded. "We'll need to recheck and see exactly how this murder compares and differs from the others. Hopefully we'll discover some similarities that we can't attribute to Monroe and give us a better idea of who we're dealing with."

They stayed a little longer, getting slightly more info from the examiner. Finally, just when Audrey couldn't stand looking at the body any longer, Will thanked the ME for her time, and after requesting photographs and findings, the three of them left the autopsy room.

"I'm sorry to have put you through that," Will said.

"No, you're not." Audrey peeled off the gown that covered her street clothes. She wasn't angry, not really. She made herself smile as she continued. "You don't regret anything that might help your case."

"Touché." He smiled. "Still, thank you."

"I didn't say or do anything either you or Agent Grayson couldn't—wouldn't—have done."

"Call me Anita. I would never think of looking at women. I still don't think we should waste our time, but I'm going to look into it because you think it's a viable option."

No pressure or anything. "Thank you." Would she look at Audrey with the same doubt Neve Graham had when she arrested Bailey? Neve had claimed she hadn't put the pieces together either, but she had expected Audrey to see it coming.

Or at least that was what Audrey *imagined* Neve had expected.

"God," she said, glancing back at the door. "Her poor parents."

"Come," Will said, putting his arm around her shoulders. "Let me buy you a drink. You can tell me about your meeting with Monroe. I want to add attempted bribery to the bastard's charges."

Audrey said yes to the drink, even though she didn't want to.

The need for a little relaxation outweighed everything else—even the fact that Jake was waiting for her. She needed to get a little numb. A warning bell went off in her head, but she ignored it. *One drink won't hurt.*

She wondered how many times her father had said the same thing.

Audrey arrived back at her hotel practically sober. She'd had two drinks and that was it. The craving to escape for a bit was too strong, and she was too aware of the long list of alcoholics in her family tree to give in.

But she did stop at a shoe store on the way back and bought a new pair of boots. Sometimes an itch just had to be scratched.

She was walking across the lobby toward the elevators, shopping bag in hand, when a man suddenly entered her periphery. He came at her with such purpose that she switched her bag to the other hand in case she had to throw a punch.

"Dr. Harte? I'm Christopher James." He held out his hand.

Audrey looked at it, then at him. He was a fairly good-looking guy—thick hair that stood up in an artful way, gray eyes, chiseled jaw. Not her type at all. Reluctantly, she accepted the handshake. "The crime writer. I apologize for not responding to your request for an interview. I've been busy. You're writing about Monroe?"

"I was, but now that there's been another killing, I've put that on the back burner until all the facts are sorted out. Right now I'm covering aspects of the trial on my website. Are the police sure this is the work of Monroe's rumored partner?"

She was so glad she wasn't drunk for this. Not because she'd give away information, but because she really would have punched him. "Another killing?" They'd only just found the body and were trying to keep it quiet for as long as they could. "A partner? Where do you get your information?"

He smiled. It was a gesture that probably worked on a lot of women—and men. Audrey found herself completely immune. "My sources are confidential."

Audrey raised a brow. "Of course they are. Guess what? So are mine." She started walking again. James followed her. Then he stepped right in front of her, blocking her path to the elevator. "Is it true that there was a note addressed to you with the body?"

She tried to move around him, but he was fast on his feet. "Mr. James, I'm seriously considering breaking your nose just because I'm in that kind of mood."

For a moment, he actually looked concerned, but that faded faster than it ought to have. He obviously had no idea just how good she was at breaking things. "So it is true."

"Does it matter? Regardless of what I say right now, you're going to infer whatever meaning you want. Why are you even bothering to harass me?"

He blinked. "Because the killer has formed a relationship with you after being dormant since Monroe's arrest."

"There's no relationship."

"So you admit that the Lewis girl was killed by Monroe's partner?"

Maybe she'd knock out a couple of his perfect teeth as well.

She straightened her shoulders. "I admit nothing, Mr. James. Now please fuck off. I've had a rough day and you're not making it any better."

"Do you think the killer feels a kinship with you because of your own past?"

Oh, for shit's sake. Audrey took a step toward him, so that there was but a couple of inches between them. She kept her voice low, so only he could hear, "If I'm the sort of person who inspires kinship in psychopaths, you probably *don't* want to be pushing my buttons." She gave him a light push out of her way and punched the call button on the elevator.

"You know, I'd love to write a book about you," James called after her as she stepped into the car.

Smirking as she gave him the finger, Audrey moved back into the car as the doors slid closed. "I'm not that interesting."

When she entered the suite, Jake met her in the entry.

"You okay?" he asked, frowning. "You have that look your father gets whenever he's about to break a chair over someone's back."

Great, she looked like a growly old man. "I'm not sure," she replied, kicking off her boots. "Today I talked to a serial killer, stood over a corpse, and got harassed by a crime writer, and it's not even seven o'clock."

"Stopped by a bar too?"

Her shoulders sagged. "Yes. Will's idea. I admit, I needed the fortification." She set her bag on the floor. "Do you ever worry about becoming a drunk like your father?"

He didn't even blink at her use of the "D" word, but then the children of alcoholics weren't as far into denial as their parents. They had different issues. "No. I realized as a kid that control was not a thing I liked to misplace, let alone lose altogether."

"Mm. I hear you. But sometimes, that numb-to-your-bones feeling is nice."

He slung his arm around her shoulders and squeezed. "C'mon, I'll run a bath."

She tilted her head back to look up at him. "Share it with me?"

He did, and by the time he was done with her, she was as limp as a dishrag and the inside of her mouth tasted vaguely of soap. Wrapped up in the thick robes provided by the hotel, they ordered room service and lounged on the bed, watching a reality TV show about ghost hunters.

"Just once, I'd like to see a ghost show up on one of these," Jake remarked, licking the spoon he'd just pulled out of the cheesecake he'd gotten for dessert. "Some hard-case ghost that just shows up and kicks their asses."

Audrey smiled. "That would be funny." His grandmother, Gracie, had believed in ghosts. She hadn't been afraid of them, but she always said that "a body oughta have the proper respect for the dead." Spirits were not to be trifled with. And of course, she'd had stories about "ghosties" that were her own, and others from her family. Jake had stories too, and so did Audrey and her mother—who was also a big fan of anything haunted. Maybe it was a cultural thing.

"How's your ice cream?" he asked.

She looked down at the pint of Häagen-Dazs in her hand.

She'd wrapped a hand towel around it so she could eat it right out of the container. She'd had a big dinner, but she felt ravenous, and simultaneously in need of comfort food. It had been one of those days. She was going to have to get some time in on one of the treadmills in the fitness center—for her mind as well as her waistline.

"Doing a better job than the booze did." She leaned into his shoulder. "Thank you for coming down here and staying with me. I think I'd be a paranoid mess without you."

"You'd be fine," he assured her. "You always are. Besides, pretty boy would have the cops watching over you, or something."

"Pretty boy?" She couldn't believe her ears. "Did you seriously just call Will Grant 'pretty boy'?"

He licked his spoon. "I believe I did."

Audrey laughed. "You're five times prettier than he is!"

"I am *not* pretty." He scowled when he said it, but it lacked any real anger. "He's got that Superman jaw and tailor-made suits. I know how much women love that stuff."

She shrugged. "I don't find Will all that attractive, to tell you the truth."

"Liar." He stuck his spoon in her ice cream and scooped out a big bite.

She slapped his hand. "Am not. When have you ever known me to want the stereotypically good-looking guy? I think I was the only girl in Edgeport who never wanted Gideon." Gideon McGann, Bailey's father, was a few years older than Audrey and she'd known him for most of her life. She'd been the only female in town not to find him attractive.

"Seriously? You never wanted Gid? What's wrong with you? All the guys wanted to be him, you know. I used to try to wear my hair like his but it always looked stupid."

"You never looked stupid to me."

"Yeah, well, that phase happened while you were in Stillwater."

Ah, yes. Her juvy prison. She'd had her past come back to haunt her more times in the last few days than she'd had in the entire time she lived in California. Of course, no one knew her in California, and Maggie had still been alive, so there had been no reason for her past to come to light.

"I'm sorry I missed it," she replied. It sounded tinny to her ears.

Jake glanced at her. He knew her moods so well. "So am I."

"Why didn't you ever come visit me there?" The question tumbled out before she even realized her mind had thought of it. Why hadn't she asked before this?

"Gran," he replied. "She asked if I would want you to visit me if the situation were reversed. I said no—that I would be embarrassed if you saw me in a place like that. She said that I shouldn't go then, because I would probably feel embarrassed for you, and that was only one step up from being embarrassed *of* you."

Audrey took a bite of ice cream. Caramel cone crunched between her teeth. "I think I *would* have been embarrassed if you showed up. I mean, all the girls would have asked about you, and you would have given them masturbatory fantasies for the next six months, but still, you would have seen me brought low, which is weird, because sometimes I think Stillwater was the best thing that ever happened to me."

"It was the first time you left Edgeport behind."

She spooned out more ice cream. It was getting melty. Her tongue burned from the cold. "Yeah. I guess I needed to get out, even then."

"You sure you want to be back in?"

"It's not like I'm there all the time."

His lips tilted to one side. "I know."

Oh, shit. This wasn't about Edgeport really, was it? "I'm glad I came back. I mean, I could have done without being a murder suspect, but the rest of it's been all right." She smiled to let him know she was teasing—as if he couldn't tell.

"Yeah, well, it's been okay having you back."

She reached up and touched the bruise around his eye. It had faded a bit since he arrived. "Do you think Lincoln will come back?"

"When he wants something." There was no bitterness in his tone, only resigned certainty.

"I still can't believe you hired my father."

"Spoke to him earlier today, he says things are working out just fine, but he had to kick Bertie Neeley out for trying to start a fight."

"With who?"

"Him." Jake grinned. "He's pretty puffed up over that one. He says he didn't even have to take a swing, just dragged Bertie out and tossed him down the steps."

"He'll be drunk on his own power now."

He inclined his head. "Better than the alternative."

There was that. Maybe she should thank Jake for giving

her father a chance, but she couldn't bring herself to do it. Her father was not her responsibility.

"He also said that you should call your mother. She's worried about you with this new murder."

"Ah, fuck. I'll call her in the morning." It wasn't a conversation she wanted to have, but since when had that mattered? The last couple of days had been full of them, what was one more?

Her phone rang. It was on her bedside table, so she took a look at the screen. "It's Nancy Scott. I'd better take it."

Jake muted the volume on the TV with the remote just as Audrey accepted the call. "Hello?"

"Dr. Harte? It's Nancy Scott. I hope I'm not calling you too late."

"No, of course not. What can I do for you?"

Hesitation. "We heard about poor Natashya Lewis on the news."

Of course they had. "Didn't ADA Grant call you to prepare you?"

"Yes, but Tori was at school. When she got home, she actually seemed a bit like her old self. She had a friend with her. The girl didn't stay long—she was borrowing a book or something. It doesn't matter. I didn't want to tell her that awful news while she seemed so light and young."

"So she heard it on TV instead." Audrey couldn't blame the woman for wanting to let her daughter have a little happiness. It was just shitty timing. "Am I correct in assuming that Tori was upset?"

"Very. She became so emotional that I had to give her two of her anti-anxiety pills. The poor thing is asleep now. She asked if she could sleep in my bed tonight." The woman's voice hitched. "Owen sometimes likes to stay up late, so he's fine sleeping in the spare room. He hates waking me up when he comes in. Anyway, before she went up, Tori asked me to call you. Do you suppose...that is, if you're not busy, could you come by tomorrow morning?"

Oddly enough, Audrey's first response was *not* to drop the phone and run screaming. After Monroe and the morgue, talking to a messed-up kid sounded fabulous. At least she stood a small chance of being helpful to Tori, and unlike Will, Mrs. Scott didn't seem to expect her to have magic powers that allowed her to see into someone's head.

"What time?" she asked.

"Ten? I'm going to let her sleep in and keep her home from school."

That was probably for the best. "Ten is fine. I'll see you then."

"Thank you so much." The relief in her voice was so heavy, Audrey practically felt it weighing down her ear. "See you then."

Audrey said good night and hung up.

"Making a house call?"

"Yeah. Tomorrow morning. Do you mind?"

"No. I'm sure I can find a way to amuse myself."

She didn't think he was lying, but she wasn't certain he was being one hundred percent honest either. Regardless, she trusted him to speak his heart and his mind as he always had.

They finished their desserts and watched more television. Finally, sometime after eleven, the day finally caught up with her and Audrey's eyelids began to droop. She pulled on a pair of boxers and a tank top and crawled under the covers. Jake joined her a few moments later.

In the dark, with his warmth spooning her back, she asked, "You're not jealous of Will, are you?"

"No." His arm tightened around her. "You're mine, Aud. And I'm yours. I don't think either one of us has a say in it, regardless. I'm okay with that. You?"

Audrey smiled, even though he couldn't see it, and wrapped her fingers around his forearm. "Yeah," she whispered. "I'm okay with that."

CHAPTER TEN

Thank you so much for coming by, Dr. Harte."

Audrey smiled reassuringly at Nancy Scott as she walked inside the house at 10:01 the following morning. "Where is Tori now?"

"In her room. In bed, I think. Since we heard the news, that's where she's spent all of her time."

"Does that seem to numb her anxiety? Her room is where she feels the most safe?"

Nancy nodded. "I think so. Certainly, when I go up, I see that she's more at ease than she is down here. Is that good?"

Audrey took off her coat. "Safety is important, but so is socialization. She's had a shock, so for now, spending time in her room might be calming her. But she obviously cannot spend the rest of her life in isolation."

The woman looked five years older than she had the last time Audrey saw her. Her concern for her daughter was obvious. "I tried telling her, but I think she feels pressured when I say it. She feels so guilty for how her experience affects me and her father. The poor thing feels as though she's let us down." She shook her head.

People with PTSD often felt guilt for the trauma, or for their own reaction to it. Tori was probably worried that Monroe's partner would come for her and finish what they started, but Audrey wasn't going to say it out loud. "Is Mr. Scott home today?"

A dull flush crept up the woman's neck. "No. He's away… on business."

Ah. He wouldn't be the first husband/father to bail on a bad situation, the dick. "Maybe you could have him call me? I would like to talk to him as well before the trial."

"Of course. Let me show you to Tori's room. Can I offer you anything to drink?"

Audrey thought for a moment. What might put Tori at ease? "Tea would be lovely."

Mrs. Scott smiled brightly, as though Audrey had just aced some sort of test. "I'll make a pot." But first, she wanted to take Audrey to her daughter's room, because she didn't know what else to do for the girl, and Audrey was her last hope. She told Audrey this as they climbed the stairs. No pressure, though.

"Tori, honey," Nancy began as she knocked. "Dr. Harte is here."

"Come in."

Tori's bedroom wasn't what Audrey expected. At seventeen, she'd kept her room fairly neat, as had been drilled into them at Stillwater. Tori's room surpassed neat and went deep into OCD territory. Everything on the makeup table was orderly and clean. Two plastic cups on the table were labeled DIRTY and CLEAN. Three makeup brushes were in the former.

Clothing wasn't all over the floor, and the carpet looked to have been recently vacuumed. The air smelled slightly of roses—an odd scent for a young girl. And the entire room was decorated in white—solid white. No pinks or purples. No posters or band paraphernalia anywhere to be seen.

There was absolutely no personality or style to it at all.

It looked nothing like a teenage girl's room, except for the teenager buried under a mound of blankets on the bed. Tori sat up when Audrey walked in. The tentative smile that curved the girl's lips was a good sign. Her mother smiled as well. "I'll go make the tea."

"Thank you. Hi, Tori," Audrey said, laying her coat over the back of the desk chair. "How are you doing?"

"A little better now. Have they caught the guy who took Natashya?"

"Not that I've heard of, but the police are working hard."

The girl looked disgusted. "They worked hard to find Ian as well, but he raped and helped kill five girls, and tried to do the same to me."

"Tori, do you remember who was with Monroe when he took you?"

"Not really. I don't know if there even was anyone with him, let alone if it was a man or a woman—they had me drugged pretty hard."

"But you definitely remember a third person?"

"I remember him talking like someone else was there, but that's it. Ian wouldn't have taken anyone there unless he trusted them, though."

"There" was Ian's family cottage just a little way up the coast. Was his partner maybe a family friend? A family member? That could explain Ian's unwillingness to give him over.

"Is he going to come after me?" Tori asked, eyes wide. "Am I in danger?"

Audrey looked into those eyes—red-rimmed and bloodshot. She looked as though she'd had trouble sleeping, been crying. She had to be medicated, because her fear was evident in her voice, but her eyes were flat. "I don't know," she answered honestly. "I do know the FBI is going to do all they can to protect you, and find the killer."

The girl nodded, rumpled blond hair falling over her shoulders. "I am. He didn't get to finish with me. He'll feel the need to finish what he started."

"Or not. Other people have gotten away and not found themselves victimized again."

Tori frowned. "That's hardly ever happened."

"Well, unfortunately a lot of people don't get away to begin with."

Glassy eyes widened even farther. "Is that supposed to make me feel better? Because it doesn't."

Audrey shifted her weight to a more relaxed posture. "Tori, I'm not saying you shouldn't be cautious or that you shouldn't be afraid. You should be cautious, and you're right to be afraid. Just don't let it rule your life. Don't go out alone, and don't accept rides from people unless you're with a group, even if you know the driver."

She sat up a little higher, a mountain of pillows at her back.

Her hair needed to be brushed. "Why not? Do they think Natashya knew the guy?"

Audrey shouldn't have said anything, but wanted the girl to be at ease, not jumping every time a car drove by. So far she hadn't done such a great job of that. She shouldn't discuss any of this with her. "I don't know. The authorities have told me very little. So why don't we talk about what's going on with you, rather than what's going on out there."

"What's going on out there *is* what's going on with me," Tori replied hotly. "With your background that should be fairly obvious."

It was a tone Audrey had heard a few times in her work, when the client wasn't getting what they wanted, or the therapist had tried changing tactics. Time to step back and let Tori direct the conversation. "What do you want to know?"

Now that Audrey was an adult, the contemptuous glances of teenagers didn't inspire the same dejection they had fifteen years ago. She arched a brow at Tori's curled lip. Fifteen years ago she would have fattened that lip, so there had been progress. Plus, ethics boards frowned upon abusing those in a therapist's care.

"I want to know what the police are doing to find him. I want to know what they're going to do to protect me. I want to know what Ian said about it."

"Why do you want to know about Ian?"

"Because he knows the truth."

"That's why he doesn't tell it. He wants something to hold over the police, like bait. Maybe if they take it, he'll get a reduced sentence or moved to a prison where there's little chance of him running into relatives of the girls he raped."

She looked horrified. "They'd never let him out, would they?"

"No. He's going to be gone for a long time."

Tori actually smiled. "Good."

Audrey watched her. PTSD manifested in strange ways, and a smile wasn't the worst she'd seen. "You know, I think fear of being abducted again is good."

"Why?" The word dripped with incredulous tones.

"Fear of dying means you want to live. When was the last time you felt like you had a future to look forward to living?"

The girl looked out the window and brought her knees up to her chest, hugging them through the blankets. "I don't know. A long time, I guess. I've been thinking about it a lot lately."

Audrey smiled. "See, that's good."

Tori smiled faintly. It didn't last long, but it was still encouraging. "Where did they find her?"

"Tori..." She had no intention of giving her the gruesome details after all she'd been through.

"Tell me. Please."

"The school." And that was all she was going to say.

"Did he pose her like the others?"

"You are I are not discussing this."

"Why not?"

"Because the FBI hasn't given me permission, and I don't think it's anything you need to hear, especially when I don't know all the facts."

"I can look it up on Google, you know."

"I know." Audrey smiled serenely, inviting her to do just that.

A battle of wills with a teenager all came down to who could be quietest the longest. Most teenage girls—not all—liked attention. Liked to talk and be talked to, especially when they themselves were the subject. Silence drove them nuts. They were sort of like psychopaths that way.

"Where in the school? Did he leave her in homeroom or something?"

Audrey caught her face before it could fall, schooling her expression to one of neutrality—she hoped. "I don't know."

Tori shook her head. "Whatever. All of the other girls were left in places that meant something to them. Tashya was smart—she loved school. Ian said they were going to leave me in a movie theater."

No emotion. Just calm acknowledgment. "Do you like movies?"

"I did. I really did. I used to go all the time. Now I watch them on my computer or downstairs. I haven't been to a movie since the police brought me home."

"Someday, you should go to one, just so you can reclaim it."

"Yeah, maybe. You're really not going to tell me anything, are you?"

Back to this again? "Have you stopped to wonder what knowing about Natashya's death means to you? How it makes you feel outside of the fear?"

"I don't know. It makes me feel less alone. Makes me glad it wasn't me. Makes me scared it will be me."

"It's not going to be you."

"You can't promise me that."

"It *won't* be you." The girl was right, she shouldn't make such a promise, but Audrey felt it in her bones.

Their gazes locked and held. Looking into Tori's eyes was something like gazing into a whirlpool; at first everything seems loose and calm, but by the time you get to the center, you've been sucked in and drowning.

"Is there anything I can do to help?" Tori asked after a few seconds, breaking the connection.

Audrey blinked. "Help with what?"

"Catching this bastard, that's what. What can I do?"

This was a new side to Tori's personality. Forceful. "I'm not sure there's anything you can do, or anything the authorities would *want* you to do, but I can tell them you'd like to help."

"Please. I feel like such a coward hiding here, but I just can't go outside. As soon as I heard Natashya was missing, I knew. I knew it had started again."

"Have you made an appointment with your therapist?" The girl couldn't go through life thinking every missing girl was related to her own abduction.

"No. I canceled this week's because I can't leave the house."

"Tori, this is not a good time to miss therapy, especially not with the anxiety you're experiencing."

The teen gazed up at her through lowered lashes. "Maybe you could be my therapist for a while?"

No! "I can't do that. I'm sorry, but as a witness for the prosecution, I'm supposed to assess, not treat. The defense could say I coached you. Besides, I haven't done clinical work in a long time." Maybe she should start again.

Tori's shoulders drooped.

"I could perhaps talk to your therapist and see what we can work out."

For the first time, there was brightness in the girl's face. "That means so much, thank you."

"Meanwhile, is the school sending your assignments home for you to do?"

"Yeah. They're pretty good about it. Sometimes too good, you know? I don't want special favors." But from the little smile on her lips, Audrey thought maybe she did like it. If the school sent work home, there was no reason for her to go at all, and she could just hide in her bedroom. "My English teacher says I have a gift for writing. I hope she means it and just isn't saying it because she feels sorry for me."

"I'm sure she wouldn't say it if it wasn't true." God, that rolled off her tongue so easily. She knew full well the teacher probably felt some degree of sympathy for the kid.

"Tea's ready," Mrs. Scott said from just outside the door. "Dr. Harte, I hope you like molasses cookies."

"Very much," Audrey replied. "Thank you." As she stood to help, she noticed a small package on the tray the older woman carried. Plain brown paper, a printed address label. No return address.

"You have mail, dear," Tori's mother told her. "A package."

Audrey's heart skipped a beat. "Mrs. Scott, I think you should let me open that."

The woman's face fell, her pleasant expression giving way to one of dawning horror. "You don't think..."

Audrey picked up the little wrapped box with the tips of her fingernails, and carefully carried it to Tori's desk. She found a small pair of scissors and used them to cut the tape. Then, she used two pens to peel back the paper. Beneath was a generic white box—much like what she'd opened when sent Cassidy's bracelet. This time, Audrey used the tips of the pens to gently pry the box open.

Inside, beneath a layer of snowy tissue paper, was a necklace— a silver chain with an intricately carved dragonfly hanging from it. She didn't need anyone else to identify it for her. She recognized it from the photographs she'd studied. It belonged to Jillian White. But it wasn't the necklace—with a blond hair still caught in its clasp—that had Audrey reaching for her phone. It was the small piece of notepaper with her own name on it.

I'm disappointed, Dr. Harte. You're not proving to be much of an opponent at all. I'm beginning to think you don't want to play. If you want to stop me, get in the fucking game, or my next pretty girl will be that little one you seem so attached to.

"What is it?" Tori asked, her voice strained.

Audrey didn't look at Tori, didn't want her to see the fear in her eyes. "It's for me."

"It's from him, isn't it?" Nancy demanded. "Hasn't he hurt Tori enough? When will you people finally put him away?"

The mother's gaze was the one Audrey could meet. "I know you're upset, but the authorities are doing all they can to find this person. I'm going to call Agent Grayson now and have her come here. You can direct your questions to her. I'm a doctor, not an investigator."

"I know that." Nancy sighed. "I know you've been dragged into this as well, Dr. Harte, and I'm sorry."

"I think you'd better call me Audrey." With that, she unlocked her cell and dialed Anita's number. As she told the agent that a package had been delivered to her, via Tori, she noticed a speck of something dull and dark on the back of the dragonfly. It looked like blood.

On the bed, Tori sat crying. How much more could the girl take? Audrey glanced at the note again. It looked like she didn't have a choice.

She was going to get into the fucking game.

It wasn't long after Audrey left for the Scott house that Jake received a call on the hotel line from Will Grant.

"Are you ready?" Grant asked.

He'd just finished tying the laces of his Doc Martens. The boots were the only comfortable footwear he owned other than a pair of flip-flops, and his feet were already itching inside his socks.

"Yeah."

"Meet me out front in five."

Jake hung up and grabbed his jacket. He made sure he had his key card before leaving the suite.

Whether or not he was doing the right—or smart—thing didn't occur to him. He did, however, realize that Audrey was probably going to be upset when she found out he had gotten himself involved. Not like he'd volunteered; Grant approached him. Generally he made it a habit to avoid anyone involved in the business of law and order, but a girl was dead and Audrey had herself all tied up in knots because of it.

He'd gotten the call yesterday, before Audrey arrived back at the hotel. Grant asked him if he'd help with a little undercover work. Jake had almost laughed, but he agreed to do what he could. It hadn't taken much enticement. As soon as Grant told him it was work that Audrey wouldn't have to do, he jumped at it.

The woman was his weakness. Always had been. From that first meeting when they were very young, when Audrey had been mad over losing her ice cream—Lincoln's fault, the bastard—and Jake got her a new one, she'd fascinated him. She'd probably end up being his downfall, but he'd resigned himself to it already. Those years they'd been apart—Stillwater and after she left for college—he'd missed her, but he hadn't realized just how much. It took her walking back into his life for him to realize that his world was a little brighter with her in it, fucked up as she was.

Not like he was any great prize, though according to her, he was prettier than Grant. Yeah, he wasn't all that sure it was a compliment. No man liked to be called "pretty," unless maybe he was in drag. Still, she was the only woman who had ever held his interest. The only person he felt like he could show his true self to.

He grabbed a coffee at the hotel shop. By the time he'd fixed it the way he liked it and exited, Grant was just pulling up to the curb. Jake opened the door of the black Audi and stepped inside. It smelled of leather with a touch of cologne. Even the guy's car was impressive. But it didn't feel like a desperate bid to prove he had a big dick.

"Good morning," Grant said.

"Yeah, hi."

"Thanks again for doing this."

Jake opened the tab on his coffee cup as the car moved toward the street. "What exactly is it you want me to do?" If it was illegal, he was going to feed the prosecutor his own teeth.

"Barry Lawson goes to the same gym three times a week for boxing training. I want you to engage him in conversation. See what you can get out of him."

Not illegal, but a little ambiguous for Jake's taste. "I thought he was a teacher. Shouldn't he be at the school?"

"He's been part-time since Monroe's arrest. He claims the treatment he received from the police, and the harassment he endured from students and faculty during the investigation, caused him grievous psychological injury. Apparently the boxing is so he can feel safe again."

Jake shrugged. "I suppose it's better than buying a gun."

"Oh, I'm fairly certain he has one of those as well."

Good to know. He owned a gun or two himself, but they were shotguns, not something a person could easily conceal beneath clothes. "So how am I supposed to 'engage' him?" He took a drink of coffee.

"I thought you could get in the ring with him."

Jake almost choked. Grant had to be fucking *joking*. "You want me to fight him?"

"Yes." The ADA glanced at him. "Was I presumptuous in thinking you are a man who can fight? I thought that black eye was a trophy."

Trophy? The only scraps Grant had ever gotten into had to

have been in his college boxing club, or something equally clean and fair. No one who had ever been in a real fight—with the intent to kick the snot out of another person—would ever see a black eye, bruise, or cut as a fucking trophy. "I can fight. How much damage do you want?"

"Damage? No, you don't have to hurt him—not much. Enough to get his respect. I'm hoping you'll befriend him enough that we can poke around in his life."

"Do I look like someone who makes friends *easily*?" Jake frowned. "Shouldn't your FBI friends do this?"

"Yes, but Anita can't get approval to go after Lawson without solid evidence after a... misunderstanding when he was arrested the first time."

Jake turned his head, taking a good measure of the man sitting beside him in an expensive suit. "Got rough with him, did they?" He'd been in the same position once or twice himself.

"Unfortunately, yes." Grant glanced at him again. "To be fair, they thought he was raping and murdering teenage girls."

"Mm." He couldn't honestly say he wouldn't have done the same thing, especially with Alisha being the same age as some of those girls had been. Vigilante justice never worked out well when carried out behind a badge. His father had been one of those sort of men who was very good at the vigilante trade, and settled scores for a lot of people over the years before his ruined, cancerous liver finally called it a day.

"You think he'll trust me after one sparring session? No offense, but I don't trust people until they've proved themselves worthy. Punching me in the face isn't part of the criteria."

"I don't expect him to trust you with his life, Mr. Tripp. I just want him to talk. Think of it as helping Audrey."

Jake stiffened. "Yeah? What would you know about helping Audrey? Since she got involved in this case, she's been stalked by a serial rapist and jerked around by a serial killer. You dragged her to a *fucking* autopsy. On top of that, some crime writer approached her, and that Scott girl's mother called late last night begging Audrey to come by."

Grant frowned, dark brows coming together over his eyes so that he looked like a brooding cologne advertisement. "Nancy Scott called her? Why didn't she tell me about that, or about James approaching her?"

"There's something you need to know about Audrey, counselor—she has a hero complex. She wants to save everybody who has ever been wronged. It's not all penance. She does it because underneath all that attitude she has the truest heart of anyone I've ever met. She will try to be what you want her to be, and she'll try to save every girl she can, even if it means allowing herself to be hurt. She doesn't know when to stop. I'm telling you this, because *you* do know when to stop. And because you're the one I'm going to blame if anything happens to her."

"Did you just threaten me?" Grant asked on a laugh. "I'm an assistant district attorney." He said it like it ought to make a difference.

Jake shrugged. He was a man, same as any other, and the title didn't matter. "An assistant district attorney whose girlfriend keeps waiting for him to propose, but he doesn't because he's banging her best friend. She's the one you really love, right? But it isn't her father who is the big shot judge who backs your political aspirations. Wonder what he'd think of you using his little girl as a career investment?"

The other man went pale. His knuckles went white as he gripped the steering wheel. Ah, the subtle pleasure of having useful information. It was so underrated. "How the *fuck* do you know about that?"

Jake smiled. Grant didn't look so much like a cologne ad with that scowl. Less perfect—more like the kind of person to whom Jake could relate. "I like to be informed. I might be backwoods, but buddy, I'm not stupid. I wasn't about to start doing you favors until I knew what you were all about."

"And what, exactly, have you decided that is?"

Another shrug. Revealing more felt like bragging. Bragging never achieved anything, except making a man look insecure. "You're ambitious and you know how to get what you want. You're just not sure if you're the kind of guy who will step on people along the way. That's respectable. But trust me, sleeping with the best friend is going to come back and bite you on the ass." He knew it firsthand.

Grant's jaw clenched so tight, Jake could see the muscle bulge just above his jaw. "I'm not discussing my private life with you."

"I don't *want* to discuss it. I don't care who you sleep with, or who the hell you marry. I care about Audrey. I'm not going to let anyone—even someone she respects—fuck her up more than she already is."

"If that's how you talk about people you care about, I can't imagine you have many friends." But there was the hint of a smile on the prosecutor's face.

"You're right. I don't, but Audrey has been my best friend for twenty-seven years, give or take, though there were times when I wasn't hers. There's not a damn thing I wouldn't do for her." Or *to* someone who hurt her.

"Here's the thing, Jake." Grant shot him a glance. "I hired Audrey. She's working with me. There may be times when I need her to do something of which you won't approve. What happens then?"

"She's a big girl, with a mind of her own. I respect her judgment, but if I think she's headed for trouble just to help you out, I suppose you and I will have to have another talk."

Grant opened his mouth, as though he wanted to say more, but then he laughed, shaking his head. "Maybe I should investigate you, return the favor."

Jake smiled. "You already have, and you found something you thought might make me useful. Otherwise we wouldn't be in this pricey car of yours, having this scintillating conversation." A surprised glance was all the proof he needed. "I told you I'm not stupid."

"I know your cousin Kenneth."

For a moment, Jake's blood ran cold, but he shook it off. Kenny wouldn't give him up—if for no other reason to protect himself. "I can't imagine the two of you run in the same circles."

"I know him from the prison. When Audrey told me the two of you were related, I reached out. He told me that you had a 'unique code of honor' and that you always kept your word. Oh, and that you could be a scary bastard."

"Did he." Not a question. Jake took another drink. "I suppose he meant it as a compliment."

"He also told me that you came to his aid a year or so ago when a couple of released inmates came after him. He said you saved his life."

Jake looked out the window as they stopped at a light. He watched a young man walking three large dogs with a narrow gaze. "Kenny exaggerates. You shouldn't believe half of what he says. Practically pathological."

"So you didn't disarm two hardened criminals single-handedly, rendering both unconscious and restraining them until the police arrived?"

The light changed. "They were stupid kids. It wasn't hard to get one over on them." He took another drink of his cooling coffee.

"They were violent kids."

"We've all been violent kids." Why was he making excuses? One of the little bastards had tried to give him a face-lift with a broken bottle. Maybe he was getting to an age where being thought scary didn't evoke the same satisfaction it once did.

"No, actually. We haven't all been violent kids. I, for one, have never felt the urge to attack a prison guard with a pipe wrench. They could have killed him."

The two had every intention of killing Kenny, or at least hurting him badly. "They didn't. It wasn't as though I took them out single-handedly. Kenny defended himself."

The ADA smiled. "You're embarrassed by his praise."

No. He was embarrassed because he'd held saving Kenny over his cousin's head and got him to put a contract out on Matt Jones. He'd blackmailed a member of his own family, a guy who was just so thankful to be alive he would have done anything Jake asked. He *did* do what Jake asked, and if Lincoln or his buddy started talking to the wrong people, Kenny could end up in a lot of trouble.

"I don't like being made out to be something I'm not," he replied. It was true.

"I'll remind you that Kenneth also said you were a bastard, if that makes you feel better."

Jake laughed. "It does, actually." But he also realized that Kenny could have told Grant that he was underhanded and manipulative, and he hadn't. He'd gotten his cousin into the mess with Jones, so if it all went south it would be on him to make sure Kenny took as little heat as possible.

They arrived at the gym a few minutes shy of ten thirty.

"Good luck," Grant said. "Remember, see if you can get him to open up, but don't be obvious."

"Yeah, I already figured that part out. You waiting out here?"

"I'll park at the coffee shop across the street. If Lawson sees me, there will be hell to pay."

Jake set his coffee cup in one of the two holders in the console. "Okay. I'll text you when I'm done. Throw that out for me, will you?" With that, he climbed out of the car and made his way up the steps to the front door of the gym.

Inside, sounds echoed. Every grunt, punch, and clatter of

equipment bounced off the walls and reverberated through the air. The air smelled of stale sweat and tasted slightly copper on his tongue. The place saw a lot more hurting than it did cleaning.

Jake walked past fitness equipment, and a woman doing jumping squats, to the ring in the far corner. He spied Lawson in front of it, talking to an older man. Lawson was maybe a couple of inches shorter than him, but they were of similar size. He was another guy who was too good-looking to be taken seriously, but Lawson's posture was defensive and rigid, like the world owed him something.

Kind of like Lincoln. Smacking him around might be satisfying after all.

"Dave's not here today," the older man told Lawson. "Sorry, Barry."

"But he's always here," Lawson argued. "Doesn't he realize how inconvenient this is? I only have certain days I can come by. You'd think he'd arrange his appointments around that."

Jake laughed. He couldn't really help it. The guy was priceless. The guy was also now looking right at him, giving him a once-over so thorough Jake wondered if Lawson was mentally fitting him for a casket.

"It's not funny," the shorter man informed him coldly. "I came here to spar only to find my sparring partner isn't here and didn't have the decency to call me."

"He's at the doctor," the other man said. "Right at this moment, actually."

Lawson made a scoffing noise. "I appreciate the effort,

George, but we both know why Dave's not here." It was an inappropriate time to think of the Cheech and Chong skit, but Jake couldn't help it. *Dave's not here, man.*

George shifted his weight. He looked like someone had tied his balls to a bear trap that could snap shut at any second. "All I know is that he said it was the only appointment he could get."

"One of you could have called me and saved me the humiliation of coming down to discover my sparring partner thinks I'm a murderer. Again."

That hadn't taken long. Or was Lawson paranoid?

"I'm sorry, Barry. I really am." George looked sincere—he also looked like Lawson's paranoia was well-founded.

"I know you are." Lawson turned to walk away.

"Hey," Jake began, capturing both of their attention again. He grinned at Lawson. "Want to fight?"

CHAPTER ELEVEN

Wearing boxing gloves to fight felt like wearing rubber boots in the bathtub. They just felt *wrong*. Still, Jake got over them fairly quickly. In his experience, failure to adapt resulted in getting your ass kicked. He'd gotten into a lot of fights as a kid—there was always someone from a neighboring town looking to scrap, or some local kid looking to draw blood. There were only three things to pass the time in a small town—drinking, fucking, and fighting. A good night was when you got to do all three. Some guys thought it a win if they could complete the trifecta with the same partner.

Lawson kept bobbing and weaving, dancing around like they were filming a cardio workout rather than trying to draw blood. It was like something on a sitcom. Had he learned how to box by watching TV?

Finally, Jake dropped his hands and stood still. "Are you here to fight or dance?" he asked.

His opponent came in with a quick jab that Jake blocked and followed with a shot to the jaw that knocked the other man backward.

Jake pointed his glove at him in warning. "Cheap shot."

Lawson smiled. "Sorry. I saw an opening. I thought we were fighting."

Jake grimaced. "*This* isn't fighting. This is tedious."

"It's what I was taught."

"You want to keep bouncing around, or do you want to learn something that will actually keep you from getting your ass kicked?"

"That one," came the immediate reply.

It hadn't taken Jake long to realize that the best way to get close to Lawson wasn't to beat the crap out of him, but to teach him how to beat the crap out of anyone who jumped him. And the schoolteacher *was* going to get jumped if people thought he'd killed that girl.

"Fine. First things first, we get rid of these gloves." He stuck his hand between his arm and body and pulled free of the humid, smelly leather.

Lawson looked panicked. "Dave is really strict about using gloves."

Jake met his gaze as he freed his left hand. "The same Dave that fucked off and didn't have the balls to tell you he didn't want to keep your appointment? I'm pretty sure that Dave deserves a punch in the face."

"I guess you're right." Grinning, Lawson pulled off his gloves as well, tossing them to the side as Jake had. "What do we do?"

"That depends. How much damage do you want to do, and how much are you willing to take?"

This time the once-over the other man gave him was a little

more respectful, although a little intense. Lawson licked his lips. "Maybe you could start out easy on me?"

"I make no promises."

For the next hour, Jake put Lawson through a crash course in fighting to win. He didn't try to beat the snot out of the guy, but he didn't go easy on him either. By the time they were done, Lawson had a bruise forming high on his cheekbone and Jake had a small cut inside his mouth. Both of them were sweating. Unfortunately, Grant hadn't thought to tell him to bring a change of clothes.

He followed Lawson into the locker room, answering the man's enthusiastic questions about violence as honestly as he could. He followed up with a question of his own. "Why do you need to know how to take someone out? You in some kind of trouble?"

Lawson's smile faded as he opened a locker. "You're not from here, are you?"

Jake shook his head. "Up near the border." It wasn't technically a lie, only Edgeport was closer to the eastern Calais crossing than the northern Houlton.

"I didn't think there was anyone in the state who didn't know who I am." Lawson pulled his damp T-shirt over his head and tossed it into the open bag in his locker. "You've heard of Ian Monroe?"

"Yeah. Who hasn't?"

"Well, I was the guy they suspected before they figured out it was Ian." He went still, as though bracing himself.

"That sucks."

"That's an understatement." Lawson's shoulders relaxed. "I had my nose broken, two teeth knocked out. And that was just what the feds did to me."

Jake arched a brow. That was more than getting a little rough. No wonder Lawson wanted to sue. "Is that why your usual partner didn't show? He thinks you had something to do with that girl they found?"

"I'd put money on it." Lawson took shampoo and a towel out of the locker. "They found her at the school—in my old classroom. I don't think it was a coincidence."

"I didn't think they said where she was found."

"Not on the news, no, but the principal couldn't wait to ask me about it just before he told me they were discussing putting me on leave—again." He closed the locker door, but not before Jake noticed the cell phone inside. "As if I'd be stupid enough to leave her there even if I did have it in me to kill someone. What's that old saying?"

"Don't shit where you eat?"

Lawson laughed—harsh and bitter. "That's right. Why would I shit where I ate?"

"You wouldn't, unless you had decided to fuck it all and go on a spree. But since we're all still alive, I'd say you haven't crossed that bridge yet."

This time his laughter was more genuine. "Not yet. I'm going to shower and then go see if I still have a job. Thanks for the lesson."

"No problem. I'm in town for a few more days if you want another."

The other man hesitated, but just for a second. Then he opened the locker again and pulled out his cell. "Give me your number."

Jake did, and while Lawson typed the numbers, he pulled the strap of the duffel bag in the locker outside. When Lawson closed the door, the strap kept it from latching. Jake wished him good luck, and then waited until he heard the shower running to snag the phone. The password protection hadn't reactivated yet, so he was able to look without signing in. He went straight to the photo gallery.

There weren't many photos, and most of them were of graffiti and vandalism apparently done to Lawson's own property. The poor bastard sure had more than his share of shit heaped upon him. Someone had smashed his car with a sledgehammer, judging from the damage. The least of the photos showed the word "Pervert" spray-painted on the door of a house he assumed to be Lawson's. The worst was what looked like shit smeared all over the front of the same house. There were piles of it on the lawn and in the drive. It looked like someone unloaded a stable's worth of manure in his yard.

Jake was just about to stop looking when a thumbnail caught his eye. He opened it. *Fuck around.* That changed things. He almost looked forward to seeing the expression on Grant's face when he saw it.

He tapped the photo to send himself a copy, then thought better of it. He pulled out his own phone and took a photo of the other screen. Then he put Lawson's phone back, moved the duffel strap, and shut the locker. He texted Grant on his way out of the gym.

The bastard had better buy him a fresh coffee for this.

*   *   *

After leaving the Scotts', Audrey called Anita Grayson and left a voice mail about the package she'd received. The jewelry, the box, and its wrapping were inside a zip-lock bag in her purse. The weight of it all was like lugging a bag of bricks over her shoulder.

She called Will, who told her that he was with Jake of all people, and that they'd meet her back at the hotel within the hour to regroup, share information, and get lunch. There was nothing else for her to do, so she returned to the hotel. She was almost to the elevator when a tall, blond woman intercepted her.

"Dr. Harte?" she asked.

Audrey looked at her face. She was a pretty woman—older than Audrey, but not by too many years. She had bright blue eyes and round cheeks. If she were twenty years younger, she'd be exactly Ian Monroe's type.

Oh, fuck. She knew who the woman was.

A slim hand was thrust in her direction. "Margot Temple."

She was raised not to be rude, and sometimes she actually remembered it. Audrey accepted the gesture with a firm and brief grip. "What can I do for you, Miss Temple?"

"Can we talk?" She twisted her torso, gesturing to the small coffee shop, while keeping her gaze on Audrey. "Just for a moment. I know you must be terribly busy."

She should say no. Tell the woman to leave her alone and go up to her suite to meet Will and Jake. Instead, Audrey heard herself say, "Sure. I have a few minutes."

"Can I buy you a coffee?" Margot asked. Audrey said she could, and the two of them went to the coffee shop. Armed with a chai latte and a scone, Audrey sat down at one of the empty tables and waited for Margot to join her.

She told herself she agreed to talk to the woman because she'd never had the opportunity to talk to someone with hybristophilia one on one before, but the real reason was that the woman seemed nice, and Audrey could use a little nice, even if it came with a side of psychological disorder.

Plus, Margot was close to Ian, and maybe she knew something useful. Maybe she was the one who had sent all the gifts, though Audrey's instincts said the woman wasn't a threat.

She hadn't thought Bailey was dangerous either. To be fair, Bailey hadn't been a danger to anyone other than herself and Maggie. Bailey hadn't been the one to beat Audrey up, or run her off the road.

"Thank you for agreeing to talk to me," Margot said as she sat down across the table. She had a huge drink topped with whipped cream and a slab of coffee cake as big as Audrey's head. Obviously she had a sweet tooth, but not when it came to men. Obviously, that was a little judgmental given Audrey's weakness for ice cream and Jake.

"Thank you for the latte and scone. What did you want to talk about?"

"Him, eventually. Do you mind?"

Audrey appreciated the candor. "I can't give you any information on Ian, Miss Temple. You're going to be disappointed if that's why you're here."

The blonde shook her head, flashing a bright smile. "No, I know. That's not my agenda at all. I really just wanted...well, to meet you. I'm not going to harp on you about speaking to the group either, just in case you were wondering. I respect you declining to meet with us."

Audrey believed her. For a woman who had romantic delusions about a serial rapist, she seemed surprisingly self-aware. And normal, though that word was a bit of a misnomer when applied to human behavior. "I appreciate that, thank you."

Margot tilted her head. "You're not going to ask me, are you?"

"Ask you what?"

"The usual—how can I care about such a monster? Why do I hate myself so much I'd think a rapist is the best man for me? What happened to make me lose touch with reality? People always ask."

Audrey pulled apart her scone. "Well, I'm not your therapist, or a loved one, so it's really not my business. Would it make you more comfortable if I did ask?" She popped the piece she'd torn off into her mouth. Oh, it was *good*.

"No. It's nice feeling like I don't have to justify myself. Plus, I don't know how or why. I couldn't explain it to you if I tried. And I've tried. A lot. Maybe I should ask you to explain it to me. I'm sure you know all about this sort of thing."

"Only you know how you feel." She broke off another piece of scone. "I could throw jargon at you if you would like, but I think you've probably done as much reading on the topic as I have—probably more."

Margot nodded. "I've tried to wrap my head around it.

Rationally, I know it doesn't make much sense. Have you ever felt that way—a connection you can't explain but you feel it down to your bones?"

Audrey chuckled. "Yeah, I know that feeling." Her humor faded. "But I am sorry to know that you feel that connection with a man incapable of ever returning your affection."

Margot tilted her head, a small frown between her brows as she scooped up a fingerful of whipped cream from her drink and popped it in her mouth. "No one has ever said that to me before. You really mean it, don't you?"

"I wouldn't have said it if I didn't." In truth, the woman struck her as more sad than mentally ill. Maybe a little naive. "Can I ask you why saving Ian is so important to you?"

"You're not the first to ask me that, but you might be the most polite." Margot smiled as she began rotating her cup in her hands. "I know he's done horrible things, but I believe there's still goodness inside him. I have to believe it. He just needs someone to love him and forgive him."

"And that person *has* to be you."

"Yes."

Their gazes held for a few seconds while Audrey pondered that. There were so many things she wanted to say—to convince Margot that her behavior was irrational, to urge her to get psychological help. But the woman had already heard it all. Audrey went for what she imagined Margot *hadn't* already been told. "I hope you're not disappointed, Miss Temple."

"Please, call me Margot. Miss Temple makes me want to start singing that 'Good Ship Lollipop' song."

Audrey had to think for a moment. "Shirley Temple, right?"

"Mm," Margot replied with a grin. "You aren't familiar with it?"

"Vaguely. She's a little out of our generation."

"My mother was a fan." She set her elbows on the table. "Do you have any idea who killed that poor girl?"

Shirley Temple? Audrey blinked. No, wait. "You mean Natashya Lewis."

"Yes." It was coupled with an apologetic smile. "Sorry, my mind skips around a lot."

Audrey took a bite of scone. She chewed thoughtfully. "I'm not part of the investigation, so I'm afraid I'm not qualified to tell you anything about it. Even if I was, I couldn't divulge information."

The blonde shrugged, still smiling. "I know."

"Especially when I know you'd just go back to Ian with it."

That got rid of the smile—and all color in the other woman's face. It would be a lie to say she wasn't a little disappointed in Margot for thinking her an easy mark. "I told him I'm not much of an actor. He thought my 'innate goodness' might seduce you."

Audrey sipped her latte. "I'm sure he thought I'd be more fascinated by you than suspicious. Also, he probably wasn't aware that I'd heard you'd been added to his visitor list."

"How did you know?"

She smiled. "I have spies everywhere. I'm sorry, Margot. I really am, but we're not going to talk about the trial, the recent murder, or anything else that might be related to Ian—unless you have evidence that might help the prosecution."

"I could lie, but that would be an insult to both of us. I do have something for you, though."

"From Ian?" Audrey cocked her head. "Margot, don't do something that might incriminate you. I know you love him, but he's a psychopath, and those people aren't capable of affection."

"I know, Dr. Harte." The woman was suddenly very serious. She looked more her age when she stopped smiling. "He only wanted me to give you a message. He said to tell you that another girl is going to be taken. He doesn't know where or exactly when, but it will be on or before the twenty-third."

Audrey's throat constricted. "That's only a few days from now."

Margot nodded. "I know. He said you should look at people close to him. Close to the investigation. And he wishes you good luck in stopping it, because if another girl goes missing, you won't find her until it's too late either."

"Margot, you have to go to the authorities with this. Let me put you in touch with the FBI. If Ian knows something about a crime that's going to be committed, you have to give evidence. You'll be expected to testify."

Margot stood up from the table with a gentle smile. "I'm not going to the FBI, Dr. Harte, though you can tell them what I said if you want. And I'm afraid trying to get me to testify against Ian isn't going to happen."

"Why? Because you want to save him?"

"No." She held out her left hand—there was a plain gold band on her ring finger. "Because he's my husband."

CHAPTER TWELVE

Jake and Will arrived at the suite shortly after Audrey. She wanted to tell them about Margot and Ian, but she put it off until Anita joined them and they were waiting for room service to be delivered.

"Wait," Will began, looking at her as though he'd misunderstood. He'd removed his suit jacket, loosened his collar, and rolled up the sleeves of his pale blue shirt. He looked like a model sitting there with one fist on his hip and the elbow of his other arm on his thigh. "Margot Temple and Ian Monroe are *married*?"

Audrey laughed. How could she not? The entire situation was unbelievable. "They are. They were married by proxy over the phone."

"Proxy marriage isn't legal in Maine."

"No, but the minister who did it lives in a proxy-legal state, and it does set them up as Common Law spouses until they can arrange a ceremony in prison."

"That's tenuous at best."

"Yeah, but contesting it will drag things out, won't it? She knew exactly what she was doing. She wouldn't help us anyway. She'd lie for him even if they hadn't pulled this stunt, but Margot made sure I knew she wouldn't be testifying against her husband right after she gave me a message from him."

"Which was?" he pressed.

Her gaze went from him to Anita and then to Jake. It would have been better if she could have told him all of this before Will and Anita. It felt like keeping secrets, telling him when she told everyone else.

"That another girl was going to go missing either on or before the twenty-third, and that we should look at people close to the trial for the potential victim. He said maybe we'd be lucky enough to save her."

"*Christ.*" Will leaned back against the chair cushions. "Another girl."

"Girls close to the trial." Anita pulled a small notebook out of her bag. "That would include the surviving rape victims, wouldn't it? Maybe he's going to go back for Amber, Petra, or Leigh."

Audrey caught her eye. "Or Tori."

"No," Anita insisted, her spine straightening beneath her fitted blouse. "That's not going to happen. I don't care if I have to sleep on the floor of the girl's room, I'm not letting that bastard have another go at her."

Audrey could have kissed her at that moment. "There's more." She took the baggie with the necklace in it out of her purse and handed it to the agent. "It was delivered to Tori, but the note inside is addressed to me."

Will went pale. "More jewelry. Was the note similar?"

She met his gaze. "More taunting me to get into the game, but we know what happened last time I got a gift."

"Monroe was right, the killer is planning on taking another girl."

"The bastard's also watching Audrey," Jake joined in, his jaw tight. "That might not be a concern for the rest of you, but it is for me. He had to have followed her to the Scott house. Either that or he knew when to have the package delivered."

Will nodded, his expression grave. It was Anita who spoke. "I've got an agent coming up from Boston to shadow Audrey. It's important we don't let the killer know that he's spooked her—or any of us. The lack of concern will hopefully drive him—or her—to slip up."

Jake scowled at her. "The fact that another kid might die doesn't bother you?"

The agent didn't even flinch. "Of course it does, Mr. Tripp. That's why I'd like to make the bastard careless, so we can catch him."

Audrey watched them stare each other down. Her money was on Anita to blink first. She wasn't going to tell them she could protect herself—she couldn't—but Jake would protect her, and she trusted him more than the FBI.

"The necklace," Will said, drawing their attention away from each other. "Do we know who it belongs to?"

"Kaylee Soto," Audrey replied. "She's wearing it in her school photo. There's a hair caught in the chain, and I think there's blood on the back of the dragonfly." She watched as Anita turned the bag over in her hands, and studied the necklace through the plastic.

"I think you're right. Damn, I don't know whether to be hopeful for a lead or brace myself for another disappointment."

"Go for both," Audrey suggested. "It always works for me."

Jake, who had been standing, came over and sat on the arm of her chair. He'd already gotten his boots and socks off, she noticed. How in the name of God did he manage to have such smooth-looking feet when he abused them as much as he did?

"On, or before, the twenty-third. Nothing like a ticking clock to raise the tension." Will turned to Jake. "Now that we're all together, please tell me you got something useful off Lawson."

"What?" Audrey's head whipped around so fast and hard, a ripple of pain ran up her neck. She winced. "You talked to Barry Lawson?"

He shrugged. "Somebody had to." His finger closed over the back of her neck, his thumb immediately finding the spot that throbbed. "He wasn't going to talk to one of you three."

A couple of hours. She left him alone for a few hours and he was already neck deep in the situation—just like he had been when Maggie was killed. The man was a murder and mayhem magnet.

She could kiss him.

Will cleared his throat. "I asked Jake to get close to Lawson, Audrey. If you're upset, direct it at me."

That little dictate jacked one of her brows so high she could have sworn it hit her hairline. "Sure, Will. I'll be sure to do that." She turned her attention back to Jake. "*Did* you get something useful?"

The arrival of lunch put a pause to the conversation, but as soon as everyone had their individual plates, Jake answered her question. "The classroom where the girl was found used to be Lawson's."

Will dumped ketchup on his fries. "That explains why the killer put her there—to call attention to Lawson again."

"He's already being treated like a pariah," Jake told them. "He might have been cleared of charges originally, but it's obvious people think he's capable of killing."

"When we first looked into him, there was a rumor he was having sex with Madison Hall, a student and one of the victims," Anita informed them. "We never found out if it was true or not, but it kept coming up while we investigated him. It turned people against him."

"Funny you should bring that up." Jake pulled his phone out of his pocket. "I believe Lawson really was having an affair with a student." He handed the phone to Audrey. "Just not the one everyone thought."

It was a photo of a phone screen. The photo was of Lawson lying in bed, shirtless. He had his arm around another man, who curled into him like a cat into a ray of sunshine. It was Ian Monroe.

"Fuck *around.*" Audrey passed the phone to Will, who had a similar reaction.

"*Monroe* was the student?" Will looked as though someone had just hit him in the face with a brick. He turned to Anita. "There's no way we got the wrong guy, is there?"

"No!" She scowled at him. "Monroe's our guy."

"And apparently he's Lawson's too," Jake quipped. "Just because he's in bed with a guy doesn't mean he's gay. He's probably bisexual."

"He *could* be gay," Audrey corrected. "If he's got guilt over it and wants to prove himself straight, it could explain the rapes."

Jake tilted his head. "He's trying to make himself *like* women by brutalizing them?"

Audrey nodded. "His first introduction to rape culture was through his grandfather's porn stash. It could be that the man instilled in Ian his own twisted ideas of what a 'real' man is."

Jake shook his head. Audrey could tell he was thinking of all the things his own father and grandfather had done, and how he'd been influenced by them, and how none of it involved hurting women or children. "Twisted."

"No wonder Lawson lost it when Monroe suggested he was the real killer." Anita gave Jake his phone. "It was a betrayal."

Jake looked around the room. "Could be why Monroe's not saying anything—he feels guilty for implicating his lover."

"Monroe's no more capable of guilt than I am of winning Miss Congeniality," Audrey drawled. "But Lawson might have used the photo as blackmail. If Monroe is really that conflicted about his sexuality, he could be coerced into just about anything to keep his secret."

"It goes both ways, though," Will reminded her. "Monroe would have been underage when that photo was taken."

"And now he's pseudo-married to the president of his damn fan club." Anita shook her head as she dipped a fry in ketchup. "Someone who will do whatever he asks and won't testify against him. He might not be the brains behind the whole thing, but he's a slippery little bastard."

Will turned to Jake. "Do you think you can continue to keep an eye on Lawson?"

He shrugged. His expression was completely neutral, as was his gaze, but Audrey had the feeling he spent more time studying Will and Anita than she did. "Sure. I have to go back to Edgeport for the weekend, but I've got his number. I told him to call if he wanted to fight again."

Anita arched a brow. "You're not afraid he might hit on you?"

Jake shot a dry glance in her direction. "I tend not to assume that everyone I meet wants to sleep with me."

She didn't look like she believed him, but didn't press it. Audrey fought a smile. Jake wasn't insecure about his looks or appeal, but his ego didn't depend upon either for support. And he wasn't a homophobe, which sometimes made him odd man out in a town like Edgeport, where you weren't legally declared a man unless you shot deer, screwed every woman you could, and drank beer—not that "light shit"—sometimes all in the same night.

"What are the feds doing?" Audrey asked.

Anita shot her a sharp glance. "Sitting on our thumbs, you know. Letting other people do our jobs. Enjoying being yanked around by a psychopath. The usual."

"Bitch, moan," she retorted. "I know you've got to be feeling the heat on this."

The older woman's shoulders slumped. "I am. We all are. Things went so badly when we were looking for Monroe, we're really getting pressured to do everything by the book, and perform magic while we're at it. The fact that we missed this guy the first time around isn't helping. We don't have much. The hair found on Natashya's shoulder is Tori's. We found another in her clothes that matches Kaylee Soto. We tried to get a warrant for the Monroes' cabin in Falmouth, but it coincidentally burned down not long after Monroe was arrested."

Audrey couldn't hide her surprise. "Seriously? Why weren't the Monroes charged?"

"Couldn't pin it on them. They were out of the state when it happened. They had to leave to escape the media. It looked like arson, but their financials didn't indicate they'd hired someone. We figured it was vandalism. But now…"

"Now you're thinking the partner did it to prevent you from finding incriminating evidence."

"Exactly."

"Imagine that," Will replied, with just enough lightness in his voice before turning serious. "So what you're saying, Anita, is that we have nothing."

"Not yet. We're not done analyzing the body and the scene."

The body. That was the part of working with police that always struck a chord with Audrey. It happened in her line of work too—you thought of people as "clients" and dehumanized them to an extent. It made it easier to look at them as bits of phobias, paraphilias, delusions. But Natashya Lewis was a woman. A young woman, and all of her hopes and dreams were gone.

Snap the fuck out of it. She could be dramatic in the courtroom, but it wasn't going to do her any good to get emotional now.

Jake gestured at Anita. "Maybe you'll get something useful off the necklace."

"I sure as hell hope so. Good work with Lawson, by the way. I'm obligated to advise you against engaging him again, just in case he is dangerous, but off the record, I'm grateful for whatever you can get us that will help us catch this bastard."

"What about vernacular?" Audrey asked. "The notes keep referencing this as a game and the killer sees me as an opponent, or at least a player. Has anyone used game-related language in an interview or written statement?"

"No," Anita responded. She frowned. "At least not that I remember. I'll go back through and double-check."

"I could go see Ian again," Audrey suggested. "Maybe I could give him some false information about Tori like Will suggested."

"Do you really think that would work?" Anita asked.

She shrugged. "I don't know. He might see through me. And he's got Margot to spy for him now. I suppose I could tell him we hadn't released details to the public."

"No." Will set his drink on the coffee table with an authoritative thud. "You're—we're—not jumping through his hoops. He'll be expecting you to visit him. Counting on it."

Audrey couldn't believe it. "It's worth it if he gives us information."

"You're the one who told me that nothing he gives us could be considered reliable. I'm not letting you jump when he snaps his fingers. I am, however, going to visit him myself, and I'm going to offer something he'll find a lot more tempting than information on Tori Scott."

"What?" Audrey asked.

His expression was grim as he met her gaze. "A plea bargain."

Which one was next?

Looking at the photographs on the screen was like studying contestants in the Miss Teen America Pageant. So blond and pretty. It was hard to decide which one had to die, but it had to be one of them; otherwise there was no poetry, no poignancy. Blue-eyed blondes were the epitome of beauty and attractiveness—Ian understood that.

Eeny. Pretty Blonde One.

Meeny. Pretty Blonde Two.

Miny. Pretty Blonde Three.

Mo. Pretty Blonde Four.

All of Ian's girls. He wouldn't like to know one of them was gone. He'd been upset enough about Natashya, but if one of *his* pretties ended up dead, all the life choked out of her, well... that would upset him. He'd be angry, helpless. He'd have no choice but to accept that he was not as smart as he thought he was—as if getting arrested hadn't already convinced him of that.

Now, which one?

Eeny. Meeny. Miny. *Mo*.

"I'm not sure how I feel about you being involved in this mess," Audrey said to Jake once they were alone later that afternoon.

He'd dragged her out of the hotel for a walk, because it was a warm afternoon and he said she needed fresh air and exercise. It was what his grandmother had always said when she wanted them out of her hair.

"I did it because you couldn't," he explained as they walked. He had her hand in his. She noticed he seemed very aware of their surroundings, as though he was keeping watch, which of course, he was. "Are you mad?"

"No." She wasn't—not really. "I guess I felt out of the loop."

"Like we were going behind your back?"

They had to pause at the intersection and wait for the light to change. "Yeah. Kinda."

"I'm sorry." No excuses. Not justifications. Just an apology. She liked that about him.

"It's all good." The walk light turned green and they stepped into the street. "Without you, we wouldn't have gotten anything from Lawson, and now we know the nature of his relationship with Monroe. Whether or not it went beyond sex is the question. Just what would Lawson be willing to do for his lover?"

"You're assuming Lawson was the victim. He didn't strike me as someone who is easily manipulated."

"But is he a psychopath?"

"I'm not sure I'd be able to tell."

"Remember Neil Le Duc?"

Jake frowned. "The kid that used to pick the wings off flies?"

"That's the one. He killed Jeannie's dog, remember? He said it was an accident, but everyone knew it wasn't."

"Yeah. His parents packed up and left town after that. Luckily they took Neil with them. Kid had empty eyes."

"*He* was a psychopath. They call it antisocial personality disorder now."

"I like 'psycho' better." Jake pushed open the door to a little coffee shop and bakery that smelled like heaven as they walked in. "It has more punch."

"It's a classic."

"Lawson didn't seem anything like Neil, but he's an adult. He's had time to learn how to fake it, right?"

"There's that." They got in line at the counter. "When you and he were fighting, did you get the feeling he intentionally wanted to hurt you?"

"No. He got frustrated, but he wanted to learn, or at least he pretended to."

Audrey shook her head as she checked out the bakery case. *Ohhh, iced scones.* "I'm not sure an actual psychopath could have faked that. I think his urge to do harm would come to the forefront when confronted with violence."

The woman in line ahead of them turned her head, giving them a questioning look. Jake smiled at her. "Psychologist."

She nodded and turned away.

"Anyway," Audrey said in a low voice, stepping close to him. "We can't rule Lawson out."

"Are you okay with going home this weekend? The twenty-third isn't far off."

"It's unlikely that our guy will send me another gift, and the police are watching the girls, Lawson, and Margot. There's really nothing I could do except sit around and worry. Being home might actually be a nice distraction."

"Your mother will be glad to see you."

"Yeah." She tried not to think about her mother much these last few days. It was too upsetting, and she needed to be focused on her job. Now that she *did* think of her, Audrey couldn't help the fear that slithered through her stomach. Realistically she knew her mother had a good chance of getting through surgery and living a long, cancer-free life, but it was still scary, because everyone knew at least one person who had been killed by cancer.

"I could bring her more brownies," he suggested. "If she's in pain, I can make them medicinal."

Audrey shook her head as he grinned. "I'll let you know." Maybe her mother would be up for it. Her father certainly would be.

They made it to the front of the line and ordered their drinks. Audrey asked for a London Fog latte, and Jake got a coffee. As they left the shop, Audrey's cell phone rang. She didn't recognize the number.

"Hello?"

"Yes, hello. Is this Dr. Audrey Harte?"

"It is. Who am I speaking to?" She could feel Jake watching her. Was he wondering if the killer had gotten her phone number? She was.

"My name is Aldous Venture. I'm Victoria Scott's therapist. Nancy Scott asked me to call you. She mentioned that you and Tori had been talking a fair bit and thought maybe you and I should meet. Both Tori and her mother have given me permission to speak openly with you. Would Monday be convenient for you?"

This was unexpected. "Yes. I have Monday afternoon free. What time works best for you?"

"One o'clock?" When Audrey said that would work, Dr. Venture offered to text her directions to his office. She thanked him and hung up.

"You look 'plexed, my dar."

Audrey smiled. Every once in a while, Jake threw one of his grandmother Gracie's colloquialisms into conversation. "Tori Scott's therapist wants to meet with me."

"That's good?"

"Yeah. Any information he can give me will help me determine if she's fit to testify, what her triggers are, and how best to handle her. Plus, I'm hoping he can clear up a few things for me."

"Like what?"

She took a sip of tea. So good. Just the right amount of bergamot and lavender. "Like whether or not certain traits have been brought on by her PTSD, or if they're part of another condition."

"Something's not sitting right with you about the kid?"

"I couldn't really name one thing, but I do wonder if she has something else going on. PTSD manifests differently in everyone, so it might be nothing. I don't want to miss anything this time, y'know?"

"Miss anything?" Jake's gaze narrowed. "You're talking about Bailey."

He wasn't impressed, she could tell. Jake didn't waste a lot of time with regret. If he could change the outcome of a situation, he would. If he couldn't, he got over it as soon as possible.

"Of course I'm talking about Bailey. And don't tell me not to blame myself, because who else can I blame?"

He stopped walking and turned to face her. They blocked the walking path and he didn't seem to care. "How about Bailey? How about Maggie? She was killed just hours after you arrived in town. Do you think you could have possibly prevented it?"

"No."

"That's right. And figuring out who killed her sooner wouldn't have changed anything. It would still be a fucking tragedy."

"Matt Jones might still be alive if I'd figured it out sooner."

"I doubt that, and the world's better off without him. I know Yancy is."

Okay, so maybe bringing up his sister's abusive boyfriend—and the guy who had taken his fists to Audrey—hadn't been a great idea. "I know no one misses him, but if I'd seen the signs..."

"You feel stupid."

She took a step back, scowling at him. "What?"

"Admit it. You're carrying this around because you're used to being the smartest person in the room—especially in Edgeport—and you're scared people think you're dumb for not figuring it out sooner. I don't need to remind you that you *were* the first person to figure it out, do I?"

"You're crazy."

"Am I right or am I wrong?"

She could tell him to fuck off. Maybe throw her latte in his smug face—if he looked smug. He didn't look any different than he normally did. Usually this was the sort of situation that would get her back up, make her do something impulsive and rash, like take a verbal or physical swing. But this was Jake, and she couldn't lie to him or be angry that he knew her as well as he did.

"You're right."

He put his arm around her shoulders and pulled her against his side as they started walking again. "Let it go, Aud. If you can't do it on your own, then go see the kid and lay it to rest. Please."

It was the "please" that got her, just like he knew it would. "Okay."

"Good." They walked a few steps in silence. "How come you never asked me if Lawson hit on me?"

"I figured you'd tell me if he had."

"Okay, but just so you know, many gay men have found me very attractive."

She laughed. God, things were so *easy* with him. Love wasn't supposed to be easy, was it? "I know. My brother thinks you're incredibly hot."

"David has good taste. Must run in the family."

"We get it from Dad. God knows Mum doesn't have any. Look who she ended up with."

They walked around the park for a while and then turned back toward the hotel. Audrey slipped the key card into the lock and opened the door to the suite. She walked in first, and tossed her purse on the couch. "That was a great idea. My head actually feels lighter. Thank you. What's wrong?"

Jake stood in the middle of the living area, as still as a deer that's heard a twig snap. He put his finger to his lips, warning her to be silent as he turned. He didn't make a sound. He walked over to the closet, pulled the door open, and reached inside.

Audrey opened her mouth to scream, but the man Jake slammed to the floor beat her to it.

CHAPTER THIRTEEN

Y ou broke my fucking nose!"

Audrey shoved a cold, wet facecloth at Christopher James. He was still on the floor—she wasn't going to let him bleed on the furniture. "You're lucky he didn't break more than that, you son of a bitch."

He blinked at her. He couldn't really be surprised that she was pissed, could he?

"How did you get in?" she demanded.

James pressed the snowy, bleach-scented cloth to his bleeding nose. "I waited for housekeeping and then pretended it was my room."

Jake crouched in front of him, eyes glittering. He didn't lose his temper very often, but his anger was a tangible thing, crackling in the air. James had no idea just how much his future quality of life was in the balance at that moment. "Why?"

The writer tipped his head back. The facecloth was mottled red now. "I just wanted to see what you had on the new murder. A little insider information to boost my site traffic."

Thank God she'd put her computer and papers in the safe

before they went out. "You asshole. Do you know how much damage you could have done if you found something? Or how much trouble you might have gotten me into?" She went to her purse and got her phone.

"What are you doing?" James asked. He started to get up, but Jake put his hand on his shoulder and forced him back into a sitting position.

"I'm calling Agent Grayson so she can arrest your ass."

"No! Please don't." His gray eyes were so wide, there was a band of white above and below each iris. "I didn't mean any harm."

Audrey met his gaze. That was bullshit. "You're not a very good liar, Mr. James. You only care about fallout now because it's on you. If we hadn't come back, you would have run your story and wouldn't have cared if it cost another girl's life, or caused a family pain. You're just a douche." Christ, what was she, twelve? Who said "douche" anymore?

Anita picked up at that moment, so she was prevented from carrying on with her monologue. Audrey filled her in on what had happened, and the detective promised to come ASAP. Then, Audrey hung up and called Will. He was even more pissed than she thought he would be. He and Anita arrived within a few moments of each other.

They didn't even ask Audrey if she wanted to press charges. Anita put James in cuffs and Will began listing possible charges to file against the writer. "Unlawful entry, interfering with a federal investigation. We'll start with those."

"Add attempted assault," Jake told him. "He was in the closet waiting for her."

Audrey gasped, her chest seizing as though he'd kicked her. She hadn't thought of that. If James had been simply searching her room, he wouldn't have had time to get into the closet before they walked in. She looked around at the suite—it looked just as it had when she left, aside from Housekeeping's cleaning. Nothing disturbed that she could see. So what was James's true intent?

"That's not true!" James insisted, voice desperate, eye twitching, skin glistening with sweat. "I would never hurt a woman."

"This is some kit you've got here, Mr. James," Anita intoned, poking through James's messenger bag. "Latex gloves, a flask, a voice recorder, a camera, and condoms. Were you a Boy Scout? Because you certainly came prepared."

Audrey stared at him. "What was your plan, then?"

He met her gaze with a shrug. "I thought maybe we'd have a drink, talk a bit..."

She arched a brow. He was kidding, right? "And what? You thought I'd be so impressed by your breaking into my room that I'd have sex with you? I think you should see a therapist about your narcissism and detachment from reality."

Jake was still there, right in the writer's face, his own a stony mask. "Or did you plan to drug her with whatever is in that flask and kill her like you did Natashya Lewis?"

Audrey's stomach rolled again. That London Fog wasn't sitting so well.

"I didn't kill that girl!" James cried, his gaze locking on each one of them. "I swear to God! I just wanted information." And then to Audrey, "And yeah. I was hoping you might be interested in sex. I thought you were alone."

Jake punched him in the throat. James choked, gasping for breath as his face turned color. Tears streamed from his eyes.

"Mr. Tripp!" That was Will. "Don't leave a mark."

Jake didn't even acknowledge him. His attention was on James. The intensity of that focus made Audrey nervous. "You slunk into her room and waited for her in a closet. I don't believe you had consent in mind."

"I don't either," Anita agreed. "I'll add attempted rape to the list."

"Wait!" James held up his handcuffed hands, one of which held the bloody facecloth. His nose veered to one side. It was definitely broken. "I sneaked in because I knew Dr. Harte wouldn't talk to me if I called. I just wanted to find out what she knew."

"And have sex," Jake added.

The man cringed. "Yes."

Jake took a couple of steps backward, putting distance between himself and James. "Get rid of him or I will."

Will's startled gaze met Audrey's. She kept her own expression neutral. If he didn't know if Jake was serious about killing James, she wasn't going to make it clear for him.

While Anita dragged James toward the door, where a police officer waited, Will approached Audrey. "Are you okay?"

She nodded. "He startled me more than anything else."

"I'm going to speak to the hotel manager when I leave. I wouldn't want to be the person who let him in."

"No," she agreed. "Thanks for coming over."

"There's no chance he saw anything connected to the trial or the Lewis girl's murder, is there?"

"None. It's all locked in the safe."

His shoulders relaxed. Even the lines of his face seemed to ease. "Good. Anita will make sure he's thoroughly processed."

"Let me know if you find anything linking him to Natashya."

"I will." He patted her on the shoulder before moving to Anita's side. Audrey stayed where she was until they'd finally taken James away. Then she went to Jake, who was staring at the door.

"You okay?" she asked.

He shook his head. "No. No, I'm really not." When he finally turned his gaze to hers, she saw anger and fear. "If I hadn't been with you..."

"They would still be taking him out in handcuffs." At least, that was what she was going to tell herself, and him. "I would have kicked the shit out of him." Well, she would have gotten a few good blows in before braining him with the nearest heavy object. Wouldn't be the first skull she bashed in.

"He could be the killer, Aud. He could have done to you what was done to that girl."

"But he didn't. And he might not be. In fact, I'll feel a whole lot better if he isn't." Because then she wouldn't think of what might have happened if Jake hadn't been with her either.

He put his arms around her, and she around him. His heart thumped hard beneath her cheek. He held her tight, as if he was afraid she might slip away.

"Would you have killed him?" she asked, glancing up.

Jake nodded. "If he meant to hurt you, yes. I would have ended him in a heartbeat."

She grabbed the front of his shirt, pulling him close before yanking the fabric out of the waistband of his jeans. She kissed him hard and hungry, steering him into the bedroom.

There was no need to tell him she would have helped him hide the body.

Audrey left Friday morning for Warren while Jake headed home to Edgeport. She'd meet up with him later that night after stopping by her parents' house, as was their usual routine. He hadn't been keen on letting her out of his sight, even though he knew exactly where she planned to stop along the way. His concern was actually sweet—and if she wasn't acutely aware of just how warranted his worry was, she might enjoy it more.

She'd checked with Will before she left, and he told her James was still in custody, and the police were looking into his alibi for the morning Natashya Lewis was abducted.

She actually looked forward to getting home. For years Edgeport was a blight on her soul that she longed to excise, but no matter how hard she tried, she never quite managed to cut it out. Now, that small, secretive little mud puddle was a haven from the rest of the world. She'd made some of the worst decisions of her life in that town. *Done* the worst thing of her life in that town, and yet she couldn't wait to get back to it and surround herself with the people on whom she'd turned her back for fourteen years.

But first, a stop by the state penitentiary to see her favorite serial rapist. Maybe Monroe would squeal on James if he was indeed the partner.

"I'm sorry, Dr. Harte, but Ian Monroe has removed you from his visitation list."

Audrey stared at the man behind the desk—a little, kind-faced man with muttonchop sideburns. "But he just added me to it."

The guard shrugged. "These guys don't get much control over their daily lives. Sometimes they like to exert it wherever they can. I'm sorry you had to drive all the way here to find out."

"Thanks, but I was passing through anyway. I'll make an appointment." The little prick would have a harder time avoiding her when she had the district attorney behind her. "Have a good weekend."

He wished her the same and Audrey walked out of the prison into the sunny, chilly October morning. Wow. It was a new low being taken off a serial rapist's visitor list, wasn't it? Seriously, what kind of rapist wouldn't want a reasonably attractive woman visiting him?

One that wanted to play head games, that was who. The guard was right—Monroe was just exerting control. Denying her visitation after sending her such a pointed, and dramatic, message via his wife was a pissing contest.

Or he could be snubbing her because of Lawson. Or James.

God, she still couldn't believe Margot had married him. She seemed like such a smart, sweet woman. What was it about Monroe that captivated her? She was aware of how strange her attraction to him seemed to everyone else. Hell, she *knew* it wasn't right, and yet she did nothing to end it. Monroe was using her, just as surely as he'd used practically everyone else in his life, and Margot allowed it.

She walked back to her car and unlocked it. Once she was inside, she unbuttoned her coat, started the engine, and set her phone to Bluetooth, slipping the earpiece into place. If it wasn't so early in LA, she'd call Angeline, but she really didn't feel like talking to her boss. There was nothing to tell her really, and it was more convenient just to e-mail her an update. Audrey was sick of talking about it. All she'd done thus far was talk. Talk to Monroe, Amber, Petra, Leigh, Tori, Margot, Will, Anita, even Jake. At least Jake was safe. She could confide just how blind she was to him.

She sat there a moment, alone in that parking lot. If James was their killer, had she been the intended victim Monroe warned her about? Had he taken her off his visitor list because he expected her to be dead? A clammy shiver ran down her spine.

Pull yourself together. James wouldn't be the first person who tried to kill you. And you really don't think he's savvy enough to be the killer.

Oddly enough, the realization actually made her feel better. Audrey buckled her seatbelt and drove out of the lot.

It was the twenty-first of the month. Normally she'd be looking forward to Halloween, getting ready for the party her friend Carrie always hosted.

She hadn't spoken to Carrie in a couple of months. It was hard to believe she'd once considered the woman her best friend given how easily their relationship dissolved. If someone asked her who her best friend was now, she wouldn't have an answer. She didn't have many friends. There was Neve, but it was awkward being friends with someone who had investigated her for murder. Maybe it was time to do something about her lack of a social life. She and Jake both spent far too much time alone. Having each other was great, and they had their families, but those relationships were sometimes shaky. Before she could stop herself, she told her phone to dial Neve. Fuck awkward.

"Well, hello, stranger," Neve said when she picked up. "You in jail or something?"

Audrey laughed. "On my way to Edgeport, so I guess you could draw some parallels. Where are you?"

"Gideon's. He went up to see Bailey today. I'm cooking so he'll have dinner when he gets back."

"How's he doing?"

"Okay. Better now that she's doing well. She'd love to hear from you."

She glanced in the rearview mirror and tried to avoid her own gaze. "I know."

Neve drew a breath. "I'm just going to be blunt. Call the kid. Visit her. She's a damn mess. Don't let her down like so many people did to you and Maggie. You had one person who made a difference in your life when you were at Stillwater. You could be that person for her."

"Are you high? I'm nobody's role model." God, her stomach cramped at the thought.

"You're so full of shit, Harte. Why are we talking?"

"I wanted to see if you were in Edgeport this weekend." She cringed at the hopefulness in her voice.

"I am. You want to get together?"

"Yeah. You?"

"Sure. Come by Gideon's at ten tomorrow morning."

"Okay. See you then." She hung up. That was easier than she had thought it was going to be after the discussion about Bailey. She liked Neve. She'd been a bit of a bitch when Audrey first came home, but only because of the murder investigation, and she hadn't wanted to be there any more than Audrey had. And now look at both of them—dating guys so firmly rooted, there they were part of the local flora.

Because of Monroe's snubbing, she arrived at her parents' house an hour earlier than she'd anticipated. Her mother and father were just having lunch.

"Hi there, babaloo," her mother greeted her as she walked into the kitchen. "I thought I heard your little car. Want some tomato soup and a grilled cheese? Your father's got the Foreman out."

God, she hadn't eaten that in years. "Croutons?"

Her mother smiled. "Asiago. Made them myself with bread your father made a few days ago."

Audrey gaped at her father. "*You* made bread?"

He made a face, gray and ginger brows knitting together. "I used a bread maker, kid. No need to soil your drawers in shock."

His wife laughed. "Go make her a sandwich, Rusty." Rusty, that was her father's nickname. Audrey hadn't heard her mother use it in some time. "Come sit by me, babe."

Audrey did as she was told, giving her mother a hug before sitting down at the table. "You look good, Mum." It was true. Her color was good, her skin and eyes bright. Her hair looked shiny, and she had a bit of mascara and lipstick on.

"I feel good." She leaned closer, as though they conspired together. "I think having a surgery date has taken a load of worry off my shoulders. I thought I'd dread it, but honestly? I'll be glad to have it over with."

"Me too," Audrey murmured, placing her hand over her mother's. She jerked her chin toward the kitchen. "How's he doing?"

"Good. *Really* good. You invite Jake to supper tonight so I can thank him for giving your dad something to keep him busy."

Audrey still wasn't convinced. "But being around all that liquor. Isn't it hard on him?"

Anne shrugged. "He said he wants to keep his head clear."

"That boy trusts me with his business!" her father yelled from the kitchen. "I don't want to let him down like that asshole brother of his."

"Stop eavesdropping, nosy!" Audrey yelled back.

"But I'm such a fascinating subject!"

She laughed. Her mother shook her head. "You two make my head hurt. Oh! Let me show you the photo Greg took of the girls the other day."

Audrey spent the next few minutes looking at pictures of Isabel and Olivia on her mother's phone, until her father returned with a bowl of soup and a sandwich for her.

"That's some good grilled cheese, old man," she allowed after the first bite. "The ratio of buttery crunch to melted goodness is almost perfect."

"Almost?" John made a scoffing noise. "Your palate has

deteriorated after so many years on the granola coast." He pointed at the sandwich in her hands. "That right there is the perfect grilled cheese."

She didn't argue, mostly because he was right, but she wasn't going to tell him that.

"When do you go for surgery?" she asked her mother.

"The twenty-eighth. I think your sister wants to coordinate with you and David to arrange babysitting duty afterward."

"Yeah, well, you'll need help for a bit afterward."

"It won't be too much," her father jumped in. "Gracie's is on winter hours, so it's only open evenings and weekends. I don't think there will be too many nights I can't be home."

"You can't do all of it, Dad." Audrey shot him a pointed look. He had a habit of taking on more than he could handle and then fucking off on it. That was not an option where her mother was concerned. "Let us help. Just think of how much fun you'll have telling Jeannie Ray what a great kid I am, coming home to look after Mum."

He smiled. "The old bat's head might explode."

"You two are evil," Anne announced.

"Says the woman who, a few months ago, blackmailed Jeannie into shutting up about me."

Her mother frowned as she smoothed her hand over the tablecloth. "That was different. She asked for it. You two are talking about baiting her."

"I'm okay with that." John picked up his wife's teacup. "I'll get you a refill, babe."

When he came back, the three of them sat at the table, working on a crossword puzzle together. It was fun.

"How in the name of G-A-W-D did you know that one?" her father demanded after Audrey supplied "cerebellum" for one of the definitions.

"I studied the brain," she replied. "What did you think I was doing all those years at Stanford?"

"Partying. At least, I hoped you were. How was I to know you were getting a decent education? Not like we talked much while you were gone."

His tone was joking, but it was apparent at the end that he realized he'd given away more than he'd intended, cut a little deeper than intended.

"No," Audrey agreed. "We didn't." And that was on both of them.

"But look at us now," he enthused. "I'm in awe of your academic prowess. What's the next clue, Mother?"

And that was the end of it. No apologies or regrets, just a rough kick to put it behind them and move on. As fascinating as it was to sometimes work out family issues and dynamics, Audrey appreciated not having to do that at the moment. The complexity of her relationship with her father was difficult to articulate on a good day, and right now she had too much other crap in her head.

Her phone rang just as they finished the puzzle. Audrey carried her dishes out to the kitchen as she accepted the call. She didn't even look to see who it was.

It was the state prison, wanting to know if she'd accept Ian Monroe's call. She knew what this was—a dominance thing. There was a chance he had information for her. There was a slim chance he might give her something they could use to stop another girl from going missing. But what was most likely was that Monroe just wanted to fuck with her.

"Dial zero to accept the call," said the computerized voice.

Audrey's thumb hovered above the keypad. This was all a game to Monroe, and he thought of himself as alpha—the one in charge of it. It was time he learned differently.

She hung up.

CHAPTER FOURTEEN

Saturday morning arrived sunny and unseasonably warm. Jake didn't seem to mind that Audrey was going to spend some time with Neve. Maybe he was glad to be rid of her for a bit after several days in a hotel room together, but he probably would have said so if that was the case. He said he was going to meet with her father at Gracie's to go over a few things before opening for the day. Audrey kissed him good-bye and left. It had rained the night before, so the dirt road was damp, the gravel packed down. Not even one pebble dared fly up from under her tires to ding the paint on her car. She turned left onto the main road and continued on to Gideon's house not far from Gracie's.

She didn't meet even one other car during the drive. Such was traffic in the big city of Edgeport.

Neve was sitting on the back steps, drinking from a travel mug, when Audrey pulled into the drive. Gideon's truck was gone, so she assumed he had to be out on a job. He was in construction and owned his own business. He always seemed to be busy doing something for someone.

He and Neve had started dating shortly after Maggie's

funeral. No one criticized them for it—at least not to their faces. Most people knew he and Maggie hadn't been close for a long time. Maggie had been the sort of person who intentionally made it difficult for a person to love them, so it wouldn't hurt so much when she drove the person away.

Audrey climbed out of the car and walked across the smooth gravel to the house. "Hey, you," she said.

Neve smiled. She was Audrey's age, with skin the color of cocoa and eyes to match. Her heart-shaped face was smooth and clear, even without makeup. *Bitch.* She had straightened her normally curly dark hair. It looked good.

"Hey, yourself." Neve stood and met her on the ground for a hug. It was quick, but comfortable. "Come for a drive with me?"

"Sure."

They climbed into Neve's car. When she wasn't driving a blue state police vehicle, she drove a silver SUV, the make of which Audrey never bothered to remember. She wouldn't even own a car if it wasn't necessary. She envied her brother, David, for living in New York and being able to walk or take some form of public transportation wherever he needed to go. He only drove when he and his boyfriend, Seth, went on road trips.

They'd been on the road for twenty minutes before Audrey said, "Neve, where the hell are we going?"

Her friend kept her gaze on the road. "Stillwater."

Audrey's blood turned to ice in her veins. Neve had tricked her, and she'd fallen right into it. "You fucking slag. Turn this car around."

"No."

"Don't make me punch you."

Neve flashed her a sweet smile. "I've got my gun, badge, and cuffs on me, sweetheart. We can do this the hard way if you want, but I'd rather not have Bailey see you in restraints and possibly bleeding."

Audrey clenched her fists so tight her nails bit hard into her palms. "This is low, you know. Even for you."

"For Christ's sake. She's a kid, and she's done absolutely nothing to you except confess her every sin. You made her feel like she had a future, that maybe she wasn't so broken after all, and then you fucked off on her. I don't care if you feel weird or guilty, or how pissed you are. Get over it by the time we arrive or I'll kick your ass."

She snorted. "You'll try."

Another smile. "Did I mention I brought my Taser too?"

"Taser, gun, and cuffs. Wow, you must think I'm some kind of badass."

"I saw the damage you did to Matt, remember? I know better than underestimate you. Plus, it would make me feel so good if I had to tase you. Seriously. I'm tempted to do it right now just for the fun of it."

"I can't believe you're my only friend. I need to widen my social circle to include more people who aren't certifiably crazy."

"That's a derogatory term. Shouldn't you say 'mentally ill'?"

"With anyone else I would, but you're not ill, you're just twisted."

"Love you too, sweetheart."

Now that the shock had worn off, Audrey had to admit, if

only to herself, that it wasn't as terrible as she first thought. In fact, it was almost a relief. Neve had taken the choice away from her and left her with no room for cold feet. She was forcing her to do what she most dreaded, and there was nothing she could do about it short of jumping out of a moving car.

And Neve had the doors locked.

The drive from Edgeport to Stillwater, which was located just north of Bangor in Orono, lasted almost two hours. It gave them time to talk, catch up, and for Audrey to prepare.

"How's she doing?"

Neve shrugged. "Better than I expected. That Ms. Kim is good."

"Reva's fabulous. They have some really good people working with the girls." Reva had been just starting out when Audrey had been sent to Stillwater.

"That's what I don't get."

"What do you mean?"

"You. You talk about wanting to make a difference, or help kids, but you hide behind that boss of yours and do everything you can to avoid *actually* helping."

"Hey, what I do makes a difference."

"What? Those acknowledgments you get in Angeline Beharrie's books for your 'tireless assistance and research'? Being on that show that makes it all out to be so tragic? Christ, Audrey, you could really make a difference if you worked *with* these kids."

"I don't do clinical work."

"Why not?"

"Because I don't want to fuck up, or say the wrong thing. You know my temper. I don't want to make things worse for them. I want to respect them." Christ, she sat across a table from a serial rapist and purposefully antagonized him. Last time she'd visited Stillwater, she told off a kid who was trying to fuck with her.

"Make things worse? Respect them? You talk like you don't understand these kids. Audrey, you are *one* of them."

Audrey's breath caught. She couldn't speak.

Neve didn't seem to notice, or mistook her silence. "Write all the books you want, research all you want, but keeping your distance isn't helping these kids. What if you'd gotten to Bailey before she got to Maggie? If she'd had you to confide in, she might not have done it. That's not on you, I'm just saying, wouldn't you rather help by preventing these kids from doing awful things rather than studying them after the damage has been done?"

"I'm not a good therapist," Audrey confided. "That's not me talking down about myself, it's the truth. I get angry when they try to bullshit me. I tell them exactly what I think."

"Maybe that's what some of them need. You're working with that Scott girl for the Monroe trial. Have you gotten angry with her?"

"That's different."

"If you say so, but I think you're a coward, and that's not the Audrey Harte who slapped Matt Jones in the mouth for calling me a nigger."

Audrey cringed. "That was twenty years ago. More."

"Well, I'll never forget it. And Maggie never forgot how you tackled Duger to the ground and pounded on him for calling her a slut."

"She was twelve. Clint was already molesting her at that time. Dugie didn't know." Duger's real name was Scott Ray. He was Jeannie's kid, and had the sparkling personality that ran in that family. He was also what was called "developmentally delayed" these days. Basically, he was an asshole that didn't know any better.

"That doesn't matter. I can count off several times you jumped in to defend some kid who needed it, even when adults wouldn't. It breaks my heart that you've lost that."

"I haven't lost it," Audrey whispered. God, her throat was so tight. She swiped at her right eye. Her fingers came away wet.

"Fuck around," Neve rasped. "Are you *crying*?"

"*No.*" She blinked. "Keep your eyes on the road." She turned her head and looked out the window.

They didn't talk for the rest of the drive.

Reva Kim, the woman who had been such a big influence in Audrey's life while at Stillwater Facility for Girls, was talking to the woman running the front desk when they walked into the main reception area. She had to be in her middle to late fifties, but she didn't look it. There was hardly a line to be seen on her expertly made up face—which brightened at the sight of Audrey.

"I didn't know you were coming to visit today!" Reva cried

as she came through the door that separated reception from the hall. She opened her arms and Audrey stepped into the embrace with a happy smile. Reva had that effect on people. She dealt with some terrible situations and people on a regular basis, but she never took it out on "her girls" and she always had an air of calm about her.

"Neither did I until I met up with Neve," Audrey replied, shooting the other woman an arch glance. "You two have met before?"

"Oh, of course," Reva replied. "We've seen quite a bit of Neve these past few months. The two of you are just in time for lunch. Would you like to join Bailey? I'm sure she'll be excited to see you."

Audrey wasn't certain about that, but she kept that to herself. Reva walked with them to the lunchroom. "I've supposed you've heard that they plan to close us down."

"*What*? No, I hadn't heard." Audrey shot a glance at Neve. "Did you know?"

Neve nodded, her expression solemn. "I thought you knew."

"I didn't." She shook her head. "Why would the state do that?"

Reva shrugged her slim shoulders, serene as ever. "You know how it goes. They're cutting funding, and there are larger facilities elsewhere that can take both girls and boys, so we're a bit of a dinosaur in that respect. Our numbers have been dwindling over the years, and we're not equipped to deal with the girls who are violent."

"You dealt with me," Audrey remarked before she could stop herself.

Reva gave her that sweet smile. "My dear girl, you weren't this kind of violent. Last month, I had a girl come at me with a shard of broken glass. She meant to cut my throat. A man who was here to visit his daughter pulled her off me." She pulled the silk scarf around her neck loose so Audrey could see the scar on her neck. "She would have killed me if not for him."

Audrey shook her head. Sweet Jesus. "My God, Reva. I'm so sorry."

"Oh, I'm fine, but I think an early retirement might not be such a bad thing after all."

It didn't feel right, the thought that Stillwater would no longer exist. The time she'd spent there had been some of the worst and some of the best of Audrey's life. She'd met Angeline there. She'd come to terms with being a murderer within those walls. She'd learned to fight and, more important, when not to. And she'd learned that she was smart—bookwise at least—and that education was her ticket out of Edgeport.

They walked into the lunchroom. During Audrey's stay there it would have been filled with girls; now there were about fifteen. The hardwood floor was scuffed, the tables and chairs worse for wear.

There were a few other adults there. Saturday used to be the busiest day for family visits, but at least half the girls there didn't have anyone with them.

"There's Bailey," Reva remarked, pointing to a table by the wall of windows. "You two go join her and I'll see about getting you some lunch." She was gone before either Audrey or Neve could even reply.

Neve nudged Audrey with her elbow. "C'mon."

Reluctantly, Audrey followed her. It was ridiculous, treating this young girl like a leper because Audrey hadn't been able to see inside her head. Hadn't she internally rolled her eyes at Will for expecting magic from her? Apparently it was perfectly fine for her to expect it from herself, though.

"You gonna eat all that?" Neve asked when they reached Bailey.

The girl looked up. She was a fifteen-year-old brunette with thick wavy hair and wide eyes. She smiled when she saw Neve, but then her gaze moved to Audrey...

Audrey tried to smile, but all the joy in the girl's face faded at the sight of her. For a moment she thought Bailey might get up and hit her, or tell her to fuck off.

She didn't expect tears, but that was what she got. Great, fat tears that rolled silently down Bailey's pale cheeks as she pushed back her chair and stood up. She threw her arms around Audrey's waist and held her so tight, Audrey could barely breathe. The girl's shoulders shook, but she still didn't make a sound. That was something else Stillwater taught a girl to do— cry her heart out without making noise, because noise got you made fun of, tortured, and sometimes hit.

Those lessons had been valuable too—in their own way.

Stillwater was where she'd learned that some people were not what they seemed. There was a very good chance she'd met Monroe's partner. A lot of times, serial killers liked to insinuate themselves into the investigation. Hadn't Monroe himself told her to look at someone close to the case?

She wasn't going to think about Monroe at that moment. He didn't matter nearly as much as the broken little girl sobbing into her shoulder.

Audrey met Neve's gaze. Her old friend's dark eyes were glossy as she blinked back tears. The former NYC cop was sentimental—Audrey never would have thought. As for herself, she did okay. Her throat was tight as she put her arms around Bailey's shoulders. The girl wasn't much shorter than her.

Bailey pulled back—just enough that Audrey would look her clearly in the eye.

"Thank you," Bailey whispered. "Thank you." And then she buried her face in Audrey's neck.

Audrey tightened her arms. A scalding tear ran down her cheek as she rested her head against the girl's. "I'm sorry," she whispered. "I'm so very sorry."

By the time she got back to Jake's that afternoon, Audrey was mentally and emotionally exhausted. The visit with Bailey had been hard, because the poor girl was coming to grips with what she had done and had felt as though Audrey—the one person she thought would understand—had abandoned her. She needed to know other people forgave her before she could forgive herself.

"God, I'm *such* a shit," she'd confessed to Neve on the drive home.

"Yeah, you are." Neve's words were softened by a smile. "A good shit, though. I haven't seen her so happy in weeks."

"Do you see her every week?"

"I try. Gideon goes up once throughout the week and then once on the weekend. I usually go with him, but I have to work tomorrow, so he'll be going up alone. I hadn't planned to go at all until you called."

"I'm glad I did."

"Me too. Although next time let's just do lunch. It's less emotional."

"Deal." She leaned her head back against the seat. "So you and Gideon, is it everything you thought it would be?"

Dark eyes narrowed. "Are you and Jake everything you thought it would be?"

"Better," she replied honestly. "There's less drama than I imagined at sixteen."

"Well, you were pretty dramatic with the whole tormented killer thing."

Audrey laughed. "Answer the question. Are you guys good?"

Neve tilted her head, as though contemplating her answer. "You know, we are. There's something about dating a man who has a kid. Did you know he cooks? I mean, he *cooks*. He does laundry—right. He ironed one of my shirts the other day. It was perfect."

"A domestic god, is he?" She wasn't really surprised. Gideon had always struck her as a very capable sort of guy.

"He is. You know what's weird? Actually, I think you'll understand this. He's strong. Like, stronger than me."

Audrey's lips curved up into a smile. "I get it." When you grew up as rural as they had, the lines of separation between the sexes were marked differently than they were in more populated areas. Sometimes men in Edgeport had antiquated ideas of how to treat a "lady" but almost every girl Audrey had known growing up could drive a four-wheeler or dirt bike. They cut wood and hunted. They worked on cars, drank, and got into fights. Neve had all of that, plus a cop for a father. The woman had noticeable muscle definition along with her enviable curves. Audrey remembered one night at a party in college, her boyfriend Kurt had gotten into a fight, and when the guy knocked Kurt down, Audrey head-butted him hard enough to break his nose and knock him out.

Kurt hadn't liked having a girlfriend that at ease with violence. And truth be told, Audrey didn't really like being with a guy so easily knocked off his feet.

"I'm kinda into it," Neve confided. "I get so caught up in being the protector that I missed out on being protected. It's nice to feel like someone's got your back."

"I wouldn't want to scrap it out with Jake." Audrey shook her head. "I don't think I'd get very far."

"Not too many would. One night at Gracie's—you weren't home that weekend—I saw him get into it with a couple of guys from Cutler—you know, the town's so small, people gotta travel just to get into a good fight."

"Same could be said about Edgeport."

"Sure, but these guys were wound up and trying to start trouble with Donalda. Lincoln jumped in and got sucker punched. Next thing you know, one of the guys is on the floor bleeding from a head wound and Jake's bouncing the other one's face off the bar. Gideon helped carry them out."

"They made two big mistakes. They messed with his staff and then his brother. God, what does it say about me that I'm actually proud of him for taking them both out so quickly and efficiently?"

Neve grinned. "It says you're still an Edgeport bitch."

"God save me." She laughed as she said it. "I've always been drawn to that part of him, you know. He'd do anything for people he cares about, even if it meant going too far."

"Yeah, well, I think that might be something the two of you have in common."

"I won't argue. So how did you determine Gideon is stronger than you? Did you have an oil wrestling match in the bathtub or something?"

They spent the rest of the drive being foolish and catching up. Audrey couldn't remember the last time she'd talked so openly with another woman. She and Neve had been good friends once, but Detective Everett Graham hadn't wanted his daughter hanging out with a murderer after Audrey came home from Stillwater. Whenever she tried making new friends, she was inevitably left with the dilemma of deciding how much of her past to reveal or conceal. With Neve she didn't have to be anyone other than exactly who she was at that moment.

Her phone buzzed in her purse as they were driving through Harrington. She pulled it out and checked the screen. It was a text from Jake: *You coming home soon?*

On the way, she responded. *We went to visit Bailey. Sorry I didn't text. Will fill you in when I get back. <3.*

Gideon's truck was home when they pulled into the driveway.

Audrey popped into the house long enough to say hi. He was marinating steaks for dinner. Neve wasn't kidding when she said he could cook. That was something he and Jake had in common, obviously.

"Thanks for going to see Bailey," Gideon said to her. "I know it meant a lot to her."

"I should have gone before this," she confessed. "I had my head up my ass over the fact that I hadn't seen how she was suffering and made it all about me instead of her. I'm sorry for that."

"You don't need to apologize to me. I spent a few weeks blaming myself, and getting so wrapped up in my own guilt that I wasn't able to be there for my kid. Neve kicked my ass, though. Got me in line." He grinned at his girlfriend, and the look that passed between them was Audrey's cue to leave. She hugged them both and promised Neve she'd call her later in the week. Then, she left the house and drove to Jake's.

There was a strange car in the driveway when she pulled in behind Jake's truck. He hadn't mentioned company in his text. She slung her bag over her shoulder as she walked to the steps. She heard laughter when she opened the door.

Jake was in the kitchen, also prepping food for dinner. He had an odd expression on his face when he looked at her. It was so strange that Audrey's heart skipped a beat. Was he angry with her? Had someone died?

"Hey," she said.

"How was the visit?" He wiped his hands on a dish towel before closing the distance between them. "We have a visitor," he murmured. "Alisha's with her."

"Who is it?" Audrey asked.

He inclined his head toward the living room. "I think it might be better if you see for yourself."

Confused, Audrey walked through to the living room, Jake behind her. When she got to the doorway, she saw Alisha sitting on the sofa with another girl. They were chattering and laughing in that manic way only teenage girls could achieve. Audrey's stomach dropped when she saw who the other girl was. What the fuck?

Tori Scott looked up with a huge grin. "Hi, Dr. Harte. We were wondering when you'd get back."

CHAPTER FIFTEEN

Tori." Audrey kept her tone neutral. "This is a surprise. What are you doing here?"

The girl looked happier than Audrey had witnessed in either of their two visits. Her cheeks were rosy—though that might have been cosmetically enhanced—and her blue eyes bright. She and Alisha had similar coloring, although Lish's hair was a lighter blond, thanks to Feria.

"You told me you were from Edgeport, so I thought I'd see it for myself. Alisha was giving me the CliffsNotes on the place. It's pretty."

"How did you know where to find me?" Audrey wanted to know who to have a word with about boundaries and privacy. This set off all kinds of warning bells in her head. Was the girl's appearance here due to transference? Or just loneliness? Was she spiraling? Why would a girl who had been afraid to leave her house drive three hours—*by herself*—to see someone she barely knew?

"Oh, I found a few Hartes in the phone book, but only one listed in this town, so I popped by. There was no one home, so

I drove into town. An old man was walking down the road so I stopped and asked if he knew you and where I could find you. He said to come back here to Jake's house." She gestured over Audrey's shoulder. She didn't need to turn; she could feel him behind her. "And here I am. Jake was nice enough to let me wait."

"That's a bit of a drive from Portland. You should have called first. I would have made sure I was here to meet you." *And send your ass back home.* "Does your mother know where you are?"

Tori averted her gaze. "I told her I was going to see a friend. She was so happy I actually left the house that she didn't ask for details."

Stupid woman. There was a predator out there that might very well decide to take a second shot at Tori, and she just let her go out? What sort of mother let her teenage daughter leave the house without asking where she was going?

What else has she been doing that her mother doesn't know about? asked the darker part of her brain. There was no way that she could spin this to make it a positive thing. It was wrong, and Tori had to know that.

"I'll give your mom a call and let her know you're all right. Lish, do you mind giving Tori and me a little privacy for a few minutes?"

Alisha's eyes widened. Audrey knew the girl wasn't familiar with this neutral, careful side of her, but she'd never met a mental health professional who'd had a positive experience with a client showing up at their house. Technically Tori wasn't a client, but she had issues, and Audrey had visited her in a professional capacity.

This was also the sort of behavior that raised red flags. It meant the client had blurred the boundaries of their relationship with the therapist, making it something more personal than what it was. Tori might have been a teenager who suffered something horrible, but she was also someone in treatment for the damage that event had triggered.

"Sure." Alisha turned to Tori. "I'll make some popcorn. Do you like butter?"

Tori grinned. It was a little too bright and toothy—like she was in a commercial. "That would be great."

Audrey moved out of the doorway so Alisha could pass. She heard her whispering softly to Jake as they walked away. Once she could no longer hear them, she stepped into the room and perched on the arm of the recliner just to her left. It brought her down a bit so Tori would remain relaxed, but kept Audrey at a position of authority.

Tori's smile faded a little. "I shouldn't have come here, should I?"

"No," Audrey said gently. "It's inappropriate, but it's also dangerous for you to be out on your own."

She nodded. "Because the killer's still out there."

"Yes."

"I thought you said I probably wouldn't be a target." There was bite in the words.

"I also advised you to be cautious." Audrey folded her arms across her chest. She needed to be careful with Tori, because she had no idea of the girl's mental state, but she also had to assume the position of authority. Being too authoritative, however, could trigger Tori's defensiveness.

"Cautious is boring."

Audrey raised a brow. That was a strange response for a girl who avoided going to school, and leaving the house altogether. Then again, contradictory behavior in PTSD victims wasn't unusual. "I know it is, but for the time being, it's also safe."

Tori's expression softened. "Am I supposed to stay a shut-in for the rest of my life? How can I get better if I'm too afraid to do anything? Coming here was the craziest thing I could think to do. And then I did it. It took two Xanax to get my hands to stop shaking on the wheel."

Hmm. She didn't look like she was under the influence of anti-anxiety meds, but her elevated stress levels could have chewed through it. Audrey didn't know enough about medications to really form an accurate opinion. However, she was pretty good at sensing when someone wasn't being completely honest.

Or at least she usually was. She hadn't been too great at it where Bailey was concerned, but even that self-disappointment couldn't stop her from wondering what Tori's agenda was.

"Why did you drive all the way up here? It wasn't just to say hello, was it? Or to do something crazy."

The girl shrugged in that boneless manner teenagers had. She gazed down at the floor, her hair falling on either side of her face like a curtain. "I wanted to see where you were from. I wanted to see the place where you killed a man."

Fair enough. Maybe not as tourist-worthy as the Paul Bunyan statue in Maine, or Lenny the Chocolate Moose in Scarborough—there wasn't even a plaque to commemorate it—but still worth a look, she supposed. But Tori hadn't said anything about driving past the house where it had happened, nor had she asked where it was. She'd come looking for Audrey, so she wanted to see her more than where the murder had taken place.

"Does my past upset you? If you're uncomfortable, the prosecution can find someone else to work with you for the trial."

Tori lifted her head, an indignant expression on her striking face. "I'm not uncomfortable. I just wanted to see the place." She made a scoffing noise. "If I had to live here, I'd probably kill somebody too."

Audrey wanted to frown, but she didn't. The remark sounded rehearsed, lacking in humor or gravity. "Small-town life isn't for everyone."

"It's not for you, is it?"

"It wasn't for a long time, no. I'm not sure what it is now. I'm going to call your mother and figure out the best way to get you home safely."

"You could drive me." Expression and voice so hopeful.

"No, I can't." In fact, there was nothing in the world at that moment that could convince her that spending two hours in an enclosed space with the girl was a good idea. She wasn't afraid of her, but her nerves were alight like someone had set a torch too close to the raw ends. She was certainly going to have a lot to discuss with Tori's doctor on Monday.

"Well, can I at least stay here until someone comes, or whatever? Or should I go sit in the car?"

Teenage hostility was a wonderful thing. How had her

mother managed to raise three kids without killing any of them? "It's not my house, but I think Jake will be okay with you staying here."

"Is he your boyfriend?"

"He's an old friend."

That sharp blue gaze locked with hers. "What's it like to have sex with someone who doesn't want to hurt you?"

Jesus. She'd been asked worse in the short course of her career, but it was still jarring. And it was a blatant ploy to take control of the situation. "I'm going to go call your mother now." Audrey stood.

"Alisha seems nice," Tori blurted out. A stall tactic. Had she not told her mother she was going out? Or did she just want to avoid having to go home? Did she think that Audrey could somehow make everything okay? No, the girl was too smart for that.

"She is," Audrey agreed.

"A little naive, though."

Inside, she bristled. Tori said it like naiveté was akin to stupidity. "There's nothing wrong with seeing the good in people."

"Yeah, look what it did for Natashya Lewis."

That was harsh. Very harsh, and said without much emotion other than mockery. Tori reached into her bag. Audrey tensed as she began to pull something out.

It was a magazine—one of those celebrity gossip ones. She threw it on the coffee table, face up, for Audrey to read. The cover photo was of Margot Temple, with a smaller photo of Ian as an inset. The headline read: MY LIFE WITH IAN.

Well, that hadn't taken very fucking long.

"Why didn't you tell me he married her?" Tori demanded.

Audrey arched a brow. "I didn't think you'd care to know. Why are you upset about it?"

"Because I deserve to know," she replied, indignant. "What if she contacted me again about talking to her group?"

"I'm sorry you are upset, Tori, but it's not my job to tell you these things. That's up to the DA or the police. Maybe your mother or your therapist thought it was for the best that you not hear about it?" Though it wasn't as if it could be kept from her forever. The kid watched TV, had the Internet, and obviously bought magazines.

"Dr. Venture?" She laughed. "That man wouldn't know what was good for someone if you gave him a list. I've already told my mother I want to fire him. I don't feel like he's helping me anymore."

"That's too bad. I can give your mother a list of names of doctors in the Portland area if you'd like." But she was still going to keep her appointment with him on Monday. And she would be interested in hearing his side of things.

"Why can't you be my therapist?"

"Because I'm working for the DA's office, and my office is in Cambridge. That's not a trip you want to make every week."

"You could move back here." There was a gleam of desperation in the girl's eyes. Audrey had no idea what was going on, but it wasn't good. Had she forgotten to take her medication? She seemed twitchy and overly reactive, neither of which was a good thing in someone with PTSD, and a one-eighty change in demeanor since Audrey arrived.

"That's not an option."

Full lips thinned. "Alisha told me you were the first one to figure out that girl killed her stepmother."

The first. Audrey paused, letting her brain catch up to her ears. She hadn't thought of it that way, but Tori wasn't the first to mention it. Maybe it had taken a visit to Bailey for her to actually hear it. She might have been slow to realize the truth about poor Bailey, but she had been the first one to see it at all. It had taken the girl's confession for other people to realize. Yes, it had taken her longer than she thought it should for her to figure out the truth, but she'd seen it faster than the girl's own father, or anyone else had.

"Yes, I suppose I was." But she wasn't discussing Bailey or Maggie with this girl. And she might have to have a little chat with Alisha about being so open to strangers.

"Why haven't you figured out who this killer is then? This one's not smarter than you, right?"

This time Audrey did frown. That was an odd question. "No, but planning to kill someone is different from an impulsive crime. Serial killers are driven by instinct and desire, but they have their plans and rituals to carry out. The killer doesn't have Ian Monroe to hide behind anymore. I'm confident the police will make an arrest soon."

Tori stood up. "Well, I'm glad you are, because every girl I know is terrified of being the next victim. One girl at school dyed her hair brown because the killer likes blondes."

"So you've been back to school?"

She averted her gaze. "I went there to pick up my assignments."

"It's more important that they don't go anywhere alone." Audrey gave her a pointed look. "Let's call your mom and see what we can work out. Meanwhile, it smells like Jake has made some cookies, and he's really good at it."

"He's cute," the girl remarked with a slight smile. "I'm sorry I ruined your day."

"He is, and you didn't." Audrey directed her to the kitchen. "Go have something to eat while I call your mom."

She watched Tori enter the kitchen, and waited until she heard the three of them talking before she got her cell phone out of her bag. She dialed the Scotts' home as she left the room—she didn't want Tori to hear the conversation. Mrs. Scott picked up on the second ring.

"Dr. Harte? Tori's gone!"

Silently, Audrey swore. Frigging teenagers and their self-absorption. "She's with me, Mrs. Scott. She drove to Edgeport to see me."

"Edgeport? Isn't that down east?"

"It is. I've already told her that she shouldn't have come here, especially not alone. Before I send her home, I need to know if you're okay with her driving the return trip by herself, or if you want me to keep her here for you to pick up."

"You can't bring her home?"

Did it also say "Taxi Service" on her business card? "No."

A sigh echoed in Audrey's ear. "Tell her to come straight home, please. And would you mind telling her that I would like for her to call me?"

"I will. She's going to have a little something to eat, but she should be on her way in fifteen or twenty minutes."

"Thank you, Dr. Harte. I'm sorry she intruded upon your private time. Was there something she wanted to discuss with you about the trial?"

What had been the reason for the visit? "I think she was hoping that I could be her therapist. She seems unhappy with Dr. Venture."

"That's odd. She's never said anything to me."

"I'm meeting with him on Monday. Maybe he'll be able to shine some light on why Tori would be unhappy with therapy. I'll tell Tori that you would like her to call when she's on her way home."

The woman thanked her and Audrey hung up. Ten minutes later, having eaten one cookie, and with three more for the road, Tori apologized to them all for interrupting their Saturday, and pulled on her coat.

"It was nice to meet you," Alisha told her.

Tori smiled. "Same. Maybe I could call you sometime?"

Alisha grinned. "Sure!" the girl enthused.

Audrey wasn't thrilled with the idea, but she couldn't say anything at the moment, and she couldn't stop Tori from calling. She'd tell Alisha what was okay to talk about and what wasn't, and she'd make sure she didn't talk about the trial in front of Jake's niece at all so nothing could get repeated. She'd also make sure Alisha didn't give away personal information either—about herself, or Audrey.

She watched as Tori left the house. Behind her, Alisha gushed about how nice Tori was. "She didn't seem messed up at all. She's a little intense, though."

A little, Audrey thought, brow arching. That might be an understatement.

As Tori got into her car, she cast a glance back at the house. Audrey frowned. Was that a smile or a smirk?

"Did you know she's a genius?" Alisha asked. "She told me she tested at 142 on the IQ test."

"Genius is 145 and higher," Audrey corrected, still looking out the window as Tori drove away. It had to have been a smile.

This one's not smarter than you, right? The question rang in Audrey's head. The last time she had her IQ tested, she hit around 130, but another time she'd scored lower. They were all subjective. Hell, there were times when she couldn't even do simple math. Was the killer smarter than her? Maybe. Probably, but Audrey wasn't going to admit that to a teenage girl.

"Neil Le Duc," she murmured, staring out into the fading afternoon.

"What was that?" Jake asked.

She shook her head as she turned away from the window. "Nothing." She smiled. "There better be some cookies left for me."

He offered her one with a smile. She took it, and listened to Alisha run through a list of movies they could watch as she chewed. Not even the melted chocolate of perfect chocolate chip cookies could completely distract her thoughts.

What was it about Tori that reminded her of a kid who got off on torturing animals?

* * *

"Did she make it home?" Jake asked a few hours later when Audrey checked her phone. They were alone in the kitchen making dinner together.

"Yes, thank God." She set her phone on the counter with the intention of not looking at it again until the next morning. "I didn't see that coming at all. I'm sorry she showed up here."

He handed her a red pepper to cut up. "Just be glad Lish was here. I wouldn't have known what the hell to do with her on my own."

"I don't have a lot of experience with PTSD, but it can result in some pretty erratic behavior. I'll have to tell Will about it. For Christ's sake, the girl was supposed to have police watching over her."

"Obviously, she ditched them. Her coming here, though, is that some kind of..." He twirled a paring knife through his fingers as he looked up. "What do you call it...transference?"

"I hope not." She peeled the grocery store sticker from the dark red pepper. "She does seem to be especially interested in the fact that I killed someone."

Jake sliced into an onion and shot her a smile. "Why would anyone find *that* interesting?"

She rolled her eyes at him. "Most people don't just boldly bring it up. Tori told me part of the reason she came here was to see the town where I killed someone."

The blade of his knife made short work of the onion. "What's that all about do you think? She can't be afraid of you, or she wouldn't have come here."

"Not necessarily." She cut the stem out of the pepper. "Some people with PTSD fly right into the face of things they should fear. Maybe she needed to see the difference between me, and Monroe and his partner."

"I would think that's abundantly clear." He dumped the onion into the pan on the stove. It sizzled when it hit the melting butter.

Audrey shrugged. "I don't know. Maybe she's romanticized what I did. It's all just speculation without her here to tell the truth."

"You mean you don't have all the answers? I'm disappointed in you, Doctor."

"It has to happen sometimes; otherwise I'm too damn perfect." She put some of the sliced pepper into the bowl beside the cutting board. "Let's talk about something else. I have to deal with this stuff all week, I don't want it to have my weekend too. Bottom line—the poor kid's fucked up, and there's nothing I can do for her. Not now at any rate." And she was going to save her darker thoughts for after talking to Dr. Venture.

"But maybe at another time?"

She shouldn't have said anything. "Neve said something to me today—that I say I want to help these kids but my job is to observe rather than get involved. I told her I wasn't good at counseling, but maybe she's right. Maybe I'm afraid. She reminded me that I got into this job because *I* was one of those fucked-up kids. I didn't forget it, but I've been pretending that the letters after my name somehow make me different and separate me from them."

Jake's smile was lopsided and sympathetic. "You're still one of 'em, Aud. Me too, but I'm no help to anybody. If you want to help them, then help them."

"I'm not sure I can do that in my current position."

"I don't know the woman, but from what I've seen, Angeline is fairly indulgent where you're concerned, which means you're valuable to her. That gives you leverage."

"I'm not going to extort my boss."

He dumped the pepper in with the onion. "All you have to do is ask. Extortion can come later if she says no."

Audrey laughed. "Right. It's been a while since I've done any clinical work. I'd have to brush up. Maybe take some classes again. Start out light."

"Trying to talk yourself out of it, or into it?"

"Not sure. So the pepper's done. What do you want me to do next?"

He slipped a finger through one of the belt loops on her jeans and tugged her closer. "C'mere."

She didn't put up a fight. When he put his arms around her, she wound hers around him. His hazel eyes were clear as she gazed into them, shifting from gold to green and flecks of every shade in between.

"You should do whatever makes you happy," he told her.

She smiled. "*You* make me happy."

"If that ever changes, promise me you'll tell me. I'm not very good at keeping the people I love, and I don't want to lose you again."

An invisible weight pressed hard against Audrey's chest. She could kick Lincoln in the balls for walking out on him like their mother had, the asshole. She'd been so wrapped up in the trial and the Lewis girl's murder to think about what he'd been going through.

Everyone Jake had ever loved left him—either by walking out or dying, and she wasn't terribly sure that he recognized the difference deep inside. She'd walked away from him fourteen years ago, but he'd made her do it. At least she came back.

"You're not going to lose me," she promised. It wasn't hard at all to make the promise. Nothing either of them ever did had been able to change that. "You're the best man I've ever known."

"I've done bad things, Aud."

"Anything worse than murder?" she asked.

He blinked. For a second he looked startled. "No."

"Then we're good." She kissed him and stepped back. She grabbed a zucchini from the stack of vegetables to cut up for stir-fry. "I wanted to kill Neve for taking me to Stillwater this morning. I think she was prepared to knock me out if she had to."

"And yet no blood was shed."

"No. I'm glad I went. It was good to see Bailey and talk to her."

"How's she doing?"

The blade of the knife slid through the vegetable like it was nothing. "All right. I think she's going to be fine, with some therapy, of course."

"If you hang up your shingle, she's going to want you to be her doctor."

"Hang up my shingle?" She couldn't stop the smile that pulled at her lips. "Do people even say that anymore?"

"Actually, smart-ass, they do. It's in the Urban Dictionary."

"Well, look at you being all hip and with it."

"Is this what the rest of our lives is going to be? You mocking me for having an old man's vocabulary in addition to his clothes?"

"If you're lucky," she replied, appreciating just how sexy he looked in his suspenders and jeans.

He turned on another burner and set a pot of water for the noodles on it. "I can live with that. Nice avoidance on the Bailey issue."

"Thanks. I thought it pretty smooth."

They ate dinner in the living room while watching a TV show on Netflix. They were working their way through *Justified*. Both of them identified way too much with both Raylan and Boyd. Halfway through a piece of coconut cream pie as big as her head, Audrey heard her phone ring.

"Are you going to get that?" Jack asked, pressing Pause on the remote.

She shook her head. "Nope. If it's family and important, they'll call the house phone. Anything else can wait."

"It might be Grant."

"Then I'm really in no hurry to pick it up." It would only be bad news. "Play the show. I want to see how Raylan gets out of this."

Jake did, and she was grateful. All she wanted was a few hours of not worrying about her mother, or her father's drinking, or a psychotic killer, or a game-playing serial rapist, or teenage girls who teetered on the verge of broken. Was that too much to ask?

Her phone stopped ringing.

Apparently it wasn't.

CHAPTER SIXTEEN

Sunday brought breakfast with Yancy and Alisha, followed by some time with Jessica and the girls. Audrey and her sister called David in New York and discussed arrangements for helping out with their mother after her surgery. He was prepared to take time off to do his part, God love him. Audrey couldn't say how long she was going to be needed in Portland, but she could promise to be home as much as possible, and that she would take some time off to stay with Anne when everything was over.

"It's not like you're part of the investigation, are you?" Jessica asked later, while making them a pot of tea. Olivia was napping and Isabel was playing in her room.

Audrey took a pan of scones out of the oven and set it on the stove top. "Not really, though the ADA's consulted with me in regards to a profile of the killer. God, these smell good."

Her sister's eyes widened. "You can do that? Like on TV?"

Audrey took a step back, holding up her potholder-covered hands. Jess looked manic. "Uh, sorta. It's not really like that."

"That Derek Morgan is so gorgeous." She set the teapot on

the trivet in the center of the table. "You know, you should work for the FBI."

Was she high? "I'm pretty sure the whole murderer thing would work against me."

Jessica paused, a bewildered look on her face. "You know I actually forgot about that?"

"Really? Because you've been pretty mindful of it for almost two decades."

"Yeah, I know." Her older sister laughed as she shook her head. Dark brown waves bounced around her cheeks. "It's good that I didn't think of it, right?"

Audrey shrugged. "Since you're not in a state of denial, I'll say it's good, sure." Really, being able to talk about it without fighting was a major win. Actually, being able to talk to her sister about anything without fighting was a major win. Everything else was just icing.

Color rose high in Jessica's cheeks. "Wow. I didn't realize how often I thought about it until I didn't." She stood there, red-faced, with her hand on her hip. "I'm not sure if I should hug you or hit you. I feel angry and stupid at the same time."

The scones were hot as Audrey picked them up and dropped them on a plate. "I wouldn't recommend taking a swing." She licked white chocolate off her thumb. "I'll kick your ass and then Isabel will want to know why I beat up her mummy."

"There's that. And I just got my nails done." She held them up. "French tips."

"Nice. Yeah, you'd be a fool to put them at risk."

The two of them looked each other in the eye, and started laughing in unison.

Audrey sat down at the table. "I never meant to hurt you or make you angry, you know."

Her sister nodded. "I know. I was so pissed off everyone wanted to talk about you. My baby sister, who stood up to a monster and stopped him for good. Like you were a hero. Or a freak. I never knew if I should be proud or ashamed, and that just made me angrier at you. Then there were people who thought *you* were the monster."

"Yeah, I've met a few of them." She reached for the jar of Devonshire cream. "Fun times."

Jess sat across from her. "I can imagine some people have been incredibly cruel to you."

Audrey glanced up, meeting her sister's direct gaze. "It was worth it."

"You don't regret it at all, do you?"

It was a conversation they'd had before, but this time Jessica sounded legitimately curious rather than accusatory. "If a magic portal to that night opened up right here in the middle of your kitchen, I'd walk through and do it all over again so young me wouldn't have to. Don't confuse regretting an action with living with one, Jess. I don't regret it, but it's cost me plenty. I've had to live with that." Not the least of which was her relationship with her sister.

Jess swallowed. "I think...I think I'm starting to understand."

Audrey smiled. "I can't ask for more than that."

They had tea and two scones each. Audrey vowed to hit the gym when she got back to Portland. Maybe she'd go for a run in the park she and Jake had explored the other day. She needed to do something to offset these trips home because she ate like a monster and didn't do anything more strenuous than sex, and while she and Jake often worked up a sweat, it wasn't a substitute for regular exercise. She was starting to feel soft and squishy, and not in a good way.

She hugged her sister before she left that afternoon. It was a little awkward, but every time they got better at it. They'd called a truce for their mother, and it was going to take time to undo all the damage and hurt they'd done to each other, but they were giving it a good go. Sometimes Audrey thought Jessica was deep in "fake it 'til she makes it" mode, but whatever worked.

Jake had invited her parents up for dinner that night. He said it was so her mother didn't hate him for monopolizing her when she came home, especially since he was spending time with her in Portland. She walked into his house to find him chopping vegetables.

"We've become entirely too domestic," she informed him before kissing his cheek. "Look at you, barefoot in the kitchen. Next thing you know I'll have you knocked up."

"Well, if anybody could do it, it would be you," he drawled. "Leave the carrots alone."

She crunched into the pilfered vegetable. "Whatcha makin'?"

"Boiled dinner. I picked up a nice ham."

"I haven't had that in years."

"Neither have I. I figured your mum and dad probably grew up with it. Apple pie for dessert."

"I'm definitely going to have to hit the hotel gym this week."

"You don't have to eat it," he said with a smile.

Audrey arched a brow. "Might as well tell the sun not to shine, my dar."

Jake hesitated.

"What?" she asked. "What's wrong?"

He shook his head, but there was a flush high on his cheeks. "You haven't called me that in a long time."

"Dar" was his grandmother's term. A mash of "dear" and "darling" that she reserved for the few people she truly liked. Jake and Audrey had used the term when they were young. In fact, she'd called him that right up until the night he screwed Maggie, and not since.

"It felt right," she said, frowning at his expression. He looked more freaked out by the term of endearment than he had been when she'd told him she loved him. Maybe he just accepted her love as a fact, like she knew he loved her.

"Aud . . ." He wiped his hands on a dish towel, turning so that the small of his back was against the sideboard. "There's something I need to tell you—"

Her phone rang. She ignored it. "What is it?"

"You should get that," he said. "I'll wait."

Her frown deepened as she walked over to where she'd hung her purse and reached inside. If it was Tori, she was going to lose her shit. The kid had texted her last night to thank her for being so nice and apologizing for dropping in on them. It had read like she was trying to make Audrey feel bad.

Audrey didn't like feeling bad.

She glanced at the screen. It was Will. She swiped her thumb across the screen. "Will?"

"Amber Gale," he blurted out. He sounded like he was in shock.

Panic gripped her chest. "Is she dead?"

"Not yet, but he's got her, Audrey. The bastard's got her."

Amber had been the correct choice out of Ian's original three. It had to be either her or Petra. Petra was far more damaged, but Amber was more poetic. She had been the original "girl that got away" from Ian. She hadn't started his obsession with sexually possessing pretty blue-eyed blondes—his cousin Colleen got that honor. Colleen, who had died at age 19 on the 23rd of April. Killing Amber, his special girl, was the perfect way to remind Ian which one of them was smarter. Superior.

Did Audrey know that Amber was gone yet? Was she worried about the sweet girl she'd interviewed only the week before? Honestly, Audrey Harte was proving to be a disappointment. She was supposed to be smart. It took brains to get a Ph.D. two years earlier than most people did. Brains and determination. All those summer classes, and a full course load every year. She pushed herself academically, but not so much in the real world.

She spent most of her professional career in the shadow of Dr. Angeline Beharrie. Outside of that show she'd been on, she hadn't done anything on her own until she helped solve that murder in Edgeport earlier in the summer. That, and her own past, was supposed to make her a respectable opponent, but so far, the psychologist hadn't done much more than stand around wringing her hands. It was frustrating. Ian had been the one to first call what they did a game. It had been silly at the time, but it fit. Not all games were silly and only for children. There were some games that required a great deal of patience and strength. Some that had a great deal at stake—like a person's life or freedom. Audrey was supposed to be a champion.

Maybe she needs better incentive.

Maybe Dr. Harte would get in the game if the life of someone she loved was at stake.

There was a knock on the door. It opened to reveal a familiar blonde with wide blue eyes. Pretty. Very pretty.

"What are you doing here?"

"I want to talk to you about Ian. He said I could find you here."

"Did he?" Of course he would turn traitor, the spineless bastard. "You'd better come in then."

The leggy blonde entered the cottage. She took one look at the girl passed out and tied up on the sofa and whirled around. "What the hell—"

A frying pan to the head shut her up—dropped her like a sack of shit.

So nice of Ian to send a gift.

Audrey left for Portland before Jake on Monday. She was going to get spoiled, spending all this time with him. She'd take all she could get. Once winter hit, there would be weekends she didn't make it home, or that he wouldn't be able to come to her.

She was tempted to stop at the state prison, but even if Monroe put her back on his list, visitation was only Thursday through Sunday, so she wouldn't be able to get in without making an appointment through the DA's office. Will might be able to pull some strings to get her in, but there was no guarantee Ian would help them.

Whatever. Audrey wanted Amber returned home safely, but she wasn't a cop, or lawyer, or any kind of agent. She had no idea how to conduct an investigation, and knew her best place to be was out of the frigging way. The FBI gave her the squirms, so she tried to avoid them as much as possible, the creepy bastards. Anita was one thing, but Will had told her more agents had arrived in Portland, their one goal to find Amber Gale.

So she was back to assessments and interviews, which suited her just fine. Will had no business dragging her into the investigation, really. She didn't resent him for it, but she could have done without seeing Natashya Lewis's corpse.

God, she hoped Amber was alive. It was probably a futile hope, and she knew it, but still . . .

Her phone rang. She'd made sure she had her Bluetooth set up before leaving Jake's dooryard.

"Hello?"

"Dr. Harte?" It was a man's voice—one she didn't recognize.

"Yes. And you are?"

"Owen Scott. My wife, Nancy, said you'd like to speak to me."

Ah, yes. The often absent Mr. Scott. "I do. I'd like to discuss the Ian Monroe trial and Tori's involvement in it with you. Is it possible for us to meet in person?"

"I really don't think that's going to be possible. I'm on the road for the next two weeks."

That was inconvenient. "What is it you do, Mr. Scott? In the file it says you work for a company called Adapteon."

"I'm a pharmaceutical rep," he replied. "It takes me away from home a fair bit. To be honest, that's for the best."

"I see."

"No, you really don't. I can tell from your tone of voice you think I'm an awful man who has walked out on his wife and daughter, just when both of them need him most."

"Actually, Mr. Scott, I wasn't thinking anything of the sort." And she wasn't. She just hadn't known what else to say. Of course, now she wanted to ask him if he thought of himself that way.

"I wish I could believe that. I also wish I felt more guilt for leaving them alone, but I don't. I feel lucky, Dr. Harte."

Fuck. He might as well be laid out on a sofa in front of her. She could smoke a pipe and ask about his childhood. "Why's that?" It was no use; she was too nosy not to ask.

"Because there are a lot of lies in that house. I've never been much of a liar. There are times I've wished I was better at it, but I just never got the hang. My wife lies like breathing, Doctor. It just rolls out of her, and Tori's the same way. I stood there and watched them lie to the FBI, and I knew they expected me to lie too."

A ball of dread had taken form in her stomach, and slowly rolled upward into her chest. Lying to the feds was a serious offense. "What did they lie about?"

He laughed—a dry, papery sound. "You mean what did *we* lie about. We lied about Tori and Ian's relationship."

The ball took up her entire torso now. It pressed against her lungs, making it hard to breathe. If the road wasn't practically deserted, she'd pull off to the side. "Tori and Ian were friends?" She knew they had gone to school together, so it made sense that they would know each other, probably even hang out.

"Friends?" Mr. Scott echoed. His voice was rough. "They weren't just friends, Dr. Harte. Tori and Ian were dating."

Audrey grabbed lunch at Panera, which she figured was healthier than a drive-thru.

She sat at a table in the back, eating a salad and wondering what the hell to do with the information Mr. Scott had given her. That Tori and her mother had lied about her relationship with Ian was as disturbing as it was understandable. Saying they were involved would take away from what Ian had done to Tori. People would assume she was willing, even if she was underage at the time. The girl probably felt stupid for not realizing earlier what Ian was. Audrey could relate to that. Nancy Scott probably wanted to protect her daughter as much as she could, knowing that the media would make Tori "The Boy Scout's Unsuspecting Girlfriend." The only thing worse than being a victim was being thought a stupid one. Now her derisive remark about Alisha being naive made sense.

No wonder Monroe asked her about Tori. He knew she'd lied. Had she lied about not knowing who his partner was? It didn't change that she was a victim, but it was going to give the defense something to use against them.

She was going to have to tell Will and Anita about this. She couldn't let them get to court and get blindsided by Monroe's defense. This, on top of Natashya Lewis's murder and Amber's abduction, was going to hit Will hard.

Christ, she wished she hadn't agreed to be involved in the trial. There was no getting out of it now—she was neck deep and sinking.

She finished her salad—it took a lot more than fucked-up teenagers to put her off her feed, unfortunately—and then she drove to Dr. Venture's office, which wasn't far from the USM campus. She parked in a lot near the building, and found Dr. Venture's suite number on the board just inside the front door. An elevator ride and a couple of turns down a corridor later, she entered the spacious and serenely decorated waiting area. There were three other people in the surprisingly comfortable-looking chairs. One was reading a magazine while the other two were engrossed in their phones.

"Dr. Audrey Harte," she told the woman behind the glass partition. "I have an appointment with Dr. Venture."

"Oh, yes." The woman—whose hair was the exact shade of blond that Audrey's first Barbie had sported—smiled. "Just have a seat and I'll let him know you're here."

Audrey thanked her and sat down. Knowing that sometimes sessions could run over, she took her phone out of her purse and checked for a text or e-mail from Will. There weren't any, which she was going to take as good news. No text meant that, for the moment, Amber Gale was still alive. Or at least she could pretend that's what it meant, and not that they just hadn't found her yet.

"Dr. Harte?"

She looked up. Standing before her was an African-American man with a shaved head and a goatee in a suit that fit him like it had been made to order. Very sharp.

Audrey stood and offered her hand. "Dr. Venture. Thank you for seeing me."

He smiled and opened the door to the inner office for her. "My office is the last on your right."

The corridor was painted pale blue-gray, with a thick cream-colored carpet and black-and-white photographs of Maine landscapes on the walls. Very nice. Angeline would give the decor a big thumbs-up.

Venture's office was just as impressive as he was. Dark furniture, a large desk, and a handful of diplomas on the wall, along with framed x-rays of inorganic items.

"Is this a Prada boot?" she asked, pointing to one that caught her eye.

Venture chuckled. "It is. My wife gave me all of these. She's a doctor. She'd like your boots."

"Fluevogs," Audrey replied, setting her bag on the floor. "I like to wear interesting footwear."

"Isn't that a saying? 'Life's too short to wear boring shoes'? Please, have a seat."

"If it's not, it should be." She sat down in an overstuffed

leather armchair. "So, of course I want to be respectful of doctor-patient confidentiality, but want to talk to you about Tori Scott's ability to testify at Ian Monroe's trial."

"Yes, of course. Tori and I have talked extensively about what happened when Monroe held her captive. Six months ago I would have been uncertain of her ability to repeat those details in front of a courtroom, but now I am almost entirely certain she would have no trouble in front of an audience."

"Really? What sort of therapy have you been doing to bring about such an improvement?"

"Oh, nothing out of the ordinary for someone having experienced violent sexual trauma, but having been her doctor for almost a year, I feel quite confident when I tell you that what you need to worry about when Tori takes the stand isn't whether or not she can testify—you need to worry about whether or not any of it is the truth."

Could this day get any worse? Audrey tilted her head. "I beg your pardon?"

"Have you ever treated someone with antisocial personality disorder, Dr. Harte?"

"I'm not a clinical psychologist. Dr. Venture, are you telling me Tori has APD?"

"Of course not, that would be a breach of confidentiality." His mouth said the words, but his gaze said something else altogether. She hadn't expected any of this. Yes, Tori had said some things that gave her pause, but APD? Sociopaths and psychopaths fell into that categorization.

Neil Le Duc eyes.

"If you haven't treated the disorder, you've interviewed people who have it, yes?"

"Well, yeah. There were probably a couple I didn't pick up on. They can be very good at hiding the condition."

He nodded. "They can be, but their cruelty and ego always come out eventually."

"The facade is difficult for them to maintain." Where exactly was he going with this?

"Take Ian Monroe, for example. I'm sure you've seen through his pretense. Of course, they often spot their own kind before any of us can, despite all our training."

He was definitely telling her that Tori had APD. Jesus. It was no wonder Audrey's warning bells went off at some of her behavior. She'd thought she was being paranoid and second-guessing herself because of Bailey, but this time her instincts had been right.

There was something wrong with Tori Scott. However, that didn't mean she hadn't suffered at the hands of Ian Monroe.

"Of course, we as medical professionals have a duty to protect our patients. We cannot divulge any crimes our patients have confessed to us."

Audrey frowned. Was he leading her? "It's almost universally accepted in the industry that we can break confidentiality if we think the client is a danger to themselves or someone else."

"Yes, entirely. It's what made me call you and arrange a meeting. It's not my patient for whom I'm worried."

Okay, so he wasn't going to just come out and say it, because he was concerned about breaching the code under which most mental health professionals operated. She was going to have to get it out of him, and she wasn't asking the right questions. Why the hell didn't he make this easier on both of them? "Dr. Venture, if you think Tori is going to hurt someone, you need to notify that person and the authorities."

"Yes, I know. That's why I'm telling you."

"I'm only working with the DA's office and the police in an advisory position. I can't report this for you."

"I'm aware of that, Dr. Harte." He sighed. "What the hell, I'm telling you this because I believe *you* are the person Tori Scott intends to harm."

CHAPTER SEVENTEEN

"Did Tori actually tell you she wanted to hurt me?" Audrey was surprisingly calm after Dr. Venture dropped his little bomb in her lap.

"Tori is a very smart young woman. Have you ever interviewed someone who is careful not to cross certain lines but flaunt others?"

"Yes." For someone who was supposed to be asking the questions, she was doing an awful lot of answering, and her mind was swimming. It felt like the mental equivalent to riding the Scrambler at the fair.

"Isn't it fascinating that some people we would classify as psychopaths keep some things close to their chest and other times brag about their superiority? For example, you might treat a young woman who tells you in generalized terms that she wishes someone might get hurt, but then give you every detail about how she once delighted in torturing a middle school teacher."

Audrey nodded. "Most know we can't reveal what they've told us they've done, but that we might report what they plan to do."

"Yes. She might say she wishes a certain person would get

hit by a car. Or that maybe if she hit the person with a base-ball bat, it might knock sense into her." His dark gaze became more pointed. "She also might say how the person makes her so angry she has fantasies about wrapping a scarf around her neck and tightening it until the person's eyes start to bulge. She might fantasize about doing this over and over to the person until she finally sees the light drain from her eyes."

Audrey's throat constricted as she swallowed. Strangulation? Was that a particularly dark coincidence? Had Tori chosen that method for her fantasies because of what Monroe had done to her? She couldn't ask Dr. Venture if Tori had ever confided in him about hurting someone, or what he knew about her inter-actions with Ian Monroe. It was obvious he wasn't going to give any of that up without a warrant. That was Anita's problem.

"I wonder if such a person might seek the company of like-minded people?" she said, using his own tactic. "Perhaps some-one a little older who could help realize her fantasies."

The glimmer in his gaze confirmed that she asked the right question. "I would think she might, if the opportunity pre-sented itself, but it's all guesswork, isn't it? We can only work with what we're given." A tight smile curved his lips. "An unknowing person might become an object of our hypothetical psychopath's obsession, which would have started before they even met. That obsession might intensify as they become bet-ter acquainted, until the patient spends an entire session talk-ing about nothing but the object of their focus—details of their life, both past and present, and the ever-growing urge to prove herself superior to that person."

Tori had been sharp with her on occasion, and there had been times when things she'd said hadn't sat right, but she'd chalked them up to the PTSD. Then there was that look she'd had on her face when she left Jake's on the weekend. That secretive, smug smile.

This one's not smarter than you, right?

No. She could not be dealing with another murderous teenage girl. It was the plot of a crazy movie or a crime drama. It wasn't real life. Tori had been Ian's victim. If she was unbalanced now, it was because of him.

But a psychopath? People didn't just turn into one of those because they'd been through something terrible and survived. It was usually present at birth, and it was very difficult to diagnose someone as a psychopath when they were under the age of eighteen. Tori was seventeen now. She'd been fifteen when the initial murders took place. That was young. So young.

You were younger than that when you killed Clint.

Yes, she had been, but she'd killed Clint to protect Maggie, and other girls in Edgeport. Clint Jones was a pedophile and an all-around douche bag. It hadn't given her pleasure to bash his head in. Sure, there had been power in it. She had been a young girl, and she brought down a full-grown man. She was the hero, and she'd liked that feeling—until she saw her mother's face. Until she realized that not everyone agreed that Clint should have died.

"Dr. Venture, are you sure about this?"

"I think you'd better call me Aldous. I've been in this field for twenty-five years, Audrey. Do you mind if I call you that?"

She shook her head. "Of course not."

"I've been in this field for twenty-five years, the first ten of which were in Milwaukee. Can you guess the name of the first psychopath I met?"

She stared at him. Maybe she was a psych nerd, or twisted, or both, but Aldous Venture suddenly became so much more than an attractive older man in a sharp suit who looked way younger than he was; he became a rock star. "Dahmer."

He nodded. "I know how good they can be at lying and faking emotion, but in the end, they are just lying and pretending, and they make mistakes. They get smug and they forget who they're talking to. Eventually they let you see the void inside."

"Do you think she's killing these girls?" It seemed impossible.

Aldous shook his head. "I can't say. And you know I can't divulge anything she's told me that doesn't pertain to you. I've already said far too much that could get me into trouble, but when Mrs. Scott and Tori herself gave me permission to speak to you, I knew I had a moral obligation to warn you. I wouldn't have told you if I didn't believe Tori might actually give in to her urges to harm you. I believe she wanted me to tell you this."

There was a voice—that angry voice—in the back of her head that wanted to tell him he didn't need to be concerned— she could take a seventeen-year-old girl. A seventeen-year-old psychopath who had shown up on Jake's doorstep and wanted to be friends with Alisha.

Blond, blue-eyed, beautiful Alisha.

Fuck.

"What else did she say she wanted to do to me?"

He grimaced. "Let me get my notes. I document every session."

While he went to the filing cabinet and started sorting through it, Audrey took out her phone and texted Will. *CALL ME. URGENT.* And then, to Alisha: *HAVE NO CONTACT WITH TORI SCOTT. IF SHE CALLS OR TEXTS, DO NOT PICK UP OR RESPOND. WILL EXPLAIN LATER.*

Aldous returned to his seat. He had a fairly thick file folder in his hands. "I know this must seem terribly old-fashioned to you, but I prefer to take notes longhand. Putting them on a computer makes me paranoid—too easy for someone to access them."

"I'm a big fan of whatever works," she replied. Her gut felt like someone was tying her intestines into intricate knots.

He began at the back of the file, flipping through pages. "Her first mention of you was several weeks ago—when you first made an appointment to stop by her house and interview her the first time. Nothing worrisome was said that day, but the following week she informed me that she had researched you and that you had killed someone when you were thirteen." He looked up at her.

"It's true," she admitted. She wasn't about to start apologizing for it now.

"I believe that was the trigger. She started by saying that she looked forward to meeting you, that you were someone who might understand her. She hoped you would be impressed by her. Then, after your first meeting, she began saying that you had been a disappointment because you wouldn't talk about yourself. She didn't feel that you had a real connection. She said she wanted to punch you in 'her lying mouth.' After that, it began to ramp up. 'I'd like to hit her in the head like she did the guys she killed until her brains spilled out.'"

"That paints a vivid picture," Audrey remarked. There was a chill just under her skin that made her shiver.

"It does. In addition to the remark about strangling you, she also expressed regret that you didn't see her as your equal, that you treated her like a kid. She said, 'If I had her alone, she'd respect me. The fucking bitch wouldn't have a choice. I'd show her which one of us was the real killer.' Finally, she said, 'When I get Audrey Harte alone, only one of us will walk out alive.'" He closed the file. "I need you to understand, Audrey, that you are the only person I've ever heard her talk about this way. She has never threatened anyone else while under my care, or I would have gone to the authorities."

"I believe you." Christ. What was it about her that attracted people who were broken? Was it a pheromone? She'd talked to kids who were killers—a lot of them. She'd been one of them. But every one of the people she'd interviewed had been incarcerated, or recently released. She'd never had someone show her the blood on their hands and expect her to keep it a secret. Not even Bailey had asked that of her.

Her phone rang. It was Will. She told Aldous who it was and then answered.

"What's going on?" Will asked.

Audrey looked at the man sitting across from her. He looked a lot closer to his age now that they'd talked. There was a weariness around his eyes she hadn't noticed before. "I'm with

Dr. Aldous Venture, Tori Scott's psychiatrist. He needs to report that Tori has threatened someone's life."

"Whose?" She should have known he'd ask. She probably should have led with that, but she'd hoped that maybe he'd drop what he was doing and come over to find out on his own.

"Mine."

There was silence for a couple of seconds. "Audrey, what the fuck is going on?"

This was a new side of Will. "She's told him she wants to kill me. She also lied about being in a relationship with Ian." Ian who had to be bisexual rather than gay—or he pretended to be gay to set up Barry Lawson. "Will, I think she's our killer."

"No. No goddamn way. She's a kid. A *kid*. She was his victim."

"A kid who had evidence of sexual intercourse, but not of violence. She didn't have a mark on her. She was calm when you found her."

"She was in shock."

"Will, why else would she threaten me? Why else would she say that I'm stupid for not seeing her for what she is? Will, her father—a pharmaceutical rep who she probably stole drugs from to subdue those girls—told me she and Monroe were dating. Look, you don't have to believe me, but you and Anita need to hear what Dr. Venture has to say. You owe it to those dead girls to entertain the idea, and I need you to hear what she's said about me in case something happens."

"In case something happens? What the hell does that mean?"

"I mean in case she tries to follow through on her threats." Strange how calm her voice sounded.

"Jesus Christ." She could picture him rubbing the back of his neck. "I'll be there as soon as I can. I'll call Anita. Don't leave before I get there." He hung up before she could answer.

Audrey smiled wanly at Aldous. "I think you might want to clear your schedule for the rest of the day."

He set the folder on his desk as he rose to his feet. "Already done. You want a drink?"

She leaned back in the chair. "I don't suppose you mean of the alcoholic persuasion?" Oh, where was her father when she needed him?

"No, but I can get you a coffee so strong you won't sleep for a week."

"That'll do."

Barry Lawson was already there when Jake arrived at the gym. He was dressed in sweats and sneakers and ready to fight. Jake quickly changed and met him in the ring.

"Thanks for coming," Lawson said.

Jake shrugged, rolling his shoulders to loosen them. "I've got nowhere I need to be."

His opponent stepped into fighting stance. "Really? No job?"

"I run my own business." There was a tenseness to Lawson's shoulders that made him wary. He'd seen it a lot in his life, especially at Gracie's. The guy was spoiling for violence.

"Must be nice." Lawson took a swing. Jake blocked it. "Being able to set your own hours."

Jake made a half-ass jab that the other man avoided. "It has its perks."

"I imagine it does." A right hook. It connected with Jake's cheekbone. "Like letting you spy for Will Grant." He swung again.

Jake dodged. Had Lawson figured it out? Or was he bluffing? "What are you talking about?"

"Do you think I don't know who you are?" Another hook—Jake saw it coming and stepped aside. "I'm not stupid. I saw you with Audrey Harte last week. I know she's working for the prosecution on the Ian Monroe trial."

Jake went still, gloves up. "You saw us? Have you been watching her?"

Lawson glared at him. "Yes."

Jake punched him in the face. Hard. "You make poor life choices." He was going to have to knock him out until the police could arrive. He didn't have any zip ties or rope to truss him up.

Lawson stumbled backward into the ropes. He didn't come back swinging. He just kind of hung there, defeated and bleeding from the nose. He looked up at Jake—there were tears in his eyes. "Why can't you people just leave me alone? Haven't I suffered enough? Paid enough? Ian Monroe set me up. I've lost friends, the respect of my peers. It doesn't matter that he was arrested; people look at me like I'm a monster. He ruined my life." He started to sob.

Jake was probably less uncomfortable than he ought to have been. One thing was certain—this guy wasn't a killer. "C'mon, man. You don't want to do this here. Let's get some paper towel and ice for your nose. Nobody looks attractive with blood and snot running down their face."

Lawson laughed, which was oddly heart-wrenching when mixed with a choked sob.

Lifting the top rope, Jake helped the other man out of the ring and into the locker room, where he wet a handful of paper towels in the sink. He squeezed the water out and handed the damp mass to Lawson. "This will help. Tilt your head back."

"You'd think I'd be used to getting hit," the teacher muttered, nasal and muffled.

Jake dried his hands on another piece of paper towel. "Been beat up a lot?"

"I hadn't been in a fight since high school when Ian set me up to take the heat off himself. After that I got punched, kicked, or slapped almost every time I left the house. Four of my students cornered me after school one day because they thought I'd raped and killed those girls. I think they would have killed me if the principal hadn't intervened."

"People are pretty quick to act when they're threatened or trying to protect their own."

Lawson rolled his eyes above the paper towel. "No shit. You just tried to smash my nose through the back of my skull."

Jake shrugged. He didn't feel like apologizing either, but he supposed he should. "I shouldn't have hit you so hard."

"Like I said, you'd think I'd be used to it. Let me guess, they asked you to snoop around and see if I had anything to do with these new murders?"

"No one asked me to do anything," he corrected. If Lawson tried to make trouble for Grant, the teacher wasn't going to have him to thank for it. "And yeah, I wanted to check you out. Audrey was getting some creepy, anonymous attention and I wanted to make sure it wasn't you." That sold the story a little better. "You don't exactly make it easy for people to think you're innocent, you know that?"

"I know. I'm distrustful and defensive."

"Maybe if you came out of the closet, you'd be more relaxed."

Lawson took the paper towel away from his face. Jake winced. His nose was already swollen. He looked around the room. Jake didn't have to look to know they were alone. "How do you know about that? Have you been following me?"

"No. I'm just observant." *And I saw the photos on your phone.* "You know admitting the truth could have taken some of the heat off you."

"I know." Lawson dabbed at his nose, wiping away the blood. "But I couldn't do it. My father would have a shit hemorrhage."

"So you pretend."

"Yeah. I made a few inappropriate remarks about girls—women—at school to sell it. It convinced people I was straight—a dog even—but it's also made me look like a pervert. I really need to give it up. It's given me an ulcer."

Jake nodded. "Being gay isn't that big a deal anymore. I'd prefer that to being thought a psycho."

"You say that, but I bet you've never had a guy threaten to beat you to death because you hit on him."

"Christ. No wonder you want to learn how to fight."

The other man laughed—a raw, bitter sound. "Exactly."

"Well, all right, let's go. The bleeding stopped?"

"You tell me." He moved the paper from his face, lifting his chin so Jake could inspect.

Jake surveyed the damage. He didn't think the nose was broken. "Looks like it. Back in the ring, then. I'm going to teach you how to protect yourself."

"Why?"

Jake's smile was grim. "Because no one else is going to."

Will wasn't happy. Anita really wasn't happy, and both of them seemed to hold Audrey responsible for it, even though she had even less reason to be joyous than they. They were in a conference room just down the hall from Venture's office.

"Hey," she finally said to Will after he'd given her what her father would call "the stink eye" for the third time. "I didn't ask for this when I signed on either."

"I should have known hiring you was a bad idea. I thought you'd bring a higher profile to the case, get it more attention. I should have known it would blow up in my face."

Had they been alone, and maybe in Edgeport, Audrey could have punched him without any witnesses. Instead, she had to keep her fists clenched by her sides. "If not for me, you wouldn't even know she was Monroe's partner because your office assumed a little girl couldn't be a killer."

He glared at her. Rationally, she knew he was more angry with himself and the situation than with her, but none of them were feeling very rational at that moment.

"We still don't know it's the Scott girl," Anita said.

Audrey frowned. "You will once that warrant for Venture's notes clears. Trust me." As soon as she'd heard Venture mention that Tori wanted to strangle her, she'd known the truth. It had taken a while to sink in, but she believed it now.

Will shook his head. His hair was a mess and his tie askew. "It can't be. Tori Scott is *not* a psychopath."

Anita glanced at him. "Saying it doesn't make it real, Will. Even if you're right, it doesn't change that she's threatened Audrey. Female serials are rare, but they're out there, and they're just as bad as their male counterparts." She turned to Audrey. "I've been doing some reading." Audrey managed a small smile.

"How did you miss this?" Will demanded, whirling around to confront Anita. He had a wildness about his features that needed to be addressed; he was losing it. "Jesus Christ, she's made fools of us all."

Audrey put her hand on his arm. "Will. *Will.*"

"What?" he barked.

Oh, that was enough of that. She scowled. "Pull yourself together. I agree this sucks, and I know it's terrible that your star witness was probably Monroe's partner, and we're all going to take some heat for it, but now you can get her too."

Anita nodded. "Her DNA was at the cabin—we overlooked

it because we thought she was Monroe's victim. We found it in the classroom where Natashya Lewis was left, but shrugged it off because she has a class in that room."

"How could a young girl pull this off?" Will asked of them. "How?"

"Young doesn't mean weak," Audrey told him. "When I was her age, I could carry another girl my size over my shoulder. She had Monroe to help with the first victims, but she picked Natashya up in a car. Probably drugged her."

"Right. You mentioned the father's a rep for Big Pharma."

Audrey nodded. She didn't think there was anything "Big" about Mr. Scott's company, but that didn't matter. "She's also got a small pharmacy's worth of anti-anxiety medication in her house. Probably sleeping pills too. It wouldn't take much to knock out someone who has never or rarely used them."

"She's a seventeen-year-old girl," Will insisted.

"She's a psychopath," Audrey countered. "She has no empathy, no remorse. Whatever sensation she gets from killing is one of the few things that she can really feel. You can't use *who* she is to understand *what* she is."

"We're a bit ahead of ourselves, aren't we?" Anita asked. "We haven't proved this kid is who we're looking for, and we can't until we see those records."

"The juvenile judge should return my call soon." Will took his phone off his belt and looked at it, as though he could magically make it ring.

"I should probably go," Audrey said to no one in particular. "It has to be against procedure for me to be here when you get the records. Dr. Venture did his duty by informing me, and he's going to have to inform the Scotts."

"We can do that when we go to talk to the girl," Anita retorted.

Audrey held up her hands. "You guys are the law, do what you've got to do." She turned to Will. "I should probably remove myself from the Monroe trial. I'm definitely too close." And when they arrested Tori, she'd be a witness. Too many conflicts of interest for her to continue on now.

And to be honest, she wanted to get as far away from this clusterfuck as she could. She'd call Angeline, explain everything to her, and then arrange to take time off to be with her mother. Honestly, it was a bit of a relief, even though she felt awful for thinking that way. She'd hide out in Edgeport and try to avoid the press. This was the second murder investigation she'd gotten sucked into in four months, of course they were going to jump on that.

Will nodded. He was beginning to look more himself. "Audrey, I owe you an apology for what I said a few minutes ago, and for getting you involved in this whole mess."

"Don't worry about it." She gave him a half smile. She liked Will, and she was trying not to take his earlier remarks to heart. "Instead of worrying about how this might look, why not think of how it will look that you helped apprehend a teenage serial-killing duo?"

His gaze turned slightly hopeful. "I can try her as an adult as well."

"That would be my recommendation." Someone as twisted

as Tori looked to be needed to be put away in maximum security rather than a juvenile facility. "Let me know if you find Amber alive?"

He nodded.

She said good-bye to Anita. On the way out, she ran into Dr. Venture and gave him her card in case he needed to get in touch. He probably already had the information, but it made her feel like she was doing something useful.

She was just about to get on the elevator when her phone rang. It was Jake.

"Hey," she said. "Are you in Portland?"

"Yeah. Aud, are you with Grant and that cop?"

"Just leaving them. God, you won't believe what happened—"

"*Aud.*"

Audrey stopped talking. The elevator doors slid shut without her. "What's wrong?"

"Go back and tell them to come to the hotel."

"Jake, why? What's happened?" She turned and started back toward Dr. Venture's office.

"I've found your missing girl."

CHAPTER EIGHTEEN

The first thing Jake noticed when he opened the door to the suite was the smell. He'd smelled it before when he and his grandfather had gone to check on Adele Pelletier after a particularly vicious snowstorm eighteen years ago. Her daughter hadn't heard from her and couldn't get out to check. He and his grandfather had gone back to the Ridge on snowmobiles, instinctively knowing where they were going despite the occasional whiteout. They'd found her dead in her bed, where she'd been for three days.

He used his elbow to flick the light switch, and kept his duffel bag over his shoulder as he slowly approached the bedroom, careful where he stepped. The lights were off in the bedroom, but the drapes were partially open. As soon as he saw the girl's legs, he stopped and dug out his cell. Thank Christ it had been he who'd found her and not Audrey.

He went back out into the corridor and called her. Normally, he would have called the cops, but that girl had to be the one they were looking for—why else would she be in Audrey's room? Grant would be able to get the cops and feds here quicker than a call to 911 would. If they didn't find the crazy doing this soon, he was going to declare open season and find the fucker himself.

How the hell had the killer gotten into the suite without a key? Had they, like Christopher James, waited for housekeeping to come by? Maybe it had been James. He could be out on bail after sneaking in the week before.

Jake leaned his back against the wall. He couldn't have been wrong about Lawson. The guy was a whiner and a bit of an ass, but he wasn't a killer. People said that anyone could be a killer if in the right circumstances, but that was bullshit, spewed to make people feel they could protect their loved ones if someone broke into their house or tried to carjack them. The truth was that some people just didn't have it in them to kill, and Lawson was one of those people. The world was probably a better place with people like him in it, but Jake wasn't in any hurry to be the guy's friend. He was much more comfortable with people who either had his back or wanted to stick a knife in it. People with whom you knew where you stood.

The person who'd left that poor girl in Audrey's suite killed for fun. He knew a few guys in Edgeport who hunted deer or moose, even bear for that same reason—they just liked to shoot things. They were also fucking idiots. The person who had done *this* wasn't an idiot.

He checked his e-mail and his texts. Still nothing from Lincoln—not that he expected to hear from his brother. Linc had developed a habit of checking in and out of Jake's life over the years. He'd be back...someday. Whether or not he'd bring trouble with him was anyone's guess. Blackmailing bastard. If he was worth a goddamn, he would be glad Yancy would never have to put up with Matt Jones and his fists ever again. In a perfect world, he'd praise his little brother for making the call. In a perfect world, Lincoln would have been the one to make that call, as was his duty as the oldest.

He'd been standing there, thinking too long, when the elevator dinged. He turned his head, sensing Audrey's presence before he saw or heard her. She stepped into the corridor like she was stepping into battle. That connection he felt with her kicked in the moment their eyes met—an electrical cord into a socket. He straightened. Her steps quickened. His feet wanted to go to her, even though it made no sense when the suite was her destination.

Her blue eye was bright, her amber one dark. "Where is she?" He pointed at the door. She glanced at it, then back to him. "Are you sure it's her?"

"As sure as I can be. As soon as I saw her, I left the suite and called you."

Grant and Grayson were a few steps behind her, along with a man Jake didn't recognize, but knew had to be another fed from the way he carried himself—like he had the biggest dick in the hotel.

Jake pulled the key card from his pocket and handed it to Grayson. "She's in the bedroom. On the bed. And no, I didn't touch anything."

The redhead gave him a nod. "Cannady and I will go in. The rest of you stay out here."

Grant frowned. "Anita—"

She held up her hand. "You're not going in until the room's been processed."

"She's right," Cannady added, not that he needed to—they all knew Grayson was the one in charge. "The fewer people in that room, the better."

When the two of them went in, Audrey shook her head. "I shouldn't have kept the suite for the weekend. I should have checked out, but they gave me a deal on an extended stay."

Jake turned to her with a frown. "Seriously? You're going to try to take responsibility for this?"

Her eyes were wide, but there was a furrow between her eyebrows. "If I hadn't kept the room, she wouldn't have been able to dump Amber here."

"She?"

"Tori Scott. We think she's the killer."

"Can we not broadcast that until we have some proof?" Will asked. He looked ready to pop.

Audrey scowled at him. "Tori went to Jake's house on the weekend looking for me, and after you put him to work on Barry Lawson, I figure he's as much a part of this as I am."

"Except that you're not anymore, remember? You quit."

Jake looked at her. "You quit?"

She nodded. He noticed now that she was a little dark under the eyes. She'd tried to cover it with makeup, but she looked tired. "Tori's psychiatrist told me today that she's talked about wanting to kill me. That's what I was going to tell you when you called."

Her words were a cinder block smashed into his chest, knocking the breath out of his lungs. "Jesus." And he had cut her off, thinking his discovery more important than what she had to say. Nothing was more important than her. *Nothing.*

"I'm too much a part of this now. Any judge would question my ability to be impartial and credible as an expert witness now that my safety has been threatened. Death threats have a way of turning a girl's head."

Always the smart-ass. Jake didn't speak. None of his words were ones he wanted Grant to hear. Instead, he put his arm about her shoulders and pulled her close. Then, he pulled out his phone and texted Alisha, suddenly needing to know she was okay. When she answered his message with a series of foolish emojis he breathed a sigh of relief.

The door to the suite opened. Grayson and the agent walked out. She had a strange look on her face. "That's not Amber Gale in there."

Audrey frowned. It was an almost comical expression when mixed with relief. "Who is it?" she and Will demanded in unison.

Grayson shook her head. "It's Margot Temple."

Had Audrey found her surprise yet? Tori wondered as she drove. Amber hadn't broken yet, and she was in a foul mood because of it. She had to leave so she could get home at the right time. Her mother might want to know what she was doing if she discovered that her daughter wasn't at the school she claimed to want to return to. It was no biggie, she still got good grades, and she had learned earlier in life to forge her mother's signature. Her mother probably had no idea how much time she spent in or out of school. The woman had a habit of helping herself to Tori's medication. It didn't matter that Tori didn't bother to take it unless she absolutely had to; it was hers. It was just one more reason for Tori to despise her. She should have killed her years ago, but then she would have been left to her father, and he was smarter than her mother.

Though her mother had been smart enough to lie for her.

She checked her phone. Nothing. Alisha had told her that Audrey planned to return to Portland on Monday. It was almost three in the afternoon and still nothing. Hadn't she made an appointment with Venture for that day as well?

Had he told Audrey what she wanted to do to her? She would have loved to see her face. Grant's too—and that FBI agent's. Had they read her file? Did they know that she'd fooled them all? Were they cursing themselves for being stupid? Or maybe they were in awe of her intelligence. She'd made them believe she was one of Ian's victims, let them believe that she was a fragile little thing, needing to drug herself before she could even leave the house.

Some of it had been incredibly tedious, like dealing with her mother, or people at school. Other times it had been a lesson in patience. How long before they caught up? And then, there had been a few times when she'd been practically livid at how they blatantly discredited her because she was a girl. She was ten times smarter and stronger than Ian, her poor, angry queer.

He tried so hard to make himself like girls, but the only time he could fuck one was if he knew she was going to die afterward.

Why hadn't Ian turned on her yet? He would soon—he'd have to. How could he not when she'd just killed his wife? Obviously he hadn't felt any real emotion for the woman, he'd only been using her, but he would still feel the loss. She'd taken one of his toys and broken it.

In a day or two, she would be the one the papers, magazines, and websites talked about. He'd be eclipsed by her glory. A teenage female serial killer who fooled the cops and psychological experts. The media would go nuts over her. They'd want to interview her, write books about her…

Maybe there'd be a movie. Not one of those made-for-TV pieces of shit, but a *real* big-screen movie. She'd like it if someone like Elle Fanning—talented and pretty—played her. Who would make a good Audrey? Maybe Mila Kunis or Lily Collins.

She had it all planned out, how the movie was going to end. She'd always known that she'd be famous. She wasn't meant for mediocrity, or worse, totally forgettable. This game could have only one winner, and if life in prison was her reward, that was fine by her. It was simple really.

Either she or Audrey Harte was going to die. She'd make sure of it.

The hotel gave Audrey another suite, of course—one that wasn't a crime scene.

"I'm pretty sure they were hoping I'd just leave," she said, setting her computer bag on the floor. At least she had her most important belongings—she'd taken them home for the weekend. She'd done laundry at Jake's and had enough clothes for a couple of days until someone could return what was still in the suite with Margot.

Maybe she'd burn it all.

Not her shoes, though.

"Probably." Jake set her suitcase by the bedroom closet. "I'm sure they're also hoping it doesn't get out that they just let a serial killer stroll through their hotel with a body. She had to walk past the front desk."

"There'd be no reason to stop her if she looked like she belonged here."

Jake slid her a sideways glance. "Would a seventeen-year-old with a big-ass suitcase belong here by herself? Didn't anyone try to help her with her luggage? Ask her what room she was in?"

"I don't know." She sat down on the edge of the bed and rubbed her forehead with her knuckles. "She must have taken the key card from my bag when she came to your place. I knew I had both of them with me when I left. I'll never keep that little envelope with the room number on it again." Stupid. She should be more paranoid than that. She usually was.

"Key card or not, she was still going to kill that woman," Jake reminded her.

She sighed. "Poor Margot. Beaten, strangled, and stuffed into a suitcase." The case had been left in the room with her.

"And left for you to find," Jake reminded her. "Like a cat dropping a mouse in its owner's slipper."

She looked up at him. "Venture said she saw me as her opponent—because I was a killer too."

"You're *nothing* like that psycho."

"I know, but Tori doesn't see it that way. Her end game is to beat me."

She let that sink in. Jake's expression hardened. "You mean she wants to kill you."

"Or be killed by me."

"Fuck."

She forced a smile. "Still want to date me?"

He sat down beside her and took her hand in his. "You're mine and I'm yours, remember. There's no going back, and I don't want to. I do, however, want to kill that little bitch."

She squeezed his fingers. "Me too." And she would—if she had to.

Someone knocked on the door. Jake slowly rose to his feet, letting go of her hand. As he left the bedroom, he picked up a baseball bat that had been leaning against the wall. Where the hell had that come from? Had he brought it with him?

Audrey stayed silent and still, holding her breath. It wasn't until she heard Anita's voice that she breathed a sigh of relief. She stood and went out to the living area.

"What now?" she asked.

Anita met her gaze. "There was a note for you left with the body." She offered Audrey her cell phone. Audrey took it and looked at the screen. In a definitely feminine hand was written, *Audrey, do I have your attention now?*

"I'd say she does." She gave the phone back to Anita.

"I know you're stepping away from the investigation, but until we take Tori Scott into custody, I'd like for you to remain here in Portland."

Audrey nodded. "My mother's sick. I have to go to Edgeport this weekend."

The agent turned her attention to Jake. "You'll be with her?"

He nodded.

She glanced at the bat in his hand. "You wouldn't hesitate to use that, would you?"

"No."

"Good." Back to Audrey. "We got the warrant for Tori's records. A car's been sent to her house to pick her up."

"She's not there," Audrey told her. "She's set this up. Everything has gone according to her checklist. She said those things to Venture knowing he'd be ethically bound to inform me and the authorities. She's got Amber holed up somewhere isolated and safe, where she can take her time. Either today or tomorrow she'll send me a clue."

Anita nodded. "Call me when she does. I don't care if it's three in the morning. Meanwhile we're going to be hunting her."

"Good." But Tori wasn't going to make it easy to find her—not until she was ready.

When she left, Audrey and Jake went back into the bedroom. Audrey flopped onto the bed. Jake joined her after he put the baseball bat aside. "Now what?" he asked.

Audrey stared up at the ceiling. "We wait."

Her phone rang an hour later. It was Anita.

"You were right. Tori's in the wind. We're trying to track her cell phone, but the GPS is off. We've got Nancy Scott's cell and the home line monitored."

"Has Nancy said anything? Maybe where Tori might be hiding?"

"She dissolved into tears when we spoke to her, and has been despondent since. I called the father, but he's in the air right now. I left a message for him to call me as soon as he lands. Hopefully he'll give us something. Meanwhile, sit tight."

Audrey hung up. A feeling of dread had wrapped around her heart and refused to let go. Where the hell was Tori? And what was the little monster going to do next?

No wonder Audrey killed someone. If Tori had grown up in a town as shit-hole-ish as Edgeport, she would have started reveling in carnage at a younger age too.

She sat in her car, just a little way down the road from the turnoff for Tripp's Cove. She had a good view of traffic on both roads—not that there was much to see.

Earlier that morning she'd driven back to Tripp's Cove, past the house where she'd seen Audrey on the weekend, back to what seemed like the end of the goddamn world. She found the little cottage in the woods, and quietly created a little sabotage in the driveway. Nothing big, just something that would take a few minutes to clear up.

She had to assume that Audrey had already warned Alisha to avoid contact with her, but they probably hadn't thought she'd drive all the way to Edgeport again. Little did they know just how convenient the crappy little town was.

A school bus lumbered toward her, slowing down as it passed by. It almost came to a pause at the end of Tripp's Cove, but then sped up and kept going. A few moments later—once the bus was out of sight—an SUV came speeding out the dirt road, its tires kicking up dust. It stopped at the pavement and the passenger door opened. A young girl jumped out. They'd cleaned the mess up faster than she thought—but not fast enough to catch the bus.

Tori smiled when the vehicle turned around and headed back down the road once more. She turned the key in the ignition and pulled out onto the street. She drove past the girl first, then stopped and backed up.

She rolled down the passenger window and leaned over the cup holder to look out. "Hey. You need a ride?"

Alisha didn't return the smile. Audrey *had* warned her. Of course she had. "No, thanks. I'm waiting for the bus."

"The school bus? It already went by. I was paying for gas at the store down there when it went by." She gestured in the direction it had gone. "Jump in. Either we'll catch it, or I'll give you a ride to school."

The girl didn't immediately do as she was told—annoying. "That's okay, really. I'll call my mom to come get me."

Tori forced a smile. "Get in the car."

Alisha took a step back. "No."

Did the little cunt think she'd come unprepared? Tori reached into her purse and pulled out her mother's pistol. She pointed it at Alisha. *"Get. In. The. Fucking. Car."*

The younger girl's face was pale, but there was a defiance in her gaze that pissed Tori off. For a second, she thought Alisha was actually going to make her shoot her. That would ruin everything.

The passenger door opened and Alisha slipped into the car, setting her bag on the floor.

"Seatbelt," Tori instructed. "And your phone."

Alisha punched her. One second she was just sitting there, and the next, something hard plowed into her jaw, and brought blood to her mouth. Fuck.

The girl dove for the pistol, but Tori pulled back her arm. She grabbed her cup from the console and threw it on Alisha, soaking her with hot coffee. She cried out. Tori hit her temple with the butt of the pistol. She slumped in the seat, out cold.

Tori put the gun away, reached across, and buckled Alisha's seatbelt. Then, she wiped her hands on her jeans. That hadn't gone the way she wanted, but the result was still the same. Tori smiled as she pulled the car out onto the road once more.

Audrey would *have* to come for her now.

CHAPTER NINETEEN

By Tuesday afternoon, they still hadn't found Tori, and Audrey was still trapped in her hotel room. She and Jake had gone to the gym earlier just to get out. He was determined not to leave her alone.

They were playing a game of cards when his phone rang.

"It's Yancy," he said, picking up. "Hey..." He frowned. "No, she's not with me. How could she be with me? I'm in Portland... Never showed up for school? I told you both to stay the fuck at home. I don't care if she had a goddamn test, Yance!"

Audrey's heart seized as his gaze met hers. She immediately grabbed her phone from the bedside table and paced out to the living room as she dialed Alisha's number. It rang three times before someone picked up.

"Alisha?" she said.

"Hello, Audrey."

The bottom of her stomach clenched and dropped. "Tori, where's Alisha?"

"She's here with me. Say hi, Alisha."

In the background Audrey could hear Alisha yelling,

"Audrey! Don't do what she wants!" The sound of her voice made her want to smile and cry at the same time.

"What do you want, Tori?"

"Come on, you don't really need to ask me that, do you? I thought you were supposed to be smart. So far, I'm not impressed."

"Well, we can't all be you." As she stood in the living area, looking into the bedroom, her gaze locked with Jake's, who was still on with Yancy. "So why don't you just spell out what I have to do to keep you from hurting Alisha."

"What about Amber? Don't you want to save her too?"

Still alive. Amber was still alive. "Is that even on the table?"

"Depends on how smart you really are. If you can find me before I decide to kill her, then I'll let her go too. But you have to find me, and Audrey—I really want to kill her. I don't have to explain it to you, though, do I? You've studied people like me. You know all about cooling-off periods and escalation. Before Natashya, it had been a long, long time since I'd been able to do this. Now that I've got two new ones under my belt, I want to keep going. It's not the same as it was with Ian, though."

"So tell me where to find you. We can get right to it."

Tori laughed. "That's no fun. It's supposed to be a game, remember? I've been bored out of my fucking head since Ian got arrested—the least you can do is put some effort into this."

Audrey wanted to scream at her. Swear. Call her every fucking name she could think of. Threaten her. "Break the rules down for me, then."

"I've left you a couple of clues to help you get started, but what I really, really want is for you to get inside my head. Where would you go if you were me, Audrey? What would you do?"

"I'd go somewhere secluded, but obviously has good cell reception."

A heartbeat of silence. "Not bad. What else?"

"How do you strangle them, Tori?" She was switching tactics now. If she was smaller, younger than she was, how would she strangle someone if she had to? She thought about the heart-shaped bruise on Natashya's chest. They would probably find one on Margot's too.

Her gaze went to the boots she'd left by the door. She had a pair in her closet in Cambridge that had heart-shaped heels.

"You plant your foot on their chest, don't you? Get a cord wrapped around their throat a couple of times and you pull. You look down at them so you can watch them suffer and panic. Watch them die."

"Oh, Audrey." Tori's voice had dropped to a purr. "I knew you were smarter than you looked. I guess footwear is something else we have in common. This might be fun after all. Don't take too long to find me, Audrey. Amber and Alisha are awaiting you in anguished alliteration." There was a beep and the call was disconnected.

She walked back into the bedroom. Jake's call had ended as well. He was on his feet, stuffing his belongings into his duffel bag.

"Are you heading home?"

He glanced up. "Yeah. Yancy needs me. Was that the bitch on the phone?"

"Yeah. Alisha's okay, but Tori won't let her go unless I come to her."

"Where is she?"

"She didn't tell me. I have to find her."

His gaze was hard as it locked with hers. "So find her."

"I'm going to." She nodded her head, trying to convince herself as much as him. "I'm so sorry, Jake." She was too afraid to even cry.

"It's not your fault." He stopped his packing and walked around the bed to hug her. "Christ, Aud, I let her into my house. Alisha befriended her. She fooled us all."

"I should have seen it."

"You did. You told me something felt off about the kid. What did you do the moment you got to my place and found her? You wanted her the hell away from Lish and me. You knew."

She nodded. "For all the good it did. I texted Alisha and told her not to go near Tori."

"She must have threatened her." His fingers bit into her shoulders, but she didn't even flinch. The pain was good— focusing. "I'm going to kill her."

"Get in line." Audrey drew a deep breath, her brain slowing, kicking into motion. "I'm going to see Monroe. Grant made me an appointment before I stepped down as their expert witness. Hopefully he didn't change it. Monroe probably knows where she's at."

"Do you think he'll see you?"

"Oh, yeah. If not out of revenge for Margot, he'll want to rub my face in it. I'm going to talk to her mother too. And I want to see those records of Venture's."

"Will the feds let you see them?"

"Anita will." She reached up and rubbed her hand over his lean jaw, stubble rasping against her palm. "Go be with Yancy. I'll let you know when I have something." Either what she found on her own or what Anita told her.

"You're not going after her alone."

"No, I'm not. When I figure out where she is, you're coming with me." They were going to handle this the right way—the way they'd known since they were kids. "I need you to give me something, though."

"What?"

She smiled as a surge of ice flooded her veins. "Your base-ball bat."

Jake left a little later. It was a long descent into night. After poring over papers and her own notes, searching for clues, Audrey couldn't sleep. She was too angry. Angry was good. She could use angry, could feed and nurture it. Angry kept scared at bay.

Finally, around four o'clock Wednesday morning, she fell asleep with the TV on. She woke up when her alarm went off at eight. She called the prison as she stumbled to the bathroom to pee. She was on the toilet when someone answered.

"This is Dr. Audrey Harte. I work with the DA's office. I need to check if I'm on the schedule to see Ian Monroe today."

There was the clacking of computer keys in the background. "Yes, you are, Dr. Harte."

"Thank you." Audrey hung up, smiling. God love Kenny.

Jake had called his cousin last night and told him about Alisha. He asked if Kenny could make sure Audrey got to talk openly to Monroe—as forcefully as needed. Hopefully he'd come through.

She checked her messages. Nothing from Anita. Had the agent spoken to Tori's father? She sent a quick text asking. Then, she jumped in the shower.

Audrey showered quickly—didn't bother to wash her hair, but instead spritzed it with some dry shampoo and twisted it into a loose bun on her crown. She dabbed on concealer, a powder foundation, some champagne eye shadow, mascara, and a deep berry lip. A bold lip color always screamed authority. She really didn't care what she looked like, but Monroe would. He'd see an unadorned face as a show of fear and weakness.

Face done, Audrey pulled on black pants, a white shirt, and boots. Then she shoved a few items into an overnight bag, just in case. By the time she pulled on her coat and grabbed Jake's bat, barely thirty minutes had gone by.

She checked her phone. She had a text from Anita: *Owen Scott has no idea where she might be. We've got a couple of leads. Will be in touch.*

That didn't give Audrey any comfort. Tori had to have found a place to take her victims after Monroe's family cottage burned down. It wasn't as though she was old enough to rent a place on her own. With her father gone most of the time, and her mother an easily manipulated space cadet, the girl had been able to come and go as she pleased, but she still had to keep up appearances. The place was probably far away from Portland. That was a lot of travel with unconscious or dead women. For Tori, the distance probably played a part in proving herself superior.

So, where would she take them? Were her parents covering for her? She could see her mother doing so, but not her father.

Think, Audrey. Where would you take them? That was easy. If she had someone she wanted to kill at her leisure, she'd take them to the camp back Tripp's Cove. It was an old hunting cottage/cabin where they hung out as kids. Located on the other side of the beach from the resort, it was surrounded by trees, and remote.

She texted Neve. Her friend had already been in touch—as soon as she heard about Alisha—and offered to help. Audrey asked her to look into any cottages or houses owned by Tori's extended family. Maybe even family friends.

She hoped Margot's murder was enough to get Ian talking.

The hotel had coffee in the lobby, along with a selection of pastries and fruit. She grabbed a croissant and a banana to go with the coffee and headed to the parking garage. Once she was in her car, with the Bluetooth connected, she left a voice mail for Anita that she was going to join Jake in Edgeport to be with the family. She had debated whether or not to do it, but she couldn't play with Alisha's safety. That said, she had no intention of sitting on her hands and letting the feds take care of it, not when she knew she could get Alisha back. It was probably going to get her arrested, but she didn't care.

"Please call me if you get any leads," she said. "I'll let you know if Tori contacts me again." She hung up and put her phone on silent before calling Jake.

He picked up on the second ring. "Hey." His voice was low.

"Hi. Are you with Yancy?"

"Yeah." She heard a door creak and shut. "She's finally asleep. Where are you?"

"On my way to Warren to see Monroe."

"You think he can help?"

"Yes. Last night Tori said she left clues for me. Where did she grab Alisha?"

"We figure from the road. They were late getting out to catch the bus. Yancy thought the bus might have been late since Lish didn't call, but the driver never picked her up."

"Alisha would never go with Tori willingly. She had to have a weapon, or she drugged her. Fucking bitch."

"I know. How are you doing?"

She laughed. "How am I? I should be asking you that. She's your niece."

"I'm pissed and terrified, and I'm ready to go hunt the little cunt down whenever you give the word."

Normally she would have cringed at the "C" word, but in this case it was excusable. "Struggling with feeling guilty. Scared. Enraged. Murderous."

"Get in line, my dar."

"The bus," she said, going back to what he'd said just a few moments ago. "Why were they late?"

"Raccoons had gotten into the garbage, knocked the can behind Yancy's Subaru."

That was it. Her heart gave a hard thump of hope. "Did she clean it up?"

"As far as I know. I didn't see anything when I got here."

"Check it out if you can. I don't think it was raccoons."

"Son of a bitch. I'll go out and check."

"Does Yancy blame me?" she asked before he could hang up. He hesitated. "Yes. And me. And herself. And Lincoln for not being here. I called him. Haven't heard back."

"You will." Their family was fucked up as much as any other, but the one thing Jake, Yancy, and Lincoln had in common was that they loved Alisha. "I'll call you when I'm done at the prison."

"Okay. Be careful."

"I will." She hung up. The rest of the drive was in silence.

Kenny was at the prison when she checked in, and he was the guard that took her to the interview room. His normally friendly face was hard, his eyes dark. "How long has Alisha been missing?" he asked.

"Since yesterday morning. I heard her in the background when her abductor called me. She sounded pissed, but okay." Or at least she was at the time.

"Whatever you and Jake need, you just let me know."

"Thanks, Kenny." She smiled at him. "I appreciate it." She didn't tell him that she knew Tori would keep Alisha alive for the time being. Tori took girls that she thought were a challenge of some sort. Lisha was a darling girl, but the only challenge she'd give someone like Tori was a physical one. No, Alisha was bait, plain and simple, and she'd be safe until Audrey got there, or until Tori got bored.

As usual, Monroe was at the table when she walked into the room.

"Dr. Harte," he greeted her with a smug smile. "Don't you look nice. To what do I owe the pleasure?"

She pulled the chair out from the table and sat down. "You don't look too upset for a widower."

His smirk faded. "What?"

Had the police not notified him? He and Margot had been legally married. "You don't know."

"Don't know what?"

Aw, fuck. Audrey folded her hands on the table. "Mr. Monroe...Ian, I'm sorry to tell you this, but Margot is dead. Tori killed her."

His face went white. For a moment, he looked like a lost little boy. "No. That wasn't...that wasn't part of the deal. We don't hurt each other."

Had he just admitted that Tori was his partner? He had, and he'd done it without hesitation. "Maybe Tori thought Margot wasn't part of the deal."

"I asked Margot to take a message to her. I wanted her to ask Tori what the hell she was up to." His dark gaze rose to hers. "She's really gone?"

Audrey nodded. "Tori left her in my hotel room."

"Bitch. That fucking bitch!" He slammed his fists down on the table, restraints rattling. "Margot was a nut, but she was *my* nut. Do you know she thought she could save me? She actually thought there was a little bit of goodness inside me. We both know how wrong she was."

"Maybe not," Audrey replied. "If Margot found her, then

you know where Tori's hiding. Tell me where she is, and Margot won't have died in vain."

Monroe's eyes narrowed. So much for that little bit of goodness. "What's in it for me?"

"Revenge," Audrey offered. "A chance to get justice for Margot. Probably a lighter sentence, and if that's not enough, how about finally proving you're smarter than Tori by turning her in."

"We promised we'd never give each other up."

"She gave you up the moment she told the police she was your victim."

Monroe tilted his head to one side—like a dog. "You're right. She did. That's still not enough reason for me to tell you where she is. You have to give me something in return, Doctor. Do something for me."

Suddenly, Kenny was right there, bending down so that his face was close to Monroe's. "You tell her what she wants to know, you little sack of shit, or I'll make sure you get some shower time with a few of the boys who think pretty-boy rapists should get a little bit of their own."

Fear—real fear—tightened Monroe's features.

"What's wrong, Ian?" Audrey asked. "I thought you liked boys. You liked Barry Lawson."

Surprise slackened his jaw, but only for a second. "Barry let me do him. I never...he never did it to me."

She smiled. "Well, maybe now you'll find out what you were missing."

Kenny had backed off a bit, but he meant business, and the three of them knew it. Monroe shot him a hesitant glance. "Her great aunt has a cottage in Eastrock."

Christ, that was one town over from Edgeport. She hadn't come to Edgeport just to see Audrey, she'd been at her hideout. "Her mother didn't mention that when the police spoke to her."

"It's been empty since her great aunt died three years ago. Her uncle owns it now and rents it out over the summer. He and Tori's father don't speak, so her family hasn't been there in years. She and I went there when we were looking for a place to . . . hang out, but decided my cottage was safer."

Hang out? That's what he called raping and killing five young women? Audrey gritted her teeth. "Where in Eastrock?"

He shook his head. "I don't know. It was touristy. There was a seafood place we walked to. Fat Freds or something."

"Fat Franks," Audrey announced. She knew it well. And the only cottages within walking distance were the ones in a little section of the town's beachfront called Garret's Rest.

"Yeah," Monroe said when she mentioned the place aloud. "That's it."

Kenny caught her gaze. "That's only twenty minutes from Edgeport."

More like fifteen, but she wasn't going to argue. Tori had balls to take Alisha somewhere so close. "Thank you, Mr. Monroe."

"You'll tell her it was me, yeah?" His dark eyes were bright with a malicious gleam. "When they've arrested her, make sure she knows it was because of me."

"I can do that." She rose from the chair and Kenny walked her from the room. "Do not tell Jake where that cottage is if he calls you."

Kenny nodded. "Right. You don't want him taking off before you can get there."

"I'm afraid of what he might do to the girl who took Alisha." Afraid that she wouldn't be there to inflict some damage of her own.

"You're right to be."

Audrey glanced at him. There was something in his tone that said he knew something she didn't, but his face and gaze were perfectly calm and clear. "Thank you for the 'incentive' you offered to get him to talk."

"I meant it."

She smiled. "Your Tripp is showing."

Kenny smiled back. "Be careful, Audrey. Let me know if there's anything else I can do."

She thanked him as they reached the reception area, then she gathered her belongings from the locker and left the prison.

With any luck she'd never see it, or Ian Monroe, again.

Jake went outside after hanging up with Audrey. He shoved his feet into the flip-flops he wore outside until it was absolutely too cold to do so. His aversion to shoes was all in his head, he knew that, but it didn't change the fact that he hated the feel of anything on his feet.

Yancy's house was similar to, but a little larger than, the

cottages farther back the road at The Cove Resort, which Jake owned and Yancy managed. There was a short driveway and a small front yard, where she planted flowers and kept it nicely groomed. Her vehicle was pulled up close to the front steps. His own truck was behind it. He walked around the vehicles and found the garbage can. It was one of those big, heavy-duty plastic ones with sturdy wheels and a handle. It was possible a couple of good-sized raccoons had tipped it—or maybe a bear, but when he opened the lid, he saw that the bag hadn't been ripped open—it had been untied.

Raccoons had nimble claws and were smart, but they weren't that nimble, or that smart. This had been done on purpose.

He stared at the bag. It stank of vegetation, but it wasn't the smell that brought tears to his eyes. He hadn't cried since his grandmother's funeral, and he wasn't about to cry now, not while Alisha was still alive.

Every instinct he had screamed for him to get his shotgun and go looking for her, but he had no idea where to look. She could be anywhere between Edgeport and Portland. And as head of the family, he couldn't just walk out on Yancy when she needed someone. Who would take care of her if he was gone? No, he couldn't run off half-cocked and looking for blood.

He pulled the bag out of the can and emptied it on the grass, then crouched down and started sifting through it. Audrey said there would be a message for her in the trash. Maybe he wouldn't know it if he found it, but looking beat the hell out of sitting around feeling castrated and useless.

Most of it was packaging that couldn't be recycled and food

scraps that should have gone in the compost bin, some feminine products tied up in their own little bag—thank God—a pair of old slippers and a small gold jewelry box with a ribbon tied around it.

Jake picked it up. The blue ribbon was damp and had a bit of brown apple peel hanging from it. How very nice of the psycho to make her message obvious. He untied the ribbon and set it aside in case they needed it later. He lifted the lid. Inside was a folded-up piece of paper and a silver bracelet. The bracelet was one of those ones with a rectangular plate attached to the chain on either side. Engraved on the front was *Tori*. When he opened the paper, he saw that it was a copy of a newspaper article, the date of which he didn't need to check: LOCAL TEENS CHARGED WITH MURDER. He didn't need to read it either. He had the original in an album that had belonged to his grandmother. She'd chronicled most of Audrey's life in that album—the good and the bad. She'd loved Audrey like she was one of her own.

His phone rang. He answered it without checking to see who it was, something he rarely did. He tucked it between his head and shoulder. "Hello?"

"It's me." Lincoln. "Any news on Lish?"

"Not yet." He set the paper and bracelet back in the box and set it aside before starting to gather up the trash. "Audrey's gone to see someone who might know where she was taken. She's going to let me know when she finds out."

"How's Yance?"

"A mess. She's sleeping now."

"You knock her out?"

"Pretty much. She hadn't slept since yesterday. I gave her a little Dramamine." Just enough to let her relax.

"What can I do?"

Jake paused in his cleanup, his gaze fixed on the ground. "We could use you here." If—when—Audrey found out where Alisha was, Jake was going to need Lincoln to watch over Yancy while he was gone. He'd never thought about killing a little girl before, but it was the only thing keeping him from falling apart at that moment. He would never, *ever* admit it, but he needed his big brother.

"I'll be there within the half hour."

"Good." Lincoln hung up before he did, but Jake didn't care. He gathered up the rest of the garbage and put the bag back in the bin. Then, he climbed into his truck and drove the few miles out to his house. He went upstairs and changed his shirt, put on some socks, and shoved his feet into his boots.

When he came downstairs, he went straight into his office. He unlocked the cabinet on the far wall, and took out his shotgun. Then he drove back to Yancy's and sat in a chair by the couch as she slept. He watched her. And waited. If he possessed one virtue, it was patience.

CHAPTER TWENTY

An hour and a half into the drive to Edgeport, Audrey called Neve.

"Are you on duty today?" she asked. Silently, she cursed the traffic ahead of her. Really? Most days you could hear crickets on the road if you had the windows down.

"Yeah. You need some help?"

"I know where Tori Scott has Alisha."

A breath of silence. That moment where Neve had to decide if she was going to report it. "Where?"

"A cottage in Eastrock. I'm on my way home now. I'm still a couple hours out."

"Woman, what are you planning? Do not tell me you're going vigilante on this."

"Why do you think I'm calling you?"

"Audrey—"

"She's got Alisha and she'll kill her if I don't show, Neve. It's me she wants, and it's me she's going to get. I need you with me so you can make sure Jake doesn't do something that will get him thrown in jail." The romance of both of them taking Tori down in a glorious bloodbath had lost some of its luster when she realized that Tori was worth killing, but not worth serving time.

"Who's going to make sure *you* don't do something that will get you thrown in jail?"

"Me." Audrey pressed a little harder on the gas. She was over the speed limit, but not going so fast that she outpaced every other car on the highway. Anxiety wanted her to drive as fast as she could, but common sense tallied up how much time being pulled over would cost her.

"So the plan is you deliver yourself into the hands of a serial killer, and then what?" She sounded as though she thought Audrey hadn't played it out a hundred times already.

"You and Jake get the girls she's holding out of there."

"Girls?"

"Yeah." Now that she was past the old woman, she switched to cruise control. "She's got another girl besides Alisha."

"Who the hell is this kid, Wonder Woman?"

"She's a seventeen-year-old psychopath with experience. She's strong and resourceful, and has access to drugs."

"And obsessed with you."

"She thinks we're the same—or at least similar."

"Jesus, Auddie, what is it about you that inspires this degree of insanity?" It was said with concern, not judgment—or at least not much.

"She's not insane. She's just not wired right. That's not an excuse. She's a fucking monster."

"Whatever. First Maggie, now this girl."

"It's transference. Sort of. Look, can I count on you?"

"You know you can." Neve sounded insulted. "I'll stick close to home. You know I'll have to call it in, though."

"I wouldn't ask you to do otherwise. I'll call you when I hit town." She said good-bye and disconnected. Then she sent a voice message to Jake letting him know what time she should arrive.

Ten minutes outside of Edgeport, she called Neve again. When she pulled into Yancy's driveway, Jake's truck and Lincoln's motorcycle were both there. It was a sunny day, but a bit cold to be driving around on a motorcycle. Not like Lincoln had the sense God gave a hamster.

She was stiff as she climbed out of the car—tension tightened her muscles to the point of discomfort. She tried to shake it off as she climbed the front steps of the little house. Before she could knock, Jake opened the door. He hugged her as soon as she stepped inside.

"Lincoln's here?"

He nodded. "He's going to stay with Yancy."

"Like fuck I am," came his brother's voice from the doorway into the living room. "I'm going with you to get Lish. Hey, Audrey."

She smiled tightly. "Hey, Linc."

Jake faced his older sibling. "No, you're not. You've got a record, and you're not getting arrested again."

"You don't care if I get fucking arrested. You just want to be the hero, like always."

"Because you were always too busy running away."

Lincoln's face twisted into a sneer. "Right, because having a guy killed in prison is so much more noble."

Audrey blinked. She turned to Jake. "You had a guy killed in prison?"

Jake's jaw tightened. He kept his attention on his brother. "This is not the time or place. Alisha is what's important right now, and I need to know Yancy is with someone I can trust."

His brother looked surprised at that, and opened his mouth to speak, but then Yancy emerged from the hallway. *"You."* She lunged at Audrey like a feral cat. Audrey threw up her arm in time to save her face from getting clawed, but the other woman laid her arm open instead. Audrey snarled in pain, but managed to step back rather than throw a punch. Lincoln had Yancy by the arms, restraining her.

"My baby's in danger because of you!" Yancy shouted. "This is all your fault! If that animal hurts her, I'll kill you! Do you hear me, I'll fucking *kill* you!"

Audrey stared at her, speechless. What the hell could she possibly say that would make any difference?

Jake stepped forward. "Yance—"

Wild eyes narrowed at him. "You are not going to defend her to me, not when Alisha is in the hands of some psycho. I want her out of my house. *Now.*"

Audrey was already on her way out the door when Jake followed after her. "Aud, wait."

"I have bandages in my car," she told him, opening the passenger door so she could easily access the glove box. She opened the kit, dug out an antiseptic wipe and antibiotic salve. She hissed when the wipe touched her torn skin, but didn't waste time being spleeny. She wiped the wound, spread salve on it and then a bandage. Jake helped her wrap gauze around her arm to finish it off.

"She'll calm down," he told her.

"Yeah, right." There was a chill in the air, and it made it more difficult to keep the tears from her eyes.

He tipped her chin up with his finger. "Hey, when we bring Lish home, Yancy will see reason."

She nodded, but she didn't believe it, not for a minute. "Tori's family has a cottage in Eastrock. Monroe thinks it's where she'd take the girls."

He shoved the first aid kit back into the glove box. "Why didn't you tell me when you called?"

She arched a brow at him. "Why didn't you tell me you had Matt Jones killed?" He looked startled. "What? Did you think I wouldn't figure out who Lincoln was talking about?"

"I didn't tell you because I didn't want you to have to lie if you were asked about it." He sighed. "I tried to tell you the other night, but Grant called."

"You should have told me when it happened. Matt was poison, just like his father. God knows what he would have done to Yancy if you hadn't stopped him."

His gaze met hers. "I didn't have him killed for Yancy."

And that was why he hadn't told her. She understood now. It had happened in the summer, during the whole thing with Maggie and Bailey, the murder and the horrible truths that came out because of it. He hadn't known how things were going to play out for them back then. Revealing what he'd done would have made him too vulnerable too early.

Having Matt killed was obviously a terrible thing, but she couldn't bring herself to be upset about it. Matt had been a complete prick who liked to beat up women like his old man. True, he'd had a bad childhood, but a lot of people did and they didn't turn out to be abusive bastards. Besides, he would have killed her if he had the chance, or at least fucked her up. He'd threatened to rape her once as well.

"Is there any way anyone can trace his death back to you?"

Jake shook his head. "Lincoln says some friend of his heard a rumor, but no one will take it seriously unless Kenny spills."

"Good." They could trust Kenny. "By the way, it was Kenny who got Monroe to talk. Gracie would have been impressed."

He nodded. "Where's this cottage?"

"Garret's Rest. Neve's seeing if she can find out where exactly."

He ran a hand through his hair. "You called Neve?"

"You bet your ass I did. She's the only thing that's going to save both of us from jail time. We can't go all backwoods here. It doesn't matter how much we both want to. This is too high profile. Tori has other crimes to answer for, and death is too good for the little twat. I want her to rot in a cell, knowing I put her there."

"Okay. Let's go."

"What about Linc?"

"I think he understands that if he comes anywhere near me right now, I'll knock his teeth out."

"All right, then." She gave him the keys. "You drive. We're meeting Neve at Fat Franks."

The drive to Eastrock wasn't long, but it felt like it. Audrey obsessively flicked her fingernails, working them underneath nail-beds until her fingers were sore, and two of them were bleeding.

Neve was already in the parking lot when they reached Fat Franks. It was closed for the season, so a car and a state police vehicle were bound to attract attention. They decided to park behind the building for that reason.

"What's the plan?" Neve asked as she approached them. She raised a brow at the bat in Jake's hand.

"I forgot my shotgun," he told her.

"That's probably for the best. I'll handle any bullets that need to be fired, that will make all of this a little easier to explain."

"Were you able to track Alisha's phone?" Audrey asked as she buttoned her coat.

"No. It's been disabled. I did, however, do a records search and found out which cottage belongs to the uncle. How do you want to proceed?"

Audrey shoved her hands into her pockets. She ought to have brought her brass knuckles along. "She's expecting me, so I'll go to the front door."

"Okay," her friend allowed, "but then what?"

Audrey shrugged. "I beat her senseless and the two of you save the girls?"

Neve stared at her, dark eyes wide. "How in the name of God have you lived this long? What if she has a gun, Jackie Chan? What then? We could barge in and get you and the girls killed."

"What if I have you on my cell when I go in? You'll be able to hear everything."

"Until psycho finds it," Jake remarked, effectively pissing on her parade.

"It's better than nothing," Neve decided. "Jake and I will go around back and find a way inside while you divert her."

"Okay, good. I'll drive down so she'll think I'm alone. Which cottage is it?"

"Number 12. It's a small bungalow with yellow siding and blue trim. Give us a five-minute head start. We'll approach from the beach."

Audrey watched the two of them skulk off before pulling out her phone and texting Anita the address for the cottage. Jake might want to do this the way they were taught, but she'd meant what she said—neither of them was going to jail because of Tori. She checked to make sure her phone was still on silent.

Five minutes later, she got into her car and drove to number 12 Garret's Rest. She recognized the car out front as one she'd seen in front of the Scott house during her two visits. She had to assume the car wasn't trackable because the cops would have been there already. By the same token, Tori must have gotten rid of or disabled her own phone as well, because Anita would have mentioned if they'd been able to locate it.

Before getting out of the car, Audrey dialed Neve, then slipped her phone into her inside coat pocket. Her stomach squeezed as she approached the door, her boot heels crunching on the gravel. She knocked and waited. A few moments later, the door opened.

A pistol was pointed at her face. Tori peered out around the door, checking for witnesses. "Get in," she said, stepping back.

Audrey crossed the threshold. "Is that gun really necessary? I'm not armed."

"Then you're a fucking idiot," the girl responded with a sneer. "Empty your pockets."

Audrey did, dumping the contents onto a small table by the door—a packet of gum, her bank card, and her car keys.

"No phone?"

She shook her head. "No."

Tori glared at her. "I hate being lied to." She pushed Audrey back against the closed door and reached inside her jacket, grabbing the cell phone from the pocket. She was right in Audrey's face, just inches away. It was now or never.

Audrey lunged.

Jake and Neve were at the back of the cottage when he heard Audrey yell and a shot ring out. He didn't think, he simply reacted. The back door was wood and splintered when he kicked it, the lock tearing through the frame under the force. He went to step inside, but Neve grabbed him and pushed past. She was the one with the gun.

The back of the cottage was a small sunporch where beach and outdoor items were stored. It smelled like sand and stale air. The girls weren't there.

He followed Neve into a dusty hallway, inching along the

wall until they encountered another door. Neve turned the knob, pushed the door open ... nothing.

There was another door across from that one. It was locked.

From the front of the house came the sounds of a fight. A female voice screamed. Audrey? His head turned toward the sound, heart in his throat. Christ, his hands were shaking.

Neve punched him in the arm. He looked at her as she scowled at him. She pointed at the door. Jake stepped back and launched himself at it, shoulder first. The impact reverberated through the marrow in his bones, but the door flew open. He staggered inside. The air that he sucked into his lungs tasted bitter.

"Uncle Jake!"

He almost fell to his knees at the sound of that voice. She was on one of the twin beds in the room, a rope around her ankle, tight enough to tear into her skin. The rope was tied to one of the legs of the bed, giving her room to get to the chamber pot at the foot of it, but no more than that.

He went to her, gathering her up in his arms. She had a cut above her left eye, but other than that, seemed whole. He hugged her tight against his chest, feeling her shoulders shake as she sobbed against his jacket. "It's okay," he whispered. "I've got you. I'm here."

"Audrey?" she asked, voice raw and muffled.

He glanced over his shoulder at the door. There was a crash from the other room. "She's okay. Let's get you out of here." God, he hoped Audrey was okay. He pulled his jackknife from his jeans pocket and opened the blade. Carefully, he slipped it between the rope and her skin. His other hand held the rope taut so he could saw through it without hurting her. The fibers jerked apart under the sharp edge of the knife, until the rope fell away entirely.

With Alisha free, he turned to help Neve with the other girl. She had a black eye and a split lip and the wound on her leg caused by the rope looked red and infected. She whimpered as he cut her free.

"Take Alisha," he told Neve. "I'll carry Amber."

Neve nodded and held out her hand to his niece. "Let's go, hon." Then to him, "I'll be right back."

He didn't acknowledge her; he just kept cutting. He had to get to Audrey, because the sounds from the other room had stopped, and he was terrified at the idea of what that might mean.

Amber had her arms around his neck and he was just about to pick her up when he heard a click from the doorway.

"Back away from her," Tori commanded.

The girl on the shabby quilt made a sound that could have been a sigh or a stifled scream. Jake backed up.

Tori entered the room. There was blood on her lower lip and a big red mark on her jaw. Audrey knew how to hit. She leveled the pistol in her hand at him. "I meant to kill Alisha to hurt Audrey, but I think it will hurt her more if I kill you."

Jake shrugged. "If you think so. How about you let Amber go? She doesn't mean anything to Audrey."

"But she does to Ian, and I know he finally betrayed me. I was counting on it. I don't know if you noticed, but Audrey's a little dim. I had to really spell it out for her so she could find me. I'm sorry to tell you that I shot her. She'll probably still be alive when the police arrive. Not sure I can say the same about you." She smiled.

He kept his gaze trained on her, rather than the shape moving up behind her. "You're going to shoot me here? Then what? Drag Audrey in here so she can watch me bleed out? That seems to lack impact."

She made a face at him. "God, what is it with you people? You talk at me like you think I'm a child. I know you're stalling."

"Actually," he said with a smile. "It was actually meant to be a diversion."

Understanding dawned on her face. As she turned around, Audrey grabbed her arm holding the gun and slammed it against the door frame as she smashed her forehead into the girl's face. The pistol clattered to the floor. Jake dove for it, coming up on his knees when he had it in his hand.

Audrey had Tori on the floor and was sitting on her chest. Her left arm hung limp at her side, blood dripping from her fingers as she drove her right fist into the girl's face. "That's for all the girls you killed with Ian." Another punch. "That's for Natashaya, and this is for Margot and Amber, and Alisha." Her fist came down hard with every name.

"And this is for putting a gun in Jake's face."

Tori's face was slick with blood, so much that it was hard to make out her features. It was obvious, however, that she was unconscious. Audrey was oblivious to the fact. For a second—just one—Jake was tempted to see how far she'd go, but he didn't need to see her do it. He already knew she'd kill the girl if he didn't stop her. And she would kill her, not for the girls she'd hurt, or even for Alisha, though that might be part of it. No, she was going to beat Tori to death because she threatened *him*.

"Audrey," he said. *"Audrey!"*

She stopped, shoulders slouching, chest heaving from rage and exertion. She looked at him, then down at the girl beneath her. She slid to the side, landing on her backside on the carpet.

"What the hell happened?" Neve demanded as she came through the door. She'd taken off her jacket. "I thought you were right behind me. Alisha's safe, and backup is on the way."

Jake shoved the pistol at her as he knelt beside Audrey. "Tori shot her and was going to shoot me until Audrey sucker punched her."

Neve's sharp brows rose. "That's quite the sucker punch."

"She's good at it. Get me a towel or something, will you?"

She tore a pillowcase off the nearest bed and handed it to him. While he wrapped the cloth around Audrey's arm to stop the bleeding, Neve rolled Tori onto her stomach and hand-cuffed her behind her back. "Ambulance is on its way, and so is your friend Grayson." Her gaze fell upon Audrey. "You okay?"

Audrey didn't speak, but she nodded. Was she in shock?

"Put your arm around my neck," Jake instructed.

She did as he asked, wrapping her right arm around his neck as he slipped one arm below her back and the other beneath her knees. He stood, lifting her up into his arms as he did so. "Let's get you out of here."

He carried Audrey to the porch where he'd kicked the door in. Alisha rushed over when she saw him. She wore Neve's coat, but there was still a bluish cast to her skin.

"Is she okay?" she asked.

Audrey smiled at her. "Takes more than a dump truck or a bullet to do me in, kiddo."

Her reference to the incident that had put her briefly in the hospital during the summer made Jake realize that this was the second, no, the third time her life had been threatened since the end of June. Maybe it was time to make some changes. Like never letting her out of the house again.

"Pull that lawn chair out for me, Lish." When she did, he set Audrey in it. "You sit down too. I'll be right back." He walked back to the room where Neve sat on the bed with Amber. Tori was starting to come out of it.

"When the ambulance gets here, you go with Audrey and the girls," Neve instructed. "I'll stay here with our prisoner and wait for the Portland crew."

Jake agreed as he grabbed the comforter and a blanket off the other bed. He took both to the porch, wrapped Audrey in the blanket and his niece in the comforter. He kissed Alisha's forehead as he tucked the thick bedding around her, bundling her up tight.

"I knew you'd come," she said. "You and Audrey. I knew you'd rescue me."

He smiled. "Always. I love you, brat."

"I love you too."

"Always have, always will," Audrey said, repeating what he'd said to her the day she told him she loved him. She gave him a loopy grin just before she passed out.

CHAPTER TWENTY-ONE

There's a pirate at our door!" Audrey exclaimed as she held out the bowl of candy with her good arm. Her left was still in a sling. The bullet Tori's gun had shot into her hadn't done any lasting damage, but it still managed to do enough that it hurt like hell and wasn't much good for anything. Thankfully, she was right-handed.

The little pirate with the askew eye patch and dubious mustache grabbed a handful of mini candy bars, thanked her, and scurried back to the car where his mother waited. The woman waved. Audrey hoisted the bowl of candy in greeting and then slipped back inside.

"I think it's going to snow," she told her mother, who was reclining on the sofa with a fuzzy blanket. She was just home from the hospital, having made it through surgery with flying colors. Now, they waited as she recovered and hoped that this was the end of the damn cancer.

"I wouldn't be surprised. Jess and Greg said they'd bring the girls by." No sooner had she said the words than the door flew open, almost taking Audrey with it. Isabelle flew inside, followed by her mother and father, who had Olivia in his arms.

She was dressed as a hot dog. Her big sister was...well, Audrey had no freaking idea.

Jess smiled at her confusion. "She couldn't decide which Disney princess to be, so she's a combination of about five of them, I think."

"Four," her husband corrected. "She left the bow and arrow at home." He leaned down and gave his mother-in-law a kiss on the cheek.

"How are you feeling?" Jessica asked their mother.

"Sore," she replied. "But good. Auddie's been taking good care of me."

"And Jake and Dad have been taking pretty decent care of both of us," Audrey added.

Greg nodded at her sling. "How much longer do you have to wear that?"

"I'm not sure. Until it stops hurting?" Getting shot was a bitch. "The therapist should be able to give me a better idea when I go for my appointment."

Isabelle's Cinderella shoes flopped around her feet as she approached Audrey. Her dress was Belle's with Ariel's tail underneath and her wig was Elsa. "Jimmy Pelletier says you were shot helping the police catch a bad person. Is that true?"

"Sort of," Audrey replied.

She grinned. "That makes you a *hero*."

Audrey ignored her family's chuckles. "I'm not a hero, sweetie."

Those odd eyes, so much like her own, widened. "You're *my* hero, Auntie Auddie."

"Ohhh," Jessica crooned as she laughed. "That's very nice of you to say, Izzy."

Audrey blinked back tears and tried to swallow with a throat that was too tight. "Thank you, Izzy. I'm honored."

"Where's Dad?" Jessica asked, saving Audrey from getting more emotional.

"Working," their mother replied. "Apparently there's a Halloween party at Gracie's tonight."

She turned to Audrey. "Why didn't you go?"

"This arm is a buzzkill. The last thing I need is a bunch of drunks bumping into me." What she didn't say was that she wanted the evening with her mother, but also that Yancy was going to be at the party, and she didn't think it would be a good idea for their paths to cross. Jake's sister was still pissed at her— to the extent that she'd forbidden Alisha to see her. It didn't seem to matter that she'd helped save Alisha; Yancy remained convinced that her daughter wouldn't have been in danger in the first place if not for Audrey, and how could she argue that when she agreed with it? She didn't take personal blame for Alisha's abduction, but there was no denying it had happened because of her.

Tori had claimed that she hadn't planned to kill Alisha, that she was just leverage to use against Audrey. It might have been the truth, because when the police found her "trophy stash," they found a pair of Audrey's earrings—also taken from her purse—but nothing of Alisha's.

Her sister and her family stayed for about an hour, and helped hand out candy when a kid came to the door. As they were leaving, Jessica cornered her by the front door. "How are you doing? Okay?"

Audrey nodded. "I'm good."

The other woman didn't look convinced. "Okay. Call me if you need anything. I'll come by tomorrow and check in."

"Jess, you don't need to check in every day. We're good."

"I'm checking in." Then, she kissed Audrey's cheek and snatched a Kit Kat from the candy bowl. "See ya tomorrow."

With them gone and the evening starting to get a bit late for trick-or-treaters, Audrey sat down in the big recliner with her laptop and pushed the seat back. She opened her browser and went straight to e-mail. There was one from Angeline telling her to take all the leave she needed. She was such a fabulous boss. Audrey felt almost guilty. Angeline had always been there for her, and was a friend as well as mentor, but Audrey couldn't tell her the truth, that she was thinking of reevaluating her career goals. She couldn't tell her, not because she was afraid, but because she had no idea what she wanted to do. Her mind changed its focus every few hours, until she didn't know if she should stay or quit or go work at Walmart—all three options had their pros and cons.

She replied to the e-mail with thanks and a promise to let her know what was going on as soon as she knew herself.

The next e-mail was from Christopher James. She almost deleted it without opening it, but something made her hesitate. Maybe it was the subject line: *Apology & A Proposition*. This should be interesting.

Dr. Harte—

Once again please allow me to apologize for my underhand-edness and unprofessional behavior a few weeks ago. It was a terrible thing to do, and my assumptions were completely off base. I hope you can forgive me. Also, I'm writing to you to make a business proposal. I think your story would make an excellent book, and several New York editors have expressed an interest if there were such a book. So, I'm proposing that you and I work on the project together as coauthors. Am I looking to exploit you? Hell yes. I have no problem being exploited in return. The both of us could make a lot of money with this project, but when I say I have more interest in tell-ing your story than I do in the money, please believe me to be sincere.

Huh. She deleted the e-mail. If she ever decided to write a book about herself, it would not be in partnership with a man who brought condoms with him when he sneaked into her room and hid in her closet. Nope.

Amber Gale sent her a note to let her know that she was doing okay and to ask about her in return. She didn't respond right away. She would reply tomorrow when she had some time alone. Amber deserved more than a quick note.

God, what she wouldn't give for a week's worth of sleep and a pint of ice cream. Tiny Snickers bars just weren't going to cut it.

After what had happened at the cottage, she'd had another fifteen minutes of fame. Reporters chased her for a few days.

She spoke to a couple who seemed reputable and declined the rest. The FBI decided not to give her a hard time for going after Tori on her own, especially when she lied and said she'd been home to take care of her mother when Tori called her and revealed she had Alisha. The fact that Tori had threatened to kill Alisha if Audrey went to the authorities helped, as did the wound she received while trying to bring in the serial killer they hadn't been able to find. Plus, they cut her some slack because she had called the state police for backup, and of course, Neve backed everything up without actually having to lie much.

Everything had worked out, so why did she feel so numb? Was it the realization that she would have killed Tori if Jake hadn't stopped her? And she would have done it because Tori had threatened him. She supposed it was the same as him having Matt killed.

God, they were so fucked up, but at least they were the same kind of fucked up.

Ian Monroe was still in jail, and hadn't been offered a plea bargain. Tori was as well—no parole. She was being charged as an adult for seven murders, and kidnapping. Monroe would still be charged with rape, but with lesser charges for the murders. It didn't matter. They were both going to spend a significant amount of their lives behind bars, if not die in prison. Tori had tried to claim Ian made her a killer, but Dr. Venture's notes revealed that she'd been the one to approach Ian. She'd been a little sketchy on the details of what they'd done, even though the admission of past crimes was protected under privilege. She'd been fifteen when she and Ian killed the first time. *Fifteen.*

Recently, Audrey had taken to studying her face in the mirror and wondering what had happened that made her believe Clint Jones had to die. Had it been her own moral compass? Or had it been Maggie? Because when she thought of Maggie lately, it was Tori's face she saw. If the girl had been a better shot, Audrey wouldn't even be alive. A good right hook had helped. Had Maggie manipulated her into killing Clint? Or had she manipulated herself. She said she'd do it all over again, and she would. But she would want to make sure her motives were her own.

The doorbell rang at nine o'clock. "Late for trick-or-treaters," she allowed as she headed for the door. A quick look out revealed their visitor to be Jake. Just the sight of him made her calm. And happy. Everything was okay when they were together. Maybe they both suffered from a little Hystobrisphilia just like Margot Temple.

Poor Margot.

"Is it too late for visiting?" he asked when she opened the door.

"No, of course not. Come in."

He did, kicking off his boots as soon as he was inside. They'd seen each other a few times since she'd been shot, and he'd stayed with her during the hours she'd spent in the hospital. He'd read her a text he got from Barry Lawson saying that he wanted to thank Jake for the fight lessons, and that he thought he needed a change of scenery and was moving to the West Coast to start over. At the time, Audrey remarked that he looked happy for Barry, to which he replied, "Everyone deserves a second chance."

She didn't know if *everyone* deserved a fresh start, but she didn't argue.

"I thought maybe you might like a little company. In exchange for letting me sneak away a bit, I'm letting your father have the rest of the night off when I get back."

"You two have it all figured out, don't you?" her mother asked from her warm cocoon, her gaze a little unfocused thanks to the pain meds. "Thank you for giving him something to occupy his time, Jake. It's done him a world of good."

"He's been a big help to me, Anne. So thank you for letting him spend so much time away from home."

"I'm getting ice cream," Audrey informed him. "Want some?"

A few minutes later, the three of them sat in the living room watching an old scary movie from the eighties. Anne groaned and cringed through most of it before falling asleep on the couch.

Smiling, Audrey turned to Jake to comment on her mother, only to find that he had fallen asleep as well. She turned off the TV and snuggled closer to his left side. Her father wouldn't care if Jake didn't return. John Harte didn't like seeing his wife and baby girl in pain. He fussed and did whatever they asked of him, but as soon as he could bolt, he did. No drinking, though. At least not yet.

She closed her eyes and pushed all thoughts of Tori and Maggie, of her career, her father, and who was or wasn't a monster, out of her head. Instead, she filled that space with things she wanted to see and do. Maybe she'd reward herself with a new pair of boots to commemorate the badass scar she was going to have from getting shot.

Tomorrow she could worry about people trying to kill her, and whether or not she needed to make some changes in her life and career. Right now all she needed was in that room. And in the town.

She was home.

She was safe.

For now.

ACKNOWLEDGMENTS

Behind every book there is a team of people who helped make that book a reality. I honestly could not have done this without them, and so I'd like to take a few minutes to thank them for being so bloody awesome.

Miriam Kriss, thank you for getting my crazy and being okay with it. You are fabulous. Devi Pillai, you are the most evil, cruel, reducer-of-people-editor of them all, and I'm only saying that because I know it will make you smile. Wendy Chan, thank you for the amazing covers you've given these books! I can't begin to tell you how much I love them. Thank you so much for getting the feel of Audrey's world and making it visual. Lauren Panepinto, I want to thank you for just being one of the coolest women I know. Ellen Wright and Alex Lencicki, thank you for promoting and supporting me and my work, and for getting copies of the books into the right hands. Also, to the rest of the fabulous Redhook crew that I have forgotten. You are appreciated! So very much.

And finally, thank you to my husband, Steve, because you gave me the shove I needed to chase my dreams. Thanks, babe.

MEET THE AUTHOR

As a child, KATE KESSLER seemed to have a knack for finding trouble, and for it finding her. A former delinquent, Kate now prefers to write about trouble rather than cause it, and spends her day writing about why people do the things they do. She lives in New England with her husband.

INTRODUCING

**If you enjoyed
TWO CAN PLAY,
look out for**
THREE STRIKES
An Audrey Harte Novel
by Kate Kessler

CHAPTER ONE

"Necromania" is defined as an obsession with death or the dead. Most of humanity has it to some degree, being very much aware from a young age that life is a temporary and fragile thing. Psychologist Dr. Audrey Harte was familiar with the term, as well as the corresponding paraphilia that sexualized corpses. Fortunately, she'd never met anyone who suffered from the disorder.

*Un*fortunately, none of her academic or professional research had ever provided a label for those people who seem to have Death obsessed with *them*—people like herself who had to have a grim reaper watching over them like others claim to have angels. It was an impossible theory to prove, but she wanted to name it, because if it *was* possible for Death to stalk a person, she wanted a restraining order. Like, yesterday.

Since returning to the East Coast just five months earlier she'd been caught up in two separate murders and had a serial killer become obsessed with her. People always thought Maine was a peaceful state, and for the most part it was, but nothing that crazy had ever happened to her when she lived in California. It made a sort of karmic sense, however, that returning to the place where she'd once murdered someone would get Death's attention. If her life was one of her sister's paranormal romances, death personified would be a gorgeous guy with a lot of muscle and incredible sexual stamina, but her life was unfortunately not a romance novel, and she was a little afraid Death was actually a guy who lived in his mother's basement and had a shrine to her in his bedroom, along with thirty-two copies of *Catcher in the Rye* and an autographed, framed photo of Ted Bundy.

She also realized that thinking she'd been singled out by Death was somewhat egomaniacal, irrational, and paranoid. So she concentrated on her mother, who was recovering from a partial hysterectomy due to cancer, instead and told herself that Death might back off if she didn't flirt so much.

"I'm going to lie down," her mother said, getting up from the table. Anne Harte was trim and youthful-looking for a woman in her sixties, who usually had a lot of energy, but fighting the cancer, worrying about her youngest daughter, and now the surgery, had slowed her. Audrey had taken time off from work to help out, which was ironic because just before her mother's surgery, she'd been shot in the left arm by a teenage psychopath, and consequently hadn't been as much help as she'd hoped.

"You need anything?" Audrey asked her, watching her tentative movements. Her mother was healing as she should, but she'd still been cut open and was uncomfortable.

"Nope. Maybe a tea in a little while." Anne tucked her graying brown hair behind one ear. "You should rest too."

She shook her head. "I'm good." It was true. It had been almost three weeks now and she felt okay. Her arm ached, but it was healing and that was all she cared about.

That and having her mother around for the next twenty or so years.

"Wake me up in an hour or so, will you, babe? I want to make cookies for when Isabelle gets home from school."

Izzy was Audrey's five-year-old niece—a fabulous kid who had her grandparents wrapped around her little finger. "Aren't there any of the ones Jake made left?"

Her mother blushed. "No."

Audrey laughed. "I'll ask him to make you some more."

"Don't you dare. That boy already feeds us more than he ought. I've probably gained ten pounds since the two of you started dating."

Dating. That was such an insipid word to describe her relationship with Jake Tripp. Regardless, her mother needed the extra calories. The cancer had taken a lot of fat off her frame, and she was only now looking more like her old self.

"He said he's bringing chicken potpie tonight. Gracie's recipe."

Anne smiled. "If he proposes, you'd better say yes."

Audrey started. She and Jake had only gotten together in June, but they'd loved each other since they were children. The idea of life without him was unfathomable, but she hadn't fantasized about marrying him since she was sixteen. Honestly, she didn't think Jake was the marrying sort. For that matter, she wasn't sure she was either. "Sure, Mum. Have a good nap."

Her mother left the room and Audrey waited until she was gone to get up from the table and clear the remnants of their late lunch from the table. Her weakened arm made the process take a little longer than it should have, but she eventually got everything put away. She took butter out of the fridge to soften for cookie-making later, and carried her laptop into the living room. Technically she was off work, but she needed to check her e-mail and make sure all was good with the Boston office. What she really wanted to do, however, was work on the proposal she planned to show her boss, Angeline Beharrie, a renowned psychologist. She'd mentioned having something she wanted to share with her and Angeline was eager to see it. Audrey wanted to give it another edit before sending it.

She was typing away, ignoring the slight ache in her arm, when her cell phone buzzed beside her on the sofa. She glanced at the screen; it was her friend Neve asking where she was and could Neve swing by? Audrey's reply was *Mum's & yes.* She hadn't seen the other woman in a few days, and she'd welcome the company. Lounging around her mother's and Jake's houses without any real purpose or direction didn't agree with her, which was why she'd gotten so much work done on the proposal for Angeline.

Neve's car—the familiar blue of all state police cars—pulled into the drive a few minutes later. Audrey opened the door before she could ring the bell or knock. "Mum's napping," she explained in a low voice when her friend raised a brow.

Neve nodded. She and Audrey were the same age and had chosen careers in which they could help people, but that was where the similarities ended for the most part—except maybe for "resting bitch face." Neve was a tiny bit shorter, her complexion several shades darker, and her hair a riot of corkscrew curls that could be achieved only through genetics. "How's she doing?" she asked as she crossed the threshold into the house.

"Better." Audrey closed the door on the cold November air. She hadn't reacclimatized to it yet. "Much better than we expected, to be honest."

The other woman toed off her boots and shrugged out of her coat. "And you? The arm doing okay?"

"Yeah, it aches a bit, but it's healing." Once Neve hung up her coat, Audrey gestured for her to walk ahead.

"Dad says you'll be tender for a while. He also said you were lucky it didn't tear through all the muscle."

"I'm sure he did," she replied dryly. Neve's father had arrested her for Clint's murder, and had been convinced she was public enemy number one ever since. He probably thought she had manipulated the bullet somehow so it hadn't hurt her more. "He needs a hobby."

"Tell me about it."

They walked into the kitchen and Audrey put the kettle on. "Biscuit?" she asked.

"Your mom's or Jake's?"

Audrey reached for the plastic container on the counter and popped the lid. "Dad's actually, but he used Gracie's recipe. Mum was not impressed with him."

"I'll try one, sure. Molasses too, please."

She rolled her eyes. "As if there is any other way to have them."

They made small talk as Neve helped her set the table and make the tea. Audrey asked about Gideon and Bailey, and Neve asked how much more time Audrey had before she had to return to Boston. She hesitated.

"*Are* you returning to Boston?" Neve asked as they sat down.

"Probably. Maybe." Audrey shrugged and reached for the sugar bowl. "I don't know. I have some things to discuss with Angeline first. I've been thinking about what you and Jake both said to me about getting more involved with kids that need help rather than just studying and interviewing them, and the more I think about it, the more I think you're right."

"Had to happen sometime," her friend replied with a smile. She pulled a biscuit in half and slathered it in butter before reaching for the molasses. "You wouldn't think I was right if it wasn't what you wanted for yourself." She took a bite.

Audrey dressed up her own biscuit. "So, what's up?"

Neve swallowed and took a sip of tea. "I got a call from a

friend of mine a couple of days ago. Before she was killed, Maggie registered with the state adoption registry. Did you know she had a kid?"

She had, and since the father of that child was also Maggie's father, it was a detail Audrey had kept to herself since finding out several months ago. She had thought about looking for the girl, but frankly, she couldn't bring herself to do it, knowing the problems the kid might have. The kind of problems that arose when your father was also your grandfather.

"I knew," she replied. "It was a few months after I went to Stillwater." Stillwater was the correctional facility where she'd spent a few years after killing Maggie's abusive father, Clint. They had been the worst and best years of her teenage life.

Neve winced. "Christ, she was that young? No wonder I didn't hear about it. Maggie probably wanted that secret to stay hidden. I don't think Gideon knew."

Gideon—Neve's boyfriend—had been married to Maggie. "He probably didn't. Did your friend say anything else?"

"Yeah. So someone requested Maggie's contact information, and the registry had to let them know she'd died."

Audrey's heart smacked against her ribs. "You think it was her daughter?"

"Probably. My friend responded to the request personally, and offered to see if she could find any family. She knew I grew up here so she called me."

She shook her head. "There's no one left. Everyone that I knew of is dead. There might be family in New Hampshire. That's where they lived before coming here."

"I checked. No one."

Audrey studied her friend carefully. Why did it feel like Neve wanted more than Maggie's family tree from her? "Is Gideon considering meeting her?" Talk about a strange situation—him meeting Maggie's daughter after she'd done so much damage to his own daughter, Bailey.

"I haven't told him yet." Neve's hand on the table curled into a fist. "The only person I could think of who might be able to tell this girl who her mother really was is you."

Ah, fuck. "I don't know..." Now that the opportunity was there, she wasn't sure she should take it. If the girl suffered birth defects from being born of father-daughter incest, she didn't want to see it. Hers would be just one more life Clint Jones had a hand in ruining. And she didn't want to have to tell the kid that she had killed her father. There was also the fact that Maggie had named the baby Audrey, which was a whole other level of discomfort.

"She's already on her way here." Neve checked her phone. "In fact, she'll be here in fifteen minutes."

"Here?" Audrey echoed. "As in, *here*?"

Neve nodded. "She drove down from Calais."

She ought to have been angry at Neve for making presumptions. She should have been pissed, because she was sitting there in sweats, with no makeup and still recovering from a gunshot wound to her left arm. Now was not a good time to meet a kid whose origins she couldn't possibly begin to explain in any way that wouldn't be upsetting to either of them.

But she *wanted* to meet the girl. And it wasn't just because

Audrey wanted to know if she was all right, but because the kid was all there was left of the Maggie who had been her best friend. The Maggie she had loved and killed to protect.

"What were you going to do with her if I hadn't been here?"

Neve shrugged. "I would have figured something out. Are you okay with this?"

She laughed. "I kind of have to be, don't I? She's going to be here any minute."

The cop didn't even have the decency to look apologetic. "If I'd given you warning, you would have found a way to avoid her."

"No, I wouldn't." She would have wanted to, but she wouldn't. "Maggie named her Audrey, did you know that?"

"Shit. No." She looked uncomfortable, which made Audrey smile a little. *Good.* "She told me her name was Mackenzie."

Weird as having the kid share her name would be, Audrey was a little disappointed the girl or her parents had changed it. "Did she seem developmentally delayed when you spoke to her?"

"I haven't actually spoken to her. We've e-mailed and texted each other." Neve's brow puckered. "I didn't make the connection that she might belong to Clint. How bad are you talking?"

"It varies." She reached for another biscuit. Even incest-induced birth defects couldn't deter her appetite. "That's why I'm nervous about meeting her. I mean, I'm not looking forward to telling her that I killed her father-grandfather, but it will be easier if I know she can fully understand why."

Neve stared down at her cup. "Shit."

"Yeah," Audrey agreed.

They sat in silence for a long moment, and then the doorbell rang, startling them both. Audrey hadn't heard a car drive in. Her heart thumped heavily against her ribs as she walked to the entryway. The doorknob was cold beneath her palm as she pulled the door open.

Standing on the step in the cold was a young woman with long dark hair and big blue eyes. She had Maggie's nose and mouth, but she was taller and not as curvy. She smiled uncertainly and extended her hand. "Dr. Harte? I'm Mackenzie Bell. Detective Graham said you could tell me about my birth mother, Maggie Jones."

Audrey swallowed, fighting the tears that burned behind her eyes. "Hi, Mackenzie," she said as she wrapped her fingers around the girl's. "I'll tell you as much as I can." But she wasn't going to have to tell that she'd killed her father, because there was little to no way the girl belonged to Clint Jones—she had no obvious physical or mental defects.

But if Clint wasn't her father, who was?

Incest didn't happen just in small rural towns, but the sheer happiness Audrey felt realizing that Mackenzie probably wasn't both Maggie's daughter *and* sister made her feel like she was trapped in a *South Park* joke.

There was no denying who her mother was, and every time Audrey looked at the girl she saw a little bit more of Maggie, but there was someone else there too and she couldn't figure out who he was.

Audrey had taken her to the kitchen where Neve waited, and made a third cup of tea. When the girl sat down at the table, after saying hello to the other woman, Audrey and Neve exchanged a glance over her head. The girl wasn't what they'd expected, and that only raised more questions.

"Thank you both for agreeing to meet with me," Mackenzie said when Audrey set a cup of tea in front of her. "I just turned eighteen a few weeks ago. I went onto the registry that same day. It was such a disappointment to find out that my birth mother died only months before I could find her."

Audrey shook her head. "I can't imagine how disappointing that must've been." But lucky too. At least she didn't have to see how messed up Maggie had been. Hearing it was going to be difficult enough.

Mackenzie glanced at Neve. "You knew her as well, didn't you? Maggie, I mean."

Neve nodded. "I've known both her and Audrey since I was young, but Maggie and Audrey were best friends."

The girl smiled, and there was Maggie again in her face. "What was she like?"

Oh, hell. That was a loaded question, but Audrey found herself smiling fondly. "When Maggie moved here I thought she was so exotic. She came all the way from New Hampshire, and I had never been outside of Maine."

Mackenzie looked at her with delight. "Did you become friends right away?"

"Yeah, we did. The best of friends." She just let that hang there, uncertain of what else to say.

"Did you stay best friends even after you killed her father?"

Audrey blinked. There was no hostility in the girl's tone, no judgment in her expression, just simple curiosity. She should have known that Mackenzie would know who she was, and what she and Maggie had done. If their situations were reversed the first thing she would've done upon finding out her birth mother's name was a Google search. "For a while. Then we grew apart."

"Did he really molest her?"

"Yes."

"She told you and you believed her?"

"Yes, but also I witnessed it."

Both women stared at her, their eyes wide. Had she never told Neve that part of the story? Hadn't her father? Everett Graham was the one who had arrested her, who had come to the house that night and found Clint's bludgeoned naked body on the floor of Maggie's bedroom. Audrey had cracked his skull open like a bone piñata.

"Jesus," Neve whispered.

Mackenzie's face was white—stark white. "Please tell me he isn't my father too."

Her relief and remorse rushed through her at the same time. She'd been so concerned about how she was going to explain to the girl the situation surrounding her birth, she hadn't entertained the idea that she would've already put it together. How long had she spent scared and dreading the truth before driving down to Edgeport?

"Maggie said he was, but I don't think that's true." Audrey braced her forearms on the table and leaned over them. "There are certain characteristics of children born of father-daughter incest that I don't see in you. I'm not a geneticist, but I have studied the psychological aspects, and I would be very surprised if you were the product of such." Though a small percent of such births did turn out perfectly healthy.

The girl made a tiny noise as her shoulders sagged. "Oh my God, you have no idea how happy that makes me. I was so scared." She wiped at her eyes. "How could he have done that to her?"

"I don't know. I'm not sure I want to."

Her dark blue gaze locked with Audrey's own. "You killed him for what he did."

She wasn't completely comfortable discussing this in front of Neve, but what the hell. She wasn't ashamed of what she'd done, and truth be told, if she could go back in time she'd probably do it again. "Yes. I didn't want him to hurt Maggie anymore, or hurt anyone else."

Mackenzie nodded. "Thank you."

Her words struck like a kick to the sternum. It was foolish, really. After all these years, hearing those words from a stranger shouldn't have any effect. She knew at the time that Maggie had appreciated what she'd done, and she was certain Maggie must've thanked her several times, but after having so much judgment piled on her for that one act, hearing those words from Maggie's daughter meant more than she could ever articulate. In fact, she had to actually take a moment to compose herself before she could reply, and even then all she could do was nod.

"Will you tell me about her? Everything about her?" Mackenzie asked. "I'm staying at The Cove for the weekend. I'd like to find out as much as I can about where I came from."

Audrey cleared her throat. "I'll tell you everything I can, but you should know that Maggie's life was not an easy one."

The girl laughed humorlessly. "Yeah, I kind of figured that out already."

"I'll bring you some of Maggie's things that Gideon has in storage," Neve said, but she looked at Audrey. Neither one of them would deny the girl the chance to know Maggie, but there were some things a daughter just didn't need to know, and it would be their jobs to weed those things out before letting her comb through Maggie's short life.

Mackenzie turned to the other woman. "His daughter killed her, didn't she?"

Neve grimaced. "Yeah, she did. Look, there's a lot you don't know…"

"And probably a lot I don't want to," the girl interjected. "I know. I don't want either of you to think I'm judging. I just want to know the truth, no matter how bad it is."

Audrey and Neve shared a glance, and both of them nodded. "Okay, then," Audrey said. "That's what you get. I'll give you as much truth about Maggie as I can."

"Do either of you have any idea who my real father is?"

The girl was asking all the hard questions, and each one was like a slap. Audrey didn't resent her for it, but she had easier conversations with psychopaths.

"I don't," Neve told her. "I knew Maggie, but we weren't that close."

"She never said anything to me," Audrey admitted. "Back then we told each other everything, or at least I thought we did. She always seemed to be in like with some guy, and she was... provocative for that age. Unfortunately, no single person stands out in my mind."

"Well, maybe there'll be some clue in her things," Mackenzie suggested so hopefully Audrey's heart twisted in an effort to get away from her vulnerability.

"Maybe," she agreed. "It's a small town, somebody must know something."

Neve made a scoffing noise. "Of course somebody knows something, just a matter of whether or not they share it."

"Why wouldn't they?" Mackenzie asked, her gaze narrowing.

Neve turned to her with a sympathetic gaze. "Small towns are weird," she explained. "There are some secrets that will become town gossip no matter how hard you try to keep them, and then there are others that should be public, that get buried so deep they might as well be part of the bedrock."

"That makes no sense," the girl argued.

Audrey's smile was grim. "Welcome to Edgeport."